BLACKENING SONG

Also by Aimée & David Thurlo

Black Mesa
Red Mesa
Second Shadow
Spirit Warrior
Timewalker

ELLA CLAH NOVELS

Death Walker
Bad Medicine
Enemy Way
Shooting Chant

BLACKENING SONG

✖ ✖ ✖ ✖ ✖

AIMÉE & DAVID THURLO

A Tom Doherty Associates Book
New York

This is a work of fiction. All the characters and events portrayed in this novel are either fictitious or are used fictitiously.

BLACKENING SONG

This book is printed on acid-free paper.

A Forge Book
Published by Tom Doherty Associates, LLC
175 Fifth Avenue
New York, NY 10010

www.tor.com

Forge® is a registered trademark of Tom Doherty Associates, LLC.

Library of Congress Cataloging-in-Publication Data

Thurlo, Aimée.
Blackening song / Aimée and David Thurlo.
p. cm.
"A Tom Doherty Associates book."
ISBN 0-312-85652-0 (hc)
ISBN 0-765-30256-X (pbk)
I. Thurlo, David. II. Title.
PS3570.H82 B58 1995
813'.54—dc20

95-4270
CIP

Printed in the United States of America

D 20 19 18 17 16 15 14 13 12

To Tony Hillerman because he never forgot
what it was like in the trenches,
and gave us a hand when we needed one.
Thanks, Tony, you're one in a million.

AUTHORS' NOTE

The rituals described herein have been abbreviated and altered slightly out of respect for the Navajo people.

BLACKENING SONG

ONE

Ella Clah sat alone in her booth in a northeast L.A. coffee shop. The laminated menu lay untouched near the end of the narrow table. She knew it by heart, having come here practically every afternoon for the past year. It was close to the Southwestern Museum, a place she visited frequently.

It was a little after five, too early for dinner, but she didn't feel like going home just yet. Today her bureau office had finally closed the fraud case they'd been working on for the last six months. Most of the other agents were celebrating at The Watering Hole, a favorite bar just a short walk from their downtown L.A. office. Ella wondered if she'd made a mistake by not going with them.

She had a reputation for being a loner, and, in truth, she rarely socialized with her fellow agents. It wasn't the company she minded; it was all the drinking. She'd seen too much of it on the reservation where she'd grown up.

Though the sale of alcohol was prohibited on the Navajo Nation, alcoholism was widespread.

She stared at the red tile flooring, lost in thought. Her life on the Rez seemed like a century ago. In the last six years, she'd moved four times. The bureau kept her on the move and away from her home in northwestern New Mexico. She'd known about and welcomed the policy, which was meant to protect agents and their integrity, to keep agents far from investigations that might involve friends and family. The job-required travel helped Ella make a break with her past and start a new and different life.

Ella watched the oleander bush in the coffee shop's courtyard sway in the hot Santa Ana wind. Tempers were short when the weather was like this. She glanced around the room, silently noting the faces of the few patrons who sat in the booths and at the tiny oak tables. Only Jeremy Jackson, the manager, seemed unaffected by the seasonal breeze. Ella had known him for months and had yet to see him in a bad mood.

Jeremy was slowly working his way toward her booth. The tall, lanky, black man's easy stride matched his casual style. He stopped by every customer, greeting each as congenially as if they were old friends, making each feel special. He was good at his job. Business had doubled at the hole-in-the-wall coffee shop since he'd taken it over.

Jeremy skirted the last few empty tables and slid into the seat across from Ella, flashing a wide grin.

"Hey, Ella. Heard on the news the local FBI office broke open a big telephone fraud operation today. You in on that?"

She nodded.

"Why're you celebrating alone again, lady?"

"You're here," she said, smiling.

"Yeah, working, as usual." He shrugged. "You'd be happier if you had someone special. I know. That's why I keep getting married." He smiled.

"Well, maybe five will be your lucky number," she answered, chuckling.

Jeremy glanced toward the entrance as the tiny bell above the door rang and a man walked into the shop. "Damn. Not again. This guy getting to be a real pain."

"Trouble?" Her view of the newcomer was blocked by the cigarette machine near the entryway.

"Nah, he's harmless, just a headache. He applied for a job about a month ago. I hired someone else, but he keeps coming back, trying to get me to change my mind."

"He must really want the job."

"No, it's more than that. I get the idea he's racist as hell and didn't like getting turned down by a black man. I better go talk to him." Jeremy walked across the room.

Ella saw the man clearly as he stepped into the middle of the diner to meet Jeremy. The guy had brown hair, brown eyes, and was no more than average in height, almost painfully ordinary. Still, eight years of fieldwork for the bureau had honed Ella's instincts to a fine point. Something made her study him more carefully.

His short-sleeved white shirt and tan corduroy pants, though clean and neat, were threadbare. He was restless, shuffling from one sneakered foot to the other, as if the wait for Jeremy was unendurable. His nervous smile seemed to flicker on and off like a neon sign. As her gaze drifted down, she noted the zippered gym bag he was clutching in a white-knuckled grip.

Instincts weren't always on target, but without even thinking about it, Ella reached beneath her cotton blazer, feeling for her nine-millimeter Sig.

Then she saw the lines of tension around the man's face vanish as he spoke to Jeremy, and she breathed a sigh of relief. She was wound too tightly, that's all. Not everyone who looked nervous was a psycho in the making.

When she heard him laugh at something Jeremy said, Ella sat back to enjoy the hamburger platter the waitress had brought her. She was off duty, for pete's sake! It was time to stop acting and thinking like a federal cop.

She bit into a forkful of french fries seasoned with ketchup. Before she could swallow, the sharp crack of a gunshot sliced through the air and the glass mirror behind the cash register counter shattered into jagged slivers.

Ella peeked around the booth partition, simultaneously reaching for her gun. Staff and customers screamed as the creep fired wildly, shattering dishes and blasting food.

She blocked out the chaos, searching for a way to get off a clear shot and bring down the perpetrator. But the man had stepped back toward the entrance, and the row of booths blocked her view. All she could see was his hand and weapon. Looking low, between the chairs and the bottoms of tables, she saw Jeremy lying still on the tiled floor, blood pumping onto the terra-cotta tiles. The gunman's gym bag, unzipped, lay open, and Ella could see that it held spare magazines for his handgun.

He kept firing, each thunderous blast deafening in the confines of the shop. The madman had either a Taurus or Beretta nine-millimeter semiauto. He'd fired off at least seven rounds; he had another seven or eight to go before he'd need to reload.

Ella worked her way closer, trying to get clear of the customers who were huddled on the floor and using the tables for cover. One woman's piercing screams rose above the gunfire. *Shut up, lady. Don't give him a reason to take it out on you!* Ella scrambled forward, still unable to see more than the hand and the pistol, which bucked every time it fired.

Abruptly, the shooting stopped. The intense silence that followed was unnerving. As Ella angled around a customer, the man stepped into view. She raised her pistol, determined to make a kill shot.

"Everyone against the counter," the gunman snapped, shifting position slightly. Now a metal post blocked her shot. "If you do what I tell you, you'll live to tell the story. I'm no murderer. All I want to do here today is make a point."

Before Ella could even take a breath, the gunman blasted two rounds through the table to his left; one round struck the waitress crouching there. "I said get moving! *Now!*"

Instead of complying, the terrified customers started screaming again. One woman tried to run to the door, but the shooter grabbed her arm, spun her around, and sent her crashing into a table. "The counter! Can't anybody here understand English?"

Ella heard sobbing from one of the two women huddled under the table in front of her. One started to obey the gunman, but the other yanked her back down.

"None of you wants to die, and I don't want to kill you," the man said calmly. "But that's what's going to happen if you don't do exactly what I say."

His voice was so matter-of-fact it sent a chill right through Ella. Gut instinct assured her he was out to make one last stand. The only adversary more dangerous than a man willing to die was one eager to find death, and this guy was a little of both.

Ella stood, carefully keeping her gun out of his line of sight, but hoping to draw the man's attention. As she did, one of the women in front of her broke loose from her companion and rushed toward the kitchen doors. The gunman started to swing around just as the middle-aged Hispanic woman slipped on spilled food and fell flat.

Before he could squeeze off a shot, Ella lunged around the customer still between them, pushing the woman into the shelter of a booth, firing as she moved. Her bullet went high, and she only managed to catch the man in the shoulder, spinning him around.

Taking a slug from a nine-millimeter hollow-point was a bit like being kicked by a horse, yet the man recaptured his balance quickly. As he returned fire, Ella ducked out of sight behind a booth. His bullet splintered into the wall just to her right.

Oblivious to pain, the lunatic dragged a woman out from under a table. Hauling her to her feet, he held her in front of him like a shield.

"Slide your gun over here, cop!" he ordered. "Then come out, or I'll blow her brains all over the floor."

The woman's terror was clear on her face, but only a tiny whimper came out of her mouth.

"You're out of time," he said calmly, raising his semi-auto to the woman's ear.

"Stop!" Ella shouted. She was as good as dead if she came out unarmed, but the hostage wouldn't have a prayer if she didn't. Ella took a deep breath and checked the .22-caliber backup pistol she kept in her boot. The tiny eleven-ounce weapon was only good for two shots, and she'd have to reach it *fast*. A mouse at a cat convention had a better chance than she did.

"Now!" the gunman snapped.

Ella pulled the clip out of her pistol. She wasn't going to give him any more ammunition. "Okay, relax. Here's my pistol," she said, sliding it across the floor toward him. "Let her go, and I'll come out."

"You're in no position to bargain."

The wail of sirens and screeching of tires reverberated in the street outside the small shop. She held her breath. "I'm the only hostage you'll need. I'm an FBI agent. Now let her go."

The psycho took a step forward, his pistol steady, the barrel still pressed to the woman's head. "Come out *now*. I won't repeat myself."

She emerged from cover slowly, half expecting to be shot where she stood. But all he did was stare at her curiously, like a rattler eyeing its next meal. She knew what he was seeing. A well-proportioned woman of slightly more than medium height, copper skin deeply tanned from her daily cross-country run, black hair and black eyes.

He threw his captive back down to the floor and casually stepped around her as she lay there, shaking.

"What the hell are you?"

The question threw her. "Huh?"

"You're not a spick or mulatto. What are you?"

She forced her voice to stay even. "Indian."

"You don't look Indian. There's no dot on your forehead. What part of India are you from?"

"New Mexico, U.S.A. I'm an American Indian—Navajo."

He smiled slowly. "Then you must hate whites. Probably as much as I hate the stinking minorities. They come here and take our jobs, like that nigger." He gestured toward Jeremy. "They make us grovel for work, forgetting that we were here first."

"My people were here thousands of years before yours. You have no quarrel with me."

"Nice try, but forget it. You slant arguments to your own advantage, just like everyone else. The cavalry should have killed all you off a hundred years ago."

A man's voice boomed through a bullhorn before she could answer. "The building is completely surrounded by police officers. Set down your weapons and come out with your hands up."

She saw the gunman tense, checking the door. She wasn't sure how he could ignore the wound in his shoulder. He didn't seem fazed by it in the slightest. Maybe he was high on something. "Let the customers go. They'll only complicate things for you. They're afraid, and you can't predict what any of them will do."

He seemed to consider it. "No," he said finally. "I have more leverage with them here."

He looked down at the woman he'd held hostage, then trained his weapon on Ella. "Get all these people facedown on the floor and tie them up." He started walking toward her.

"With what?" The blood stain on his shirt had spread. The river of crimson flowed downward, coloring his tan slacks.

"Cords from the curtains, their belts, whatever. And hurry it up. Otherwise I'll shoot a few more." He stopped just short of arm's length away and wiggled the barrel of his Beretta.

Ella looked at the frightened group. Four customers and the cook were still unharmed. She'd do her best to keep it that way. With the gunman a few steps behind her, she knelt beside the woman he had used as a shield. The one-time hostage wore slacks with an elastic waist, no belt.

"You want me to tie her up? Then give me a knife so I can cut some cords from the blinds."

"What kind of a fool do I look like? Give you a knife?" He laughed coldly.

"Then get the cords yourself, if you want her tied up." Ella hoped he would stand next to the window. A sharpshooter could take him out in the blink of an eye.

"Okay, forget tying them up," he snapped. "I'm not going anywhere near the windows. Those cops outside can't wait to blow me away." He turned to the huddled group. "Lie facedown on the floor and stay there."

The same cop's voice boomed over the loudspeaker again, echoing loudly in the small shop. "I'm going to call you on the telephone. Pick it up and we can talk."

The psycho motioned Ella to the phone. "You answer it. Tell them that I'll kill everyone here if they move in."

Ella picked up the ringing phone and identified herself, repeating the message word for word. There was a hesitation, then the officer, in a terse, drill sergeant's tone, ordered her to repeat her I.D.

After another short pause, the officer spoke again. "I'll ask the young man," Ella said clearly into the receiver, taking the opportunity to let the police know what they were up against. She turned back to the shooter. "They want to know what your demands are."

"I want . . . I just want what's due me. A job, respect," he muttered, then glanced up and met her eyes. "Tell them to call back in five minutes. Then hang up."

She complied, itching for the opportunity to reach for her gun. "You can't get a job or respect like this. Think about what you're doing."

"What do *you* know about it? The feds hired you, didn't they? Probably had some sort of quota to take ten Indians that day. I tried to join the police force once, but they wouldn't take me. Too busy hiring people like you and this loser." He took a step toward Jeremy and nudged his body hard with his boot.

Jeremy twitched and she heard him groan softly. He was still alive! Ella moved toward the black man without thinking.

"Stand still!" the gunman clipped.

She froze. "Relax." She held his gaze and straightened to her full five-foot-six height. "I've never taken anything away from you or anyone else. I worked my butt off for everything I've ever had, believe it."

"You people get all kinds of financial help and advantages white folks never have."

"Advantages? Like hauling all your water thirty miles in old oil drums? Riding a bus sixty miles a day to get to school? Not even a fan to cool you on a hundred-degree day because you have no electricity at home? Those don't qualify as advantages in my book, but that's a big portion of the Rez, pal. The only reason we have a Rez at all was because the land was so poor nobody else wanted it."

"So why didn't you stay where you belong and make things better?"

"My job makes its own contribution. People belong wherever they can make a place for themselves. That's something you should have learned."

"There's no place for me."

"There can be." This guy intended to die and take as many of them with him as possible. She knew that with a certainty that alarmed her. She had to keep him talking until a chance came to act. "What's your name? Mine's Ella Clah."

"Joe."

"Joe what? You have a last name?" The lifelessness in his gaze stunned her. She had to be very careful not to push him too far.

"Joe Campbell."

"Tell me about your family, Joe."

"I don't have one anymore," he snapped. "Now shut up and lie down on the floor with the others."

If she could distract him for just a few seconds—that's all the time she'd need to get her backup pistol.

The phone began ringing again. "Do you want me to get that for you?" she asked, an idea forming in her mind.

"Yeah, but make it quick. Tell them I'm not ready to talk to them yet."

"You'll be better off if you give them something to work with. How about medical attention for your shoulder? You'll also need safe passage out of the city." She had to make him think of life instead of death. That could shift the odds in their favor.

"Passage to where?" he muttered under his breath. "Just do as I say," he ordered loudly. "Tell them I'm not ready to talk."

As she stepped around the athletic bag on the floor near him, she glanced inside. Adrenaline shot through her as her heart slammed against her rib cage. Besides spare clips for his pistol, the bag also contained explosives. It didn't take an Einstein to guess his next move. The moment the SWAT team fired in tear gas or stormed the place, they'd all go up in a ball of fire and smoke. There wouldn't be enough left for the coroner to I.D.

As Ella approached the phone, he followed closely, glancing at the wounded with clinical detachment.

"Why don't you release them?" she suggested pleasantly. "They're absolutely no good to you here, and the cops might see it as a gesture of goodwill and ease up a bit."

"No. Tell them that we've got two wounded hostages. If they try anything, I'll finish them off. That'll keep them on their toes."

What it would do was get them to act faster, but arguing with him wasn't going to get her anywhere. He was on the edge as it was.

Grabbing at the phone, being deliberately clumsy, she knocked it off the desk. As the instrument clattered to the floor, the gunman flinched and brought the Beretta to within a foot of her head. "My fault," she said quickly. "I'm just nervous."

"Pick it up."

Ella bent down, slid her hand into her boot, and palmed the tiny derringer. Turning, she extended her right arm into his surprised face, and fired twice.

Somebody screamed, but it wasn't Joe. She'd hit him with both rounds in the left eye. His mouth opened, but he was dead before his body reached the floor.

Ella heard a soft whimper, and saw the injured waitress trying to crawl away from the corpse. "It's okay. It's over." She didn't blame the woman for wanting to move. Though personally she didn't share the Navajo belief in the *chindi,* the evil in a man that remained earthbound after death, bodies still gave her the creeps.

"Don't move around too much," she cautioned, crouching at the waitress's side. "I'll have a medical team here in a flash." From the amount of blood on her clothes, Ella was surprised the woman hadn't gone into shock.

"Thank God it's over," one of the men said, struggling to stand.

"No! Everyone stay down and don't move until the SWAT team says it's okay," Ella announced. "When they come in they won't know who any of us is. They could shoot somebody by mistake."

She grabbed the receiver from the floor. The cop had held on. "It's over, guys. The perp is down. Come on in, we need two med teams fast!"

She pocketed the derringer and moved to Jeremy's side. A bullet had pierced his rib cage. He was unconscious, but his breathing was steady. He'd make it. She'd seen others come through worse and Jeremy was a fighter. "Hang in there, buddy."

Within seconds, cops were all over the coffee shop. Ella stood aside, watching the paramedics work while the officers helped the unharmed hostages to their feet and took their statements.

Ella leaned against the wall, relieved that the only life lost had been the gunman's.

A plainclothes detective came to take her statement, commenting, "You'll undoubtedly get a commendation for what you did. This could have been a real bloodbath." His gaze fell on the bag with the ammunition and explosives. Its contents had already been rendered safe by a SWAT team ordnance specialist. "He was ready for a siege."

"Worse. He wanted to become a martyr, one guy fighting the system."

The coffee shop patrons were being led out by police officers. Most flashed grateful smiles or asked to shake her hand. One elderly woman stopped and gave her a hug. "Thank you so very much," she said, in tears. "I'll be praying for you—and for that poor man's soul."

As the woman left, Ella spotted her partner entering the diner. "Dennis, I'm over here." She waved briefly.

Dennis Anderson looked like the ex-Marine, ex-college quarterback he'd been before getting into law enforcement. With his well-fitting suit and regulation dark glasses, he had *FBI agent* stamped all over him.

"So much for your quiet supper after a tough day," he commented. "Lucky for the patrons that this is your favorite hangout."

She nodded slowly, her gaze drifting over to one of the pools of blood that had started to congeal on the tile floor. "What are you doing here? Don't tell me you were in the neighborhood and decided to drop by."

"The special agent in charge asked me to find you. He's been trying to raise you on the radio."

"What's the boss want with me?"

"He was probably trying to verify your whereabouts. My guess is that he got a call that you were involved in a hostage situation."

"Yeah, that makes sense."

"Let me give you a ride downtown to the bureau offices. You're in no shape to drive. I hate to be the one to break it to you, but you look like shit warmed over."

"Gee, thanks. I think you look like crap too," she countered with a wry grin.

"I'm serious. Finish giving the detective your statement, then let's get rolling."

"Sorry, Agent Anderson," the police detective said, joining them. "But we'll need Agent Clah to come down and help wrap this up for our captain. I doubt she'll be going anywhere until very late tonight."

"How about extending a little professional courtesy here? She can come in tomorrow."

"No way. The captain wants to get a full account while it's all fresh in her mind. He wants any statement he releases to the public to be complete and accurate. We also need your weapons for a ballistic comparison," he said to Ella, holding out his hand.

"Wait a second," Dennis Anderson clipped. "Our agents are required to be armed at all times."

"Then the bureau can drop off replacements at the station," the detective countered.

Ella glanced at Dennis. "A derringer and my Sig. Both are bureau-approved, so they'll have replacements."

Dennis nodded. "I'll make sure new weapons are waiting for you when you leave."

"Thanks, Dennis," Ella answered.

"Come on," the detective said, glancing at Ella. "I'll give you a ride downtown."

"No, thanks. I'll follow you in my car." She was tired, and in no mood to be agreeable. Besides, once they were finished with her, she didn't intend to hang around, waiting for a lift back to her vehicle. She'd go home, call her boss, then sleep for the next twelve hours.

It was close to midnight by the time the honchos in the downtown L.A. station had asked their last question. Ella drove carefully to her apartment, concentrating on staying awake.

Bone weary, she inserted the key in the lock of the thick metal door and turned the heavy deadbolt back with a thud. As she stepped into the room, Ella heard the beep of her answering machine.

"Now what?" she mumbled, automatically sweeping her gaze around the kitchen/dining/living room of her tiny apartment to see if anything had been disturbed. Her little color TV and cassette player were still in place. They would be the first things taken. Break-ins were an everyday occurrence in the city, and her instincts never slowed, even at home. Navajos learned as children that the world was a dangerous place, and Los Angeles was a perfect example.

Ignoring the incessant beep and flashing red light of the machine, Ella took a precautionary stroll around the place before slipping off her holster and dropping the new pistol onto the bed.

Except for a few photos of her family on her tiny desk, the furnished apartment was pretty much as it had been the day she moved in. Neat, clean, and simple, the way she liked it. Ella kicked off her shoes and strolled back into the other room, stopping at her machine. There were two messages, at least one probably from her office.

Pressing the rewind button, she reached for the volume control and turned it up. "Ella?" the message began, then there was a sound that could have been a sob. Ella's heart fell into her stomach, and she turned up the volume even more. She hated those in-the-middle-of-the-night calls; they were never good news.

There was a long pause, then the message continued. "This is your mother . . . there's been . . . something terrible has happened . . . uh . . . please call me right away . . ."

Without waiting for the next message, Ella turned off the machine and grabbed the phone, punching out the numbers automatically. Her hand was shaking, and she had to redial twice. Finally there was a distant sound of ringing, as if she were really listening to the family phone back in New Mexico. Her mother picked up on the second ring.

"Hello. Ella? Is that you?" Her mother's voice was weak and strained.

"Yes, I just got home. What's wrong?" Ella tried not to

let the fear show in her voice. "Has Dad been in an accident?"

"No, not an accident. It's . . ." Rose began sobbing, and Ella's mouth suddenly went very dry. "Could you come home? He's been murdered."

"I'm coming, Mom, right away. I'll call back in a few minutes and let you know when. Bye." Ella hung up and started thumbing through the yellow pages, her hands shaking so badly she could barely hold on to it. This was the first time her mother had ever asked her for anything.

Then she remembered the second message. Setting down the phone book, open to the airline section, she played the other message. Just as she'd figured, it was the special agent in charge, asking her to call as soon as she got in.

Dialing, Ella tried to clear her throat. Whatever it was would have to wait. No matter the cost, job or no job, she was going to New Mexico tomorrow.

TWO

The next morning Ella arrived at the bureau offices half an hour earlier than usual. Last night, she'd verified the police reports using the bureau's resources and knew for certain that her father had been the victim of a homicide. An intense numbing shock blunted the sorrow she should have been feeling. The coffee shop incident still seemed more vivid and real to her than anything else.

At the moment, she was going through the motions, her feelings packed away like winter clothes in Southern California. She'd spent most of the night preparing what she hoped would be a convincing argument, one meant to allow her to take part in any investigation involving her father.

As she reached her desk in the agents' common office space, she saw Henry Estrada, the special agent in charge, come to his doorway. "Ella, my office, please." If she'd described him to anyone, Henry would have sounded like the hero of a romance novel: tall, broad-shouldered, dark-haired, with chiseled features and a square jaw. But somehow, in Henry, the total was less than the sum of the parts. He looked like a Cro-Magnon who'd taken up weight lifting.

"You talk to anyone back on the reservation yet?" he asked softly when Ella stepped into his office.

"I spoke to my mother last night. I also telephoned tribal police headquarters in Window Rock," she answered, determined to keep her voice even and cool. "They wouldn't give me any details about the murder, but they implied the case was far from ordinary. That didn't exactly come as a surprise. When the murder of a Navajo preacher makes the Los Angeles newspapers . . ."

"You did a helluva job yesterday, on and off duty. I'm really sorry about your father." He slid an open file across his desk. The topmost fax was a copy of the Navajo tribal police report. "I'm doing this as a courtesy, Ella. But this isn't, nor will it be, your case. Is that understood?"

"But the bureau *will* get involved. It's within our jurisdiction."

"Yes, but you won't be working on the case. That's bureau policy."

She studied the file. The coroner's report was preliminary, mostly listing the condition of the body when it had been found. Yet even those sketchy details were enough to make bile rise to the back of her throat. It took all her willpower to school her face into neutrality. "Unless you have a member of our tribe handling this, you'll get nowhere," she said at last. "There are unusual facets to this case. It isn't easy for an outsider to conduct *any* investigation on the Rez. But this one will be impossible."

"You have an idea who killed him?" Estrada's eyebrows rose.

"No. All I can tell you is that my father's religious vocation, and the zealous way he pursued it, angered many Navajos. My mother wrote me less than a month ago about some anonymous threats made against him. When I called home, he told me it was the work of some old enemies. They were upset because his preaching was leading the People away from traditional beliefs. He didn't think anything would come of it.

"It's an age-old problem. But to find my father's enemies, you'll have to understand the Dineh and our ways."

"That problem is being dealt with. The bureau will work hand in hand with the tribal police."

"When will the coroner's report be complete?"

"I don't know, but there's no reason for you to see that." He looked her right in the eye and held her gaze.

She knew this was her boss's way of warning her to stay away from the investigation. To Navajos, eye-to-eye contact was considered a confrontation, and Estrada knew that. Still, Ella couldn't back off.

"I need an extended leave of absence. I'll have to get my father's affairs in order and help my mother cope with what's happened."

"You can have up to a week with pay."

"I appreciate that, but I'll need longer, even without pay."

"How long?"

She couldn't afford to pull her punches now. "Sir, I helped crack the fraud case that kept this office tied up for months, and I worked alone to resolve that hostage situation yesterday. Thirty days shouldn't be out of the question under the circumstances."

Estrada took a deep breath, then let it out again. "If I hear that you're investigating the case, I'll have the local police bring you up on charges for obstructing justice. Clear?"

"Abundantly."

He continued to hold her gaze with an unblinking one of his own. "Thirty days is pushing it. I'll approve your request, but anything more than that could jeopardize your career."

Relief began to uncoil the knots in her stomach. It hadn't been as hard as she'd expected. "Thank you, Henry."

He steepled his fingers beneath his chin. "Let me know as soon as you're ready to come back. If you can make it in three weeks or less, so much the better."

She nodded once. "Can you tell me who has been assigned to the case?"

"No, but it'll be someone from the New Mexico office, or a resident agent near the reservation. I'm sure you'll be contacted. Help with background on your father will be appreciated. Interference will not." Estrada's voice was firm.

Ella left his office and quickly filled out the reports and request forms she needed. By the end of the morning, she intended to have a full load of gear, including extra weapons and ammunition, ready to ship next-day delivery to her mother's home. Then she'd book the next flight there.

As she worked, Ella found herself wishing she could honor Estrada's order not to get involved. But her boss didn't understand—she was already involved. The facts she'd gleaned from the police report suggested the murder had ritualistic overtones, things no Navajo would ever discuss with an outsider. Ella was the only hope of catching her father's killer.

* * *

She arrived in Farmington the following morning, feeling as rumpled and stale as week-old laundry. Though she'd slept on the red-eye special out of Los Angeles, she'd been stuck with a three-hour layover in Albuquerque. The final leg of the journey had been the worst. The thirty-minute flight had been a bumpy, quick climb, and a roller-coaster descent.

As she stepped out of the plane and walked across the concrete runway to the small Farmington terminal, doubts crowded her mind. She hadn't been home in six years, and for a brief moment she felt again like the shy, insecure girl she'd been most of her life. But as she glanced across the green San Juan River valley city of Farmington, the feeling passed. Those days were gone. She was a woman now, aware of her capabilities and her limitations. In accepting both, she'd found her strength.

She was on her way to claim her one suitcase when a face, and a voice, from the past startled her.

"Hey, little cousin! I had to come to Farmington today to mail off some evidence to the state lab, so your mother asked me to give you a ride home. Sorry to welcome you back to civilization under these circumstances, though."

She glanced at Peterson Yazzie's khaki-brown uniform, noting that he was now a tribal police sergeant. According to her mother, he hoped to someday become tribal police chief.

"Good to see you again," she said, knowing Peterson was stationed at the Shiprock office. He might be able to tell her if any new evidence had been uncovered. She retrieved her suitcase quickly. "I'm going to be involved in the investigation," Ella added, choosing to leave out the fact that this was in no way an official involvement. "What's been happening here?"

"I wish I had answers for you," he said guardedly.

"I've been away for a long time, but we *are* cousins," she said, trying to keep barriers from being erected. She was aware that some of the people she'd known on the Rez thought she'd become an outsider.

"We don't really know much. Your dad was on the way home from the site where he plans . . . planned to build his church. He'd been having open-air services there already. For some reason, he stopped a few miles from home and got out of his pickup. We found his body fifteen feet from the road."

"He wouldn't have stopped without a darned good reason. There'd been threats against him."

"What threats?"

"Nobody told you?" She exhaled softly. "I should have figured that."

"Fill me in."

"Mother wrote me that he'd gotten some threatening phone calls, and that he'd received some notes."

"Why didn't he come to us?"

"Dad didn't take it seriously. He blamed it on the traditionalists. It's the same fight they've been having since I was a kid. To be honest, I didn't take it seriously either."

Peterson nodded slowly. "But now it's a lead we can't afford to ignore. Can you get your mother to turn over those notes to me?"

"She may not still have them, but I'll ask."

Ella followed Peterson to his tribal police car. She'd intended to rent a vehicle, but for the time being this suited her better. She wanted to get all the information she could before Peterson realized she wasn't actually assigned to the case. She'd made no false claims, so she didn't feel too bad about the subterfuge.

"I understand that my father's murder had some unusual, maybe even ritualistic, elements. Can you tell me what you know about that?"

He turned away, and she could see how hard he worked to not let his feelings show. That effort frightened her more than anything he could have said. "I'll take you to view the body. I'd rather you see this for yourself."

To handle the body of someone who'd met a violent death was thought to be dangerous, for the *chindi* was said to linger nearby. Ella didn't believe in the *chindi*, and she was certain Peterson didn't completely believe either, but some traditions were too ingrained to cast aside easily.

"Has my aunt Merilyn come to stay with my mom? I don't think Clifford will be much help."

"He isn't," Peterson said, then shook his head. "What I meant to say is that we haven't been able to locate him. But that doesn't necessarily mean anything. He goes off by himself for weeks at a time."

Something about Peterson's tone made Ella's throat go dry. "How long has he been gone?"

Peterson took a long, deep breath. "The last time anyone saw him was the night of your father's murder."

Forty minutes later, they arrived at the coroner's office, a small cubicle down a side corridor at the public health hospital in Shiprock. By then a thick, uncomfortable silence had descended between them. Although Peterson hadn't said anything more, the implication was clear. Ella's brother Clifford had fought against everything their father stood for. Obviously, he was a suspect.

Ella followed Peterson down an empty corridor filled with the overwhelming scent of pine disinfectant. She hated morgues. No matter how many times investigations brought her to such places, she couldn't get used to them. Death seemed to echo back at her with each hollow clack her shoes made on the sealed concrete floor.

Her father was dead—she knew that, yet in defiance of logic she still hoped to discover that it had all been a horrible mistake, that some other man's body was lying on the metal table inside.

"I'm glad you're here," Peterson said, interrupting her thoughts. "I wasn't looking forward to working with that *bilagáana* agent, Blalock. He demands instant answers, and never understands when none is given."

Ella stopped by the door to the morgue. To not correct his assumption now would be the same as lying to him, but to correct it would mean risking losing her chance at first-hand investigation. She had to see her father's body, both to honor a duty to her mother and father and to gather the most information possible. Nothing could stand in the way of that.

As she reached for the door, Peterson spoke. "Prepare yourself. His body was . . . mutilated."

For one insane moment she felt the floor beneath her feet tilting. "A pattern?" she asked, relieved when she managed to keep her voice steady.

"Too early to tell." He led the way inside, then nodded to the technician sitting behind a desk.

The Hispanic man opened the door to an adjoining room, and went in. The cold air that seeped out was even more chilling because of what Ella knew the place contained. She wouldn't be looking at a stranger this time. She suppressed a shudder as she saw how the floor sloped toward the large drains in the center of the room. Her knees felt wobbly, but she forced herself to remain calm and still as the attendant rolled out a gurney carrying a covered body.

Ella steeled herself as the sheet was pulled back, but when she saw the bloody, dissected wreckage that had once been her father, she ran to the sink against the wall. Her father's enemies had been more savage than she'd dreamed. For a moment, she thought she was going to be violently ill, but after taking several deep breaths, she brought herself back under control.

Turning back around, she noted gratefully that the remains were once again covered by the thin sheet. "This wasn't—"

She broke off as a tall, brown-haired Anglo, wearing a dark gray suit and maroon tie, strode into the room. "Who's Peterson Yazzle?"

She knew instantly that the intruder was Blalock, the FBI agent assigned to the case. One glance told her he was wrong for the job. He looked as if he'd arrived by limo from a Washington, D.C., boardroom.

Peterson stared coldly at him. "I'm Sergeant *Yazzie.* I assume you're Blalock. May I see some identification, please?"

The man flashed his gold badge, his manner condescending, as if he seriously doubted the intelligence of everyone in the room. "I'm the agent in charge of this case. Who is this woman and what is she doing here? The body has already been identified."

Peterson glanced at Ella, then back at the man. "There seems to have been a mix-up. Meet FBI agent Ella Clah. Her father was the victim."

"Dwayne Blalock," he said and shook her hand. "I'd like to speak to you in private, Agent Clah."

She stepped to the side of the room with Blalock. He had

one brown eye and one green one. She found the oddity distracting, but pushed it from her mind.

Since she already knew what he was going to say, Ella figured she'd save him the trouble. "Look, this is just a misunderstanding. The sergeant is my cousin, and I had a few questions to ask him. It was professional courtesy."

"Don't B.S. me, Clah. I've been briefed about you. You're said to be a good agent, but so am I. Don't try to get involved in my case. You have orders to stay away. You don't want to blow your career."

"My father has been killed. What would you do if you were in my place?" she challenged.

"*I* will arrest whoever murdered him," he said, avoiding the question. "I won't have you slowing me down."

"Listen to me, Blalock. Take a good look around you. You're an outsider here, no matter how long you've been in New Mexico. To make any headway on this case, you're going to need some cooperation. Have you ever worked a case on Native American land before?"

"I've been in this wretched backwater for two years—in other words, forever. I do whatever it takes to get the job done. Bet on it."

"You'll need contacts on a case like this, lots of them. Very few people on the Rez will talk to strangers about crimes like this one."

"I'd rather work alone," Blalock said, "but I'll use the tribal police if I have to. I've got to tell you, though, I've learned not to expect too much from them or their methods."

"You'll need more than the help of the tribal police," Ella insisted. "To get anywhere, you're going to need someone like me, someone who is part of this world and yours."

"No deal. Right now this Yazzie guy is going to give me

a full briefing. Then I'll know what progress has been made. The tribal police chief is going to be meeting me here in a few minutes. You and I will meet later today and you'll give me whatever information you've got. After that, you stay out of it."

Blalock paused for breath, but whatever he intended to say was cut off when the door opened and Tribal Police Chief Randall Clah stepped into the room. His presence was imposing. Navajos tended to be taller than their Pueblo Indian neighbors in the Southwest, but Randall was big even for a Navajo. Standing six feet three, he was a barrel-chested man with broad, strong shoulders.

His gaze took in everything in the room, passing over Peterson and focusing on Ella and Blalock. His eyes were hooded, revealing nothing except perhaps polite indifference.

Randall Clah was Ella's former father-in-law. His greeting was as cool as she'd expected.

"What kind of operation are you running here, Chief?" Blalock demanded loudly. "The sergeant brings relatives in for a briefing without any authorization. We're going to have to set down some procedures and have a little discipline here."

Ella clearly saw the effect Blalock's booming voice and tone had on the others. Their stiff silences spoke volumes to her, though she was certain that Blalock hadn't noticed. He probably thought he was impressing them with his take-charge style.

Wordlessly, she slipped out of the room. Blalock's aggressiveness probably worked fine most of the time, but here, he'd just alienate everyone. On the Rez, things moved at their own pace and in their own way. Unless Blalock changed his tactics fast, official support would be grudging, if given at all. She was surprised he'd been assigned to the Four Corners post.

Ella loitered near the front entrance of the hospital, wondering whom to phone for a ride. She didn't want to bother her mom just yet, and her cousin might be tied up for hours.

Hearing footsteps coming up from behind, she turned to see Peterson hurrying to catch up with her. "You pulled a fast one on me, letting me think you were working with Blalock. But it's my own fault. I shouldn't have assumed anything."

"I had to find out for myself what was going on. My mother and brother need my help."

He nodded slowly. "You're not going to stay out of it?"

She gave him a long glance. "Would you, if you were me?"

"You always did answer one question with another." Peterson gave her a wry smile. "But I'll admit it—if someone had attacked my parents, I'd use every skill I had to bring them down."

"We obviously think alike, but that's to be expected."

"Yeah. We're both in law enforcement," he answered.

She shook her head. "It's more than that. We're both Navajo, and this is a Navajo situation. How has Blalock managed to last this long out here?"

"He gets along with the Anglo politicians, I guess," Peterson conceded with a shrug. "I'll have to tell you someday about his record on *our* land. He forgets that once he enters the Rez, he's in our world, not his, and he sticks out like a sore thumb." Peterson pulled out a set of keys. "Come on. I'll drive you to the station. You can borrow my pickup to get home. I won't need it until tonight, and I can arrange to swing by your mom's place later."

"Thanks, I appreciate it."

THREE

Ella drove south, then east, up a dirt track that led to her mother's house at the base of a low mesa. Still some distance away, she slowed, then braked to a full stop. For several minutes she stared at the familiar old house. It hadn't changed in twenty years. The flat-roofed, sand-colored adobe dwelling, with its four one-room-at-a-time additions, resembled the building block structures kids often erected. The house was no different from hundreds of others scattered throughout the reservation, but it conjured a string of memories, like beads on a string, that made it special to her. And daunting, as well.

She stared pensively at the bright yellow sunflowers that lined the front porch. She'd helped her father plant their ancestors during her senior year in high school. That had been a difficult time for all of them. Clifford, already eighteen, had turned against their father's adopted religion. In an act of rebellion, he'd built the old-style hogan that stood behind the house.

As Ella thought about her older brother, she worried about him. Was he out in a ditch somewhere, carved up like her father?

Ella pressed on the accelerator and drove the rest of the way to the house. When she reached the end of the track, her mother stepped out onto the porch. Beside her was Wilson Joe, a friend of Clifford's from the old days, when they'd all attended Shiprock High.

Rose Destea rushed to her daughter's side and hugged her tight. "I'm glad you're finally home."

"I got here as soon as I could."

Rose eased her hold and stepped back. "Wilson came to offer his help."

He gave Ella a quick half-smile. "I figured I might be of some use until you arrived," he said.

"Thanks," Ella answered. She was glad that her mom hadn't been alone, but wondered about Wilson's willingness to come. The cloud of suspicion that rested over her family would make them virtual pariahs and might extend to anyone they associated with—until the truth came out. His presence might have been comforting to her mother, but it raised many questions in her own mind.

Ella and Wilson stood face-to-face for a moment. She'd had a crush on him all through high school, and he hadn't changed much since then. He was as handsome as ever, tall and broad-shouldered, with a solid, though not overly muscular, build. His face mirrored the inner strength and pride that was so much a part of him. Despite her training, she found him as difficult to read as ever. Although he said the right things, he seemed to be wrapped in an impenetrable shell. She wondered why he needed it.

"If there's anything you or your mother need, let me know. She has my telephone number. I teach at the college these days, and I'm usually there or at home. And you can always leave a message on my answering machine."

"Thank you," Ella said.

Ella watched him walk to an old pickup parked near the rear of the house, get in, and drive away. When she turned to her mother, the serene mask Rose had worn in front of Wilson had vanished. Deep, dark lines of despair framed her face.

"I'm so sorry, Mother," Ella managed to say, though her throat had suddenly constricted painfully. "I should have come home immediately after you told me about the threats."

"No, don't take responsibility for this. You've always been too quick to shoulder the blame for things that were beyond your control. Come inside. We have to talk."

Her mother wore a traditional long skirt and a simple yellow blouse. An intricate turquoise-and-silver squash blossom hung around her neck. It had been a gift from her mother's mother, and Rose seldom took it off.

On the surface, everything looked the same. Yet, as often happened, that casual observation was deceptive. As Ella stepped inside the house, sadness overwhelmed her and for the first time tears came to her eyes. What had been taken from them had left a gap that would never again be filled. Even their home seemed changed. A stillness had settled over it as if it waited, listening for the footsteps of one who would never return.

Rose walked to the kitchen, and in what had been almost a ritual for as far back as Ella could remember, began fixing Ella a snack.

"Mom, you don't have to do that," Ella said, drying her tears with a tissue. "Come sit and talk to me."

"We can talk, but you need to eat. You look even thinner

than the last time I saw you, and you were practically skin and bones then."

Ella had put on fifteen pounds in the last six years from too much chocolate ice cream. Only her daily running kept more poundage at bay, but in her mother's eyes she'd always been too thin. "I spoke to Peterson. Dad didn't say anything to the tribal police about the threats."

Rose sighed and poured Ella a glass of a special tea she made from plants from her herb garden. Ella knew the mixture of herbs and water had steeped all day in a gallon jar sitting out in the sun.

Chilled, it was wonderfully refreshing, with a pleasant, nutty flavor. "I bought some of your favorite ice cream, and made oatmeal-raisin cookies and chocolate cake."

"Mom, you shouldn't have done that." Hurt flashed in her mother's eyes and Ella instantly regretted her words. "But I'm glad you did. I am hungry." She took a large mouthful of the cake her mother brought, her mind only vaguely registering the rich, buttery taste. "Tell me what's been happening."

"Your father wanted to build his church close to where the new community college is going to be. Some of our people were very angry about it. Both your brother and I could feel danger surrounding him, pressing in from every side. But he refused to listen to us. You know how stubborn he could be. He insisted his god would protect him."

Although her father had adopted Christianity, her mother had kept her traditional Navajo beliefs. Ella noticed how her mother had avoided the use of her father's proper name.

"Why did people object to another church? Dad wouldn't have forced his religion on anyone." Even when her mother had refused to follow Christianity, her father had respected her choice, never pressuring her to do otherwise.

"No, but you know he always tried his best to influence those whose beliefs weren't strong. That's why some in the tribe began seeing him as a threat. You see, people are finally realizing that our kids know very little about who they are. That's become a big concern."

"But it always was, to one extent or another."

"Yes, but those willing to fight for what we're losing have never been as organized as they are now."

"What do you mean?"

"A new faction actively opposes plans to build the new college. They want some of the money the tribe would spend on that used instead to pay some of our people to teach the Dineh's history and beliefs."

"But what's that got to do with Dad?"

"Your father's outspoken support of the college, and his insistence on building a new church close by, made them furious. They saw him as a traitor. They made him a symbol of what those who value our ways hated most." Rose paused as her voice trembled. "That's a simplified version. There's more to it, but his insistence on challenging our ways lay at the root of the problem."

"Where did Clifford stand on this?" Ella asked, though she suspected she knew the answer already.

Rose sighed. "He hasn't changed a bit since you last saw him, and he won't. Like me, he feels we have enough colleges and too many churches. It's time to spend our energies bringing the old ways back, and teaching others our beliefs, before what makes us Navajo is lost forever."

"Only Clifford was far more vocal than you, right?"

"Yes. That's his way. I never openly opposed your father because I knew he was doing what he thought was best."

"Clifford hasn't agreed with Dad on anything, as far back as I can remember. And like Dad, he's very blunt."

Her mother smiled, but pain was clearly mirrored in her eyes. "You were always close to your father, disagreeing with Clifford and everything he stood for. But now your brother will need your support, and maybe your help. Can you set aside your differences?"

Ella started to answer when she heard the sound of a vehicle driving up. Glancing outside, she saw the tribal police Jeep park near the front of the house. Blalock threw open the passenger door and started up the path. Police Chief Clah, respecting the Navajo custom not to approach a dwelling until invited, hung back. Ella saw him gesture, trying to get Blalock to return, but Blalock didn't even slow down.

Ella glanced at her mother. "It's my father-in-law. He's brought Agent Blalock, the Anglo investigating father's death. Blalock is a little hard to take . . ."

"The man and his habits are well known, especially in this household. Don't worry. If there's one thing I've learned over the years, it's patience."

"You'll need it with this guy." Ella tried to hide her distaste as Blalock approached the front door. He peered at her through the screen. "I'd like to come in and talk to your mother."

"She's here." Ella beckoned him and Randall Clah in.

Rose nodded at the men. "Make yourselves comfortable." They perched on the couch.

Blalock turned to Ella. "I'd like to talk to your mother alone."

"Really? Well, we don't always get what we want," Ella answered calmly.

Clah's mouth twitched, but the smile in his eyes never quite reached his lips. "We want to know where your son is, Mrs. Destea," the Navajo police chief said softly. "We hope you can help us."

"I can't," Rose answered flatly.

"You must have some idea where he could be found," Blalock insisted. "Ma'am, the longer he stays at large, the worse off he's going to be. We *will* catch him, and once the courts are told how he tried to elude justice—"

"One second," Ella interjected. "Are you assuming Clifford killed our father?" She gave him an incredulous look. "You are out of your mind."

Blalock shot her an icy glance. "He ran from the police when they went to question him. And dozens of witnesses heard him threaten your father. He vowed to stop your father from building his church on Navajo land."

"So what? They argued all the time. So do lots of other fathers and sons. You have no case."

"There are other things."

"Like what?"

"You're not an attorney, and I don't have to present my evidence to you. You were instructed not to interfere, Agent Clah. I suggest you remember that."

Ella turned to her father-in-law. "You and I have had our differences. That's no reason for you to allow him to come in here and treat my mother with so little respect."

Clah held her gaze for a long moment. "This has nothing to do with you and me."

"I wish you'd remember that," she shot back.

Blalock held up one hand. "Hey, I'm trying to question someone here, okay? Drop the family discussion." He turned to Rose. "Apparently your son has some radical religious beliefs that have made him enemies among the Christian community."

"Not as many as you've already made," Rose answered calmly. "I know about you, Agent Blalock, and I won't answer any more questions. Please leave my house."

"Obstructing justice is a crime, Mrs. Destea."

Randall Clah stood up and grabbed Blalock's arm. "A moment with you, please," he said in a low voice and took Blalock aside.

Ella watched the two men standing at the far side of the room. Clah's voice was too soft for her to hear, but his eyes flashed with cold fire. Ella puzzled for a moment about her mother's comment to Blalock. What did she know about him? Earlier, Peterson had alluded to something involving the agent. Navajos were slow to anger, but remembered their enemies forever. Ella made a mental note to ask about Blalock at the first opportunity.

As Ella seated herself beside her mother, her gaze settled on the framed snapshot on the coffee table. It showed her father in a T-shirt, basketball under one arm. It had been taken during a Fourth of July picnic. Good times like that were elusive memories now. The ghastly image of her father's corpse remained in her mind, obliterating everything else.

As she tried to banish it, something niggled at her memory, a vague impression of a conversation she'd had with Clifford a long time ago, like a name that hung at the tip of your tongue. He'd mentioned skinwalkers, Navajo witches, but she couldn't remember the specifics. Navajos never discussed the subject openly, and at the time she'd wanted nothing more than to forget what he'd said.

When Blalock turned back toward them, his manner

was less abrasive. "Mrs. Destea, I know both you and your husband are well thought of in this community. But Clifford must turn himself in; it's the best chance he's got. If you see or hear from him, will you call us?"

"If it's the right thing to do at the time."

Ella had to give him credit; Blalock was good enough at his job to know when he was being stonewalled. He glanced at Ella and cocked his head, motioning for her to follow him outside.

She went out to the porch with him. "You're using the wrong approach, Blalock, and you've apparently had that problem for some time. Change your attitude, or you'll get so lost you won't be able to find your butt with both hands and a full-length mirror."

"I don't need your advice, or your bullshit. What I want is information. Is your brother into witchcraft?"

It took all her willpower not to punch him for that. "My brother is a *hataalii,* a medicine man. What you're suggesting is unspeakably obscene."

"All I know is that he's acquired quite a following, and that he's reputed to have some vague supernatural powers. I heard one of the tribal cops on the case muttering about witchcraft, but he wouldn't elaborate. I don't believe in that crock, and I know you don't either. I've looked into your background. You're a no-nonsense, show-me-results agent. So let's cut the mysticism crap and get down to basics. *A*—Reverend Destea is killed in some ritualistic fashion. *B*—your brother ran from the cops. *C*—coincidentally your brother is a self-styled mystic who opposes everything your father stood for. That all adds up to *D*—Clifford is our most likely suspect. Now where is he?"

"I have no idea."

"When you find out, and I have no doubt you will, I

want you to call me. If he's innocent, he's jeopardizing our chances of catching the real murderer."

"As you've pointed out to me, I'm not here as an agent. Now it seems you want me to do some investigating for you. Does this mean you've changed your mind about having me involved?"

"And countermand my supervisors? Forget it, lady. I have my career to think about. If I can solve this case, I might finally get transferred out of this wasteland. If you block me in any way, I'll see you spend the next decade sharpening pencils in some jurisdiction even worse than this one."

"Don't threaten me, Blalock. Ever. You don't outrank me, and it's extremely unlikely you ever will."

He held her gaze. "Don't stand in my way. Ever."

He strode off and joined Clah by the Jeep. Ella waited until they were out of sight, then stepped back inside.

Her mother was absently tracing the pattern of the fabric on the arm of the sofa with her index finger. "They just don't understand. Clifford and your father have been arguing for years. If your father said the grass was green, Clifford claimed he was color blind. It meant nothing. Although their beliefs were radically different, both of them saw violence as repugnant. Murder—unspeakable."

"Don't let Blalock upset you. He doesn't know enough about our culture or our family. But he's going after Clifford, so I have to find him first, Mom. Help me, please. Tell me what you know."

"Where do your loyalties lie?" Rose watched her daughter carefully.

"With those of us who've been robbed of someone we love. Whoever killed dad will pay for it."

"And will you believe all that that Anglo tells you? He'd have you arrest your own brother."

"I know Clifford isn't guilty of murder, but he must have knowledge of the crime or he wouldn't be hiding. Maybe he can give me some leads." She paused, searching for a way to make her mother understand. "What scares me is that I think he's going to try to handle this on his own. That'll be a big mistake."

"I agree with you. I suspect the same thing. But I still can't help you. Clifford didn't say where he was going, probably because he was afraid I might tell you."

"Mom, none of this makes sense. My brother fears no one. He's never run away from a confrontation in his life." She shook her head slowly. "He knows his influence here on the Rez is considerable. They couldn't railroad him even if they wanted to."

"Clifford may not be thinking right," Rose answered slowly. "He's still unsettled by the loss of his son."

Ella nodded. She had heard the news a month ago, and had called to comfort Clifford. The child, his first, had been stillborn.

"That very nearly broke him, and his wife hasn't been the same since. In a way, I think Loretta blames him, but he did everything he could. He used all the knowledge he possessed as a *hataalii* to ensure the safety of his child." Her mother stared out the window at the mesa as if answers could be found there. "It wasn't enough."

"How good was the clinic where Loretta delivered?" Ella asked pointedly.

Rose's gaze turned hard. "Pride would not have kept Clifford from seeking the best medical help for his child. You should know that. But the last few months of pregnancy were hard on Loretta. Nobody was able to do anything."

Ella leaned back in the chair, trying to focus her thinking. Clifford had used all his beliefs and prayers to help his wife and unborn child, yet still he had failed. That blow struck at the very roots of everything he was. "I thought he had put the hurt aside by now."

"No one blamed Clifford at first. He'd done what the progressives believed was necessary, taking Loretta to the hospital for prenatal checks. He'd also used our ceremonies and done all that the traditionalists expected. He was very careful not to make any mistakes in our rituals. But then, some very ugly rumors began to spread about him." Her mother's voice dropped to a hushed whisper. "Do you remember anything about skinwalkers?"

Ella blinked, taken by surprise to hear her mother broach the subject. "They're evil witches. They wear the hide of a coyote or wolf and they're supposed to be able to transform themselves into the animal. That's how they got their name. But what's this got to do with Clifford?"

"One way for a person to become a skinwalker is to sacrifice a relative."

FOUR

Ella tried to hide her emotions, walking over to the window and looking outside so her mother wouldn't see her face. Heat shimmered in waves over the sand, rocks, and sage that stretched out to the late-afternoon horizon. Her mom's old mutt was lying by the side of the house fast asleep, oblivious to the chaos those around him were experiencing.

"I can't believe that anyone made such a vile, stupid accusation about my brother. Who's responsible for starting that gossip, do you know?"

"We tried to find out, but it turned out to be impossible to trace," Rose answered.

"Clifford's a *hataalii*. He's supposed to be our tribe's best defense against witches."

"*Is*—not 'is supposed to be,' " Rose countered sternly. "That accusation was meant to undermine him. They started that story after the loss of his child, when he was the most vulnerable!" Anger swept through Rose like a flash flood in a narrow arroyo, and she took several deep breaths.

"A good tactic on their part," Ella admitted. "Who had the most to gain by undermining him?"

"These skinwalkers have covered themselves well. I can't even guess." Rose covered her face with one hand. "Clifford is a strong man. He kept his hurt inside him, but the baby's death almost finished Loretta. She lost her son, then began to hear that her husband had caused the tragedy." Overwhelmed by emotion, Rose fell silent, clasping her hands together tightly.

"Is that why Clifford is hiding? Have others become so afraid of him that they are threatening his life?" Ella started sorting through possible motives.

Rose shook her head. "Your brother is afraid of no man. He has many friends and followers. They believe him. He knows that."

Ella turned from the window and joined her mother on the sofa. "Then something else must have frightened him." She lapsed into a thoughtful silence. "Could it be somehow linked to the death of his child?"

"Possibly, but that's one connection you may never be able to see."

"Why not?"

"You never paid attention to what I taught you of our people's beliefs, so even if it stares you in the face, you may not know, or believe enough, to realize it."

"You'd be surprised how much I remember. I may not believe in it, like Clifford and you, but what counts is knowing the way he thinks, and what actions he'll take because of it."

"Spoken like a *bilagáana*." Her mother smiled, her eyes eagle sharp as they rested on Ella. "Daughter, you may be fooling others, but not me. You're afraid of exactly the same things Clifford is: evils that resist control. In the world you've chosen to live in, those evils are easily defined. Here, that's not always so. But in your own ways, both you and your brother are committed to restoring harmony. And neither of you would ever betray the trust others place in you. You have more in common with your brother than you think."

Ella bit back her response, but denied the accusation hotly in her mind. Her brother certainly had abilities, some would say gifts. He would walk into a room and instantly become the center of attention. Like a master politician and a magician rolled into one, he could become anything to the people around him. Many thought he possessed real magic. Ella knew it was just insight and charisma, and craftiness. She'd seen it all before, especially in con men and charismatic preachers, but it was a striking talent nevertheless.

The thought of going up against whatever or whoever had forced her brother to run terrified her. But he was her brother, and she had to help, and that meant first she had to find him. She tried to put herself in his place. He must have told someone what his plans were. "I have to talk to Loretta."

"She's at the hogan Clifford built for her just before the baby. Her relatives are with her. It's about three miles from here, on the other side of the mesa. But you'll have a hard time driving there—the road is washed out again."

"Good. That'll slow Blalock down. I guarantee he'll want to question her, and I'd like to talk to her before he does. I can walk."

"You don't trust Blalock, I see." Rose's tone showed rare approval.

"What do you know about him?" Ella asked, eager for her mother's perceptions.

"He's been assigned to this area for a long time and he hates it. He wants us to conform to his ways and doesn't seem to understand that he has to do the adapting. He's not a very likable man, and he makes enemies far more easily than friends." Rose shrugged. "From what you've said, I gather you don't have much faith in him either."

"I just don't think he'll get anywhere on this case. He may not realize it, but he's in over his head." Ella sighed. "Now tell me again. How do I find the hogan?"

"Do you remember the cliff face the kids spray-painted one year?"

"Yeah."

"Your brother's hogan is a little south of that place, near a stand of junipers. Runoff from the summer rains will have deepened some of the arroyos, so walking will be slow. Still, it'll be faster than driving."

"I better get started; it'll be dark before long."

The lines on her mother's face sharpened and fear swept over her features. "Wait. Go tomorrow instead."

"I can't. By then Blalock might have spoken to her. I need to do this tonight." She knew instinctively that it wasn't the terrain her mother feared. "Do you think our family's enemies will come after me?" she asked, realizing that in a way she hoped they would. They'd learn she was no one's easy prey.

"Nights are dangerous here. Now more than ever."

She exhaled softly. There was so much her mother would never say openly to her. Ella's refusal to accept the old ways stood as an unbridgeable chasm between them at times. She needed facts, but her mother's facts were often rooted in beliefs that Rose didn't want to expose to Ella's coldly logical viewpoint. "I'll take my pistol, don't worry. It should be in the trunk I shipped ahead."

She went down the hall to what had once been her room. Her childhood books still filled the shelves. A maroon and silver Shiprock Chieftains banner was proudly displayed on the whitewashed walls, along with a watercolor painting of Shiprock she'd done back in the eighth grade. That her mother had chosen to keep all of her treasures warmed Ella's spirits. As her gaze drifted to the far wall, she saw the crucifix that hung over the bed.

Ella stared at it. She'd never quite believed in the Christian god, but then again, she wasn't certain about the Navajo gods either. She could understand Clifford's aversion to the religion the missionaries had brought into the Southwest. Navajo fear of the *chindi* was strong, and the stories she'd heard as a child made it difficult for her to imagine the apostles feeling anything but stark terror when Jesus visited them after the crucifixion.

"I put your trunk in the closet," Rose said from close behind Ella.

Ella retrieved it by the leather handle and unlocked the lid. Grabbing her windbreaker, she rummaged among the clothing and retrieved her pistol, ammunition, and running shoes. "I'll be back," she said, taking off her street shoes and lacing up the sneakers. She slipped the pancake holster through her belt and adjusted it. "Please don't worry."

Her mother said nothing, but concern was evident in her stiff, disapproving stance.

Ella headed down the dirt track. It was easier to go this way until the track dead-ended. Although she was in good physical shape, hiking across the uneven desert terrain was always tiring.

It had been a wet summer; the desert received almost all its rain in July and August, and afternoon thunderstorms were very common. Ella glanced around her, seeing the results of those rains. Water had carried away tons of sediment, leaving large furrows that would be extremely jarring to passengers in a car or truck riding over them. She picked her path carefully from among the natural ditches that bordered the dirt track. Hearing a loud rumble of thunder, she looked up at the gathering clouds. It was likely to rain again soon.

As Ella walked, she sorted her thoughts and tried to come to terms with the world she'd reentered. Dusk settled over the Colorado Plateau, the ground becoming shrouded in increasingly deeper and darker shadows. The hum of night insects rose to a droning crescendo, and the air became sticky, almost humid.

Struggling mentally with the events of the past two days, Ella reached the top of a rise, then started downhill. She was watching a large jackrabbit scamper away when some sixth sense compelled her to turn around. At the top of the little hill stood a large animal. She tried to make out some details, but the creature was indistinct against the purple and gray backdrop of the twilight sky.

It was too large to be her mother's dog, or any dog for that matter. A bear was a possibility, but it was the wrong shape. Cougars were rare in this area, so she ruled them out too. She took a step toward the creature to get a better look, and as she did her skin prickled uncomfortably. Ella stopped as the animal moved back into the shadows and vanished. She wondered if it might have been a wolf.

Abruptly an old black pickup appeared at the same spot where the animal had been only seconds before. The truck started down the rutted incline, bouncing and sliding, the engine revving. Ella stared in disbelief as the vehicle careened directly toward her, ripping through the sagebrush and piñon.

She started running, as fast as she could, heading for the next rise. If she could get there with a few seconds to spare, she might be able to fire off a few shots and either disable the truck or its driver.

Ella glanced behind her and realized the pickup was gaining ground too quickly. She'd never get away. She'd have to make her stand right where she was.

She whirled and pulled out her pistol, going quickly into a two-handed combat stance. In the semidarkness, hitting the driver of the jouncing truck would be nearly impossible. Her only chance was to wait until it was almost upon her. She swallowed her fear and took careful aim.

As she started to squeeze the trigger, the pickup suddenly veered away to her right. A cloud of sand, gravel, and dirt rose in the air, all but obscuring it from her sight. Coughing, she fired twice, aiming at a rear tire. The vehicle continued to speed away. She'd missed.

The motor sound abruptly stopped when the pickup disappeared over the hill. Suspecting a trick, Ella remained still, visually searching the area. After a few minutes, she moved cautiously in the direction the truck had gone, trying to avoid silhouetting herself on the hilltop. To her surprise, the pickup was nowhere to be seen. That was impossible; it couldn't have simply vanished.

As she circled around, curiously looking for tire tracks, a light drizzling rain began. She zipped up her windbreaker. It was futile to remain here searching for the truck. It would be completely dark soon. The truck had probably coasted down the hill and gone to ground in an arroyo, joyriders frightened away by her shots. They'd probably been just as scared as she was. Soldiers learned to hide tanks in the desert. Certainly an old truck could be made to disappear. The best she could do now was stay alert and make it to Loretta's as fast as she could.

Breaking into a cautious run, Ella looked toward the top of the next rise. Her heart suddenly lodged in her throat. The shadowy creature she'd seen before stood there, gazing down at her. She picked up speed, wanting to get a closer look, but before she drew near, it moved away, and dark gray shadows closed in around it.

Ella's heart was beating overtime. She was nearly certain that the creature was a coyote, or a wolf. She shook her head, forcing herself to become detached and analytical. It was just too dark. She hadn't seen it clearly enough to be sure of more than a general shape. It was pointless to assume anything. She cursed her imagination. That's what she got for listening to her mother's stories about skinwalkers. The animal probably belonged to the man in the pickup, at worst set loose just to unnerve her.

Ella looked back at the point where the truck had disappeared. Rain was already softening and obliterating the pickup's tracks. Soon they'd be gone. She'd have no evidence and no witnesses.

Things just didn't add up. How had the truck managed to hurtle those arroyos? They were no more than two feet deep, but they should have been sufficient to stop any normal vehicle going that fast. And where had it gone so quickly?

She tried to make some sense of it. He knew which path to take. She was dealing with someone who knew the land like the back of his hand. The darkness and her own imagination had conspired against her. That was all. Checking her pistol and gaining confidence from the feel of cold, dry steel, Ella continued toward Loretta's hogan.

* * *

By the time she arrived, she was thoroughly cold, wet, and tired. The hogan, illuminated from within by the flickering light of a kerosene lamp, looked inviting, and more to the point, safe. Except for the dark pickup parked near the door. Warily, Ella edged closer, trying to make sure it wasn't the same vehicle that had tried to run her over.

A tall man stepped down out of the truck. Ella recognized Blalock's bulky shape and stiff-backed stance. She cursed the jerk in the truck, cursed herself for being distracted by stories of skinwalkers. He had beaten her to the punch. Then she smiled. He hadn't been invited in yet. She still had a chance to speak to Loretta first. Ella went up to Blalock. "How did you find this place?"

"Good investigating," he answered. "But it took hours to drive here." He gave her a speculative look. "Jeez, Clah, you look like something the cat barfed up."

Ella glanced down at herself. From her knees down, she was covered with mud and plant debris. In contrast, Blalock looked like a recruiting poster despite the rain: water beaded up and rolled off his coat. Probably waterproofed. His hair seemed to curl rather than plaster itself down on his scalp as the heavy drizzle continued.

"You're annoying," she answered at last.

He grinned. "Yeah, I've been told that before."

"How come you're waiting out here? You didn't do that at my mother's place."

"Your mother lives in a regular house, not something traditional like this hogan," he said, then paused. "I have learned a *few* things since I took up this post. Besides, the police chief warned me that if I kept walking up to doors around here, someone was likely to shoot me with a deer rifle."

Ella bit her lip to keep from smiling. It sounded like her father-in-law had managed to penetrate Blalock's devotion to procedure with a new idea. "He's right. You have to honor our customs, particularly during times like these."

"Yeah, well I've been waiting for forty minutes."

"They know you're here. If they haven't come out, they don't want to talk to you."

"*That* I figured. How about a trade, Ella?"

"I know you want me to get you in," she said, "but what are you willing to give me in exchange?"

"What do you want?"

"A look at the M.E.'s report."

He considered it. "It'll have to stay between us."

"Okay by me."

"You've got yourself a deal."

"Stay here. I'll signal you in a few minutes." She walked around the car and stood in plain view of the eastern-facing doorway to the hogan. An old, heavy-set woman wearing a long red skirt and a tan, long-sleeved blouse appeared at the entrance, pushing aside the heavy blanket that served as a door. She waved at Ella, gesturing for her to come in.

Ella accepted the invitation briskly, glad to get out of the cold rain. It was warm inside the hogan, and food had been set out on a blanket. A small, damp circle of ground directly below the smoke hole was the only place moisture had penetrated the sturdy log and mud structure.

She remembered to head to the left. The south end of a hogan traditionally "belong" to the women, and Loretta and her grandmother were seated there. Loretta's brother, the only other person in the hogan, nodded silently to Ella but didn't move from where he was seated, just north of the entrance.

Loretta spoke first. "We've finished eating, but there's still some of the fry bread and stew grandmother brought. Help yourself to whatever you like." Loretta was young, perhaps twenty years old, and had pretty, almost Asian features. Her hair was arranged in one large braid down her back and she was dressed in a traditionally styled burgundy velveteen dress and deerskin boots.

Ella nodded in thanks, then spooned a small helping of mutton stew onto a plate. It would help take the chill out of her. She sat down on the dirt floor and looked at her sister-in-law and her family. Loretta was by nature outgoing and friendly, but even to Ella it was clear that tonight she was just going through the motions. She had the haggard look of a deer among wolves.

Ella studied everything, from prayer sticks she felt certain her brother had made to the sacred pollen scattered about for protection. A Winchester thirty-thirty rested across Loretta's brother's jeans-clad hip.

"Is FB-*Eyes* still out there?" Loretta asked, explaining the emphasis with a slow blink.

Ella nodded. Strangers and friends, Navajo or non-Navajo, were often given nicknames by the Dineh. "He would like a chance to ask you some questions."

"My husband, your brother, is not the man the police should be looking for." Loretta's voice held a hard edge. Ella knew at once that her sister-in-law stood firm in her belief that Clifford was innocent.

"I know." Ella finished the last of the stew and set the plate aside. The food had revitalized her. "If you talk to FB-Eyes, maybe he'll see that he's wasting time looking for my brother while the real killer escapes."

"Then I'll speak to him," Loretta said, her eyes tired.

Her brother's head snapped around and he glared at the women. "You're going to invite him in? He's not your husband's friend. He believes all the lies planted by our enemies."

"No," Ella countered in a soft voice. "He's after the truth, like I am. But to find it, he has to recognize the right trail. That often means taking a wrong turn now and then." She watched the heavy-set Navajo man, with his short-cropped jet black hair, measure her words.

Making up his mind at last, he shook his head, then turned to Loretta. "Little sister, you shouldn't speak to this man. He'll only make things much worse for all of us."

Loretta turned to her grandmother, who sat quietly, staring toward the entrance. They were avoiding the use of names in accordance with tradition. Names had power, and to use them often would wear them out.

Loretta shifted her gaze back to Ella. "If I have you invite FB-Eyes in, you'll be responsible for his behavior. Do you accept that?"

Ella nodded. "Before I call him, *do* you know where my brother is?"

"No, of course not. He would never place us in danger by telling us that. You know the way he is."

She nodded, accepting the undeniable truth. *Hataaliis,* even under normal circumstances, made secrecy second nature. They claimed to be particularly sensitive to the risks knowledge often carried. Information about rituals, gained inadvertently by outsiders, had sometimes even resulted in death, so Ella had never underestimated the power belief alone could have over people. The unknown always commanded more respect and fear than the known.

Ella went to the entrance of the hogan, pushed aside the

damp blanket, and waved at Blalock. If he did anything to offend anyone, she'd kick him out and worry about the M.E.'s report later.

As Blalock entered, he glanced warily at the armed man.

"This is their home," Ella warned in a whisper. "You're a guest. Chill." She motioned him toward the north end, and fortunately the man complied.

Following Ella's lead, Blalock reluctantly lowered himself to the dirt floor. "Ma'am, I need to find your husband. Your father-in-law's death was a ritual killing of some kind. If your husband has knowledge of why it was done that way, he could be in a great deal of danger."

"I know nothing of the murder, and I assure you I don't know where my husband is."

"You were with him when he ran from the police. Can you tell me why he did that?"

"My husband has many enemies, as did his father. I suggest you search there for the answers."

"Where? Who are your husband's enemies?"

"Those whose ways seek to harm the tribe," Loretta said flatly.

Ella looked at Blalock, wondering if the implication had occurred to him as well. Loretta could have been referring to a third faction, those not allied with Clifford or their father. A statement like Loretta's raised more questions than it answered.

"Can you be more specific?" Blalock insisted.

"My husband wanted to teach our people the old ways. There are some who say that that doesn't matter anymore, that clinging to the past only holds us back. It's within that faction that I believe you'll find the murderer."

"But that's the side your father-in-law was on. He had

no quarrel with them. Why would they kill him?" Blalock persevered.

"That group is prepared to do whatever it takes to reach their goals. They would sacrifice one of their own if they believed it would discredit those of us who stand against them."

Ella studied Loretta speculatively, wondering how broad an interpretation to give her accusation. Instinct was telling her that the same might be said of either side.

Blalock's expression shifted to one of open skepticism. "Are you familiar with the silver concha belt your husband frequently wore? I understand he made it himself."

"Yes, he did. Silversmithing is certainly not a crime. Why do you ask?"

"A silver concha etched with what several people identified as his mark was found near the body. Can you explain how it got there?"

Ella felt the blood drain from her face and her mouth go completely dry. Could Clifford have had something to do with the murder? She glanced at Loretta, hoping she'd have an answer that would satisfy Blalock.

To her credit, Loretta didn't even flinch. "I think it would be obvious. Someone is trying to frame my husband."

FIVE

Ella could see that Blalock was getting impatient. He'd learned nothing new, despite some rather inspired questioning.

Suddenly he changed tactics. "Ma'am, are you acquainted with your husband's religious practices? Specifically, ritual sacrifices and that sort of thing?"

Even in the lantern light Ella saw Loretta's face grow several shades paler. "That isn't an acceptable subject—"

Ella felt the cold stare Loretta's brother gave her. She stood and motioned Blalock outside. Blalock remained rock still, ignoring her. Annoyed, Ella crossed the hogan and nudged his shoulder with her knee, bumping into him until he stood.

"Cut the crap, will you?" he growled. Looking at the impassive, closed faces around him, he grudgingly left the hogan.

Ella knew that the inference that Clifford had been involved with witchcraft had not only offended but frightened those in the hogan. To speak of a powerful evil was to invite it into your life. Ella was frustrated that superstition was interfering with the investigation, but she knew pushing further now would accomplish nothing. She tried to apologize to Loretta.

"Sister-in-law, have you become so much a part of their world that you vouch for them so easily?" Loretta asked.

When she tried to answer, Ella found that the words lodged in her throat. As Ella walked outside, Loretta moved to stand beside her brother, blocking the doorway. Ella knew with certainty she wouldn't be welcomed back.

She joined Blalock by his truck. "You blew it big-time—for both of us. You're not that new around here. You know better than to pull a stunt like that!"

"I was getting non-answers, and you know it. I had to press the issue," Blalock complained.

"How do you figure you're going to get anywhere by ignoring our ways?"

"Oh, please. I handled her with kid gloves."

"You insulted her, and everyone in there. And since I made the mistake of vouching for you, your actions fall on me too."

"I'm investigating a ritual murder. I need to know what motivated the killer."

"Let me see the M.E.'s report."

"Not here. I prefer someplace out of rifle range of this hut. There's a diner along the main highway, just off the reservation." He motioned her inside his vehicle.

"You want to go to my mother's place instead of the diner? The ride's bumpy, but it's a lot closer."

"No offense, but I prefer neutral ground, where I won't have to mince my words or be politically correct," Blalock grumbled.

Moments later they were under way. "It's a good thing my pickup has four-wheel drive. The ruts in the road are the size of the Grand Canyon." Blalock paused. "This is your home, Clah, not mine. You want to love it, ruts and all, that's fine. All I want is a murderer brought to justice. How about giving me something to go on? This is no ordinary heat-of-passion murder. There are things going on here that nobody, not even the chief of police, will talk about."

"You're dealing with ancient taboos, things that are hard for any of us to speak openly about."

"Oh, come on," he said incredulously. "The people back in that hogan might have that problem, but you don't. I was told you don't even speak Navajo, that you're more Anglo than the Anglos. That's practically a quote."

"From my father-in-law?"

"So, Randall Clah, the chief of police, is your father-in-law?" he observed. "I wondered about the last names."

"I married his son right after high school graduation. Then Eugene went into the Army Rangers. After months of surviving dangerous training exercises, he died in a traffic accident off base."

"Tough break." Blalock lapsed into a thoughtful silence.

Ella stared into the darkness. Eugene's death had left her feeling so lost! Yet working through that time of pain, she'd found a new direction for her life, and strength she'd never thought she had. Something good had sprung from the bitter ashes. She hoped her mother would eventually be able to put her own life back together again, but she held little hope that anything positive would come from her father's death.

Blalock cursed as the pickup bounced in and out of a particularly nasty hole. "So much for the suspension."

"Slow down or we'll end up walking."

He eased off the accelerator. "Tell me something. If your brother is so traditional, why does he have an ordinary name like Clifford? And why the hell doesn't anyone ever call him Cliff? In fact, one thing I've noticed around here is that people may use nicknames, but they never shorten a proper name."

"Names are believed to have power. Why shorten them? In fact, that's why so many have nicknames. You avoid using a name whenever you can."

"But why 'Clifford'?" he insisted.

"That's his legal name. War names are secret and are considered to have a special power of their own. Using Clifford in public makes life easier."

Blalock lapsed into thought as the miles stretched out. "This is the worst post I've ever had," he commented at last. "To make things even worse, I get the idea that they've never thought much of the feds around here."

"That's true," Ella admitted. "My father-in-law was really annoyed when I joined the bureau. But let's face it, very few local authorities welcome FBI agents with open arms, regardless of the community."

"It's more than that. I'm also a white man, or as Clah says, an 'Anglo.' "

"That's certainly one factor working against you," she conceded.

Blalock leaned forward as they came to a low spot crisscrossed with deeply cut channels. "Keep an eye out, will ya? I don't want to drive headlong into one of these arroyos."

Ella strained to see ahead. The moon had gone behind the clouds, leaving them surrounded by thick blackness.

The headlights sliced narrow, momentary paths through it, but the darkness eventually won, sealing itself as they passed.

The cry of an owl filled the night, unnerving her. "To a traditional Navajo that signifies death," she muttered.

"Only if you happen to be a mouse," Blalock countered.

She considered telling him about the animal she'd seen earlier, and the truck that had come from nowhere and disappeared. Some people would claim that run-in had supernatural implications, but Ella just wondered how the stunt had been pulled off.

She was weighing what, if anything, to tell him when the distinctive crack of a rifle shot shattered the stillness of the night. Simultaneously the windshield flowered into a spiderweb pattern, a nickel-sized hole in the center.

Blalock uttered a single expletive, then swerved and braked suddenly, slamming them against their seat belts. Throwing open their doors, they both dove into the damp cover of a stand of tall brush.

Ella, pistol in hand, peered out carefully and noted the bullet had gone clear through the cab and out the rear window. "Did you see where it came from?"

"No. But he can't be too far away. The sound reached us about the same time as the bullet did."

She looked into the blackness without much hope of seeing anyone. "Well, at least the vehicle isn't disabled."

"We're damn lucky." He peered into the darkness, muttered a curse. "I can't see anything. I'm calling this in and getting my rifle. There's a nightscope on it."

"Turn off the dome light first."

"I'm not a rookie, Clah."

As Blalock carefully made his way into the truck, Ella

sharpened her senses. The moonlight filtering through the clouds was barely enough to allow her to make out even the largest obstacles around them. She listened carefully for any sounds that didn't belong, but all she could hear was an occasional distant rumble of thunder.

Blalock joined her again, rifle under his arm. "I asked for assistance, but it'll take officers an hour to find us. I couldn't give them very good directions." He slowly scanned the area with his nightscope. "If he's still out there, I don't see him."

"He's probably long gone. I don't believe the attack was meant to kill either of us. Only one shot was fired, and it passed between us."

"Maybe the sniper just missed. Your relatives weren't too happy with me."

"Nor with me, but it's highly doubtful they could have made it out here ahead of us," she snapped. "Keep in mind that they were on foot."

"Maybe someone was in place already." After waiting for several minutes, they came out from cover and ran to the truck. Ella studied the bullet hole.

"If you were playing the odds, wouldn't you say I was the intended target?" Blalock asked. "I've made some enemies the past few years."

"Who knows?" she answered slowly. "I have my own enemies here."

"You think this might all be clan-related? Family ties seem to be strong on the reservation. Maybe two opposing clans are out to settle some score."

"I can't say yes or no at this point, but my hunch is that's not the answer." She studied the rear glass. "It's too bad we won't be able to track down that bullet, but it's long gone."

"Time to get rolling," he said, placing the vehicle in gear. "I don't want to be anyone's sitting duck. I'll call in and tell the Navajo Police we're out of danger."

Half an hour later they reached the small diner, well past the fence and simple road sign that marked the reservation's boundaries. Few customers here would even give them a second glance. Blalock took a briefcase from behind his seat and carried it inside.

Ella picked a table that would give them both a clear view of the room. "This'll do," she told the waitress, a middle-aged Hispanic woman.

Blalock ordered coffee for both of them, then waited until they had been served and were alone again. "Listen, you know how graphic a medical examiner's report can be. Are you sure you want to deal with it?"

"I've already seen the body," she said, forcing her voice to stay calm and clear.

"Yeah, but you didn't stand there and study it. This is more clinical and . . . well, worse." He opened his briefcase and pulled out a manila folder. "Don't say I didn't warn you."

She opened it. At least photos weren't included. She read the report, her stomach churning painfully. Her father had been speared and stabbed to death with edged weapons, then scalped. His ears had been cut off and were missing. All the tendons from his legs, arms, and neck had also been taken.

She swallowed convulsively. Anger and sorrow mingled within her until she could barely draw in a breath. Wordlessly, she closed the folder and slid it back across the table. Without looking at Blalock, she stood and went directly to the ladies' room. By the time she got there, her legs were shaking and she could barely stand. She leaned against the wall, gulping air, and sank slowly to the floor.

Tears rolled down her cheeks. The magnitude of what had been done to her father hit her full force. The cold, matter-of-fact detachment of the report combined with the vivid image her father's corpse had branded in her mind to fill her with black despair. She'd known about the threats. How could she have failed her own family so miserably? She sobbed for what seemed like forever, then finally forced herself to stop. She would continue to fail them unless she got up, washed her face, and went back out there. Blalock didn't have a prayer of solving this case alone. No one would talk to him about the things he'd need to know, and even if they did, she doubted he'd understand any of it. She might not believe, but at least she understood.

Ella washed her face, straightened her clothes and hair as best she could, then returned to the table. Blalock watched her speculatively, as if trying to assess how big a mistake he'd made by showing her the report.

She sat down and leaned back, doing her best to look calm and professional. Her mouth was still dry, but she rejected the idea of trying to pick up her coffee cup just yet. "Let's start with what you need to know. What's on that report doesn't explain what you're dealing with."

"I gathered that."

"Traditionally, a mutilation like this was done to a slain enemy warrior who'd fought bravely. A medicine man could use the stolen items for his medicine bundle. This was supposed to be a powerful ward against the medicine man's enemies."

Blalock's eyes narrowed. "Do you realize the implications of what you're saying?"

"I am *not* telling you that my brother did it. What I am telling you is that whoever framed him knows a great deal about old Navajo medicine and traditions."

"We have evidence that places your brother at the scene. Remember the concha from his belt?"

"That concha might have been one he crafted as a gift or a spare. Or maybe it was one stolen or lost weeks or even months ago. What you have is nothing more than circumstantial. Don't try to lead me into any false conclusions with fancy footwork. It won't work."

Blalock shrugged. "Tell me this. Do you believe your brother is capable of killing someone?"

"His father? No."

"How about in self-defense?"

"Even if my father had attacked him—and I assure you he wouldn't have done that—Clifford would have offered no resistance."

"Is it possible he might have killed his father to increase his own powers as a medicine man?"

Ella struggled to keep her temper in check. "You're looking at it wrong. Clifford isn't that kind of medicine man. Murder would be the undoing of everything he claims to be, everything he's worked for and represents to the People."

"So you're saying that there's another Navajo medicine man out there, who wanted some extra power?"

"Not a Singer," she answered softly. "Today this type of crime can only be associated with skinwalkers. They traditionally gather power by whatever means they can. They subvert rituals and use them to hurt others. Traditional beliefs give them a very strong hold over people and can do a great deal of harm." She took a swallow of water, trying to keep her voice even. "Someone may be using our ways to put bizarre twists on what might otherwise be a straightforward case," she added softly.

"You still believe, at least partly, in this kind of stuff, don't you?" Blalock asked.

"I acknowledge the harm it can do. That's reality and has nothing to do with beliefs."

Blalock locked the report in his briefcase. "You've had a good career in the bureau, so don't screw it up now. Stay out of this. If you hear anything, come to me and let me handle it."

They walked back to his truck. "You won't be able to solve this on your own. You're dealing with too many things you don't understand," Ella insisted.

"Once the tribal police realize I'm going to be right there, every step of the way, I'll get their cooperation. They want this solved too."

"They'll investigate, but what makes you think they'll take you into their confidence?" Ella asked pointedly.

Blalock smiled slowly as he started the pickup. "They don't want an outsider's interference, and the only way they're going to get rid of me is to help me find answers."

Not far from the Destea home, Ella asked Blalock to pull over. "I can walk from here," she said. "It's less than a quarter of a mile to the door."

"I don't think that's a good idea," he warned. "You don't know who might be hiding out there."

"That's why I want to be on foot," she answered. "I'm much less likely to be noticed."

"You're sure?"

"Yeah. Driving with your headlights on, you make the better target."

Blalock muttered a curse as Ella swung out of the truck's cab. He drove off and she started to jog home. She didn't want to stay outside any longer than absolutely necessary. Cold desert air filled her lungs as she crossed the canyon, stopping briefly every so often to look around.

Her mother was sitting on the porch, the mutt at her feet; both stood up as she approached. "What happened to you?"

"Nothing. Blalock. Did you know they call him FB-Eyes?" She pointed to her own, emphasizing the meaning, but failed to coax a smile from her mother.

"I don't like that man," Rose said soberly. "He understands very little for a man who knows it all."

As usual, her mother's observation was right on target. "He'll learn. He has to."

"No, I don't think he will." The women went inside. "He hasn't so far, despite his mistakes."

"There's more than what you've told me already, isn't there?"

Rose nodded slowly. "A while back he went after one of our people, a young man who belonged to your father's church. The boy had been homesick and came home from the navy without leave." Rose's expression hardened in anger.

"Mom, according to the law, the FBI can arrest someone for that," Ella said warily. "What happened?"

"The boy saw him, started to run, and Blalock grabbed him. Broke his arm in two places. His brothers were so mad FB-Eyes had to call the police for help. Nothing was done to Blalock—he said he was attacked and used force in self-defense. He got away with it."

"Don't judge all agents by this one, Mom. He's a very bitter man, but a good investigator. He's just out of his element here."

"Let's not talk about him any more." Rose crossed her

arms across her chest. "By the way, Peterson stopped by to pick up his truck. I reminded him that we must bury our dead, but he told me it'll be a little bit longer." Rose shook her head as she and Ella sat down together on the sofa. "I'm very worried about this. There are things that need to be attended to. His favorite belongings, like that old pipe you called his 'Sherlock Homes' pipe, are part of his essence, of everything he was. They must be buried with him. For him to find peace, we have to do our part."

"Will our relatives be gathering to receive some of Dad's things?"

"No. They're afraid, because of the way he died. But there will be a Christian ceremony. The congregation from his church wants one, and I will respect that for the sake of his memory."

"Not a graveside service, surely." She couldn't imagine any Navajos going to that. They'd want to stay as far away from a burial as possible. According to age-old teachings, even to look upon the dead was hazardous.

"No, no, a memorial service at Reverend Williamson's church, where your father preached. I'd like you to come with me if you will. It's tomorrow morning."

"Of course." Ella knew that only the dedicated Christians among the Navajos would attend the service, and she wanted to see who they were. Loretta's suspicions could be correct.

"I expect it will be a small gathering," she said wearily. "What time will it start?"

"At eight. Since we can't take the truck, thanks to all this rain, we'll have to leave just after sunrise. It's a long walk. Peterson offered to pick us up at the highway and drop us off at the church, but he was hoping I would say no. I did."

Ella nodded. She was beginning to remember just how much walking one did on the reservation. "Sunrise, then."

Rose prepared a hearty breakfast of scrambled eggs with green chiles, black coffee, and fry bread, then ate almost nothing. Ella washed the dishes, then she and her mother left for Reverend Williamson's church. As they crossed the rugged landscape, heading for the main highway, Ella asked, "Mother, what do you believe? Will Dad be in the Heaven he always spoke of? Or did our relatives guide him to the Underworld?"

Her mother smiled wanly. "If they did, he probably fought them every step of the way. Your father never liked to admit when he was wrong."

There was a huge lump in the back of Ella's throat. "I really miss him. He'd always help me think things through, then let me make up my own mind. He never put down my opinions, even when he didn't agree."

"He loved you very much. He would have never admitted it, but you were his favorite child. He missed you terribly, but he always publicly supported your decision to make a life for yourself outside the reservation, particularly after your husband died. He even understood your wish to stay away. Or at least he thought he did."

"What do you mean?" Ella asked, instantly on her guard. Sometimes her mother's intuition was unsettling.

"Your reasons for leaving and staying away were . . . complex, far beyond what your father believed. I've always known that."

"What do you think my reasons were?" she asked softly.

"Your father believed that life here wasn't challenging

enough for you." Rose lifted her long blue velveteen skirt as they crossed an area filled with stunted junipers. The buckskin squaw boots she wore were much more suited to walking than Ella's black flats. "But I knew that was only a small part of it. You were trying to avoid things you didn't understand or want to face."

"Doesn't everyone do that, to one extent or another?" she whispered.

"No," Rose answered gently. "Your brother faced fears and uncertainties of his own, yet he chose to learn the way of the *hataalii* and study Navajo medicine to protect us and the tribe."

"But he wasn't always successful," Ella observed softly.

"No, not always."

They continued in silence until they finally reached the highway. As they walked along the gravel shoulder, an occasional car or truck roared by; the passengers often staring openly at the two women. Almost without exception, those cars were from out of state. Most New Mexicans, Indian or not, were used to seeing her people walking along roads in what appeared to be the middle of nowhere.

Ella was glad she'd decided to wear slacks. If she'd opted for a long skirt, like the one her mother was wearing, she'd probably have fallen on her face by now. The ground was soft and slippery in places where the shoulder was narrow or eroded away.

Ella and her mother were certainly a sharp contrast. Ella was dressed for work in the city, complete with coordinating jacket to hide the pistol at her waistband. Her mother wore a traditional blouse and skirt, concha belt, and many turquoise strands, or *heishi,* as a necklace. Rose's hair was in a tight bun while Ella allowed hers to fall loosely around her shoulders.

The church's tall steeple loomed in the distance. "Your father gave his first sermon there," Rose said sadly. "He devoted his entire life to spreading the gospel to the Dineh, but his god wasn't powerful enough to protect him."

"Ours wouldn't have either," Ella answered gently. "I remember something you told me once." Her voice dropped to a reverent whisper as she recalled part of the Navajo creation story. "When our god Slayer went out to kill the monsters that preyed on the land, he met Cold, Hunger, Poverty, and Death. Cold warned Slayer that without him, it would always be hot. There would be no snow, no water in the summer. Slayer had to let him live, and that's why we still have cold.

"Then Slayer turned to Hunger, who said that without him, the people would lose their appetites. Slayer knew that he couldn't destroy Hunger.

"Poverty, unlike the others, *asked* to be killed, but also said that if he was destroyed, old clothes would never wear out and all people would be ragged and filthy like him. Slayer allowed him to leave unharmed.

"Finally, Slayer faced Death. Slayer wanted to destroy him, but Death said that without him old men wouldn't die and give up their places to the young. He assured Slayer that he really wasn't his enemy, but a friend. Slayer spared him, and that's why we still have death."

"I told you that story when you were a child. I'm surprised you remembered it all so well. You seemed to think it was like . . . what did you call it? . . . a fable."

"And Daddy was angry with you for telling it to me."

"But he accepted my reminder that you had a right to know both his way and mine."

"You see? I do remember the things you taught me about the People."

"I should have told you more. There's so much you need to know now. There's danger all around us."

Ella's skin prickled at the change in her mother's tone. She was certain that the dangers Rose spoke of transcended magic or legends and were somehow connected to Clifford. Yet asking her mother directly would be a waste of time. Rose Destea wouldn't give out information until she was good and ready.

Ella set her mind to trying to find some answers. Recalling Wilson Joe's visit, she noted that despite Clifford's absence, her mother hadn't shown any undue interest or concern about his whereabouts. Wilson and Clifford had once been very close friends; there was no reason to think that had changed. Maybe Ella had missed a connection that had been staring her in the face all along.

They reached the church. The graveled parking lot was one-third full with mostly pickups. Mother and daughter entered the small church.

Rose introduced her daughter to the Anglo missionaries who'd provided her father with a place to minister to the Navajos. Their leader, Reverend Williamson, always conducted the main service at eleven. Her father had generally led the earlier nine A.M. service, in Navajo.

Ella greeted the members of the congregation who'd assembled for the memorial service. The group of Navajos was small, and treated both Ella and her mother with polite reserve, aware that neither of them would have been there if given a choice.

Reverend Williamson gave the eulogy. As she listened, Ella couldn't quite believe he was speaking of the man she'd known. He'd been a loving father, but certainly not the saint being described.

Ella noticed that every time her father was mentioned

by name, the Navajos became restless. Soon it was obvious to her that they were anxious for the ceremony to be finished. She didn't blame them. Some beliefs were so deeply rooted, they'd become a part of the People. To mention the name of one recently deceased was said to summon his *chindi.* If called, a *chindi* might return to once-beloved places, bringing only misery to the living.

Ella studied the mourners as the service continued. Grief was visible on a few faces, but even more pronounced were the furtive glances cast toward Ella and Rose. Clearly the jury was still out, and no one was sure whether Ella or her mother could be trusted. That caution made people guarded and their expressions, by and large, unreadable. She wouldn't glean much information here.

When the memorial service finally concluded, Ella heard a sigh of relief go around the room. As Ella stood, glancing toward the rear of the church, she spotted Wilson Joe, his back ramrod stiff, his gaze glued on her mother. Uneasiness spread through Ella. Wilson Joe wasn't Christian.

The worshipers proceeded to a covered patio, where the women's auxiliary served a simple lunch of fried chicken, biscuits, and salad. Ella saw her mother talking privately to Wilson. As Ella approached, their topic of conversation abruptly shifted to the weather.

Her heart felt heavy—her own mother didn't really trust her. Ella glanced at Wilson, wondering if she could count on his support, but one look convinced her otherwise. Wilson's guarded expression told her that as far as he was concerned, she was only a cut above an outsider. If she wanted his trust, she'd have to earn it.

"Did I interrupt something?" Ellas asked, barely masking her hurt.

"No," Rose answered, "but I should go and acknowledge the others now. They were all your father's friends."

Wilson never took his eyes off Rose as she walked away, and it dawned on Ella that he was here to guard her mother.

"You two shouldn't have walked here alone," Wilson said, his eyes as cold as a February breeze.

"Do you have reason to believe my mother is in danger?"

"I don't know that she isn't. Do you?"

"I'm capable of protecting my mother from physical harm. Don't underestimate me," she responded sharply.

"Are you? You're attuned to only one kind of danger," he countered, his gaze never leaving Rose.

Ella stayed beside Wilson as he discreetly followed her mother around the patio. "Did my brother ask you to keep an eye on her?"

"For him to have asked me would mean I've been in contact with him," he answered, careful not to confirm or deny. "Trickery," he added, shaking his head. "Is that what you've learned from your police friends?"

"I've learned to win, old friend," she said, her voice hard.

A sudden, angry shout from a parishioner caused her to reach for her pistol. Wilson did a double take at her response, but Ella scarcely noticed as she whirled toward the source of the noise.

In the parking lot, Blalock sat in his car, camera in hand. "Bureau business," he said to Ella as she strode up. He continued to snap pictures as people stared at him in contempt.

A cloud of rage engulfed her. She would have expected more discretion and common sense from one of her colleagues. He could have easily videotaped those leaving or arriving at the church from a hiding place across the road. The way he'd chosen to do this was deliberately insulting.

Ella removed her jacket and used it to block Blalock's next shot. It took all her willpower not to knock the camera from his hands and stomp it to pieces on the pavement. "Leave right now," she ordered.

"No way."

Blalock slipped his camera into the glove compartment, slid out the other side of the car, and approached Willy Ute, a Navajo man who'd been a friend of Ella's father since their childhood. Ella saw an unmistakable and uncharacteristic flash of anger in Willy's eyes as Blalock asked for his name.

Wilson Joe stepped forward and placed a hand on Blalock's shoulder.

Blalock spun around. In one fluid motion he grabbed Wilson's arm, twisted it in a hammerlock, and slammed him into the car.

Ella dove between the men, forcing Blalock to either attack her or release Wilson. Blalock glowered at her as he stepped back.

Wilson moved toward Blalock, still angry, but Ella held up her hand to ward him off. "Check on my mother instead," she said calmly.

Concern flashed across Wilson's features. Reluctantly he backed off and walked away, searching for Rose.

"What do you think you're doing?" Blalock demanded in a harsh whisper.

"What do you think *you're* doing?" she countered, leading him away from the church. "If you want to ask questions, do it somewhere else. Use your brain for a change, and lose this macho act. You're disturbing the peace, and you can be arrested for that."

Blalock stepped closer to her. "Taking photos is standard operating procedure, and I wasn't trespassing. I parked just outside the property the church leases from the tribe. I know; I checked. Now stop being a fool. Someone took a shot at us yesterday. That person could very well be here right now."

She moved away again, Blalock following. She studied his expression carefully. "I understand what you're doing. You're trying to provoke them into unguarded answers. But that tactic won't work with these people. They'll clam up even more."

"The real problem is that you want me to cut you some slack because your family's involved. But you're interfering with my case. Keep it up and you'll be the one behind bars."

Before she could answer, Peterson Yazzie drove up in his squad car. "Agent Blalock, the chief would like to meet with you back in his office."

"I'll be there as soon as possible."

"No, sir. You have to leave immediately." Yazzie signaled another tribal patrolman, who'd pulled up in a second squad car. "I believe it's important. Follow Officer Todacheene. He'll show you the quickest way."

Blalock glared at Ella. "You blew it for me today. I'll make sure to point that out in my next report."

As Blalock went back to his vehicle, Yazzie strode to his unit. Standing by the door, Yazzie flashed Ella a quick half smile. Ella realized then that he'd been keeping watch over the church. She gave him a barely perceptible nod, grateful that she had at least one friend here.

After Blalock drove away, Wilson joined her. "Your mother was upset, but she's okay now. You were right to be concerned about her, but not about me. I could have handled myself with FB-Eyes. You shouldn't have come between us. I fight my own battles."

She held his gaze. "This is one you would have lost. He wanted to provoke a confrontation, and you walked right into it. Don't underestimate him. He intends to find answers even if he has to put a dozen people in jail—or the hospital."

Wilson shook his head wordlessly and walked back to the church. Ella noticed that Peterson was speaking to Rose. Finishing, he approached Ella.

"The body hasn't been released," he said in a barely audible voice, "but I wanted you both to know I'm doing my best. I know your family needs to have him buried."

His veiled reference to the *chindi* made her realize that Peterson was a traditionalist. "Thank you, I appreciate that. This memorial service will help Dad's converts, but my mother's ways deserve to be honored too."

He nodded. "I'll also do whatever I can to help you with your own investigation, but it'll have to stay unofficial. Don't approach me at the station or where others might notice. That'll just make things difficult."

"Understood. And thank you," she said, trying to convey with her gaze what words couldn't adequately express.

"One more word of advice; you can take it or leave it. Wilson's pretty free with his fists. Don't let him bring unwanted attention down on you, and try to remember that your father had friends as well as enemies."

The words echoed in her mind as he walked away. Her father's enemies were her own, but her father's friends were not necessarily hers as well. That could create problems.

"It's time for us to go home," Rose said, joining Ella.

"Would you like to try to catch a ride?"

"No. I prefer to walk. It's not so far. Does it seem so to you?"

"I can make it," Ella said, smiling, "but it is hot."

"That's the desert. Nothing can be done," Rose answered with a shrug. "Shall we go?"

As they started away, Ella glanced back. Wilson Joe was twenty yards or so behind the women, but there was no doubt in Ella's mind that he was following them.

"I know he's there," Rose said without turning.

"Why is he doing this?"

"Out of friendship for your brother, and respect for your father. Your father trusted Wilson like he did you and his own son."

Wilson Joe was still angry, and he couldn't decide what bothered him the most. The Anglo giant some of the Dineh called FB-Eyes had been a real asshole and needed someone to punch his lights out. He'd hoped to do it himself, but had been denied the opportunity.

Ella was almost as hard to take. Navajo women, in his opinion, tended to be rough and independent, but Ella went way overboard. She was assertive and annoying, and probably could have knocked him on his butt. He hated that in a woman.

What bothered him the most was that he'd made an idiot of himself in front of her. He'd promised to protect Mrs. Destea. But as Ella had indicated, he'd screwed that up, left her alone and unprotected when he let FB-Eyes get to him.

Ella's control—of the situation and of him—had challenged him on a very basic level. A surge of heat coursed through his body. After all these years, Ella could still fill him with an almost overwhelming desire to conquer—or was it to possess?

That undercurrent of attraction between them had existed as far back as he could remember. Yet he'd never pushed it, finding it difficult to forget she was his best friend's little sister.

Now they were man and woman, but the passage of time, and the choices they'd made in their lives, stood between them, a more insurmountable barrier than youth had ever been.

Ella and her mother walked in silence for several miles, Ella brooding the entire time. Even her mother didn't trust her. How could she expect to get any of the answers she needed when her own family refused to confide in her? If the People remained guarded, she wouldn't get any farther than Blalock on the case. It was time to start tearing down barriers. She needed to get on the inside track and stay there. But how?

Ella weighed her options. At long last, she decided to start by clearing the air. "I'm not the enemy. Why do you keep secrets from me?"

Rose glanced at her. "No one thinks of you as the enemy. But until you're sure of where your loyalty lies, the friendship you offer has limitations. That's why people are so guarded around you."

"And you feel this way too?"

"Yes, more so than most. I want to protect you; you're my daughter. I wouldn't have you torn between what you feel you *must* do and what you *want* to do."

"Then you know where Clifford is?"

"No, I do not."

"But if you had to, you could get a message to him."

"Perhaps."

Ella glanced back, checking on Wilson. He was at the

bottom of the small canyon they'd just crossed. She hated to admit it, but even though he was a wild card, his presence was oddly reassuring. He made her feel as if she had a wall behind her, guarding her back. She knew it was nothing personal; his loyalty was to Clifford, not necessarily to her, but the feeling persisted.

As the miles passed, Ella became increasingly vigilant, her gaze darting around as she remained protectively close to her mother. She'd faced danger many times before, but the stakes had never been this high.

So far the faceless one who'd torn apart her family had the odds in his favor. She had to find a way to turn that around before someone else was hurt or killed.

SIX

Ella sat at her father's desk, sorting his papers and searching for clues. She'd felt she'd done nothing useful in the two days since the memorial service. Peterson had called yesterday to tell her Blalock had ordered a fingerprint check on the concha found at the crime scene in hopes of further implicating Clifford, but the lab hadn't been able to lift any prints. Time was slipping through their fingers and no one was making progress.

It was ten in the morning and the temperature was already past eighty degrees. She leaned back as memories of her father filled her mind.

This was his room, his domain, where he'd spent hour upon hour planning sermons and outings for the members of the church he'd loved. She remembered sitting on the woven red-and-black area rug a few feet away, reading and keeping him company. He'd devote time every evening to preparing his service or studying the Bible, but no one in his family had ever been neglected.

Still, being his kid hadn't been easy for either Clifford or Ella. So much had been expected of them! Raymond Destea had wanted his children to learn and accept his adopted religion, but Rose had insisted that they make their own choice. Consequently, Rose had taught them Navajo beliefs, while Raymond instructed them about Christianity.

In the end, both Ella and her brother had disappointed their father. Clifford had chosen the old ways, turning from his father's path. And as children often did when their parents pressed them in opposite directions, Ella had refused to choose. Being guided by her own sense of right had been enough for her, at least for a while. About a year and a half ago, when she'd come to her brother's wedding, she'd realized just how different she'd become from everyone she cared about. Though she had her career, and the satisfaction she derived from it, something was missing from the center of her life.

Ella had kept busy since then, volunteering for every assignment that had come her way. But in the back of her mind, uncertainty about her life choices had continued to grow. Now, choices she'd avoided were demanding her attention. She could feel the pressure building with each passing day.

Her mother entered the room and sat down on the chair near the window. "Peterson called earlier, when you were out searching your father's pickup. He told me the body would be released soon."

"He'll do his best for us, Mom. He understands what we're going through." Ella replaced the contents of the file drawer she'd searched. "Will you help me with something?" Seeing her mother's nod, she continued. "I haven't been able to find any of the threatening notes you said Dad received."

"Your father threw them out. He never took them seriously." Rose walked to the small bookcase that held a snapshot of her husband, taken years ago. She touched his image lovingly. "He was stubborn, and impossible to deal with. But I do miss him."

Ella felt her mother's sadness as keenly as she felt her own. She would find her father's killer. Whoever was threatening her family would soon learn that Ella made a dangerous and relentless enemy.

"Don't try to hide from your sorrow by burying it under your work," Rose said softly. "You have to let your feelings out before you can be free of them."

"I can't run away from the pain, I know that," Ella agreed. "I only wish there was something I could do to make things easier for you."

"I have to face this in my own way. No one can help me with that." Rose leaned against the wall and stared outside. Heat distorted the land with shimmering, undulating waves. "There's a ground-breaking ceremony and a barbecue today at the site of the new college. Your father and I were expected to attend. I'm exhausted inside as well as out. I need time to think. Will you go in my place?"

Sensing that her mother wanted time alone, Ella nodded. Her mother seldom asked anything of her. "I'll be glad to."

"You'll be asked if I'm in favor of the construction of the new church. Tell anyone who wants to know that I've agreed to lend my support to the project since it meant so much to your father."

"Who else knows your position on this?" Ella asked, remembering Wilson's concern for her mother's safety.

"The ones from his church," Rose answered with a

shrug. "I made my feelings clear to all who attended his memorial service."

Ella felt her stomach tighten. Her training warned her to expect trouble. That she wasn't sure what form it would take made her all the more uneasy. "I wish you hadn't said anything."

"You shouldn't worry. My association with the religious aspect of the new church is minimal. As acting building committee chairman—or chairperson—my involvement starts and ends with the actual construction. It's something I'm doing strictly in deference to your father's wishes. Everyone knows my beliefs are different." She took a deep breath, then let it out again. "Please don't feel you have to stand and watch over me every moment. I am, and will be, all right."

"That's not what Wilson Joe thinks," Ella commented.

"He means well, but his concerns are not valid."

"Why do you say that?"

"If there was danger, I would feel it," she answered simply. "Trust my judgment on this. You should attend the barbecue. Many people will be there, it's an excellent place for you to continue your search for answers."

She couldn't argue with her mother's logic, though she was surprised at her matter-of-fact acceptance of Ella's investigation during what should be a period of mourning. But Ella wasn't willing to trust her mother's safety to a premonition. "It would help me if we went together. To many people, I'm just a stranger, someone they don't know enough to trust. I may have a difficult time getting anyone to talk to me unless you're there."

"I'm staying here." Rose's voice was firm.

She'd heard that tone before. Trying to talk her mother

out of anything after she'd made up her mind was impossible. Her father had been extremely flexible by comparison—and he was as stubborn as a mule. "Okay. I'll go alone," she answered, struggling to accept what she couldn't change.

Ella showered, brushed her ebony hair until it shone, and prepared to go. Her dark green slacks and cream-colored silk blouse looked good on her, and took the middle road between dressy and casual. She secured her small derringer inside her boot using a strap of Velcro. The feel of the gun above her ankle would act as a constant reminder of what she was really there to do. Since there was no way to conceal it, her duty pistol would remain locked in the family truck.

Ella walked to the living room, where her mother was knitting a colorful wool sash, probably for a ceremonial costume. "I'm taking the truck."

Rose nodded, not looking up from her work.

At the door, Ella turned back to her mother. "Will you be okay?"

"Go." An order, but an indulgent one.

Ella drove down the dirt track. Home would never be the same without her father. She couldn't even begin to imagine what her mother was going through. Anger rose in her as she thought of the person responsible. She'd bring him down for what he'd done.

No matter what Ella did, her mother would continue to suffer. Pangs of guilt and second thoughts assailed Ella as she thought of her mother—alone at the house with just the mutt to keep watch. But there were times everyone needed privacy.

Wilson had to be wrong; her mother couldn't have any enemies. Both traditionalists and progressives loved her.

The traditionalists admired her because she'd held on to her beliefs despite the path her husband had chosen. The progressives respected the way she'd learned to live in both worlds, a goal they often professed to hold.

Reassuring herself, Ella drove across an empty span of alkali soil, a barren flatland she'd known about for years. It was a lonely route, but the terrain would make it difficult for anyone to ambush her. There weren't many places to hide.

She arrived at the newly developed housing area around noon. The three-bedroom stucco houses each had one or two vehicles parked in the dirt driveways or along the washboard streets. Though the houses had carports, the People used them more often as covered porches or to store hay.

Curbs had been installed, but asphalt roads were months or years away, if ever. Sidewalks were probably out of the question; Navajos simply walked straight where they wanted to go. Maybe the college would have them. Anglos liked sidewalks. Ella saw the advantages, though she still wasn't fond of them herself. Then again, even walking down some L.A. streets was out of the question. In many ways, the simpler Navajo lifestyle had a lot to be said for it.

Ella viewed the changes on the reservation with mixed feelings. Progress was often a two-edged sword. This brand-new community had risen up in an area where her ancestors had left only moccasin prints. A mile from here the new community college would be built. It saddened her to see miniature cities cluttering up what had once been beautiful open country.

She wished she felt more sure that the tribe was moving

in the right direction. The changes facing the People had left many trapped in an in-between world that lacked the firm foundation the old ways had given them. For instance, murder had been extremely rare among them a decade ago, but now power and greed strengthened their hold with each passing day. What her father had viewed as progress could yet become the tribe's death warrant.

A large gathering of cars encircled the site of the ceremony. Fortunately, the customary cloud of choking dust that usually enveloped such an event had not yet materialized. The rain had indeed been a gift of the gods this time. The amplified ramblings of a local politician filled the air, and the aroma of barbecued ribs, wafting through her open window, made her mouth water. Ella parked in a field, at the end of a long row of vehicles. A country-western band was setting up on a low wooden stage. A large half circle of people, mostly Navajos, stood facing a wide speaker's platform.

Ella approached the obviously restless but silent crowd. It was past lunchtime, and she knew most of the people had come for the food and entertainment rather than the speeches and political strutting associated with these events. The men and women, many with children at their sides, were clad in traditional Navajo or western wear.

Ella moved on the fringes of the gathering, wondering what to do next. People who knew her nodded slightly in acknowledgment. The uneasiness in their eyes told Ella some were probably grateful for the irritating speech that allowed them to avoid speaking with her.

Ella noted that the last folding chair to the right on the speaker's platform was unoccupied, and deduced hopefully that the other six dignitaries seated there had spoken already. Maybe she had timed her arrival properly after all.

The politician, a tribal council member whose name she'd forgotten, ended his speech in English, then began again in Navajo. Ella crossed her fingers, hoping it had been brief, because the Navajo version was usually at least twice as long in duration. She had to concentrate to get the gist of his message. It was something about the children and the future of the Dineh, and the preservation of the Way.

Ella realized how long it had been since she'd spoken her native tongue, except to her relatives on the phone. Her Navajo was embarrassingly rusty.

As she studied the crowd, Ella saw one of her older cousins, Anna Goodluck. Anna was pregnant again. Ella had lost count of how many children she and her husband, Ronald, had. Ronald, an electrician, worked at the big power plant just off the Rez. Anna caught Ella's eye and motioned her over with a wave.

"I heard you were back," Anna whispered, ignoring a frown from Ronald, who was holding an infant in his arms. "I'm sorry about your father." She gave Ella a big hug and a smile.

"Thanks, cousin. It's good to see a friendly face. I see you haven't changed." Ella glanced down at Anna's swollen belly, then winked.

"We needed another daughter. With four boys and only one girl . . . we Goodluck women are outnumbered." Anna nudged her husband with her elbow, and Ronald tried unsuccessfully not to smile while pretending to listen to the speech.

"I wish you all the . . ." Ella mumbled, remembering the words she'd used to tease her cousin after she'd married Ronald.

"I know, good luck." Anna laughed. "And when are you going to get lucky and find the man of your nightmares . . . uh, dreams?" Anna responded, looking to make sure Ronald had heard. This time he managed to not smile.

"Aren't they all taken?" Ella suggested, looking around as if taking the measure of the men in the crowd. Ella envied Anna her husband and children, wondering if putting her career above everything else was really right for her after all. She was so alone when she was by herself, with only her thoughts for company.

"There's an eligible one, I hear," Anna gestured toward Wilson Joe, who stood near the bandstand. "Go say hi. I'll talk to you later, when we eat."

Wilson was looking at Ella. Like many of the Navajo men, he was wearing a new white straw cowboy hat and a colorful western shirt. His new snakeskin boots were buffed to a shine. He looked prosperous; Ella wondered what Clifford would have thought of that. If you looked too well heeled, Navajos, particularly traditionalists, soon began to wonder what you'd been up to. Then again, maybe she was being too cynical. He could just be trying to impress someone. She joined him.

"If I'd known you wanted to come, I would have offered to give you a ride," Wilson said.

"To be honest, I didn't know I was coming until an hour ago. My mother suggested it."

He nodded slowly. "There's a lot you can learn here if you listen to the right people."

"We'll see," she answered, painfully aware that except for a few relatives and former classmates, most would avoid her. Knowing that fear of the accusations against her brother, and respect for the trouble her family was experiencing, lay at the root of it didn't make it any easier to accept.

The last speech ended, and the grateful crowd applauded loudly. Most were already heading for the serving tables, where women stood by large kettles of hot mutton stew and pots laden with barbecued beef. Golden fry bread was heaped in small mountains on metal trays, and more was being prepared in enormous pans of oil kept hot on portable stoves. The aroma enveloped Ella, and fond memories came to mind.

As they stood in a long food line, Wilson was greeted warmly, but few of the people they met were willing to say more than a few words to Ella. Her sense of alienation grew. "I'm still one of them, yet they can't see that," Ella muttered in despair.

"You're not one of us anymore," Wilson Joe said quietly.

"How can you say that?" She whirled and faced Wilson angrily. "You studied off the reservation longer than I did. From Mom's letters, I know that you only recently returned to live here."

"If you can't understand why these people feel uncomfortable around you, and you have no patience with that," he said harshly, "then you're *not* one of us, despite what you think." He regarded her coldly.

She exhaled softly, conceding his point. "That's exactly what my brother would have said," she observed ruefully.

"I know."

"You were always closer to Clifford than I was."

"It was easier for me to be his friend, since I wasn't uncomfortable around him."

His comment struck a nerve, and she stepped out of the food line, moving away from the crowd. Wilson followed, and she turned back to him. "You think I was?"

"Don't forget how long I've known you and your family," he answered gently. "I realize you love your brother, but you've always been a little in awe of him, maybe even a bit frightened. At first you avoided any ceremonies he took part in. Eventually you stayed away from anything to do with our traditions. Those who didn't know you very well thought you were doing that because you'd become a Christian like your father. But that wasn't true at all."

"My beliefs, or lack of them, are my business. They shouldn't concern anyone else."

"No, but your behavior prior to your leaving is all they have to remember you by. You haven't even been back here since your brother's wedding." He shook his head slowly. "You need them to trust you, but that won't happen, at least not right away. Do you realize how much of a stranger you've allowed yourself to become? You haven't lived on the reservation since you were eighteen."

"I know all that. Yet I hoped our people would help me, though they won't help the bureau. I have to break this case fast. I'm afraid for my family," she said honestly.

"Your brother is in a great deal of trouble," Wilson conceded.

"Why did he disappear? He's making himself look guilty, and believe me, the circumstantial evidence against him is impressive. He's got to face this squarely, or he's going to be in so deep no jury will ever believe him."

After a brief pause, Wilson said, "The danger to his life is real. The ones who killed your father also want your brother dead."

"Wait a minute. He and my dad were on opposite sides of every argument. Why would they have the same enemies?"

Wilson pursed his lips and regarded her thoughtfully, as if trying to make up his mind. Finally he spoke again. "I don't think either of us is in the mood for food right now.

Let's take a walk." He led Ella away from the gathering, uphill through a rugged stretch of sagebrush and buffalo grass.

"Where are we going?"

"To the site where your father wanted to build his new church. The trouble starts there."

"His insistence on building a church so close to the community college led to some anonymous threats. Do you know who was behind those?" she asked, watching Wilson out of the corners of her eyes.

"No, but I guarantee Clifford had nothing to do with them. It's not his style to do things behind anyone's back."

"You're right. Clifford has never been shy about voicing his opinions." She smiled ruefully.

They reached the top of the long, gently sloping hill. Wilson gestured down into the canyon. "Your brother spoke out publicly against the Anglo church and was trying to find legal means to stop its construction." A small, leveled section partway up the reverse slope contained the ruins of a building at least a century old.

"Do you know about this place?" Wilson asked.

"Clifford said something about it once, but I don't recall what. I know he didn't like to come around here."

Wilson glanced back at the gathering, a half mile or more behind them, then turned again to look at the ruins below. "Let's go a little closer," he said, with a trace of reluctance.

Ella could tell, from the lines of tension around his eyes and the rigid cast of his shoulders, that he was apprehensive. Maybe he was worried about losing visual contact with the others. That could lead to gossip that might damage his standing as a professor. She discarded the thought almost immediately. Wilson wasn't like that.

"Tell me about the ruins," she said softly.

"About one hundred years ago, a Christian church was built there. During the first service, lightning struck the steeple. Several people died, trapped by the rubble or burned to death."

"So the site was abandoned, considered to be contaminated by the dead. That explains why nobody ever really talks about this place, and why Clifford would have been uneasy here."

He nodded. "It was a long time ago, but people moved away, and most avoided coming around again. It's only recently that construction started coming closer to it. Then your father decided that the new church should be built right here. To him, it was a way of showing everyone how his chosen religion could triumph over paganism."

She shook her head. "Now I know why this church became such an issue. Dad never told me his plans. I should have asked what the problem was, but I didn't take the time. Clifford, of course, would have opposed him with everything he had."

"Our Way clearly teaches that any place tainted by death is dangerous to the living."

"Why didn't they do a Blessing Way, a purifying rite, over the spot?" Ella kicked one of the loose bricks that were scattered everywhere. The fact that no one had scavenged any salvageable building materials attested to the strength of the cloud of fear that surrounded the place.

"It's not that simple. There are other problems that would also have to be dealt with."

"Like what?" She leaned back against one of the many boulders that littered the sides of the canyon. The coolness of the rock, and the solid feel of it pressed against her back, helped push away the fear that seeped through her. This was why she'd left. Here, rules shaped by logic and nature sometimes twisted, forming a different reality.

"Six months ago, we started to find slaughtered—not butchered—livestock in this area. Lately, people in nearby communities have been reporting instances of animals being born deformed."

"Do you really believe this place is cursed?"

Wilson hesitated. "I know that evil comes in many guises. It can be an intangible force that can only be recognized by the results it produces. Bad things have happened here. That's an indisputable fact. By insisting on building his church here, your father was challenging forces he didn't understand."

"He understood them, all right—he just didn't believe they had power over him," Ella explained.

"And now he's gone."

Wilson moved away from the circle of debris. He had helped her, and in deference to his obvious reluctance to linger, Ella followed. The tip of her boot struck something hard, and she stumbled. She managed to break her fall with her shoulder, but as her hand slammed into the rocky soil, something sliced into her palm.

With a cry, she jerked her hand away. "Son of a gun, that hurts!" Ella rose to her feet slowly and looked at her palm. Blood flowed from a long cut. She kicked at the sand, trying to figure out what had cut her. "What the heck is down there?"

A metallic something caught the sunlight, shimmering brightly. She tried to pry it loose with her boot, but it resisted. "It's stuck fast."

"Are you okay?" Wilson asked, his gaze on her hand.

"Yeah, the cut's not very deep; it just smarts, that's all."

"Let me see what's buried there, then." Wilson quickly dug free a belt buckle. As he started to pull it out, they saw it was attached to the tattered remains of a leather belt.

"Not everyone is afraid of this place." Venturing a silent guess on how a man's belt might have been lost in that remote area, Ella smiled.

Wilson used his handkerchief to wipe the surface of the buckle clean. "The leather's been damaged, but the buckle's in good shape." He glanced at the inscription on it, then dropped the belt as if it were scalding hot. Disgust was etched clearly on his face.

Ella, who'd been tying a handkerchief around her hand, stopped and stared at him. "What's wrong?"

"That's a prize rodeo buckle. It's got Ernie Billey's name on it."

She searched her memory for the name. It sounded vaguely familiar, but she couldn't quite place it. "Let's take it back with us. Maybe we can find him."

Wilson shook his head. "I hope we never even come close to finding him. That man's been dead for ten years. His grave is halfway across the reservation. This was buried with him; he wore it all the time—when he was alive."

"Someone dug him up?" She glanced around her quickly. "But where's the rest of him?"

"Like I said, I don't want to know!" His eyes narrowed as he glanced around them. "This is the work of skinwalkers. They rob graves."

Ella retrieved the belt and started to roll it up.

Wilson stared at her. "What are you doing? You shouldn't touch that."

"It's evidence."

"It proves nothing. Besides, you can't take that among all those people! You'll create a panic. Have you forgotten everything you were ever taught? You'd be endangering yourself *and* others."

She considered what he said. Finding the belt indicated that grave-robbing had taken place, but that was it. There was no way of telling how long the belt had lain there, or who'd brought it. Wilson had wiped it clean when he'd pulled it from the ground. "What would you like to do with it?"

"Take it farther down and bury it."

"Why not put it back right here?"

"Disturb *this* ground again? No way." Wilson used his handkerchief to take the belt from her, then, holding it at arm's length, he headed around the bend of the canyon.

A hot, dry wind from a halfhearted whirlwind passed by and blasted them with heat.

"S-s-su!" Wilson muttered.

She recognized the expression. It was the equivalent of "scat." Dust devils were said to be animated by evil spirits. What a time for one to appear!

Wilson's presence helped her push back some of her uneasiness. Old, shadowy fears, sprung from rituals she'd never truly understood, were now resurfacing, demanding she face them squarely. She wished she could find someone with a sensible explanation for what was going on. She thought of a new tack to take. "My brother is much better equipped to deal with the type of trouble we're facing. I wish he wasn't in hiding."

"He would be very surprised to hear you say that you want him around, but he would be pleased."

"I love my brother, but I will never be completely comfortable around him," she admitted slowly.

"Why? You know he would never harm anyone, particularly you."

She paused, measuring her words carefully, wanting Wilson to understand. "The things he does make me feel . . . off balance." Her hands grew clammy as her mind drifted to the past. "When we were kids, he could make people overlook objects that were right in front of them, or make them see illusions. He could never manage it with me. I knew it was some kind of magician's trick, but I could never figure out how he did it. He always scared me."

"He's a very special *hataalii.* He uses all his abilities to heal, and to restore harmony."

She glanced around her. "I have to admit Clifford belongs here; he's part of everything, the tribe, the desert. I've always felt like a guest, one who has nothing special to offer and can never quite figure out a way to fit in."

"You've kept yourself separate—you still do—but you're not alone." He captured her gaze and held it. "You have a place here. What you have to do is find it."

The strength behind his steady gaze bathed her with new confidence. Without stopping to think of the consequences, she asked the question that had been in her mind since her arrival. "Are you truly my friend, or am I one more obligation you're fulfilling for the sake of my brother?"

"I'm here with you now. My friendship with your brother doesn't require that."

"If you are my friend, then why don't you trust me?"

"Why do you ask me for something you can't give me in return? To walk in beauty, there has to be balance."

He was right. There was nothing else she could say. Time was what they needed most, and what they most lacked.

Wilson stopped at a soft, sandy spot halfway up a hill. "We'll rebury the belt here. Then we'll go back."

He dug a hole with a stout branch, then dropped in the belt, along with the handkerchief he'd used to handle it. Once he'd covered them with dirt, he reached into his pocket and brought out a small pouch of pollen. He touched a pinch of pollen to her lips, then to his own, while uttering a prayer. Then, he released the yellow dust, scattering it to the winds. "May our trail be in pollen."

She remembered the ritual blessing. Pollen was light. It signified peace and prosperity. It was hope because from it came life. For that one instant, she felt the power of beliefs that were as old as the Dineh. Once again, she was part of what she'd left behind.

As they started back, a feather floated across her path. Ella said, "The dust devil swept something good toward us. I remember my brother teaching me that feathers stand for beauty and happiness, and are present whenever a transformation is about to take place." She reached for the feather, had just grasped it, when Wilson said, "Let it go."

"Why? It's beautiful. Look at the brown and white markings. It's almost striped."

She held it toward him, but he brushed it out of her hand. Seeing the surprise on her face, he pursed his lips, pointing Navajo style. The rotting carcass of a dead owl, covered in similar feathers and bursting with maggots, lay at the base of a nearby piñon tree.

"That bird is a sign of ill omen to the Dineh; surely you know that." Wilson took Ella's hand and, led her away.

"Then it's a good sign that the owl is dead, right?" Ella asked.

"I wish I could answer that," Wilson mumbled as they walked back toward the crowd and safety.

SEVEN

It was early afternoon when Ella returned home. Her mother was crouched by the flower bed, her long blue denim skirt spread out around her. Her cloth gardening gloves were stained with soil. The mutt lay by her side, absently sniffing the four-inch-tall herbs Rose was planting.

"You're back early," Rose observed, disapprovingly eyeing the pistol Ella was carrying. "I hope you didn't cut your time short because of me."

"I didn't, not really," Ella answered, knowing she wasn't being completely truthful.

Rose shook her head. "I suppose that means yes, at least partly."

"You can't expect me to go off and not even give you a thought," Ella replied, patting the dog. The animal had been around for a decade. Nobody had ever decided on a name for him, so he was just Dog. Sometimes her dad, in a burst of inspiration, had referred to him as Boy.

Rose patted down the dirt around the last plant, then stood, brushed off her skirt, and walked over to turn on the garden hose. "Did you see Wilson?"

"Yes, of course. He and I had a long talk." Ella wondered now, had they just wandered into each other, or had Wilson sought her out?

Rose placed the hose, running at a trickle, so it would soak the area she'd just planted. She studied her daughter's expression. "You're beginning to understand. I'm glad to see that."

"Understand? What do you mean?" Ella asked, thrown by her mother's statement.

"You know precisely what I mean. That boy's been interested in you since high school."

Ella gave her mother an incredulous look. "No way. He didn't even know I was alive."

Rose laughed. "My daughter the great detective! You miss what's right in front of your face!"

"I don't see it because it's not there," Ella argued. Clearly she couldn't discuss her doubts about Wilson with her mother without affecting their own relationship.

Rose Destea laughed again, then led the way inside. Ella dropped her pistol in her room. "How can you be so smart and still so blind!"

"Mom, he dated almost everyone *but* me! In fact, he'd avoid me even when he came over to visit with Clifford."

"Exactly." Rose walked to the kitchen and poured them each a glass of her special blend of iced tea.

"I don't get it."

"You were Clifford's little sister. He was very careful not to do anything that might strain their friendship. Brothers can be very protective."

"Well, maybe that was some of it, but he certainly wasn't interested in me, not in a boy-girl-type way."

Rose's eyes twinkled. "Should I assume you've also managed to miss his interest in you now?" A tiny smile played on her lips.

Ella averted her gaze, shifting uncomfortably in her chair. She considered protesting, then changed her mind. Better that her mom thought it was a budding romance than a direct consequence of the murder.

"No answer?" Rose insisted playfully.

Ella shrugged.

Rose chuckled. "There's hope for you yet."

Ella couldn't believe that her mother was teasing her. It had been ages since she'd done that. As Ella looked around for a coaster to place under her moisture-covered glass of tea, she noted that sacred pollen had been sprinkled everywhere. A thin yellow trail lay on the windowsills, and in each corner of the room.

"Did you have company while I was gone?" she asked suddenly, suspecting Clifford had been around.

"Company? No guests have been here."

"Don't be evasive, Mom. Someone's blessed the house."

"Oh, so you see that!" Rose smiled.

"Mom!" Ella tried to make her voice sound sharp, but failed miserably. She sounded like a child, not a top investigator. "Was my brother here?" Had he been watching the house and seen her leave, or had someone tipped him off?

"You came to that conclusion from a little corn pollen? Our tribe has more than one *hataalii,* daughter." Rose filled a plate with cookies.

"Yes, but not in this chapter. And you still haven't answered my question. Was Clifford here?"

"It seems you've already made up your mind. Why bother asking me?"

Ella sighed. She was getting nowhere. Her mother could dodge questions better than any criminal she'd ever met. She smiled, remembering how Peterson Yazzie had claimed the same applied to her.

"Tell me about the barbecue," Rose said, setting the plate of cookies on the table in front of Ella.

She hesitated, wondering how much her mother was prepared to know. "It was . . . interesting."

Rose sat up straight. "Tell me what happened."

Ella told her about meeting and talking with Anna, then described the discovery Wilson and she had made, gauging her mother's calm reaction carefully. "Why aren't you surprised?"

"That area around the new church *is* evil. I've always felt it, and so have many others. Nothing that you found there would shock me."

"Is what's happening at that site linked to the reason Clifford is on the run?"

"As a *hataalii,* your brother is the sworn enemy of any skinwalker. Keep that firmly in mind while you search for your answers."

"And what do you think I'll find?" Ella asked, certain her mother knew far more than she was admitting.

"You'll have to decide for yourself." Rose paused. "I received a phone call earlier from Loretta's brother, Paul. It seems the police have started watching her. When Paul took her to the market, they saw a car with two men following them."

"Were they certain the men were police officers?"

Rose nodded. "Paul recognized one of them—and he thinks he's being followed too. He saw some lights behind him when he went to the pharmacy last night. From what I've heard, the police have been questioning all of Clifford's friends, trying to find out where he's hiding."

"Wilson didn't mention that," Ella said thoughtfully, wondering why he hadn't. "Maybe they haven't gotten to him yet," she added. She'd ask Peterson about it later.

It occurred to Ella that except for Wilson, she didn't know who Clifford's friends were. It was part of the price she'd paid for being out of touch for so long with her family.

Ella heard a vehicle driving up the dirt track. Moving to the side of the window, she peered out. "It's Wilson."

Rose grinned. "See, he misses you already."

"Right, Mom," Ella answered, knowing that she was being teased. "Just an hour without me was too hard for him to bear."

"Poor love-struck man!"

"Oh, puh-leese!"

Rose nodded toward the door. "Go greet him. It's you he came to see."

"How do you know?"

Rose gave her a steady look and smiled. "My intuition is better than yours. More years, more experience."

She realized that her mother was right. Ella's own intuition hadn't done her much good on this case. She had to start thinking like a cop, not a victim.

Ella waved to Wilson from the porch. Watching him walk, she realized that something was worrying him, and her trained instincts focused on discovering what he was hiding.

"You should have stayed a little longer at the barbecue," he said quietly when he reached her.

Ella glanced into the house. Her mother was still in the

kitchen. "What happened?" she asked, her voice deliberately low.

"FB-Eyes showed up."

Ella grimaced. "What's Blalock done now?"

"He badgered everyone about Clifford. He tried to act polite, but everybody knows that with him, it *is* an act. He's convinced your brother's being hidden by his traditionalist friends, and he wants to stir the progressives into betraying him."

"He'll keep putting pressure on people, offering deals or making threats. He won't let up until he gets some leads," Ella said ruefully.

"It doesn't matter what he does. He still won't get anywhere. Your mother told you about FB-Eyes' big AWOL arrest, didn't she?"

She nodded, then narrowed her eyes and studied Wilson speculatively. "You're awful damn sure that Blalock won't get anywhere. Does that mean that you think my brother really is acting entirely on his own, or that you think people would never betray him to Blalock?"

"Ah, the Blalock school of endless interrogation. I see I'm with a graduate."

"Well, we both trained in the same place. I'm just not as rude as he is." Ella smiled. "Talk to me. You know I'm the best chance Clifford's got."

"Not if you turn him in."

"Turning him in may be the best shot *he's* got."

"If you really understood what was going on, you wouldn't be so quick to say that."

"So enlighten me." Ella knew she was making progress with Wilson. He was at least talking to her about Clifford.

He took a deep breath, then let it out again. "I've got a better idea. Let me take you on a little drive. By the time we finish, I promise you'll have answers to many of your questions."

"Where do you want to go?" Ella's training told her to be wary. She wasn't going anywhere without both eyes open.

"You'll have to trust me."

"All right. Just let me tell Mother I'm leaving." After Ella spoke to her mother, she retrieved her gun and pocketed some extra ammunition before rejoining her guide. "I'm ready."

Wilson led her to his pickup, then held out his hand. "Your weapon, please."

"Why do you need it?"

"A precaution."

"Against what? You're in no danger from me. I'm sure you know that."

"Your choice," Wilson maintained. "Either give me your weapon or we stay here."

She reached underneath her windbreaker and handed him her pistol. "Satisfied?" She could feel her backup weapon safely inside her boot.

Nodding, he placed the pistol in the glove compartment. "A sign of trust between us; the gun won't be far from your reach."

Ella could feel that she wasn't in any danger. By playing along, she might finally get some answers.

Wilson drove toward the highway. The truck bounced hard, tossing them everywhere. She gripped the dashboard with one hand. Before the main road became visible ahead, Wilson pulled over.

"What's wrong?"

"From this point on, you'll have to cover your eyes." He offered her a clean blue bandanna.

"What?"

"That's the only way we can proceed. I'm sorry, but it's for your own protection. Trust me, please."

"What's to keep me from removing the blindfold, or do you plan to tie my hands too?"

Wilson shook his head. "Your word will be good enough for me."

"Fine. You have it." She had the gut feeling he was taking her to see Clifford, and this was the chance she'd been waiting for. She fully intended to use her training to keep the upper hand. He might have thought he was in control, but he was wrong. Ella shifted in her seat, angling away from him so he could tie the handkerchief over her eyes. She didn't like the feeling, but knowing her hands would remain free made her feel partially better.

"You know that you're in no danger. Your gun is in the glove compartment, and your hands are untied. Just do nothing until I tell you."

Ella shifted again until her back was against the seat. "I'm trusting you," she said reassuringly. She was less helpless than he thought.

"I won't betray you," Wilson answered. "I'm going to reach across you know and refasten your seat belt."

Although she was perfectly capable of doing it for herself, even blindfolded, she allowed him to help. Ella felt the warmth of Wilson's body as he leaned over her. His aftershave was musky and masculine. Shrugging off the pleasant warmth she felt from his nearness, she concentrated on the fact that his scent would help her ascertain his position if he moved away from her while she was still blindfolded.

She felt tension in the air, like an intense, unexpected storm.

Finally he sat back and restarted the engine. The truck jerked forward.

Ella forced herself to concentrate, memorizing every bump in the road, trying to ascertain the direction in which they were traveling from the warmth of the sun on her face. She kept track of animal sounds, the rush of wind through a canyon, anything that might give her a clue. She heard the distant sound of a lone oil well amidst the sound of birds. From that, and the scent of piñons, she grew confident that she'd be able to find the area again.

After they'd traveled for what seemed like an hour, she began to feel restless. She had a feeling that Wilson had anticipated her effort to gather clues from the land itself and had driven them in circles for a while. She knew it for sure when the pickup dipped sharply to the right and the underside collided with a sharp crack against a rock. That had happened before.

"We'll reach our destination soon," he said encouragingly.

"Try to miss a few of the bumps."

"Impossible out here. Sorry about that."

She felt the pickup slow down, then brake to a stop. "Why didn't you bring me here directly from the ceremony?" Ella asked, her voice taut. "Did you need someone's permission first?"

"You'll know the answer to that soon enough."

Wilson came around the truck and helped her down, then led her forward. She heard another set of footsteps. The strides were measured, and soft as a skilled hunter's. They were steps she recognized.

Wilson removed her blindfold, and she shaded her eyes with one hand, trying to adjust to the sudden influx of light.

When she could finally see, she nodded a greeting to her brother, Clifford, who was standing to her right.

His back was ramrod straight; a tiny smile played on his wide mouth. He was dressed in jeans and a chambray shirt that hung loosely outside his pants. Except for the medicine pouch on his belt, he was dressed like any of a thousand young Navajos. But Ella could sense the special charisma that gave Clifford his power over others.

Despite that power, he looked tired. There were dark circles around his eyes, and an aura of intense wariness that reminded her of the hunted, almost feral look she'd seen on many fugitives over the years. It attested to sleepless nights and the toll fear took when it became a constant companion.

Concern filled her as Clifford's gaze darted over the terrain behind her, searching with the thoroughness of a hunter who suddenly recognizes that he is the prey. "Why didn't you have Wilson bring me to see you sooner?" Ella asked, breaking the silence that had shrouded them all.

"Always criticizing, little sister," he teased softly, holding her hands for a moment.

Ella fought a sudden urge to hug him, respecting the tribal custom that discouraged physical contact between a man and a woman of the same clan. "You're in so much trouble! Will you let me help you?"

"I'm the one who has to protect *you*." Clifford gestured toward a small, somehow familiar-looking old-style hogan hidden among a stand of tall pines halfway up the long slope the pickup had climbed. "Come inside."

Ella followed him in, then sat across from him on the cool dirt floor, glancing around. A two-burner gasoline stove and a box of canned goods suggested he'd been there for some time. The lack of new ashes in the fire pit told her he'd been careful about smoke. Were they close to other hogans? Realizing that Wilson had remained outside, she glanced at her brother questioningly. His eyes were half closed. Ella wondered how long it had been since he'd slept.

"He'll keep watch and make sure no one comes up unexpectedly. It's a necessary precaution." Clifford rubbed his eyes.

"Tell me what's going on."

"Our father is dead because he refused to believe the truth. Don't repeat his mistake. You have to listen to what I tell you with an open mind."

"I promise that I'll do whatever I can to help you. Remember, I'm trained to be observant and objective. I have no preconceptions."

He leaned back against the earthen and pine log sides of the small hogan. It was a type of structure called *Tzin-yah'-dee klin'*, or logs stacked up. Constructing it required no woodworking tools. Navajo warriors in the story of the Cub Mountain Chant had occupied this kind of hogan in defense against the Utes. Ella knew she'd seen this place before, but it had been years. Damn her memory!

The hogan suited Clifford's traditionalist nature. He remained quiet for a few seconds, looking at her with eyes half open but very perceptive.

"Throughout your career, you've found a way to avoid the things you feared the most," he said. "Intangibles have always frightened you far more than anything you could visualize and define. What I have to say will make you remember what you've fought hard to forget."

"My memory's better than you think," she answered quietly. How like Clifford to put things in mystical or magical terms! She'd listen to his explanation, then make up her own mind.

Clifford nodded. "We're fighting an ancient evil. It uses the skinwalkers for its own purposes."

"What do you think that purpose is?" She kept her voice cool, nonjudgmental, trying to maintain the poker face of a successful agent. She wanted him to keep talking. Many times her ability to listen without revealing her own thoughts had helped put witnesses at ease and aided her work.

"I don't know, not precisely. But evil always works at the expense of the majority." This time, when his eyes narrowed, it was from outrage and frustration, not lack of sleep. Ella could feel Clifford's struggle not to let negative emotions like anger cloud his thinking.

"Evil or not, whoever killed our father is as human as you and me. I have to catch that butcher before he harms anyone else." Ella took a deep breath. "In the meantime, I'm worried about you and the rest of our family.

"Our enemies are human, true, but what drives them goes far beyond that. Everything exists in two parts; there's evil and good in each of us. When something happens to upset that balance, a *hataalii* is needed to restore harmony." Clifford crossed his arms.

Ella knew from Clifford's rigid stance and stony gaze that his mind was made up. Still, she had scored a partial victory. She'd gotten him to talk openly about the situation, and that was the first step.

She studied the hogan carefully. Clifford's old model 94 Winchester rifle was propped up near the door, alongside two boxes of .30-.30 cartridges, and across the hogan, a Ruger Blackhawk revolver sat in a leather holster on a blanket roll. The pistol looked to be a nine-millimeter. If need arose, she and her brother could share pistol ammunition.

Her heart pounded as she realized the implications of this analysis.

Clifford had followed her gaze. Ella was sure that he could sense her tension and the urgency that was driving her. "Do you have any idea who we should be looking for? These skinwalkers have to be people who live in the area."

Clifford shrugged, uncrossing his arms and clasping his hands. He was nervous. "I can't make wild guesses—you know what would happen if I accused someone who was innocent."

Ella smiled grimly. "Yeah, they'd be hiding out somewhere in an old hogan with half the world out to get them." She took a peek out the door to make a point.

"I'll give you the names and backgrounds of a few people I've had run-ins with and the name of someone our father had bad dealings with on occasion. Be very discreet when you look into this. These people could all be innocent."

Ella handed him her pocket notebook and a pen, but he already had the list and thumbnail descriptions written on a piece of brown paper torn from a grocery sack. She was grateful that he'd had enough confidence in her investigative abilities to prepare the list beforehand. She glanced at the names and pocketed the list. She'd follow these up soon. Right now there was another urgent matter to handle.

"Thanks. Now let's get back to your situation. It's my opinion, as a law enforcement officer, that you'd be better off turning yourself in. At least you'd be safe and I could devote my time to finding the real criminals instead of worrying about you."

Clifford shook his head immediately. "My—our—enemies are everywhere. It's a lot easier to get into a jail than out of one. I'd be dead overnight. Besides, I have to fight for our People from the outside. Here, I can do the ceremonies needed to protect all of us. There's magic that needs to be countered."

"Let me do my job and track down the killers. Even Houdini couldn't get away from me once I had my hands on him. Give yourself up. I'll escort you in and make sure you're placed in protective custody." Ella knew his mind was made up, but she had to try.

"You're not *listening.* To succeed, we have to fight on two fronts," Clifford said, his voice rising slightly. "You deny the existence of the unknown, which is my area of strength."

"I prefer to keep my goals straightforward and simple." She wasn't going to let an argument about spiritual or religious matters cloud her thinking. "Talk to me. Tell me how to find the one who killed our father. My strength is in tracking down criminals, not ghosts."

"I *am* telling you!" Clifford held up his hand. "I can't believe this. You're still the only person I know who can make me lose my temper." He turned away, gathering his composure again. Ella watched his shoulders slump. "I don't know who the murderer is. I only know where we have to look to find him."

She glanced at the battered old suitcase by the bedroll. "But you're thinking they might find you first."

"I have to be prepared to fight them any way I can. They'll come after me because as a *hataalii* I'm the biggest threat against them. They also know their actions against my family have ensured that I'll do my best to destroy them, not just what they represent. I have to use every kind of weapon to ensure my own survival. Every morning I prepare myself physically and mentally. I've also fortified this hogan with *hozonji,* our Good Luck Songs, and I've sprinkled it with sacred corn pollen. I've done the same thing for the homes of our friends and relatives."

"Do you know why our father was chosen as their victim?"

"A symbol mostly, but anyone involved with the new church or the college is in danger. That entire area is infused with evil. The skinwalkers have chosen it as their home and will not give it up to anyone. You've been to the site of the church; Wilson told me. Didn't you feel something while you were there, a wrongness about that place?"

Ella wanted to deny it, but she couldn't. "Spooky stories can bother anyone," she replied with a shrug. "It made me nervous."

"I know what you found there. You should be afraid. Can't you understand that it's all interwoven?"

"I'll tell you what I do see. The evidence against you is mounting. The police have a silver concha with your mark on it. Did you know that?"

"I don't see how. All of mine are accounted for. I took two off my belt and melted them down to make a bracelet for our baby." He twisted around to show her the two spaces on his belt, and his voice dropped to a whisper. "The bracelet is now buried with the child. There are no others that I know about."

"I'm so very sorry for what happened," Ella said, her voice strangled. She took a deep breath to steady herself. She had to maintain her objectivity as an agent to continue questioning him effectively. "Have you been to the church site recently?"

He remained silent for a few moments. "The last time I went there was to do a Blackening Song to exorcise the evil, or at least weaken its power. Before I could complete the ceremony, Paul came to find me. Loretta had gone into labor. My son was . . ."

"I know," Ella said gently.

"The evil in that place has already caused the death of our father, and my tiny son. My enemies are now after my wife. I need your help, little sister."

"Loretta's being looked after, and I'll watch over Mom. Can you identify the people trying to stop construction of the new church? If you're right, they're the ones who murdered Dad."

"Why do you insist on only seeing half the problem?" Clifford asked wearily.

Ella considered her reply carefully. The power of magic, of skinwalkers, was bolstered by the people involved in those activities—and by those who feared them. She toned down her answer. "Evil needs to be in people to do harm," she responded, keeping her voice coolly logical. "I've been trained to track down criminals. I'll go after the people; you can take care of the other half of that equation. If you won't turn yourself in, that's the only deal I can offer you."

He nodded. "All right, but don't trust anyone outside our family except Wilson. Until we know who the skinwalkers are, they have the advantage."

"Do you know anything about the threats made against Dad? Unsigned notes were sent to him, warning him to drop the idea of building a church. If only I had known how far they were willing to go!" Emotions reverberated in Ella's voice. Then she realized from the puzzled look in Clifford's eyes that her father hadn't trusted Clifford not to side with his enemies.

"I don't blame you for assuming the notes were nothing more than a way to scare him . . ." His voice trailed off.

"There's a 'but' in there someplace."

He shook his head slowly. "I wish you'd never chosen to leave our land. There's so much you haven't learned. Now you're vulnerable."

"I followed the life's walk that was right for me. I don't regret my decision."

"Then you shouldn't have returned. You're not prepared to handle any of this. Go back to the world you adopted."

She struggled to forgive the hurt his words caused her, because she knew they'd been spoken out of concern for her safety. "I can carry my own weight. Just because you don't see what part I'm to play in what's happening, don't discount me. Isn't that what you've always said about traditional beliefs?"

Clifford's eyebrows rose slightly. "You argue well, but this is no parlor game."

"No," she replied somberly. "This is my job. It's what I'm trained for. That's why you can't afford to turn down my help. In a life-or-death situation, you use every weapon in your arsenal."

Slowly he nodded in acquiescence. "All right. As long you agree to do the same."

EIGHT

Wilson blindfolded Ella again. "Do you understand why this is still necessary?"

"You're trying to keep me from being an accessory, and from the danger that knowledge of Clifford's whereabouts can bring. Still, I don't agree. I'm perfectly capable of taking care of myself."

"I respect the training you've had, but none of us can face this on our own. The odds against us are bad enough. Let's not make them even worse."

It was the conviction in his voice that worried her most. Fear was a strange thing, an unpredictable force that could take on a life of its own. It could cause people to go off half-cocked. She'd hate to think that the most pressing danger they'd be facing would stem from their own worries.

As they drove away from Clifford's hogan, the sun playing on Ella's face guided her, mapping a trail in her mind. She was certain that, if necessary, she'd be able to identify the general area where her brother was hiding. She'd noted the position of the mountains in the distance as she'd left the hogan.

Suddenly Wilson braked and veered sharply to the right. Ella reached for the dashboard to steady herself. "What the heck are you doing?"

"There's a police car parked ahead of us. I'm going to have to avoid it."

"At least that's proof they don't know where Clifford is," she commented.

The pickup headed up a steep slope. The truck slowed, and Wilson commented, "The ground is muddy from the recent rains."

"You have four-wheel?"

"Sure, we'll make it."

Instinct told her differently. She could feel the truck's speed become erratic as the tires bogged down, extracted themselves, then repeated the process; the rear end of the vehicle fishtailed drunkenly. "Can't you find firmer ground?"

"I'm trying, but it's not easy."

They traveled downslope slowly, the truck sliding dizzily. "Look, maybe you should let me take the blindfold off. I could help you keep an eye out."

"No. We'll be fine. Have confidence in me."

Abruptly the truck's nose plummeted, practically tearing Ella out of the seat belt. She gritted her teeth. The pickup was still, canted on an angle.

"Are you okay?" Wilson asked quickly, concern evident in his voice.

"Yeah, but why do I get the feeling that we've fallen into a ditch?"

"ESP?"

She exhaled softly. "It's already late afternoon. If you're

going to dig us out all by yourself, you're going to have to do it pretty soon. I don't want to have to walk out of here blindfolded if you can't get us unstuck, especially in the dark when *you* won't be able to see . . ." She let the sentence trail off, hoping he'd concluded that he needed her help.

"Wait here while I go take a look."

She heard squishing footsteps as Wilson made his way around the truck. It sounded like a swamp outside. She shifted, listening intently.

He came around to her side. "Here, let me take the blindfold off."

Ella squinted for a moment, but the sun was behind a gathering thundercloud, and easy on her eyes. She glanced around, grimacing. "Jeez, you really had to look to find this lousy place."

"Thanks a lot. I didn't plan to get stuck out here in the middle of nowhere . . ." He gave her a playful glance. "Then again, the company's not half bad."

"Aw gee, thanks. But save your flattery for better surroundings."

He handed her a shovel. "You're right. Here."

"Hold it, buddy boy. What will you be doing while I'm digging?"

"I'm going to chop some brush. I've got an ax in the back. We'll need to put something under the tires for traction." He studied the muddy, reddish-colored sediment that surrounded them. "You won't be able to really dig; the ground is too soft and the mud will only flow back. So try to uproot some grass and weeds that we can place in front of the wheels."

They spent forty minutes building a path for the tires, laying down lines of vegetation and branches. The mud seemed to claim each piece, swallowing it as soon as the truck's weight hit it, and the vehicle bogged down repeatedly.

Ella rubbed her back. "I need a break. Let's take five, okay?"

Wilson nodded. "I suppose it's okay. We're making good time."

Ella stretched, unkinking her sore muscles. "I'm going to walk around a bit."

"Trying to figure out where we are?"

She shot him a cold look. "I *know* where we are. We're stuck in the muddiest wash I've ever seen on the reservation." As a matter of fact, Ella did recognize the particular wash they were trapped in. She'd been there before, though not recently.

Wilson cringed. "How about letting me walk with you? Or would you prefer me to throw myself in the mud to provide traction so you can drive away?"

She pretended to consider it, then gave him a grudging smile. "Come on." She cocked her head. "Let's get out of the sun."

Searching for the coolness of shade, she led the way to a cluster of junipers. "At least this didn't happen before the clouds came. We would have roasted."

"Too much city air-conditioning?" he goaded playfully. "I thought FBI agents were supposed to be hardened and tough."

"Tough, yes, but smart too," she clipped. "Our work is hard enough without inviting extra hardship."

He laughed apologetically. "Oops. I think I struck a nerve."

She gave him a quick half smile. "Maybe you did. I'm protective about the bureau." Ella looked around, hoping to pinpoint the exact location for future reference.

They approached a circular, hollowed-out circle in the middle of an expanse of rocks. Wilson stopped abruptly, saying, "I don't like this. Let's go back."

"Let me check this place out first," Ella said, curiously studying the big bowl-shaped feature. "It looks like a place where cattle have lain. Am I right?"

"No. Come on. It's going to rain soon, and I want us out of here by then."

She crouched down on the far side of the circle, trying to make out a pattern in the ashes that had been strewn there. "It almost looks like a dry painting, but it's made from ashes, not sand. Here's something that looks like a bird. And what's this?" She pointed to a human-looking figure with two faces.

"Those are used in skinwalker rituals," Wilson said, his voice barely audible. "It depicts the person they intend to harm or kill. Come away from there."

Ella ignored his warning and studied the picture carefully. "It's so faint now, I can barely make anything out. The winds have almost obliterated it."

"Don't touch it."

"No one's here," she reassured him calmly, "and it's not raining. Don't worry." Wilson seemed increasingly edgy. Was he really that superstitious, or did he have some other motive for wanting her to leave?

"Your brother is right about you," Wilson grumbled. "You're just plain stubborn."

Ella was at a loss to explain how, but without any warning, the feel of the place suddenly changed, and she felt cold all over. She stood, suddenly uneasy, as some sixth sense worked overtime to alert her to danger. "Let's get back to the truck."

Wilson nodded. "Something's wrong. I sense it too."

"Keep your eyes open." Ella was angry now. Was Wilson's mind-set about evil making her feel threatened, or was it something about the place? She'd had this feeling before, with no ghosts in the vicinity. She recalled how the man in the diner had set her teeth on edge just before he'd started blasting away. Maybe her instincts for survival *did* function after all.

They strode back to the truck quickly. Working fast, motivated by a strong desire to leave, they extricated the pickup from the mud. Wilson accelerated slowly until they were out of the muddy arroyo, then braked to a stop, leaving the motor running. "I'm going to make sure the tires are still intact."

Ella took her pistol out of the glove compartment, fastened the holster to her belt, then stepped out of the truck. Her hair stood on end, as if she were about to be struck by lightning. She'd felt this way before, usually before a case went really sour. "The truck will make it now. Let's get going," she urged, looking around for someone who might be standing in the tree line. A sniper could pick them off quite easily.

Wilson was just coming from the rear of the vehicle when Ella spotted an elderly man coming down the arroyo to their left. Wilson saw him too. "I don't recognize him," he said warily.

"His face is hidden in the folds of that blanket," Ella commented, worried that Wilson, who had lived here most of his life, should not recognize the man despite the blanket. Her body was tense, her muscles so tight they screamed with the strain. There was the possibility that Wilson and Clifford had planned this whole encounter, for reasons she couldn't begin to guess.

The man approached to within twenty feet, then

stopped and pointed his gnarled finger directly at them. "You can't escape what surrounds you," he warned, his voice hollow, as if he were speaking from a cave. "Death wraps itself around you even now." He began a bizarre, incomprehensible chant, which grew progressively louder as he repeated each stanza. It sounded somehow familiar, yet not.

Wilson backed up a step, then, seeing that Ella had held her ground, reached out and pulled her back. "Stay away from him."

"Yeah, he's crazy," Ella said softly. "But there's nothing supernatural about him. He's human like you or me." The volume of the man's chant had increased to an ear-shattering pitch.

Wilson stepped in front of her and scattered pollen into the air, invoking Changing Woman's protection.

The man's face contorted in rage, and he reached into a fold of the blanket.

Ella instinctively unsnapped the strap of her holster and reached for her pistol.

Suddenly the man threw something large at them. Gun in hand, Ella dodged as Wilson jumped back. With a dull thud, the object landed by Ella's feet. The chant continued unabated, like the wailing of an animal.

Ella glanced down at the thing and shuddered. It was the head of a recently killed goat. The beast had been born deformed, without eyes. "Back away," she ordered Wilson. "I've got you covered."

Wilson started to move closer to the truck, never turning away from the old man. "We need to leave. Now," he shouted over the man's screams.

The chant echoed in the confines of the canyon. The fanatical mystic reached inside the blanket and pulled out a desiccated, skeletal human hand. Ella raised her pistol; Wilson reached into the cab of the truck, groping for his rifle.

The old man held up the bony hand, continuing to chant, then abruptly threw the hand at Ella. Though she jumped back, the thing brushed her extended gun arm. Her skin prickled; she shuddered with disgust and rubbed at her skin to remove all traces of the foul thing.

"That's it. I've had it," Wilson growled. He raised the rifle and fired two rounds into the air. The sharp cracks reverberated back and forth from the earthen walls around them.

To Ella's surprise, the old man tumbled to the ground. She glanced back at Wilson, but the barrel of his rifle was still pointed toward the sky. Ella broke into a run, wondering if the man had suffered a heart attack.

"No! Don't go any closer," Wilson yelled.

"I've got to!" she yelled back.

Wilson ran to catch up with her. Ella stopped three feet away from the bundle of blanket and cloth that lay crumpled on the sand. Scarcely breathing, she studied the shape. Something was very wrong with it, she realized, heart pounding. There was no body—nothing lay beneath the blanket except ground. Before Wilson could stop her, she tossed the blanket aside and stared in mute shock at the expanse of grayish sand beneath. No prints or marks marred the smooth surface.

"What the . . .," Ella whispered.

"Get away from there," Wilson said sharply, then handed her a small piece of flint from the medicine bundle tied to his belt.

She stared at the flint for a moment. "Protection from

the *chindi?* That man was as real as you and I." Her tone was too shaky to pass as genuine conviction, but that was just from excitement.

"You're wrong," Wilson insisted. "Only a very powerful skinwalker could have done something like this."

"Or a trickster." Like her brother. Ella looked around, searching for anything that would provide her with a logical answer. "A holographic projection of some sort, perhaps."

"Not everything can be explained rationally."

Ella clung stubbornly to logic. "He was an illusionist, a good one," she said flatly, "but that's all." She wondered again, glancing at Wilson, if he'd set her up, perhaps with Clifford's help. Wilson, after all, was the only one who had known where she'd be at this time. Maybe it was all a scheme to make a believer out of her.

"I'll take the blanket with us as evidence," she said finally. "Maybe we can learn something about the identity of the owner from hair, or cloth fibers."

Wilson grabbed her hand. "Forget it. You're not putting that thing into my truck."

"But it's just . . ."

"No. This isn't open to discussion. Now let's leave."

She didn't have much choice, but gave in gracefully. Silently, Ella vowed to come back for the blanket later, as soon as she could borrow the truck from her mom. Sitting beside Wilson as he slowly drove away, she could sense his disapproval. He obviously wanted her to admit that what they'd seen was a perfect example of a skinwalker's powers. The problem was, she knew better. Superstition could cloud anyone's thinking, and she had no intention of letting it affect her assessment of this case. What surprised her the most was Wilson's eagerness to believe in things that defied reason. Maybe it was all an act for her benefit. Maybe he was as much a con man as her brother. If not, despite the honesty and caring on his face, the gap of understanding between them would grow wider with each denial she made.

Ella stared across the cab at Wilson, who stubbornly kept his eyes on the road. She decided to give him a chance to come clean. "I'm going to uncover the truth, count on it. Someone's playing with me, and I don't like it. Whoever's behind this is about to find out what a mistake it is to take me on."

"First, consider what your brother said."

"What do you mean?"

"This isn't the time for you to start to learn about things that have always frightened you," Wilson said softly, his eyes shimmering with emotion. "You're not equipped to fight the evil that's at war with your family. Leave the reservation while you still can."

"I know you're worried, but you don't have to be," she assured him calmly, her mind rapidly sorting through various reasons Wilson might have for wanting her to leave. "I've been in some tight spots, and always come out ahead."

"It's not your courage that's in question," he insisted. "It's your safety . . ."

"My family deserves my loyalty and my protection. Whoever we're fighting attacked me, too, by killing my father. I won't back away."

He nodded reluctantly. "Then we'd both better learn to be more careful." They'd reached the Destea house. Wilson walked her to the front gate, then wordlessly returned to his truck.

Ella watched him leave. Her mother's old mutt came up

to her, tail wagging hesitantly. She patted him on the head. Together, Ella and the animal walked to the front porch.

"You're back early," Rose said, opening the door. "I'm just getting ready to fix dinner."

"I feel like I've been gone for a long, long time," she muttered, following her mother into the kitchen. Ella sat at the table, sketching a crude map of her afternoon journey so she could find the place later.

Dinner that night was a simple meal, leftover mutton stew and fry bread. Neither woman seemed in the mood for chitchat, and long silences filled the house. Ella had no intention of discussing the day's events with her mother. The last thing she needed was more mumbo jumbo, or someone else telling her to leave the Rez. Still, the kitchen felt homey, and Ella was able to relax and unwind. The dog curled up in front of the back door, and Ella briefly wondered if the animal for some reason had decided to keep a closer eye on its owner.

Thinking about the list of names Clifford had given her, Ella decided to ask Peterson do a background check on each person.

Whoever had killed her father had a strong motive. Was it someone who stood to gain by taking her father's place in his church, like Reverend Williamson? According to Clifford's notes, he'd never truly accepted her father's role in the church, preferring to run things totally on his own. Or perhaps it was a traditionalist, someone who benefited by Clifford's becoming a fugitive.

Finally, Rose spoke. "You've seen your brother."

"How did you know that?"

"Whenever something bothers you, or when you feel uncertain, you draw into yourself."

"He wants me to leave the reservation," Ella volunteered flatly, studying her mother's reaction to see if Clifford had been discussing strategy with her mother.

Rose was restless, toying with her iced-tea glass and silverware. "Perhaps you should leave," she conceded, "but I know that you won't. Everything you believed in is being threatened by what has happened in the past week. Your beliefs about yourself, about life, are all changing, and that's hard to deal with. You're a fighter, and you're going to be tested to the limit. The process has already begun."

Ella felt a shudder travel up her spine. She wished someone around her would talk sense, not superstition. Like dominoes stacked in a row, events were tumbling down at an alarming rate. She was suddenly certain it was much too late to walk away.

"I need to run an errand tomorrow morning. Will you need Dad's . . . the truck?" She couldn't go out tonight without worrying her mother, but tomorrow she'd retrieve the blanket. She'd also pay Peterson a visit.

Rose shook her head. "Use it as long as you'd like," she said resignedly.

After dinner, Ella sat with her mother in the living room, listening to the Navajo radio station. The silence between them, filled only by the music playing softly in the background, left her nerves on edge. Finally she replaced the old crafts magazine she'd been paging through on the table and stood up. "I'm tired, Mom. I'm going to bed early."

Rose glanced up from her knitting. "I'll be up a while longer—the nights feel too long for me alone. But you sleep well."

Ella walked to her room, keenly feeling her mother's sadness. Her father's absence lay heavily over them, a tangible weight, as if the house itself was mourning the loss of one of its own.

She sat by her bedroom window, lights off. The full moon bathed the nightscape in a soft, silvery light. The desert seemed so barren, yet life teemed within its desolate stretches. Prairie dogs scurried about, foraging for food. A jackrabbit hopped through the brush, making its nightly rounds.

Yes, tomorrow she'd return to the place where they'd seen the old man. She'd get the blanket and try to identify the weave, the maker, and eventually its owner. Maybe she could even get Peterson or Blalock to send it out for laboratory analysis. There might be something to tie it to the murder. Ella crawled into bed and pulled the covers in around her. As the old mattress sagged comfortably beneath her, Ella closed her eyes, but sleep refused to come. She tossed and turned restlessly. Everything seemed oppressive—even the weight of her blanket against her toes annoyed her and kept her from drifting off.

When sleep finally came, it was void of rest. Eerie images haunted her dreams, making them a vivid study in terror. She was walking among the ruins of the old church, and shadows began to move on their own, transforming to people she recognized. The first was a Navajo warrior. He held a bloody knife in one hand. From the other, dangling by its long hair, hung a severed head. The head appeared to be Ella's father. The warrior was first Peterson, then Blalock, speaking Navajolike gibberish. He laughed, and pointed to the head. Instead of her father, however, the severed head was now Wilson's.

The nightmare grew even more bizarre as Wilson's head began to speak in a soft, seductive tone, offering to make love to her. The warrior, no longer Blalock, but a stranger she couldn't place, groaned in disgust and threw the head at her. She caught it, and looked down in terror at her own face.

Ella woke with a start, and couldn't get back to sleep for an hour. By the time the first rays of light peered through the cracks in her curtains, Ella felt more exhausted than when she'd first gone to bed. She got up and dressed quietly. It was barely eight o'clock, and the house was still. At least her mother had finally gone to bed. Ella had heard Rose moving around all night, as if she'd dreaded the cold emptiness of the bed she'd shared with her mate. Ella understood that particular feeling well. Although her marriage to Eugene had only lasted eighteen months, after he'd died she'd slept on the sofa for months.

Ella went to the kitchen, her thoughts racing as she anticipated the long journey ahead. She had no intention of getting stuck in the mud out there like Wilson had.

After a quick breakfast, she grabbed a few paper grocery bags to protect whatever evidence she found and took the pickup's key from the hook in the kitchen. Just then her mother came out of her bedroom. Rose's eyes were red and puffy, as if she'd spent the night crying.

"Mom, would you like me to stay and fix breakfast?"

Rose shook her head. "I'll be fine. I have to find my own way around this sorrow. There's nothing you can do."

Ella left hesitantly, although in her heart she knew her mother really did need time alone. Rose would have to delve deep within herself to find the strength to make a new life.

By the time Ella made it down the dirt track to the highway, it was nearly nine. As she started to pull out, she saw Wilson's familiar truck approaching.

"Where are you off to?" he asked, pulling up beside her.

"I was just on my way over. I thought you might need some wheels, so I was going to put myself and my truck at your disposal."

"I appreciate the thought, but I don't think you want to come with me on this trip."

His face immediately grew somber. "I had a gut feeling about this, that's why I came early. Let me guess. You're on your way to where we saw the skinwalker, right?"

"I want that blanket," she answered simply.

"What makes you think you can learn anything from it? I saw nothing to indicate it was unique in any way."

"I've been trained to find things that convey information and lead to suspects. I want to take a closer look at it."

He slammed his hand against the steering wheel, his lips pursed and his eyes narrowed. "You won't listen to me on this, will you?" He glanced at her, and exhaled softly. "Never mind, that was a wasted question. Let's go back to your mother's house. You can leave your father's truck there. I'll take you in mine."

"I'll take my mom's truck, and go by myself. I have other business to attend to anyway." Ella wondered if he was trying to keep her from investigating on her own. Was Wilson afraid she might discover the old man's disappearance was a trick?

"If I don't go with you, I'll worry," Wilson insisted.

"Worry, then. I've got a job to do, and you're slowing me down," Ella said curtly, driving off quickly before he could answer back.

He followed her anyway, but stayed far behind, apparently hoping she wouldn't notice. Amateurs, Ella sighed to herself. Sometimes, she realized, people forgot what she did for a living.

Half an hour later, as she drew near the spot, Wilson's

pickup closed the gap between them. She reluctantly slowed to a stop.

Wilson pulled up alongside, smiling grimly. "I had to make sure you could find the place."

"There's nothing I can do about your being here, but if you really want to help, stay out of my way. Better yet, stay in your truck." Ella wasn't about to be led around or misdirected by Wilson.

"I'll stay out of your way," he grumbled. Ella noticed that despite his gruffness, Wilson was gripping the steering wheel so hard that his knuckles had turned a pearly white.

"Don't worry, it won't be long."

"No," Wilson said, swallowing. "We'll go together, and I'm taking my rifle, just in case."

They went down into the narrow canyon. Ella glanced around, perplexed. There was no sign of the blanket. "If memory serves me, it should be right around here." She walked a slow circle around the area, looking for signs of gadgets or wires she might associate with trickery.

"Yeah, I thought this was the place too." Wilson gripped his rifle tightly.

"Stay here, and keep a sharp lookout.

He gave her a long, speculative look. "Where are *you* going?"

"I'm going to search a little further down the wash. Since we're on higher ground here, you should be able to keep me covered."

He nodded in agreement.

Ella walked away slowly, studying the ground and listening. As far as she could tell, the only footprints around were Wilson's and hers, from the day before. She crouched, searching for the old man's tracks, but only the vaguest of impressions remained on the soft sand. Thinking back, she couldn't remember having seen his feet; they'd been hidden beneath the blanket. Maybe he'd worn moccasins and the dragging blanket had wiped out his tracks.

The goat's head was still on the ground. She stared at it. If the old man had only been a projection, or an illusion, where had this very real goat's head come from? She stared at the bloody remains, now crawling with maggots and flies. Not far away lay the bloody hand, covered with ants. Opting not to touch either, at least for the moment, she continued searching for the spot where the man had fallen.

She couldn't find it, only vague suggestions of where footprints might have been made. Where had the blanket gone? No one could have removed it, not unless they'd floated there.

"What's wrong?" Wilson called out.

"I can't find the blanket," she answered. A skillful tracker like Clifford, or one of a dozen Navajo hunters, could walk without leaving obvious tracks. But she couldn't conceive of her brother, or Wilson for that matter, digging up somebody's hand.

Wilson looked around slowly, then jogged toward her. "Maybe someone came and took it." He studied the ground. "No, forget that."

"It's got to be here. Maybe we're not looking in the right place."

"Let me help you look."

They walked on. Suddenly Wilson crouched on the dry, sandy ground. "What've you got?" Ella asked.

"I'm not sure."

She bent over him. A thin layer of gray ash covered the sand. She reached out to touch it, but Wilson grabbed her hand.

"To scatter ashes in daytime is an insult to Sun."

"I remember," Ella said. She decided to humor Wilson, drew back her hand, and added thoughtfully, "It also leaves a trail for Poverty to find you." She stared at the ground pensively. "This is where the blanket was."

"Yes. But all that remains are these ashes."

"Someone seems intent on using fear to confuse our thinking. There's no trace of a fire, and no footprints." She pursed her lips. "Of course, a skilled tracker could have obliterated his trail." She stood up. "Who do you know who could have concealed his passage like this?" Ella asked bluntly.

"I could do this, if I was very careful. So could your brother, and a few of the old *hataaliis*. Your father-in-law, the police chief, used to be quite a hunter, but he's put on some weight." Wilson was pensive.

"How about cops, like Peterson Yazzie, for instance? Or some of the deer hunters you've gone hunting with?" Ella probed, eager for names.

"Peterson isn't as crafty as he'd like you to believe. You could lose him in a closet. But, now that you mention it, Samuel Pete and Herman Cloud have done some bow-hunting. You've got to be good to try that," Wilson concluded. "Paul Sells, Loretta's brother, is supposed to be a very good hunter too."

"Thanks. That's food for thought."

What bothered Ella most was knowing she was being manipulated and led astray. She couldn't quite shake the spidery sense that someone was looking over her shoulder. She had learned, in her years as an FBI agent, that when things got risky you hedged your bets and waited for backup. In this situation only friends and family could be counted on for help—and she didn't have many friends on the Rez. Her own brother was wanted by the law. She had to plan her counter moves carefully.

"Don't tell anyone what we've seen. It will only play into the hands of those who want to use confusion and superstitious fear to their advantage," she said.

"Agreed."

"I will not allow these people to defeat me this easily. If I go down, it'll be fighting them every step of the way." She saw Wilson smile. "What the hell are you grinning about?"

"You haven't changed a bit. You have more courage than any ten people put together. And it's still based on sheer, undisguised stubbornness."

Ella laughed. "Yeah, I guess I am a bit stubborn. But in my line of work, that's a real asset." It felt good to laugh, even at herself.

"I've always admired that in you, Ella—your courage, that is. I could do without the stubbornness. I can't think of anyone I'd rather have on my side in a fight."

"Except maybe Clifford," she mused. "You know, he may hold the solution to all this. Once he clears his name, we can use him to counter any fear tactics the skinwalkers use. People trust him. That's undoubtedly a big part of why they want to get him out of the way."

"Let's hope people around here don't find out what we're really facing, at least not yet," Wilson said softly. "The last thing we need is a pack of vigilantes on a witch-hunt. Innocent lives could be lost."

Ella nodded somberly. "You know, to find out who's involved, I'm going to have to learn more about skinwalkers. The bad guys are obviously putting a lot of effort into making people believe they're truly magical. What do you know about skinwalker practices and rituals?"

"Probably more than most," Wilson admitted quietly. "I've studied the subject for years. But speaking of the unspeakable will invite their attention."

"I don't think we need to worry about it. It's pretty obvious we already have their attention."

Wilson nodded slowly. "I suppose you're right."

"So tell me what you know."

"Not out here. They've obviously made this place theirs. Come over to my place after you finish your other business. I'll make lunch and we can talk." Ella agreed, and Wilson climbed into his truck and drove away.

Once he was gone, Ella retrieved the skeletal hand, using a couple of sticks to pick it up and place it in the paper bag. Setting the bag on the passenger-side floorboards of her pickup, she drove to the police station. Peterson's squad car wasn't there, nor Blalock's. Ella continued down the road to check the closest diner, and sure enough, Peterson was there.

Ella walked into the lobby and bought a newspaper, making sure Peterson saw her. Returning to the pickup, she started reading. Five minutes later, Peterson wandered by.

"Hi, Ella. You wanted to see me?" he said cheerfully.

"Yes. Have a seat, but watch out for the bag on the floor, okay?" Ella gestured. "I need some info on these people." She handed him the list of four names, which she'd recopied.

Peterson glanced at it. "Reverend Williamson we both know is a pain, but harmless as far as I can tell. Gene Sorrelhorse is trouble. He's a self-styled vigilante who has a tendency to solve problems with his fists, kind of like Wilson Joe. Willy Ute is an old friend of your father's, one of his converts too—in fact, I think he's taken over the earlier service at the church. There's nothing particularly noteworthy about Charley Atcitty. He works construction, that's all I know. What makes you suspect these particular people?"

"I didn't say I did. Their names have come up as I spoke to others, and I wanted to know more about them."

"I'll do background checks if you want, see if anything turns up."

"Please."

"Anything else? I've got to be going before one of our units drives by."

"You could have one of the forensic people write up a report on what's in the bag by your foot."

"Jeez, it smells," Peterson complained, looking down at it. A big blue fly clung to the side of the bag. "What's in there?"

"Somebody's hand." Ella shrugged. Before she could explain, Peterson jumped out of the pickup as if his pants were on fire.

"Dammit! Why didn't you tell me before I sat right next to it?"

Ella told him about meeting a skinwalker, but left out Wilson and the other details.

Peterson looked at her skeptically. Finally he took the bag, gingerly, and agreed to see what he could find out about recent grave-robbings.

He drove off quickly when a police car appeared. Ella waited until the unit drove by, then left herself.

NINE

Ella spent a nervous hour driving to Wilson's home—a lonely trek southeast, toward Gallup. She tried to both dismiss her unease as a by-product of her nearly sleepless night and remain alert to any possible ambush. Soon, however, the natural serenity around her began to weave a comforting spell. Sage and purple asters bloomed as far as the eye could see, lining the valleys that stretched between flat-topped ridges and isolated sandstone mesas. The desert, renewed by the summer rains, was flecked in yellows and blue-grays that reached all the way to the horizon.

"I never figured you'd live so far from the community," Ella said after greeting Wilson. "I pictured you nearer the college."

Wilson shook his head. "I deal with people and students all the day long. After I finish my workday, I need a retreat of sorts. Time alone is at a premium when you're teaching."

"Do you like it?"

"Teaching, or living alone?"

"Both," Ella answered.

"I really enjoy teaching. The sense of satisfaction in the job is very rewarding. I'm helping people learn how to learn and how to make their thoughts clear to themselves and others. That, in turn, shapes lives."

Relaxing inside the adobe one-story home, nestled near the base of a mesa, Ella understood why he'd chosen to live there. The soothing quiet was interrupted only by the occasional cry of a bird and the soft sounds of the breeze rustling through the piñons. "I've grown so accustomed to hearing traffic outside, I'd forgotten there were places like this," she commented.

"I remember hearing you complain, back in high school, that your parents lived too close to the highway. You loved to go off by yourself and hike in the desert."

She smiled, surprised he remembered. "I'd spend hours dreaming of what I'd be, or what I'd do with my life." Ella had also gained experience in orienting herself outdoors, a skill she had used the day before, when Wilson had tried to confuse her by driving in circles.

Ella glanced around the living room. Care had been taken to make this home special. Each piece of furniture had a distinctive touch. The leather sofa had intricately carved oak sides. The design was repeated on the armoire, and on the legs and arms of a nearby easy chair.

"These must be antiques," Ella commented. "They just don't make furniture like this anymore. How long have you been a collector?"

"I made most of the furniture here. It took me the better part of a year to carve the Navajo designs into the wood."

Standing beside Wilson, Ella studied the carvings on the doors of the armoire. She recognized the beings that represented the cardinal points within the Sacred Mountains. "I remember these. Darkness Woman, Evening Twilight Woman, Dawn Man, and Horizontal Blue Man."

"Some paint in colors. I create in wood." Wilson waved a hand, indicating his work.

"This place really has your mark on it," Ella observed with undisguised admiration. The whitewashed walls and the openness of the living room created a sense of freedom. "You've made a good home for yourself."

"Tell me about your home in the city."

"It's just an apartment, a place I use mostly to sleep and shower. I don't even own the furniture. I found my center in my work."

Wilson had started to say something when his stomach growled. "Oops." He laughed. "My stomach's never been much for silent suffering. Let's see if there's anything in the kitchen that will make a decent sandwich."

Ella helped him assemble thick sandwiches of cold cuts, lettuce, and tomato. The kitchen was fully equipped with modern conveniences, and Ella knew that his gas appliances depended upon a propane tank in the back. That's the way it always was in outer areas of the Rez.

"Tell me about your life," Wilson urged. "Is working for the FBI all you thought it would be when you joined?"

"In a way, it's more. I've enjoyed traveling, seeing new places, learning new things." Ella grew pensive. "That's what I had thought my life would be like when I got married, but fate stepped in."

"I heard about the accident. It must have been very hard on you," he said sympathetically. "I really admired the way you got yourself together afterward."

"I didn't have a choice." She reminded herself not to use her deceased husband's name to avoid worrying or offending Wilson. "I'd found my identity through being his wife. When that was abruptly taken away from me, I had no idea what to do with myself. I came home for a while, to sort out my thoughts and my life."

"I remember. I tried to visit, but Clifford said you weren't seeing anyone."

"I needed to figure things out in my own head, and I didn't want anyone's help. For once I was determined to find my own answers."

"But you'd always done that," Wilson protested.

"No, not really," Ella answered with a sad smile. "I reacted to what was going on around me, that's all. I knew I was different from Clifford, and not in total agreement with either my mother or my father on the issues that affected our family most. So I avoided any decisions that might have restricted my options."

"How did you finally settle on law enforcement?"

"It seemed to suit me perfectly. Right and wrong are clearly marked. There are rules, and the opportunity to restore order. I decided to go to college and earn my degree, then apply to the bureau under a minority recruitment program. The bureau taught me to stand on my own, and gave me confidence I never had before. I realized I was capable of accomplishing anything I set my mind to. I made a place for myself, and I made a difference there." Ella carried the plates of sandwiches and potato chips to a small circular table.

Wilson set down two tall glasses of cold lemonade. "I've always known I belonged on the Rez, and I always wanted to teach. I went to college and graduate school in Albuquerque, but came home as soon as I could. A few months ago I was finally offered a full professorship at the new community college and I jumped at the chance."

"So you *are* in favor of the college," Ella commented.

Wilson hesitated. "The college itself is a very good idea, though I do agree with Clifford that the choice of location is a poor one. I also wish your father had never insisted on building a church there."

Ella finished her sandwich, then sat back and regarded Wilson speculatively. The openness of their discussion had done a lot to dull her suspicions. "Do you realize we've talked all around the one subject I came here to discuss?"

"Yes," he admitted, the smile in his eyes never quite reaching his lips.

"We can't avoid it," she said quietly. "I need to know more about the ones I'm fighting."

Wilson leaned on the table, steepling his fingers beneath his chin. "Didn't your brother ever talk to you about this?"

"Only once, and in very general terms. At least that's all I remember."

Wilson looked past her and out the window that faced the rugged side of the mesa. "Do you think you could stand a long drive, then a little hike? There's something I'd like to show you, but there's no way I'm going to that place after nightfall."

"Where do you have in mind?"

"A site skinwalkers used at one time. Though they abandoned it years back, you might still be able to learn something from it. We'll take my truck."

"I'm ready whenever you are." She picked up the last few potato chip crumbs on her plate. "But how sure are you that they're not meeting there anymore?" Ella wondered why he would agree to take her to such a place, yet still speak of skinwalkers in a such a roundabout way. What was he really up to?

"Your brother did a special ceremony to make sure they wouldn't return."

Questions filled her mind, like how and when had they found it, and what had they found there. Still, she remained quiet, knowing Wilson would tell her at his own pace.

The drive, cross-country over rough terrain, took nearly an hour. Wilson's grip on the wheel was firm but not white-knuckled, as it had been the day before. Still, when Wilson at last braked the truck to a stop, the muscles at the corners of his mouth twitched nervously, matching the accelerated rate of Ella's pulse. "Come on. It's not far from here, but we'll have to walk." He pulled out a flashlight from the glove compartment.

"Tell me about this place."

"Your brother, brother-in-law Paul, and I encountered something here during spring break our senior year in high school. We'd gone on a hike, and Clifford and I were bragging to Paul how we knew this country like the back of our hands. He laughed and asked if we'd like to put that to a test. We foolishly agreed, so he had us tie handkerchiefs over our eyes. Then he led us around blindfolded for half an hour. When he took the blindfolds off, we walked in circles for a long time, trying to find our camp. Paul just grinned, telling us to use our skills to find the way. Finally we decided to take a break." Wilson looked away, clearly uncomfortable.

"What happened?" Ella prompted him.

"We heard several people talking nearby. Clifford was curious. He insisted on sneaking up to find out what was going on. I just wanted to get the heck out of there, but I couldn't leave him behind. Paul was with your brother, so I did what they wanted."

"Clifford always had a knack for sticking his nose where it didn't belong," she commented.

Wilson led her around a deep, narrow arroyo, then up a small slope littered with jagged boulders and sage. The uneven ground made walking difficult, and Ella had to concentrate to keep her balance. Thankfully it was much too hot for rattlesnakes to be roving about. Her boots were comfortable for walking, but definitely not thick enough to ward off a bite.

"It's just up ahead."

Looking where he gestured, Ella saw a narrow opening covered with spiderwebs, leading into the earth. Traces of pollen were visible on the ground, and four weather-worn prayer sticks were placed around the hole. "We'll go in there," Wilson said.

"Inside that hole?" The thought revolted her. She'd never much liked confined spaces, and even thinking of climbing into that narrow pit made her feel slightly nauseated.

"It's a tunnel, not a hole. Once you're in, it's about four feet wide—plenty of room."

She considered asking him to describe the site to her, but she'd been pushing him for concrete information. This was no time to back down out of groundless squeamishness. "Is it safe? I mean, it won't collapse or anything, right?"

"No, it's sturdy."

"How do you know?"

"Your brother came here right before he went into hiding, to help himself start thinking like his enemies. He blessed it again; I suppose you noticed the pollen."

Ella was pleased, Wilson was trusting her with information about Clifford's movements. But she still didn't care for heading underground.

As they descended, she could feel the dampness of the cool, subsurface earth. Wilson led the way, lighting their path with his flashlight. The tunnel had been plastered with clay and dug well. They proceeded slowly, on their hands and knees. Unexpectedly, Ella saw a tattered white cotton curtain ahead. "Is that where we're going?"

"We'll go past two curtains like that," he answered, "before we reach the place I want you to see."

The sound of his voice reverberated inside the earthen tunnel, becoming distorted. She fought a sudden, sharp fear that they might be buried alive. The air was stale and filled with a strange smell like rotting leaves, but there were no plants around. She tried hard not to speculate on what else might be rotting nearby.

Wilson pushed aside the second curtain. Like the first, it was made of an old flour sack, opened along its seams. Just past it, the tunnel expanded into a rounded, cavernous area about twelve feet high and twenty feet across. Ashes from a small fire pit were still visible, and strange dark markings on the hard-packed floor of the cave were crisscrossed with sacred pollen. Clifford had also been here recently, it appeared. The chamber seemed unnaturally cold. The intense chill pierced her marrow and left her feeling violated and somehow soiled.

"They were there," Wilson said in a hushed whisper, indicating a half circle that flanked the opening. Hollowed-out, sandy impressions on the ground suggested the cave had been used quite frequently. "About a dozen or so of them, naked. They were singing. The sound was monotonous and off-key, but rhythmic and compelling in an odd way. I mean, it *made* you listen."

"You recognize anyone?" Ella asked, hoping for a name.

"A girl, about twenty years old, right on the other side of the fire. Her name was Allison Begay. She had a reputation for sleeping around. I guess it's natural that I remember her—naked and all. The others were hunched over, their faces in shadow. But to be honest, Clifford and Pete and I were all looking at Allison." Wilson scratched his head, as if trying to remember more. "It happened so long ago, and we never talked about it, not to anybody."

"How come they didn't see you?" she asked. The curtain was so light, it was almost transparent. Then again, perhaps the years had made it threadbare.

"No one looked up. They were all staring at a feather on the ground." His voice dropped even more. "It was dancing."

"Dancing?"

"What else would you call it?" Wilson challenged. "It was standing on end, moving up and down." He shuddered, then forced his body to become still. When he continued, his voice was flat and unemotional. "We heard them say that as long as it was upright, the skinwalker out in the night was still alive. If it fell, it meant he was dead."

"What happened then?"

"One of them—Allison, in fact"—Wilson laughed shortly—"finally looked up and saw us." He gestured back down the tunnel. "Come on. I'll tell you the rest once we're back outside."

She wasn't going to argue with him. There was nothing she wanted more at that moment than to be out in the open, taking in lungfuls of clean air. He'd certainly picked a prime spot for spooky storytelling. The larger cavern, instead of reducing her feeling of confinement, had actually made it worse. The air was still and heavy. She'd had to continually fight the feeling that she was slowly suffocating. Forcing her breathing to remain even, she followed Wilson back to the surface.

When she finally felt the sun on her face, she sighed in relief. "It's hideous down there."

"It's more than the enclosure. There's something disgusting about going deep inside the earth to conduct profane ceremonies."

She nodded in complete agreement. As far as she was concerned, it was disgusting to go there for any reason. "Tell me what happened after they saw you."

Wilson quickened his steps back to the truck, as if he wanted to outrun the memories by leaving the area as soon as possible. "They saw your brother first. He was ahead of me, and Paul was behind. Clifford said something I couldn't make out, and suddenly the skinwalkers stopped. They were still for only a few precious seconds, but, fortunately, that was enough to help us escape. We ran and ran, and finally ended up at Fred Benally's hogan. He was there working for a patient."

Benally was the *hataalii* who'd instructed Clifford. "I know Clifford decided to become a Singer his senior year in high school. Was this incident with the skinwalkers the reason for it?"

Wilson considered it. "No, but I think it helped him define his own priorities. You see, the encounter scared both of us. Up till that time, neither of us had paid much attention to the stories about skinwalkers. We'd figured that they were just a way to explain things like sickness and bad times."

"Clifford never mentioned any of this to me."

"He didn't tell your father either. The only person who knew was your mother. She warned Clifford back then that his real battle with the skinwalkers was yet to be fought. That scared him. He made up his mind to develop all his skills, because he felt certain that someday his life would depend on them. He told me that your mother didn't usually get those feelings, but when she did, they could be counted on."

The story surprised Ella. There was so much about her own family she'd never known. Raymond Destea's love for the Christian religion had effectively discouraged open discussion on subjects that, in retrospect, should have been addressed in detail to clarify potential choices. Customs that related to the native religion had never been quite clear to her.

Ella stole glances at Wilson as they journeyed back to his home. Although he wasn't outwardly aggressive, he was as strong as Shiprock itself. It had obviously taken a great deal of courage for him to return here, but he hadn't hesitated, knowing she'd need his help and guidance to understand the threat he claimed they were facing. A man who stood by his words and actions was very rare. She wanted to believe Wilson was such a man.

"Paul said he and Loretta are being watched by the police. You better stay on the lookout too," Ella warned. "Remember, if nothing else, you're guilty of harboring a fugitive, and Blalock would have you arrested on that charge in an instant if he thought he could use it to break this case open."

"He'd do the same to you," he countered.

"You bet. I'm more guilty. I'm violating the law I've sworn to uphold."

"You're being torn in two," Wilson observed sadly. "I wish there had been some way to spare you that."

"I have no regrets about my decisions. There are some

loyalties that supersede even my allegiance to the letter of the law. But I'll need your help and Clifford's cooperation to see that the spirit of the law is upheld, and that the ones who killed my father are caught and punished."

He nodded once, but she couldn't tell whether it was in acknowledgment or approval. Despite his honesty, Wilson was still an enigma to her. Every time he'd been with her, he had in effect tried to frighten her away from the investigation. Was Wilson sincerely afraid for her, or was he literally using "scare tactics" to manipulate her?

Ella realized that she should have asked for a background check on Wilson too. She'd take care of that as soon as possible. She had a feeling Peterson would jump at the chance, but suspected Blalock would give a less biased report.

One thing was very clear. Whoever Ella asked to investigate Wilson Joe would have to do it without his knowledge. He seemed to be, at least for now, one of her few allies, and she couldn't afford to lose his trust or help.

TEN

When they got back to Wilson's home, he offered Ella a glass of lemonade as they walked into the kitchen.

"I'd like that," she said, glad for the coolness provided by the house's thick adobe walls. Her mouth felt parched, partly from the fear that had threatened to overwhelm her back in the cavern and partly because of the three-digit temperatures outside. "Let me give you a hand."

As he brought out glasses, she pulled the pitcher from the fridge. They sat there in silence, comfortable enough with each other not to feel the need to talk. The day's experiences and revelations had been exhausting.

Once Ella finished her drink, she stood and carried her glass to the sink. "It's time for me to go. I have to check in with the police and see when they're going to release my father's body. If they can't give me a time, I'm going to have to start putting pressure on them."

"Why don't I follow you to the tribal police office? Maybe I can help out. I know some of the officers."

The offer was tempting. Ella had no desire to have a confrontation of any kind with her father-in-law. Having Wilson there would keep the conversation on track, away from unresolved issues from the past. But this was her responsibility, not Wilson's, and she'd have to deal with it.

Randall and she had never agreed on much, that was certain. She'd been told by more than one relative that the chief had blamed her for his son's enlistment. Randall Clah maintained Eugene had joined the army to impress Ella. There was no truth to it—Eugene had set his own goals in life, and he'd never worried about impressing anyone. Ella had also heard that, extending his logic, Randall Clah held her partially responsible for the accident that had claimed Eugene's life. After Ella had joined the bureau, the rift between them had widened even more.

"I appreciate your offer, but I need to do this myself," Ella said. "I may have to get nasty and ugly, and you shouldn't be associated with that. By now the labs have done all the tests they need. I have a feeling Randall hasn't released the body for other reasons."

"Like what?"

"He's against anything I do or want. That story goes back a long way," she answered softly.

"I've heard," he admitted.

Wilson followed her to her own vehicle and waved good-bye as she drove away. It was shortly after three when Ella pulled into the police station parking lot.

Parking, Ella speculated for a moment, wondering if Randall should be considered a potential suspect. But what motive could he have had? His only tie with her family had died with Eugene. If ambition and control were driving factors for the skinwalkers, Randall certainly stood nothing to gain. As police chief, he was already top cop.

At the door, Ella practically collided with him.

Chief Clah glared at her. "What are you doing here? I warn you, any more 'misunderstandings' like the one you pulled at the morgue and I'll have you arrested."

"I came to see you, Father-in-Law," she answered flatly. Ella refused to allow herself to get angry, but she couldn't resist annoying her stuffy father-in-law a little.

"What about? I don't have the time to talk right now."

"My father's body."

His expression changed from hostile to guarded. "I called Hector Silva earlier. He'll bury your father if you want him placed in the Christian cemetery."

"You didn't have to do that," she said, surprised. "But thanks." She meant it.

"I did it out of respect for your mother. I wanted to present her with solutions, not problems, when I called to tell her the body had been released."

Ella had expected a fight, been braced for one. She wasn't sure if she was disappointed or relieved by her effortless success. "Would it be all right with you if I went inside and used a telephone? I'd like to call home and make sure Mom's okay."

"Ask the officer at the front desk to let you use one of the lines there. Now I've got to go," Randall snapped.

As Clah strode out the door, Peterson Yazzie came down the hall; the trace of a smile on his face told Ella he had overheard. She shrugged and said, "I guess he's used up all his civility for the year. At least I don't have to wonder about how *he* feels about me." Peterson almost laughed.

"You won't have any privacy at the front desk. Use the phone in my office." He led her to a tiny, windowless room.

"Help yourself. I'll wait out here in the hall. Dial nine to get an outside line."

Ella stepped inside. Yazzie's office was no larger than a closet, but he'd obviously spent time making it personal. Achievement certificates hung on the wall, alongside commendations he'd received throughout his years on the force. There was a photo of him shaking the hand of the current tribal chairman. Another showed him at the All-Indian Rodeo, standing near the state governor.

She'd been told how ambitious Peterson was, and these photos made that easy to believe. He had undoubtedly pressured the chief to get the office. Small or not, it was a mark of prestige. The department's facilities were extremely limited. Her mother's letters had often mentioned Peterson's efforts to become chief of police. She'd wondered how her father-in-law felt about that, especially because her own parents had always been quite close to Peterson.

Ella sat behind the desk and dialed home quickly. Then, assured her mother had handled the news of the release of Ella's father's body well, she opened the door. Peterson stepped into the office, half closing the door behind him.

"I haven't been able to get any more background information on the people you wanted." He spoke quietly. "Your father-in-law has pulled the files on just about everyone who knew your father. If he catches me going through them, I'm history."

"He doesn't plan on working the case alone, does he?" Ella had heard that Randall Clah was a good cop, but it was felt that as chief of police he should be delegating more responsibility to his staff.

Peterson shrugged. "Don't worry, I'll get a look at the files. The chief only locks his office when he leaves the station. Next time he's here, as soon as I'm sure he'll be away from his desk for a little while, I'll borrow the files. Ten minutes, and I'll have copies for you." Peterson was whispering. Hearing footsteps in the hall, he cleared his throat to warn Ella. The radio dispatcher, a young Navajo woman in her early twenties, walked past. She gave Peterson a big smile and didn't seem to notice Ella at all.

"Silva has retrieved my father's body from the morgue," Ella said in a normal tone. "Reverend Williamson will say a prayer as they inter the body."

When Ella arrived home, Wilson was waiting on the front porch, and Rose was tending her garden. As Ella came up the walk, Wilson stood and nodded a greeting.

Ella returned the nod. She said quietly, "It's my duty to gather some of my father's possessions so they can be buried with him."

"I'll drive you and your mother to the church grounds. That's why I came over here."

Ella wasn't surprised that Wilson knew about the release of her father's body, but his offer of a ride did surprise her. Attending a graveside service was something few Navajos did willingly. But she refused to become suspicious of Wilson. She needed the support. Even her mother had declined to be present; her own beliefs made different requirements of her.

"You've been a good friend to my brother, and to me. But if you'd rather, there's something else you could do to help me. My mother won't be attending this service. I wish you'd stay here and make sure she's handling things okay."

"I don't think she's going to need me as much as you

will. You're really all alone here. Unless I'm very much mistaken," he said softly, "this duty is going to be difficult for you."

"I won't deny that," Ella admitted.

"Then let me come with you."

Maybe she should have argued a bit more and released him from the offer. Yet, the truth was, she wanted him there. Facing her father's burial alone, with only Mr. Silva and the Christian minister present, left her feeling as cold as if she'd been standing naked in a snowstorm. "I'd be grateful if you'd come."

"Then the matter's settled."

Almost three hours later, they stood side by side at the grave site. The sun was sinking quickly into the horizon as the preacher concluded his prayer. His wife was by his side, holding a Bible. While the coffin was lowered into the ground, gruesome images of what the killers had done to her father's body flashed through Ella's mind. Ella dropped the blanket-wrapped bundle of her father's possessions onto the coffin. It landed with a dull, hollow thud that echoed the way she felt inside. She nodded at Mr. Silva, who began to fill the grave.

Orange and lavender lit up the sky as the sun began its final surrender to the gathering night. "I'll meet you back at your truck in a minute," she told Wilson after the casket was completely covered.

Ella picked a handful of the wild sunflowers that grew near the fence, then placed them over the dark soil of the newly covered grave. "I *will* get the ones who did this to you. You would have said my motive is revenge, and asked instead that I forgive. But evil can't be left unchecked; otherwise it continues to destroy. The scales must be balanced."

Ella rose to her feet, resolve and purpose strengthening her, to discover Reverend Williamson hovering a discreet distance away. His wife had gone back to the rectory.

The Anglo minister approached her hesitantly. "It really wasn't necessary for those items to be buried with him."

"Not to you," she answered. "Our family feels the need, however."

The reverend shook his head. "What I meant was that your father is at peace. He was a good man. You should be proud of him."

"I am," Ella replied simply.

"Tell your mother she will always be welcome at our services. And you too, if you choose to remain here."

"Thanks for the offer, but I wouldn't count on either of us attending," Ella said gently. "My mother respected my father's choice while he lived and always supported him, but her own religion will sustain her now."

"And you?"

"I don't share either of my parents' beliefs."

The minister nodded pensively. "Tell Rose that I'll always keep her in my prayers."

"Thank you, Reverend." Ella managed a smile. "By the way, Reverend, my mother and I were discussing the church and we were wondering who would minister to the Navajo congregation now. I understand Willy Ute will be taking over?" Ella tried to make the question as nonthreatening as possible.

"He would like to, but he doesn't have enough training. I've given this some thought. I worked closely with Raymond for years, and I believe I share his compassion for your people. I'm going to step into his footsteps, for now at least. I think he would have wanted it that way."

"I wish you the best of luck, then, Reverend. Thank you for your candor." Ella nodded to Williamson, then walked away. If Williamson was an ambitious man, and she knew that some evangelists were, then Williamson definitely remained a suspect. With her father's murder, Williamson had doubled his congregation.

Ella joined Wilson in his pickup. Feeling a little bit guilty, she confessed, "I've never liked that man."

"Why?"

"I don't know. Maybe it's a holdover from when I was a kid. I used to resent when he telephoned and interrupted Dad at home in the evenings. That was the only time we had with him." She shrugged. "But that's not all of it. He's so sanctimonious sometimes, he sets my teeth on edge. The only beliefs he respects are his own. I don't have anything against his religion, but I resent his attitude."

"I've heard others question his tolerance." As the miles stretched out before them, Wilson broke the silence. "Something's on your mind. What is it?"

"I've been considering asking my mother to stay with relatives. I just don't know how safe she'll be all alone at the house as I continue to investigate, especially considering what has already happened to us."

"I doubt she'll go anywhere, or allow anyone to come stay with her. I expect she'd see it as admitting she couldn't take care of herself, and there's no way she's going to do that."

"Maybe she could move in with Loretta for a while," Ella countered. "That's not too far from home, and I could tell her I'm worried about Loretta."

"Then the risk to each of them would double. It could

tempt others to try and kidnap them both and force your brother out of hiding."

"Good point." Wilson thought almost anything that forced Clifford to come forward was a pretty good idea, but even she wouldn't recommend this tack.

"You could talk to your mom, maybe convince her to go visit your Aunt Merilyn, at least for a few days. They've always been fond of each other." Wilson came to a stop in Rose's driveway.

"I can try. And thanks again for being there for me this afternoon." Ella smiled as she stepped out of Wilson's pickup.

As Wilson drove away, Rose hurried out to the front porch. Suspecting trouble, Ella held her breath, searching her mother's eyes for a sign. When her mother smiled, Ella breathed again.

Ella almost ran up the steps to her mother. "Is everything all right?"

"Stop worrying. I was just hoping to catch Wilson before he drove away. I could use some help with the water pump. The handle's stuck. I've tried oiling it, but it doesn't make any difference."

"I'll take a look at it."

"Someone has to force it, then it'll start working again. This has happened before."

"You probably just need a new handle." Ella remembered when the red pump had first been installed, when she was in grade school. The paint had long since been rubbed and weathered away.

"No, I'll just keep fixing it. No sense in replacing something that's still working."

Ella smiled. Some things never changed. Her mother never threw out anything. What became obsolete was always kept in reserve—just in case. The question "in case of what" had never been answered. Items broken were likely to remain broken. Every once in a while, something would serve an alternate purpose. A spare tire became a swing for years, and an old leaky washtub, a planter.

"I'd better get to it now," Ella said. "It'll be dark soon."

Ella walked around to the back of the house, where the pump was. They had running water in the house; this pump provided water for her mother's garden. Ella tried the handle with one hand, then both, but it was stuck fast. Placing her entire weight on it, she leaned into the curved metal. Slowly the handle gave.

Ella worked the handle up and down a few more times to test it. As she brushed her hair away from her eyes, she caught a glimpse of a figure, high on the mesa behind the house.

She stepped to one side, pretending to study the pump from a different angle, then stole another furtive look. She couldn't tell whether it was a man or an animal. All she could see was a vague outline.

Ella made a snap decision. She'd face whoever was out there. First she draped her windbreaker over the handle. Maybe it was already dark enough that, from a distance, it would look like she was still working on the pump. Then she patted her waist where her pistol rested, for reassurance.

Ella had never mastered the traditional hunting skills Wilson and Clifford set such store by, but she was light on her feet and had been trained to proceed cautiously, conserving her energy. She circled around the base of the hill and reached the summit of the mesa less than five minutes later.

The mesa's top sported only a few patches of waist-high gray sage and grass; it was impossible for anyone to hide effectively. Yet there was no one there. She realized she wasn't likely to find any tracks on the rocky ground.

Still, she searched the slope that led downhill to the west. But it was just too rough, and in the low light, not even her own prints could be discerned.

The howl of a coyote rose high in the air. The sound was so cold, it pierced her like a needle. Its pitch fluctuated like unearthly laughter.

Turning toward the sound, she saw movement on the next mesa. The phantom figure was hard to discern. It was taller than the brush, but certainly not a man. Feeling unnerved, she fingered her gun.

Ella glanced down at her mother's home. For the first time she was truly glad it had the added protection of the pollen blessing. If nothing else, the ones who were using traditional beliefs to create fear might respect that, if only to avoid revealing the fact that they were fakes. She knew she would be unable to get any closer to whoever or whatever was out there. Either there were two of them, or she was awfully slow.

Ella looked back down the hill. The brightly lit house beckoned invitingly. More than ever, it looked like a haven. Frustrated, she was ready to go back. She'd lost this round.

The coyote's cry rose again, mocking her. She was beaten for now, and she knew it. But tomorrow she'd see how fast she could turn the hunter into the hunted.

Whoever was behind all these stunts was going to pay.

ELEVEN

It was close to lunchtime the next day when Ella drove home, hurrying back from a fruitless meeting with Yazzie and a more rewarding visit to the grocery store. At least they'd be able to eat for a while. Her mother wasn't feeling well so Ella hadn't lingered over her errands. Ella could tell that the strain was beginning to wear on her mother. First her husband had been taken from her, and now she was denied the comfort of her son's company and support. Ella couldn't understand why Clifford was being so unreasonable. But then, she never had understood her brother.

Ella couldn't shake the feeling that her mother was disappointed by her inability to produce evidence that would clear Clifford. To Rose, it was unthinkable that anyone could suspect her son.

Lost in thought, Ella drummed her fingers against the steering wheel as she steered down the narrow asphalt road. The beauty of the Colorado plateau, washed in reds, yellows, and browns, was only a momentary distraction. The longer the case went unresolved, the more it would sap her mother's strength. Ella needed to make real progress soon.

Seeing flashing lights in her rearview mirror, Ella pulled over, her pursuer a dark blue pickup she recognized as Blalock's. The FBI man approached casually. Ella got out of the truck to meet him. "What's up?"

Blalock regarded her for a long moment, as if trying to make up his mind about something. "I've been waiting for a chance to talk to you alone," he said at last, looking up and down the empty highway. "Come sit in my car."

Settling into the passenger seat, Ella tried to appear unconcerned, but she was intensely aware that no one knew where she was, or who she was with. If Blalock was one of her enemies, she was making a big mistake. "What's this all about?"

Blalock reached under the driver's seat.

Ella unobtrusively moved her hand closer to her sidearm.

He pulled out a large padded manila envelope. "Here."

"What's this?" she asked, opening it to peer inside.

"A formal letter of apology to your mother for the incident at the church. Also, as keepsakes for her, I've had copies made of all the official letters of commendation you've received throughout your career."

Ella smiled, disarmed by his blunt kindness. It was totally unexpected. "You didn't have to go to all this trouble." He was being uncharacteristically nice.

"Yes, I did. Believe me, it's as much for me as it is for her. I've got to live with myself." He met her gaze. "And that's as close to an apology as you're going to get."

"I appreciate this, and so will my mother."

"I realize you've got a vested interested in this case, and the help you've given me so far has been useful. My problem is that I can't just ignore direct orders from the Albuquerque office. That's why I'm reluctant to tell you anything that can be traced back to me."

"Look at it this way. It's to our advantage to work together. The sooner you close this case, the quicker you'll get transferred back to your kind of civilization. It doesn't take a mind reader to know you're unhappy out here," she said.

"You're not totally at home here either; don't kid me."

"That's true, but this is where I was born and raised. I may not like many of the things here, but at least I'm used to them."

Blalock nodded thoughtfully. "Okay. We'll pool our information. I know you've been investigating unofficially. What have you uncovered?"

"First, what have you got to trade?" Ella knew better than to trade something for nothing.

"For now, not much at all. I admit, I'm at a standstill. But I'm pursuing a few angles that might pan out. For one thing, I'm trying to establish where everyone even remotely connected to your father was that night. It's taking some time, because names keep popping up."

"You'll let me in on those?"

"Count on it. What have you got?"

"Nothing solid, just guesses and feelings. Add Wilson Joe to that list you're checking out, but please do that one yourself." Blalock nodded, and Ella continued, "It's not that I suspect him of anything, I just want to know where *everyone* fits in. Also, add Allison Begay to your list. I hear she used to be involved in some, let's say, 'superstitious' behavior around here. If I turn up anything else, I'll let you know."

Blalock glared at her. There's something you're not telling me."

"It's nothing you can deal with, trust me."

"If we work at cross purposes, we're going to jeopardize this entire investigation," Blalock warned.

"Believe me, the leads I'm following are closed to non-Navajos. They involve our religious practices and beliefs."

"Are they linked to the case?"

"Probably not directly. I'll have to see it through and let you know."

"You're still not playing ball. I made a gesture of good faith, and you're throwing it back in my face."

"No, not at all. I *am* cooperating with you." Ella opened the door and stepped out of his car. "I gave you a name I'm willing to bet you haven't come across in your investigation. When I have something concrete, I'll contact you."

"Yeah, sure, only I better not hold my breath."

"I want an arrest made and this case closed as soon as possible. I have much more at stake here than you do. Don't forget that."

As Ella headed back to her mother's truck, Blalock whipped his car around and drove off, leaving a trail of dust and the smell of burning rubber in the air. She hoped she hadn't just lost a valuable source of information. His instincts had been right—she was keeping things from him. Blalock would have laughed in her face if she'd mentioned skinwalkers, or he would have decided they were like a terrorist organization and turned the reservation upside down looking for them. Doing that would create a panic that would give even a stupid crook enough time to hide . . . and her opponent was anything but stupid.

Although Ella knew she'd done the right thing, she still felt a little guilty. Blalock had gone through a lot of bureau paperwork to make up that packet for her mother. He had even had the commendations bound into a portfolio. She leafed through the papers quickly, memories of past successes filling her mind and giving her confidence a much-needed boost. Ella took a deep breath. She slid the folder back into the envelope, set it on the seat, and resumed the drive home.

When she got there, Ella saw her mother, sitting on the porch knitting, with Loretta in the chair beside her. Ella felt her stomach muscles tense with nervousness. If her sister-in-law would give her a chance, Ella would try to mend fences with Loretta.

It looked like she wasn't going to get that chance. Loretta had stepped off the porch and was walking away, in the direction of her home. "Don't go!" Ella called, hurrying to catch up to her.

Loretta waited for Ella. Her expression was unforgiving. "I just came to visit your mother, and let her know *she* is welcome to stay with us."

"What did she say to that?" Ella asked.

"She changed the topic," Loretta admitted. "I don't think she'll come."

Ella nodded slowly. "I figured as much, but it was nice of you to make the offer." She paused for a moment, trying to figure out how to proceed. "I've been hoping for a chance to talk to you. I want to apologize for what happened with FB-Eyes."

Loretta's face lost some of its hard edge. "This has been hard on all of us. I know you're doing your best to help."

Loretta looked as if she'd aged ten years since the last time Ella had seen her. Yet she was still hanging tough. In her own way, she was as proud as Rose, and wouldn't accept consoling words easily. "I'm going to do whatever it takes to clear my brother's name," Ella said firmly. "But I need your help. I don't want dissension between us at a time when we need to maintain a united front." Ella paused. "I love my brother, though he makes me crazy sometimes."

Loretta's expression softened and she smiled sadly. "You make him crazy too, you know. You're both too set in your own ways."

Ella smiled back. "Okay, I'll admit that."

"Truth is always hard to refute," Loretta baited her. "For me too. So forgive my anger toward you. There's no place for that now, as you say."

Ella glanced back at the house. "How did Mom seem to you?"

"She's a strong woman. You don't have to worry about her. She'll go on with her life. You already have her thinking of the future. She has many hopes for you and Wilson."

Ella groaned. "There's nothing to hope for!"

"Maybe, but it's a distraction, a pleasant one, that keeps her mind occupied. There's no harm in it."

Ella wasn't convinced, but decided not to argue the point. "If you hear anything helpful, or if you need anything, please call me?"

Loretta nodded. "I will. I want my husband back as soon as possible. I miss him."

The words were spoken simply, but the raw emotion behind them communicated clearly to Ella. "Would you like me to walk home with you?"

"No, it's not necessary. My uncle will meet me soon."

Loretta headed up the mesa. Ella waved and went back to the truck for the groceries. Putting them away in the kitchen, Ella noticed three iced-tea glasses in the sink. Rose came into the room and rinsed the glasses.

"Wilson drop by again?" Ella asked.

Rose nodded. "I hope you two are getting along okay. He usually stays longer than he did today."

Ella sighed. "It might be a good thing that he left early. If Wilson's around all the time, he's going to start interfering with what I have to do."

"There's more going on between you than the search for answers. You know it as well as I do."

She hated to do it, but she couldn't allow her mother to build false hopes. "Wilson and I are friends, but that's all it'll ever be. He loves the reservation, and his teaching post here. My career will always keep me away. We've both made choices, and my job is as important to me as his is to him. When summer's over and classes begin in the fall, we'll both be too busy to do anything but write an occasional letter."

Rose shook her head. "You inherited every bit of your father's stubbornness, but he had more sense."

Ella followed her mother to the living room. Rose sat in the easy chair next to the lamp and began to knit. The only sound in the room was the clicking of her needles. Ella picked up a crafts magazine from the coffee table and leafed through it.

After an eternity, Rose glanced up. "I didn't mean to speak harshly to you."

"It's okay, Mom."

"I miss your brother—you know that—and Wilson's presence has helped. I don't know what I would have done if you hadn't come home. The house seems very, very empty when I'm here alone, yet this is my home, where I belong."

Ella felt tears welling in her eyes. She remembered, all

too vividly, what it was like to face the death of your mate. After Eugene had died, she'd wandered aimlessly around their apartment. What her mother was going through was far worse. She'd lost the man with whom she'd shared her entire adult life. Her mother and father had been like counterweights that balanced each other, and now, with his senseless murder, everything was off-kilter.

Ella gave her mother a hug. "We've both had our losses. After mine, I was lost too. But I learned there were many reasons to pick up the pieces and go on. You have even more hope and support than I did. You have Clifford and me, and your own home. Lean on us, but never give up hope. The hurting will stop."

"You're right, of course. I'll eventually find new things to fill the empty spaces inside me." Rose walked to her husband's desk and sat down heavily. "But right now, our whole family is in trouble."

Ella glanced at the commendation binder Blalock had given her, which she'd left on the table closest to the door. She considered showing it to her mother in hopes of distracting her, then discarded the idea. This was no time to remind her mother of that disastrous church service. As her mother turned to look out the large bay window, Ella placed the binder on a bookshelf.

"Did my daughter-in-law tell you what's been happening?" Rose asked.

"You mean about the police following her?" Ella said, gesturing for her mom to join her on the couch.

"No. This is more serious. I think she's in trouble, though she doesn't fully realize that yet."

"How so?"

"After FB-Eyes came back to ask more questions, she insisted on leaving the hogan and moving in with her brother, Paul. They've both seen coyotes around the house at night. They stay just out of rifle range, in the shadows."

Ella suppressed the shudder that traveled up her spine. "They must be after the sheep."

"Paul's not sure what to do. He called earlier, asking for you."

"I'll go call him back."

Rose shook her head. "He's not home. By now, he's at the chapter house. He said he'd be there until six."

Ella remembered Navajo-style local government. Chapter houses were like grange halls in a lot of ways, places where many of the Dineh came together to voice problems and complaints. "Paul used to be one of the headmen. Is he still?"

"Yes, and he has more influence than ever. He's the one who reports to the Tribal Council on local affairs."

"I'll drive over to the chapter house and meet him there." Ella hadn't thought of Paul as a possible suspect because he idolized Clifford. But he was in a position of power, or at least influence, and that could corrupt almost anyone. There were enough politicians—on and off the Rez—to back up that notion. She assumed Paul was on somebody's list of involved parties and made a mental note to look at his file, if he had one.

"Good idea. He said he was just going over to do some paperwork. You'll have all the privacy you need."

"Mom, have you noticed anything or anyone around our home when I'm gone?"

"No, nor when you're asleep. I keep watch sometimes."

Her mother's admission that she hadn't been sleeping was distressing. "You know, if you ever want to talk, come and wake me. I don't mind, really."

Rose shook her head. "It's all a process."

"Of grieving?"

"That, and of learning how to cope with this new life I'm forced to lead." Her smile was broken, mirroring the pain inside.

At that moment, Ella wanted to arrest the man who'd taken her father's life more than she had ever wanted anything in her life. She'd never seen anyone look so alone.

"There's something else you should know. I think Paul's really afraid. If you weren't my daughter, I don't think he'd go to you for help. He's afraid of trusting anyone, particularly the police and that man, FB-Eyes."

Ella nodded, remembering Blalock's behavior at the hogan. She couldn't blame Paul for his reaction, particularly given Blalock's history with Navajo suspects. "I'll be back as soon as I can, Mom."

"Do your investigating and stop worrying about me. I'm not the helpless old woman you sometimes think me to be."

"I never . . ."

Rose held up a hand. "Go. I'm counting on you to clear your brother."

"I *will* do that, though it may take me some time if Clifford won't come forward and speak for himself. Don't lose faith in me, please." Ella knew she had failed her mother once, by not acting on the threats against her father. She wouldn't be able to stand it if her mother thought all her help would be so ineffective.

Rose answered her unspoken thought. "You're my daughter. My love for you isn't measured in what you accomplish or fail to achieve. It's there. Always."

Ella hugged her mother tightly. Knowing the strength of her mother's love revitalized her, but she wanted respect too. "Just hold on, okay? All this will end soon, and Clifford will return."

A few minutes later, Ella drove slowly away, trying to make sure she didn't come across any hidden arroyos or holes as she headed cross-country. She'd save at least forty-five minutes going this way, if she could stand the bouncy ride, and she was eager to meet with Paul. Maybe he could give her a new lead. At the moment she was desperate to find a trail that would yield positive results.

As she slowed down to traverse an area crisscrossed with rain-spawned furrows, she caught a flash of a mirror or windshield in her rearview mirror. Someone was tailing her. She drove over the next hill and stopped the truck, engine still running, near the cover of some boulders. She glimpsed Blalock's pickup coming up the slope behind her. In the blink of an eye, he killed the engine and coasted behind a cluster of tall brush, gliding out of her line of vision.

Crafty, but not enough. He probably hadn't expected her to take such an isolated shortcut. Ella downshifted and headed straight into a big canyon she knew practically by heart. She'd camped there many times when she was in the Girl Scouts. The area was a maze of hairpin curves, and arroyos so deep they could swallow a vehicle whole. Hard ground, where sandstone had been exposed would hide her tracks. To the southwest, Shiprock seemed to nod its approval as she drove into the wash.

Ella headed directly into the narrowest part and smiled, thinking she could almost hear Blalock cursing her now. The canyon split into three channels and he'd have no idea which one she'd selected. Sooner or later, he'd learn that she was on her own turf and that the bureau was wrong about one thing: being an outsider was no advantage here.

Despite that, Ella had to give him credit. He was a

skilled agent. Clearly his instincts had told him she was withholding information. That's why he was trying to follow her now.

After long minutes detouring around red and orange cliff faces that could hide entire stacks of buses, she stopped and turned around in the seat, searching out the rear cab window. There was no sign of Blalock. Unless he'd followed her tracks precisely, she'd be willing to bet he was stuck in the mud in a side channel. There was a section at the base of one of the cliffs that was famous locally for its soft sand beds, which ran for a quarter of a mile or more.

She slowly wound her way back to her original route. If Blalock didn't surface by early evening, she'd come back for him. No sense in letting him walk the fifteen miles back to town.

Satisfied that she was now free to go to her meeting unwatched, she increased her speed. Though she'd lost time eluding Blalock, she should still make it to the chapter house before Paul left.

Ella had almost crossed a two-mile stretch of alkali flats when she noticed another vehicle in the distance. Although it hung back a quarter of a mile and was moving slowly, she thought she recognized the pickup as the one that had tried to run her down on her first night home. Her flesh prickled uneasily and she reached down to touch the butt of her handgun.

It was impossible for her to tell at this distance if it was the same truck, but she couldn't banish the thought, and her uneasiness increased. Blalock *might* have hedged his bet and arranged for a two-car tail, yet some intuition warned her that whoever was following her had far more deadly intentions than FB-Eyes.

Ella stopped and quickly jumped out of her truck.

Before the dust settled, she was standing in the bed of the vehicle, looking back. Wishing she had a pair of binoculars, Ella strained her eyes toward the black pickup, hoping to determine the make and model. But it had stopped as soon as the driver realized she was no longer moving.

For several minutes they played a waiting game, then Ella broke the stalemate, resuming her journey. She increased speed slightly. The pickup stayed well behind, maintaining the distance between them, never completely out of sight. After several minutes, she began to suspect the driver was only trying to rattle her.

She turned, heading directly for the bluffs. The sand would be hard-packed there, and the mesas and slopes would make it easier for her to hide or shake off the vehicle behind her.

Ella spent twenty minutes using every trick she'd ever learned, but no matter what she tried, the truck remained with her. He was second-guessing her with unerring accuracy. Panic rose inside her, but she quickly squelched it with anger. If he'd really wanted to do anything more than scare her, he could have easily gone on the offensive.

Still, as the cat-and-mouse game continued, Ella's confidence began to wane. She was going to miss her meeting with Paul unless she headed in the right direction again soon. She turned north, heading toward a canyon she was certain she recognized. As she drove through the narrow gap, she realized she'd made a deadly mistake—it was a box canyon, with no escape ahead. She slammed on the brakes, spinning the car around, certain she'd just trapped herself, but the pickup had hung well back, perhaps suspecting she'd been laying a trap for him. Without hesitation, she sped back out to open ground. She couldn't ditch him; whoever was following her knew the land better than she did.

Ella decided to head for the highway. She'd taken courses in pursuit driving. Maybe on a flat stretch she'd be able to use those skills to outsmart him.

Ella sped across the uneven ground, taking the closest and most direct route to the main highway, though the truck pitched and bounced viciously. The moment she reached the paved roadway, she pressed down on the accelerator, widening the gap between her and the dark pickup. She had no intention of losing him now, however. This was her chance to turn the tables, and that was exactly what she intended to do.

In her side mirror, she saw the truck hit the asphalt. He followed at a moderate pace, letting the distance between them grow. Ella let up on the gas pedal, hoping he'd catch up, but the truck took the turnoff leading to Four Corners.

Now it was her turn to give chase, something she was very good at. She turned her vehicle sharply and pressed hard on the gas pedal. Ella had a good chance of catching up to him, and when she did, she'd get some answers, one way or another.

She took the turnoff curve at sixty miles per hour. All those hours of combat driving, plus a few harrowing ones running down fugitives, were paying off. As she reached the summit of a long hill, she studied the area below and ahead. The pickup had disappeared!

Ella chided herself for her overconfidence. The driver of the pickup had once again anticipated her move, and had undoubtedly pulled off the road into a ditch or arroyo.

He'd had only a few minutes' lead, at most. He had to be nearby. She slowed the truck to a crawl, unholstered her pistol, and laid it on the seat beside her. She'd find him. He was around; she had no doubt about it. Slowly Ella drove a half mile farther, searching the shoulders of the road meticulously. There were no tracks, no evidence that he'd even been by here. She reversed directions and backtracked for a mile, looking for tire marks or likely hiding places.

Finally she gave up. He'd vanished, just like before, only this time he'd done it in broad daylight.

There was a possibility that the pickup had a souped-up engine. Then he might have outdistanced her in so short a time.

She glanced at her watch and sighed. To make matters worse, it was now far too late for her to meet Paul at the chapter house. For a moment she contemplated going there anyway, in case he was running late, but she couldn't risk it. She wasn't sure where the dark pickup had gone. If it had managed to hide rather than outrun her, she'd lead the driver straight to Paul and put him in danger.

She slowed considerably, almost inviting the dark pickup to reappear, but it didn't. Once in Shiprock, she drove past the chapter house. The parking lot was empty—Paul had gone home.

Ella glanced at Shiprock High School as she went by, then turned left and drove across the new San Juan River bridge. The old silver-painted steel truss-style bridge on the north carried traffic the other direction. During her childhood, it had been the only crossing, and Ella remembered standing on the southern walkway and dropping pebbles down into the river.

The new bridge was sleek, modern, and concrete. She hated it.

A half mile east, on the south side of the highway, was the old tribal-operated café. Pulling into the parking lot, she saw that only a few cars were parked there. It was still a bit early for dinner. As she went inside, she spotted Peterson sitting at a counter stool.

She eased up onto the seat beside him. "Hi. I didn't expect to run into you here, but I'm glad I did."

"Hey, this is still our generation's favorite haunt. It's too crowded around dinner, so I always come in a bit early." He studied her face, then picked up his hamburger platter and carried it to one of the booths, motioning her to join him. When they were seated, he asked her, "What happened?"

"How do you know anything did?" she countered.

"Your face is flushed, and you've got that spark in your eyes. It doesn't take a genius to figure out that you've been up to something."

Ella filled him in, her voice low. When she was done, Peterson nodded slowly, then pushed his side order of french fries to the center of the table for her to share. "I could talk to Paul for you. He and I have known each other all our lives. He trusts me."

"That would be great—only please don't talk to him about this in front of Loretta. She's got enough to worry about right now."

"Is there any specific message you'd like me to give him?"

"No, just tell him that I tried to come see him, but I had a tail on me and couldn't shake him. If he'll say, find out what he wanted, and how I can help him."

"Paul will talk to me."

"Did you manage to get a look at those files, the ones my father-in-law had in his office?"

"I'm afraid not. He's suddenly started locking his office every time he leaves it. I've checked the knob twice now, and almost got caught when the dispatcher walked by. It's like the chief read our minds." Peterson apologized in a whisper, his eyes darting around to see if anyone else was listening.

"Don't get caught, but keep your eyes open for an opportunity. If he's just changed his habit, he's likely to forget at least once." Ella hoped she was right.

"Will do."

"What about the hand? Anything from forensics?"

"There haven't been any reports of grave-robbing; I've checked that. Forensics is another matter. I have to go through the back door on that, so to speak, but I have a cousin who works in that department, and he owes me a favor."

"Sounds like you've got things covered."

Peterson laid several bills on the table, waved to the half-asleep waitress, and stood, picking up what was left of his burger. "I'll go over to Paul's house right now and catch up with you later."

As he walked out, Ella glanced at the clock across the restaurant. She wanted to call police headquarters and find out if Blalock had returned or called in. If he hadn't, she'd have to go back for him.

Ella used the phone in the lobby, and spoke to the woman at the information desk. She smiled when she heard that Blalock had called to say he'd been delayed, but expected to be in shortly. She decided against leaving a message. His pride stung, he was probably in no mood to hear from her.

Ella ordered a soft drink and a burger to go, now anxious to get back home. She didn't think her mother was in great danger. Those who were after Clifford had no need to terrorize his mother. Still uneasy, however, she drove home via a circuitous route, eating her dinner on the way.

From now on, she'd make sure to vary her patterns. She carefully maintained a route that allowed her a clear view in any direction. It would be impossible for anyone to either ambush or tail her without her spotting them.

Rose came out onto the porch as soon as Ella pulled into the driveway. "Wilson called. He said he'd call again this evening, and for you not to worry." Rose smiled.

"What's that smile all about, Mother?" Ella asked, her eyes narrowed.

Rose shrugged, the smile still in her eyes. "Nothing."

"Mom, don't start seeing things that aren't there," Ella cautioned as they went inside the house.

"I never do," Rose answered with a Cheshire cat smile.

Later that evening, in the living room, Rose knitted a sweater for Clifford while Ella tried to read the morning paper. Somewhere an owl called, and everything became very still for a moment. Ella glanced up surreptitiously to see if her mother had noticed, then realized that Rose too was pretending not to have heard.

Soon the steady drone of night insects picked up momentum, and inactivity, coupled with that sound, began grating on Ella's nerves. She set down the newspaper she'd been scanning and walked to the bookshelf. Her father had been addicted to action-adventure novels, and the shelves were filled with them. At the moment though, she wanted some light fiction. She found a shelf that contained a stack of her mother's favorite nighttime reading, *Time* and *Life* magazines dating back to the 1940s. Rose had collected them for years, picking them up at garage sales and fund-raisers. Picking out one that featured moviemaking in the Southwest, Ella sat in the chair nearest the window—after discreetly but carefully checking that she wouldn't be visible from outside. A cool breeze wafted through the curtain.

She began reading about westerns filmed in Monument Valley, Arizona, but the insect chorus outside continued to draw her mind away from the printed page. A vague feeling of disquiet increased her restlessness.

Ella finally closed the magazine and stared through a corner of the window. She couldn't shake the prickly, nerve-tingling sensation that the house was being watched. She surveyed the surrounding desert with eagle-sharp thoroughness. The moon was full and bright, bathing everything in a silvery glow. She could see no one moving around out there.

Still, the feeling persisted. She fought it for as long as she could, telling herself that it was just nerves. Finally, unable to remain seated, Ella stood up.

"Mom, I'm going out for a walk. I won't go far, but I need some fresh air to clear my thoughts."

Rose shook her head. "You really shouldn't wander around outside at night. It's too dangerous."

"I'll stay within sight of the house, I promise. But if I don't get some exercise, I'm going to go stir-crazy."

"Just like your father!" Rose muttered.

Ella smiled, then kissed her mother. "I'll be back in ten minutes."

Switching off the kitchen light, Ella waited for her eyes to adjust to the darkness, then stepped out the back door. She stood rock still, her gaze taking in everything. She could feel a watcher's eyes on her. When her instincts were this strong, they were seldom wrong. It suddenly occurred to her that the dog was nowhere to be seen. Even at night, he seldom ventured far from the house.

Ella walked a little farther, passing a stand of junipers that blocked one side of the house. As she did, she caught a brief glimpse of a figure on the other side of the belt of trees.

Setting aside any pretense of stealth, Ella charged forward, reaching for her gun. The figure stepped back quickly, moving behind some of the boulders that littered the canyon floor. Seconds later she reached the spot, but no one was in sight. However, in the bright moonlight, she could make out vague footprints, and determined from their size, and the depth and length of stride, that they'd been made by a man.

As she stood up she heard brush rustling ahead. The sage and tumbleweeds swayed slightly. She surged forward and caught a brief glimpse of a running figure. She shouted, "I'm a federal agent. Stop where you are."

The person ran into a thicket. She raced after him, but he soon became lost in the shadows and the bramble. Ella increased her pace, oblivious to the scratches the brush was leaving on her skin.

By the time she broke through to the other side, the man had disappeared. Her heart slammed against her ribs, her senses alive. He was somewhere close. She could almost smell him.

Remembering the skinwalker and his vast array of tricks, she ducked down and waited. If he couldn't see her, maybe he'd come toward her. As she waited, she sensed danger surrounding her, pressing in on her like a tangible presence. Her heart hammered against her ribs.

After what seemed an eternity, she heard sniffing sounds, like those made by a dog or a coyote, coming closer with each passing second, searching for prey. She held her gun steady, peering through the bushes. Ella's trigger finger itched, and she held her breath, body poised for confrontation. A heartbeat later, her mother's mutt came into plain view.

She lowered her pistol, exhaling loudly. "Dog, you almost got yourself shot," she scolded, then stopped, giving him a wary look. Her father's enemies and illusions; in this investigation, the two went hand in hand. Was this her mother's dog, or something sent to get her out into the open?

The animal came up, tail wagging, and rolled onto its back, asking to be scratched. This was no illusion. Ella breathed a sigh of relief. "Maybe it's a good thing you came, Dog. At the moment, the last thing I want to be is all alone out here." She petted the old hound, then stood up. "Let's go home."

The dog shook itself, licked her hand, and scampered back toward the house. Ella followed it, angrily conceding another victory to her faceless enemy. Before she could take another step, she heard the sound of a large animal moving rapidly through the brush behind her. The mutt stopped, then came to stand by her side. Ella was surprised to hear the low, deep, guttural snarl that came from the dog. Hair stood up along his backbone. This was the first time she'd ever known him to show any aggression.

"Come on, boy," she urged and headed quickly back to the house.

TWELVE

Midmorning the following day, Ella loaded boxes filled with her father's clothing into the back of the truck. She'd volunteered to take them to Reverend Williamson, who'd donate them to poor non-Navajos. Navajos wouldn't want things that had belonged to the dead.

The drive to the church helped her relax. She hadn't slept after discovering that someone had been keeping tabs on her and watching the house. The incident had shaken her belief that her mother was safe. Then, to make matters even more frustrating, she'd missed a call from Peterson. She'd tried to reach him at home, but he wasn't there. Now she was forced to wait for him to call back.

Ella drove slowly, trying to organize her thoughts. Her mother would not allow any of their male relatives to stay at the house for her protection, nor would she go and stay with her sister Merilyn. Rose steadfastly maintained that Ella herself was the one in need of protection. Ella had begun to wonder if her mother was right. So far her successes had been few, and her own life had been threatened more than once.

The church parking lot was deserted, except for a van and the garishly painted church bus. Reverend Williamson was doing carpentry work by the entrance. Seeing Ella drive up, he climbed down the ladder and smiled. "I see you brought the clothing."

"Yes. My mother said you'd find a use for my father's things," she said, climbing out of the pickup's cab.

"I sure can. I give them to a mission in Farmington. No sense throwing out perfectly good clothing."

Despite her rational belief that the clothes were harmless, it seemed creepy to give away clothing that had belonged to the dead. Out of respect for her father's beliefs, and for the sake of harmony, she decided not to say anything about it. "If you'll tell me where to put the boxes, I'll unload them."

"Just leave them on the patio. As soon as my wife returns, we'll load them into our van and take them to town."

Ella worked quickly, eager to leave as soon as possible. As she set down the last box, Williamson returned. He said, "Have you made any progress in the investigation?"

"It's not my case, officially," she answered, surprised he'd asked. Maybe Williamson had realized that he, now in her father's position, could be the next target, if stopping the church was the murderer's goal.

"I know that, but I can't imagine that buffoon, what's-his-name, Blalock, getting anywhere without your help."

Ella had to smile. Even Anglos were having a hard time accepting Blalock.

"He's certainly not very personable, but he's quite competent," she said out of respect for a professional colleague.

"I certainly hope so," the reverend muttered, a trace of uncertainty in his voice.

Ella patted the top of the box. "This is everything," she said, fastening her cop's scrutiny on the reverend's face. He could be putting on an act. After all, he was the only person she knew so far who had gained from her father's death. "I'll be on my way now."

As she turned away, she caught a glimpse of a figure standing on the hill behind the church, watching. Sudden anger shot through her, and she strode toward her truck. Williamson shouted something, but she didn't take notice. She hopped behind the wheel and in a flash was under way, tires spinning in the gravel. She raced straight uphill, hoping the wildly fishtailing truck would stay together. "I've got you now, buddy boy," she muttered under her breath.

Seconds later, she slammed to a stop. A cloud of gravel rose around her as she leaped out, gun in hand. "Come out from behind the rocks. Now!"

Two elderly Navajo men stepped forward slowly, eyes wide.

"Is this the way all FB-Eyes introduce themselves?" the older of the two asked. His coal-black eyes transfixed her coldly.

Ella studied him carefully, returning her pistol to its holster. The man wore his long gray hair tied back. A silver and turquoise squash blossom hung from his neck. There was an authoritative air about him, and despite his age, he stood ramrod straight.

"Who are you, and why were you watching us?" she demanded, less sure of herself now. He seemed indignant, but not threatening.

"I'm Samuel Pete," he answered calmly. "We're here because of you."

"What do you mean?" Ella asked, remembering Wilson had said this man was an excellent bow-hunter, skilled in tracking—someone who could have managed the skin-walker's illusion.

"I'm Herman Cloud," the other man said. "We were curious about you. There's been a lot of talk."

Ella's gaze shifted to him. Cloud's hair was salt and pepper, his face lined with deep furrows that attested to long days in the sun. He wore old work jeans and a long-sleeved chambray work shirt. His belly hung over the thick silver belt buckle at his waist.

"Everyone knows we're on your brother's side," Samuel Pete added sternly, "except you, it seems. You don't lack confidence, L.A. Woman, but you do lack common sense."

She stared at him aghast. So that's what she'd been dubbed. "Why do you call me L.A. Woman? This is my home too."

The man chuckled softly. "You don't act that way." He glanced down at her gold Seiko watch, a gift she'd given herself years ago, after she'd closed her first case. It had taken months to pay off on her only credit card.

"I am part of the Dineh."

"In some ways, maybe."

"How long have you been watching me?"

"Long enough to know that you rush headlong into things you don't understand. In the FBI, don't they teach you how to survive?"

"I'm still here, aren't I?" she countered, rankled by his attitude, especially since he was right. "Were you keeping watch over my home last night?"

"No, but we do try to keep an eye on your mother during the day. It's the least we can do for your brother. At night, once you're there, your mother shouldn't need extra protection," Samuel Pete answered.

They appeared to be sincere. "Will you help me? Do you have any idea who might be trying to frame my brother for my father's murder? Perhaps you've heard others talking . . ." She allowed her words to trail off, hoping one of the men would fill the silence.

"We know your brother has made enemies, but we don't know who's doing this to him. If we did, we would pass the word, and our people would handle it themselves. We don't need you," Samuel said.

"Handling things yourselves would be a mistake. Unless my brother is cleared in a way that the courts accept, he'll never be free to go on with his life."

"We'll do our best to help him, but we can't give you answers we don't have."

Ella knew that these men could be a wealth of information if they chose, but getting them to trust her was another matter. "Can I count on you for help if I find out anything?"

"Your brother has many friends," Samuel Pete responded, without giving a clear answer. "We'll be around." The two men turned and walked off.

"Wait! At least tell me where I can find you if I need you."

Neither man slowed. They walked off down the side of the highway. Ella kicked the right front tire of the truck, hard. Instead of gaining needed support, she was losing ground.

Dejected, she got back into the truck and coasted down to the church. Reverend Williamson was sitting on a wrought-iron bench. "I tried to tell you," he said, coming over to the truck. "I'd spotted them before, hanging around.

Either they knew you were coming, or else they followed you here."

"They didn't follow me," she said flatly. "Did you tell anyone I was coming?"

"My wife knew, and some of the women's auxiliary." He paused. "I think that's all."

Which meant everyone had known. You had to work hard to keep secrets on the Rez. "No harm done, Reverend."

"Thanks for bringing the clothing by."

"You're welcome." Ella headed back to Shiprock, passing Cloud and Pete by the side of the road. Engaged in conversation, they never looked her way.

Since she had to pass the college, she decided to look for Wilson. With luck, maybe she'd run into Blalock somewhere along the way. She wanted to see if he'd completed the background check on Wilson. On second thought, perhaps she should wait. He was probably still annoyed with her for losing him in the desert.

She went by the old college—a wing of the old boarding school—and saw Wilson's vehicle in the parking lot. Ella maneuvered her truck into a visitor's parking space. Inside the building, she walked the empty halls until she found his name on a door.

The minute he saw her, Wilson's smile widened. "Hey. I tried to call you this morning, but you'd already left."

She was getting tired of being snubbed and treated like a pariah. Wilson's warmth was invigorating. "I was hoping you can tell me more about Samuel Pete and Herman Cloud." Ella told him about her encounter.

"Pete lives on a little farm just west of the Hogback, but he's always on top of things. I figure he's in his late sixties, but it's not slowing him down. It's too bad you couldn't get him to open up to you. He probably doesn't know anything that you could take to court, but I'd be willing to bet he's heard plenty."

"And the other one?"

"Herman is about ten years younger than Samuel, and the two have been fast friends for several decades. Both are staunch traditionalists. They've always supported your brother in spite of his youth because he's very dedicated to the old ways."

"Can they be trusted?" Later she'd see if her mother and Peterson shared Wilson's evaluation. Although she liked Wilson, she still wasn't 100 percent sure he was trustworthy.

"Yes, I'm certain of it. They'd also make formidable allies—if you could earn their trust."

"I can try," she answered. "By the way, have you heard they've nicknamed me L.A. Woman?"

He chuckled. "The college kids started that, after hearing stories about you from their parents."

"I suppose it could be worse."

"Oh, far worse," he agreed, then chuckled again. "Besides, I always liked the Doors."

She shot him a stony look. "Is there any chance that you can talk to Samuel or Herman and find out what they've overheard or suspect? Maybe you could persuade them to talk to me."

"I can talk to them, but I doubt they'll tell me any more than they told you. I know them because of Clifford, but they don't approve of some of the life choices I've made. I don't hold to the old ways as much as they think a teacher should."

"Well, that's that, then." She took a seat at one of the student desks.

"By the way, I ran into Paul Sells at the gas station. He was scared, shaking like a leaf. Peterson had come to see him, apparently on your behalf, to pick up a message Paul had for you. But Paul doesn't want to talk to a cop, even Yazzie, so he just said somebody was following him."

"What was Paul's real message to me?" Ella watched Wilson carefully. "Did he say?"

"Yeah. He told me to tell you to concentrate on taking care of yourself. He would take care of his sister."

"Did you try to find out why he was so scared?"

"I did. I figured the stakes were too high not to ask. He and Loretta have been seeing packs of coyotes, late at night. Only he's convinced it isn't real coyotes, but skinwalkers in coyote shape. Apparently he picked up a small swatch of cured pelt that had been snagged by a juniper behind Loretta's home."

"What's he going to do?"

"He's armed to the teeth. No one could sneak up on that house. Someone's always keeping watch. He and his uncles take turns."

"Good."

There was a light knock at the door, and an elderly Navajo woman, wearing dark slacks and a cotton blouse, entered. Wilson took a small bundle of Navajo-language textbooks from her hands. The woman eyed Ella skeptically. Ella suddenly remembered what it felt like to be sent to the principal's office.

Wilson quickly introduced them. "Bessie Tso, this is Ella Clah."

"L.A. Woman," Bessie said softly, and nodded. "I've heard about you."

"Bessie is our cultural anthropology professor," Wilson added.

Ella studied Bessie Tso. Her face was remarkably free of wrinkles. Her eyes glowed with an unmistakable fire. This was a bright, alert woman who'd fought to attain whatever she had. Despite her weight, Bessie's movements were limber, and Ella had the impression that Bessie's body wouldn't dare disobey her. One thing perplexed Ella, however. This woman seemed as modern as Ella herself, yet seemed vaguely disapproving of her. "Pleasure to meet you, Professor."

"I've heard a great deal of talk about you, but I'm still not certain where you stand."

"On what?"

"The church for one, and the college."

"I think it's up to the community to decide what it wants," Ella answered.

"Yes, but do *you* think both should be erected, and that they'll fulfill a useful function?"

"They will to those who want them."

"Oh, come on! Only a politician gives nonanswers like that. You must have an opinion of your own."

"I *am* giving you answers, though obviously not the ones you want to hear," Ella said a little more sharply than she'd intended.

"No matter how long you straddle the fence on issues like these, sooner or later you'll be forced to make a choice. Be prepared. It's not enough to stand aside and let things take their course."

Bessie walked out. Ella said to Wilson, "Is she always like that, or do I bring it out in her?"

Wilson chuckled. "She's always like that. Plus you bring out her fighting instincts. With your family involved on both sides of the issues, people have been speculating on where you stand. She was looking for answers."

"I wasn't being evasive—that really is my position. I feel very strongly about the people's right to choose."

Wilson shrugged. "Even so, you're hedging. If one side *had* to take precedence over the other, which would you support?"

Ella met his gaze. "I'd be starting a third group, and insisting that all parties involved reach a compromise. Don't you see? I *really* don't favor one over the other. What I do favor is the right to free choice."

"You *really* should think about it and decide whether building—or not building—the college and church better suits the needs of the tribe. Making that decision will help you keep things in focus." Wilson placed the books Bessie had brought on the bookshelf. "Like you, I've lived in both worlds for many years. My heart is with the old ways, but I know we need the new to survive as a people. You have to find your own balance point. As far as I can tell, you haven't."

"I choose not to choose. Since I don't live here, I don't feel it's my right to interfere. Besides, it'll help me keep my objectivity throughout this investigation."

"Maybe it's easier for me to take a stand, since whatever happens affects me directly. Working with the students has also helped me focus my thinking." He paused, gave her a long, speculative look, then continued, "I'm giving an orientation workshop this afternoon for incoming students. Why don't you stay? You can be a guest speaker. You're a prime example of the range of educational and employment possibilities open to our people these days."

"But I don't have anything prepared," she said, surprised by his request.

"Have you done any public speaking?"

She nodded. "The bureau encourages their agents to

take an active part in community affairs. I've given talks at high schools and community centers."

"This won't be that different. It's very informal. If it makes you feel more comfortable, you can summarize your academic background and then turn it into a question-and-answer session."

There was no graceful way to decline, not after all the help he'd given her. Even if he intended to put her on the spot, she could turn it to her advantage. Radical groups often recruited from students, and this would give her a chance to meet some of them. "I'll give it my best shot," she agreed, hoping the time would fly by.

Ella watched Wilson closely as he gave his opening remarks. She envied the way he positioned himself in both the progressive and traditional worlds. What surprised her most was that he seemed comfortable everywhere. He'd learned to live with the differences, without compromising his own views.

"In conclusion," Wilson said, "education is necessary to protect and preserve the old—language, culture, and religion—and keep it a living part of our modern world. As a service to our community, Special Agent Clah has consented to speak to us today. She's made the most of the grants and scholarships our tribe offers, using them to help achieve her goals and contribute a life of service."

Ella glanced at the group of thirty incoming freshmen. She synopsized her education and all her training to become an agent. Then she opened the floor to questions.

"Members of your own family are in a great deal of trouble," one young Navajo man said slowly. "Will you use your connections as a law enforcement officer to help them?" The noise in the room stilled, and Ella could hear people breathing.

The unexpected question threw her momentarily, but she quickly recovered. "If I could, I probably would, but that's just not the way it works. I'm officially prohibited from being involved in the investigation. My interest is personal, and not a part of my duties as an FBI agent."

"Many believe that your brother is the key to the problems the area around the new college has been having." The young woman speaking looked at the others as she spoke. "Deformed animals are being born, and troubles plague the community near there. Would you bring him in, if you knew where he was?"

Ella glanced at Wilson; he returned her look calmly. Clearly this was her show as far as he was concerned. Good—because she intended to respond to the challenge these kids were issuing. "I'd be legally bound to take some action, like anyone else in this room. But I wouldn't make such an arrest myself. As I said, I'm not working this case. I'm here as a private citizen."

"Are your loyalties to the bureau greater than those you feel for the Dineh?" another co-ed asked.

"The two don't conflict," she answered. "The bureau is an investigative service, which serves the People as well as others."

"How does your being a federal agent help the tribe? Isn't it a form of disloyalty to use tribal scholarships to get an education that will benefit those outside the Rez more than us?"

"Our ways teach that everything is interrelated; one event always affects another. What I do outside the Rez isn't separate from what happens here; it's all part of the balance," Ella said, a bit surprised by the tack the student had taken. The room grew silent.

"Thanks for talking to us, Agent Clah," Wilson said, taking the opportunity to step forward. Ella went to the back of the classroom and waited while Wilson finished his lecture. Finally he directed the group to adjacent rooms, to speak with other professors. When the students had all left, Wilson came toward Ella, hands spread apologetically.

"It wasn't my intention, but your session turned out to be a trial by fire," he commented ruefully. "That deserves at least a soft drink on the house," he added with a wry smile.

"I accept. My mouth has definitely gone dry."

They went down the hall to the faculty lounge. Although the room was barely the size of a large closet, it looked comfortable, filled with worn, thickly padded easy chairs and a threadbare sofa. A large window faced the river, framing a vista of the small fields lining the old flood plain of the San Juan River. Above the valley, dry mesas stretched beyond sight into the clear sky.

Wilson handed her a can of soda from a vending machine, then sat beside her on the sofa. "You did an excellent job with the students. I really didn't expect them to ask those kinds of questions, but I figured it'd do more harm than good if I asked them to change the topic."

"I agree."

"But you handled it beautifully. You were completely calm and in control."

Ella shook her head and averted her gaze. "No, that's not true. I've learned to project confidence, my own brand of illusion. Underneath, I was really nervous. Of course, a person does her best dodging when under fire."

"I'll have to remember that." Wilson laughed. "But truly, you spoke very well."

"I envy your students—or maybe I should say I envy their outlooks on life. Things seem to be more black and white to them."

"That's the way it usually is when you're young and idealistic. You have all the answers . . . if only someone would listen," he observed.

"You know, not many people around here would have asked me to talk to any group of Navajos. Most seem to want to disassociate themselves from me. You're one of the few who have made me feel at home since the day I returned."

"I'll stand by you and your family, no matter what lies ahead. You can count on that." Wilson smiled.

Ella took a sip of her cola. Bessie Tso walked into the lounge, shaking her head. "More bad news," Bessie said. "Have you heard?"

"What's happened?" Wilson asked quickly.

Bessie clicked her teeth indignantly, then sighed. "Two people have reported seeing someone wearing animal skins hanging around the college construction site."

"Who reported it?"

"I'm not sure—I heard the story from my sister. She says that when the tribal police went out, all they found were several disemboweled sheep."

Ella managed to look calm and professional, though her throat had gone dry again. "Where exactly?"

Bessie gave her simple directions. "Are you going out there to look?"

"That's right."

Wilson stood up. "I'm finished here for the day. I'll go with you."

Bessie looked at him skeptically. "Be careful what you rush into," she warned, then left the lounge.

"She's right," Ella said. "There's no need for you to come along on something this unpleasant. If there are answers to be found there, I'll spot them."

"You sure?" Wilson asked. "There are things people won't say to cops."

"There are also things my special training helps me spot that someone else may not consider. Thanks for offering, though." Ella walked away before he could answer.

THIRTEEN

Ella arrived at the site a little past four-thirty. Seeing two squad cars ahead, she drove up and parked about fifty feet from them. She noted with relief that the sun was still high in the west. She didn't relish the thought of trying to investigate a site like this after sundown.

As she approached the raw circle of earth that had been cleared of vegetation, she saw Peterson studying the carcass of one of the mutilated animals. Blood and low, black heaps of entrails stained the sand.

Spotting Ella, Peterson rose to his feet and went over to join her. "You want a look?"

"If it's okay with you."

"Sure. We're covered. Jim Goodluck won't carry tales back to the office."

Ella stepped carefully around the gate and crouched next to the slaughtered sheep. "These tracks leading over here, they look like a wolf's, but there's something odd about them. The stride is all wrong."

"Yeah, the wolf would have had to be walking on his hind legs," he answered.

Ella studied them carefully. "That's what I was thinking. Someone has done a great job faking this to look like—"

"Skinwalkers," he interrupted softly. "The story's going to get around now. No telling what harm it's going to do."

"People who're afraid are capable of doing some damned bizarre things," Ella agreed. "Whoever is behind this is clever, using crowd psychology. Isn't there any way to keep this quiet?"

He gave her an incredulous look. "You haven't been away *that* long. News and gossip fly faster than a laser beam on the Rez."

"Yeah, you're right. Any idea who might be behind this?"

"No, that's the worst of it. We don't have a clue except what you see here. The other incidents have been similar. People are already looking at their neighbors funny and speculating about those they don't like. We're in for a lot of trouble."

"Someone must know *something*," Ella commented, glancing at the residential community a mile away. "The tracks lead in that direction."

"Right. And should we canvass the people there? That's going to get us nowhere. No one is going to talk to us about something like this."

"You have to try."

"We intend to, but we have our own ways of working—you know that. We'll talk to people later, unofficially. Ask questions. Mostly listen. That's our way—the only way that's going to work. It might take longer than your methods, but your methods won't work at all."

"Blalock does know about this, doesn't he?" she asked, glancing around.

"He's not coming. According to him, dead animals aren't a priority. Killing sheep isn't a federal offense. He said he'd read our report when we return to the station."

Ella sighed. "He really should be out here. Too many things like this have happened lately for it to be mere coincidence."

"I think Blalock is spending too much time sending us to do his job while he sits at a desk and calls the shots."

Ella smiled. "Has he alienated everyone at the department in the couple of years he's been here?"

Peterson nodded. "You know how hard your father-in-law is to read? Well, when Blalock's around, that's no problem. The chief's face changes color every time FB-Eyes enters his office. It's like a thermometer."

"From what I've heard, Blalock's had major problems with the tribe. My mother told me about his breaking one young man's arm, but talking about it upset her a great deal. What can you tell me about that incident?"

Peterson glanced around to reassure himself they were alone. "Things were really tense around here for a while after that. Your father based a sermon on what had happened, asking for community restraint but demanding that FB-Eyes be held accountable. One of the tribal newspaper reporters heard about the sermon and did a story on it. Your brother took your father's side, and was quoted in the article, asking for Blalock's badge. By the time the smoke cleared, FB-Eyes had been raked across the coals more than once."

"So Blalock had it in for both my father *and* my brother," Ella concluded.

"In a big way. I wouldn't trust the man. It would suit him just fine to arrest one for the murder of the other. Proving that one of his main attackers was a murderer might improve Blalock's standing with the regional office and earn him a chance out of here, which he badly wants," Peterson advised.

"An interesting angle. Thanks for filling me in." It didn't mesh with her own assessment of Blalock, but she had no reason to dismiss it out of hand. It was worth checking into.

Ella caught a glimpse of someone standing in the shade of a cottonwood tree, hidden in the shadows—Eddie Buck, a man she'd gone to school with. She decided not to seek him out until Yazzie and the other officer left.

"Come on," Peterson said. "While Goodluck talks to the construction people, let's follow the tracks. With both of us tracking, we might see something he missed."

It was a pointless exercise. The tracks led into a ravine and just disappeared.

"This person sure knows how to hide his tracks," Peterson commented. "I'm almost certain he scooped up sand with his hand, then threw it over most of the tracks he'd made."

"He also used some of the brush," Ella answered. "I saw some marks where he hurried too much." She exhaled softly. "The question is, now what?"

"Nothing else to do, except talk to some of the people who live near here, when the time's right."

"The vicious way these animals were killed is meant to inspire fear. It makes me wonder if the butchers are trying to divert our attention from something else that's going on. What do you think?"

"That you've been around the *bilagáanas* too long. You're starting to sound like FB-Eyes."

Ella shook her head. "No, listen. I've heard all about skinwalkers, but face it, this isn't one of the things they normally do. Take a human life, rob the dead, and even commit bestiality, yes, but this stuff doesn't fit—until you remember that our Way teaches that to look upon the body of a dead animal is hazardous. Someone is using these incidents to create fear and divert attention. It's a good plan, but not quite good enough."

Peterson rubbed his jaw pensively. "You may have a point, cousin."

Ella said good-bye to Peterson, watched as he and Officer Goodluck drove away. She looked for Eddie Buck, who had apparently managed to keep from being interviewed by Officer Goodluck.

If her mother's gossip was current and accurate, Eddie had had too many run-ins with the police lately. It was no secret in the community that he liked to tip the bottle with regularity.

Ella strolled over. She'd known Eddie practically all his life. They'd never been good friends, but Ella was sure she could get Eddie's cooperation if she approached him in the right way. Years of training and field experience often enabled her to get the most reluctant witnesses to open up to her.

Ella casually joined Eddie in the shade of the cottonwood. "Hi, Eddie. I didn't know you were working construction here. Remember me? I'm Clifford's sister, Ella."

"Sure, I remember. The smartest student in the school is

now a Fibby agent in L.A. People starting to call you L.A. Woman, have you heard?" Eddie smiled.

"Beats some of the nicknames you and I used to hear. How's the construction industry doing these days?"

"Good jobs have been hard to find—on or off the Rez," Eddie commented.

"They say it'll get better again," Ella said. "Especially with the college coming. I don't know if I would have the guts to work around here, though. There have been some strange stories about this place recently."

"It's been weird, all right. Sometimes when I hear what's going around, it really gives me the creeps. What about Charley Atcitty? You can't tell me that was just coincidence."

"What happened to Charley? I hadn't heard." Charley had been a classmate of theirs too.

"Well, only a few of the guys around here know, and they're not likely to talk much about it."

Ella knew that if she prodded now, she'd get nowhere. She forced herself to wait, grabbing a paper cup and filling it with ice water from a nearby cooler. She sipped at the cool liquid. An eternity later, Eddie spoke again.

"Charley lived in that trailer." He gestured at a small, white metal structure resting on cinder blocks. "He was hired to watch over the equipment and supplies. One morning he came out with a bandage on his arm. He told the guys he'd been shot the night before, walking back from his girlfriend's house. He figured someone had been out hunting, or shooting at some tins cans, and one of their bullets strayed and grazed his arm. He went to the public health clinic later that day. I don't know what happened, but he came back in a panic, insisting he had to find a Singer right away. With your brother gone, the closest one is about a day's drive from here."

"Wait a minute; back up. Charley was in a panic *after* they treated him at the clinic?"

"Yeah. I tried to talk to him, but he wouldn't say a word. He was really scared. Then FB-Eyes came to talk to him. You know what that Anglo is like. Charley was really worried that he'd be locked up, and he wouldn't be able to get to the Singer. I think Charley just clammed up, because when I saw FB-Eyes leave Charley's trailer, he was really pissed."

"What do you think scared Charley? This place?"

"I think he saw something he wasn't supposed to and that's why he got shot at. Charley's not too smart. He may not have realized what he saw until later. That's the only thing that makes sense."

"Where's Charley now?"

"I don't know. The next day, he came and got his things and left. Someone said that maybe he'd gone home, but not even his family has seen him."

"I haven't seen Charley in years. Was he the kind who'd normally go to a Singer?"

"Charley? You've got to be kidding! He thought all that traditional stuff was bullshit. That's why he agreed to live in the trailer."

"It was good talking to you," Ella said. "You be careful out here," she added, wadding up her empty paper cup and sticking it into her pocket.

It was time to pay a little visit to the public health clinic. Gunshot wounds had to be reported, and the doctor's name would be on the report.

* * *

By the time Ella arrived at the public health clinic, half an hour later, she'd decided to capitalize on Blalock's unpopularity and take a chance that he wouldn't find out that she'd come here today. Stepping up to the main desk, Ella lowered her voice conspiratorially and produced her badge.

"I need to find out which doctor treated a gunshot victim recently." Ella shrugged, then smiled sympathetically. "I figured it would be easier for everyone here to deal with me than with FB-Eyes," she added in a conciliatory tone.

The Navajo woman at the desk nodded, and without saying a word pointed to a name on the placard. Ella breathed a sigh of relief. The Navajo woman doctor had been a good friend of her family's for years. She was also the medical examiner.

Ella walked down the brightly lit corridor. The small clinic was still familiar; it wasn't hard to remember the location of Carolyn Roanhorse's office. The office door was open, and Carolyn was behind the desk. The portly woman was engrossed in reading a medical journal, but glanced up as Ella knocked lightly on the door.

"I was wondering if anyone would *ever* come around asking questions," Carolyn said with a marked lack of surprise when Ella explained her purpose. "I suppose you read my M.E. report on your father. I'm sorry. It was very hard for me to do."

Ella sat down in the chair across from Carolyn's desk. "I did, and I appreciate what you went through. But now I have to do my job—find the killer or killers."

"Yes, I know. I'm relieved to see you. From what I've heard, I'd rather not have anything more to do with FB-Eyes than is absolutely necessary."

"What can you tell me about Charley?"

"He came in with what he claimed was an accidental gunshot wound, but there were things about that injury that didn't add up." Carolyn paused, then added softly, shaking her head, "And when I told him what I'd learned, that poor man became really frightened."

"I'm not asking out of idle curiosity, you know," Ella said, noting Carolyn's hesitancy.

"You're a professional, and I've known your family for years," Carolyn said after a moment. "I'll trust you with the whole story, providing you don't tell anyone where you got the information unless you clear it with me first. Agreed?"

"You've got it." Ella nodded.

Carolyn got up and shut the door. "I found bone fragments in the wound. That really bothered me, because the bullet had only grazed muscle. So I sent him down to X ray, which confirmed that the bone was intact. Those bone fragments had nothing to do with his wound."

"Bone ammunition?" Ella asked in a shocked whisper. Whoever had shot Charley had done some homework. Bone was the weapon of choice for Navajo skinwalkers.

FOURTEEN

Ella drove to the police station. She had to find a way to make Blalock understand that a group of people using the tribe's natural fear of skinwalkers was at the heart of the case. The pattern of events was starting to look more like a conspiracy than crimes committed by any single perpetrator acting on his own.

As Ella walked into the station, she heard Blalock's voice booming from the other end of the building. From what he was saying, it was clear he felt he wasn't getting the correct amount of cooperation. Of course, if he kept this up, he wouldn't be likely to get any at all.

Blalock glared at Ella as she entered the room. "What are you doing here?"

"Good to see you too," she answered.

"Cut the crap. What do you want?"

"I've got a lead for you." Ella lowered her voice while she recounted what she knew about Charley Atcitty's wound, without giving Blalock details that would reveal her source.

"I've already heard about that. I hate to tell you, but it points to your brother more than ever. In my opinion this Navajo mumbo jumbo is just part of the smokescreen that cults usually throw up to make themselves seem less revolting than they are."

"Listen to me: this has nothing to do with cults. Navajo beliefs are just as valid as your Christian religions. Sometime, try walking into a Catholic church and calling the parishioners members of a cult and see if anybody is offended. What I am talking about is rooted in ancient Navajo beliefs. Check and see if any grave-robbing has recently been discovered in the Rez or the surrounding area."

"Give me a break; a psycho is a psycho. I'm here to find out who killed your father and bring the guy in. To do that, all I have to do is follow the trail of evidence, and that leads to your brother."

"Then your evidence leads to the wrong man," she insisted.

"Look," Blalock said, clearly exasperated. "I checked out the names you gave me. Allison Begay hasn't been around for years. She moved away from the Rez in the early eighties. Wilson Joe is slightly more interesting, but not by much. Peterson Yazzie hauled him in for beating the crap out of someone in a parking lot, but charges were dropped. The two men were related. Wilson Joe has a violent temper, but not much else to make him a serious suspect."

Ella made a mental note to ask Peterson about the fight. This was the second or third time she'd heard about Wilson's darker side, but she'd yet to see concrete evidence of it. "You're too convinced it's my brother, and that's clouding your investigation."

"Thanks for your opinion." He stood by the door. "Now I've got work to do."

"You sure you're being objective about this?" Ella said challengingly. "I heard you may have personal reasons for wanting my brother locked up." Her family had certainly made things hard for Blalock. Had he found a way to get back at them? Rogue FBI agents were very rare, but they existed.

"I don't care what you've heard about me. This is my case, lady. I'll make the judgment calls."

Ella strode out of the office. Blalock was going to continue getting nowhere if he wasn't willing to keep an open mind. Unless he never intended to get anywhere in the first place. The idea seemed far-fetched, and Ella decided to pursue a more likely direction.

Thinking of another way to follow up on what Carolyn Roanhorse had told her, Ella remembered Ernie Leighton. The Anglo man ran a gun shop just off the main highway. He'd know who in the area had the expertise and equipment to construct reliable bone "ammunition."

It took her most of the afternoon—Ernie liked to talk—but she finally was able to get three names. One of them, Eddie Buck, was the man who had given her the information about Charley Atcitty.

"Do you know where Eddie Buck is living these days?"

"The same trailer Charley Atcitty was using. Once Atcitty moved out, Eddie asked for his job. The company said yes right away. I think they were very relieved to have someone else volunteer to stay on the site."

"And Eddie's a hunter?"

"All his life. He's good too. He wins the turkey shoot every November."

As she drove to the college construction site, speculations crowded Ella's mind. Eddie was a crack shot, but also a friend of Charley's. If Eddie was responsible for shooting Charlie, it fit her theory that the immediate goal of those pretending to be skinwalkers was to create fear.

A stakeout was called for, and with a depressing lack of clues to run down, Ella had time on her hands. There was no reason why she couldn't shadow Eddie for the next few days and see what he was up to.

Ella stopped by the pay phone and dialed home. She gave her mother only a vague idea of what she intended to do, but Rose was perceptive. By the time Ella replaced the receiver, she was certain her mother had understood precisely.

Ella hated stakeout duty with its long, boring hours of fighting to stay alert. Pulling it without a partner was twice as dangerous. She couldn't afford to let her guard down for even a moment.

As darkness enveloped the desert, Ella maintained a sharp lookout. All was quiet, except for the usual sounds: night crickets, mosquitoes, rustling leaves. She was seated behind some brush on a hillside that offered a perfect, unobstructed view of Eddie's trailer. Infrared scope in hand, she forced herself to be patient. If Eddie was involved with skinwalkers, real or fake, it was possible he'd be leaving soon. Night was their time.

The minutes dragged on, turning into hours. It was nearly midnight before there were signs of activity below. The single light in the trailer went dark. Five minutes later, Eddie emerged, glanced around, then walked to his truck.

Ella ran to her vehicle and within seconds was following Eddie, making sure to give him plenty of room. The task was harder than she'd expected. It wasn't like tailing someone during the daytime, or in the city, where streetlights and traffic helped you keep track of a suspect. Only brief glimpses of red brake lights cut through the darkness as they both traveled without headlights. Ella used the nightscope to guide herself, but even so, within five minutes she had lost Eddie completely. She stopped on a hill and scanned the vicinity but was unable to pick up his trail.

Cursing her luck, Ella returned home. Once the sun came up, she'd return and follow his tracks until she learned exactly where he'd gone.

Rose was asleep when Ella returned. Wilson had slipped a note under the front door. He was taking some supplies to the hogan around lunchtime the next day. Though he hadn't specified, she knew they'd be for Clifford.

Ella stripped and crawled into bed. She planned to be back on the road at sunrise, and needed to sleep, but her thoughts kept her awake. She couldn't stop speculating about where Eddie had gone. Possibilities paraded before her mind's eye in an endless circle. Hours ticked by. Finally, an intense weariness overcame her, and Ella welcomed the yawning void.

She felt as if she'd just fallen asleep when the alarm on her wristwatch went off. She opened her eyes slowly. It was five in the morning; the sun would be rising soon, with Mountain Daylight time in effect. She dressed quickly, left a note assuring her mother she'd be fine, and raided the kitchen for breakfast. She headed out carrying a thermos of tea and a dozen chocolate chip—oatmeal cookies. It was a good crunchy snack, and even nutritious.

When she arrived at the hillside behind the construction

site, the sun was still below the horizon. She'd checked the area where she'd lost Eddie, but the past night's brief but heavy thunderstorm had effectively obliterated his tracks. Frustration had made her muscles tighten until they ached. She selected her vantage point carefully. A short time later, Eddie came out of the trailer and sat on the porch steps, cereal bowl in hand.

"You got away from me once, buddy boy, but not again," Ella muttered, nibbling on a cookie. "Today I'm sticking to you like bubble gum on a hot sidewalk."

Hours passed and the temperature soared; she crouched beneath the meager shade of a small juniper. She was getting no place in a hurry. Still, instinct told her not to give up.

As the midday sun baked the desert in ninety-degree heat, Ella began to wonder if maybe her instincts were wrong. Then she saw Eddie get into his old car and drive off. She started up her pickup and followed from a distance, driving slowly enough to avoid raising much dust. The way her luck was running, he was probably going into town for groceries. She'd have the golden opportunity to see him buy canned pop, then return home.

In the daylight it wasn't hard to tail him. He slowed down at the end of a dirt track, then turned and headed cross-country. Ella smiled. Her stakeout was about to pay off after all.

The pace he set was fast for the route they were taking, and she watched the ground carefully, wincing every time she heard rocks and solid-packed dirt scrape against the bottom of her pickup.

Moving in a mostly parallel course, she stayed out of his sight while keeping his car in range. Finally, Eddie approached a decrepit wood-framed, tar-papered shack. A hole in the north side signified that a death had occurred in the shack. North was the direction associated with evil, so that was the way a body was removed from a house. Ella parked behind some large boulders and crept forward on foot, stopping about fifty feet from the shack, behind cover. The wind was blowing the voices of those inside the shack to her. She smiled, thinking that her traditional brother would have said that the Wind People were helping her. Wind always reported the truth.

Ella hugged the ground and listened.

"It worked." The voice sounded vaguely familiar, but strange, as if the person was excited or drugged. She tried to identify the speaker, but distance altered the tone.

"So we know where he is?" another man asked. This voice was deeper, but also distorted.

"Yes. The homing device helped, like I knew it would."

The voices were impossible for her to identify at this distance. She fought the temptation to go in closer. Beyond this point, there was nothing that would provide her with cover. Her approach would be too easy to detect.

Ella stayed very still, holding her breath and listening carefully. Something was going down, and she had to know more.

"Despite all his precautions, Wilson Joe couldn't do a thing against this," another laughed. "He's a fool."

Hearing Wilson's name made her skin prickle with fear. The sound of her own heartbeat grew so loud she had to strain to hear each word.

"Do we make our move against Clifford Destea tonight?" the first man said.

A shiver raced up Ella's spine. They had found her brother! She had to get out of here and warn him before these men reached him.

"No. His magic is dangerous. We have to take him by surprise. That means striking while it's daylight."

The wind rose in stronger gusts, rendering some words indistinct. Desperate to learn their plans, Ella inched forward on her stomach, staying low to the ground.

". . . and we'll rely on our guns. The last thing Destea will expect is an attack while the sun is still up."

"He may . . . be alone . . . and . . ."

"It's possible Wilson Joe . . . but so what? He's . . . What can he do?"

"Then let's get . . . others. We'll meet at . . . near the arroyo in two hours."

Ella moved away. It sounded like they were about to adjourn. She hurried back to her car at a jog, using whatever cover the ground provided. Minutes later, she sped across the terrain. This was no time to play it safe. Her brother's life, and Wilson's, were at stake. A shortcut across ground suitable only for a tank saved her at least twenty minutes of driving. Thirty minutes later, Ella reached the highway. On the pavement, she could at least double her speed.

It would probably be a waste of time trying to phone or locate Wilson for directions. He was either still at the hogan, or on the road. She had to find Clifford's hogan fast, relying only on her memory of the position of the sun, her instincts, and the few clues she'd managed to get during her previous visit. The odds weren't favorable, but she had one advantage. The sameness of the terrain would make it nearly impossible for a stranger to discern the differences between areas, but she knew how to search them out. She remembered the color of the soil, the turns, the arroyo where Wilson's truck had become trapped in a section of sticky, clayish mud. She headed there, knowing it would be her best starting point.

Ella glanced at her watch, painfully aware she was racing against time. She reached the canyon nineteen minutes later. By anyone's standards, she'd made remarkably good time. Now she had to find her way to the hogan. Ella followed the route that seemed the most likely, looking for tracks and landmarks, trying hard to remember the number of turns Wilson had made, and the feel of the ground underneath the wheels. She remembered the strong scent of junipers right before they reached the hogan. There had been piñons where Clifford was, however. What she needed to find was a large stand of junipers just below where piñon pines could be found.

Twice she went off course, winding up surrounded by piñons. The color of the rocks and the ground were not what they should have been. Searching her mind for places rich in the sticky reddish clay around the hogan, she headed north.

Ella tried desperately not to give in to growing panic as her search continued without yielding results. Time was passing, and she still had not found either her brother or Wilson. Frantic, she parked the truck at the base of a hill and took several deep breaths.

She had to stop trying to reason it out and instead rely on intuition and gut instincts. There were times when letting go was the only way to get things done. Ella closed her eyes and forced herself to relax. Her breathing became even, her muscles uncoiled. Slowly her thinking became more focused. Guided by a certainty she couldn't explain, she headed east and uphill, new confidence assuring her that she was on the right track.

Ella soon began to recognize her surroundings. She wasn't far from a place where Clifford and she had tracked mule deer as children. It had been their father's favorite camping area. Memories painted vivid images in her mind, and she recalled a time when the whole family had been gathered under a tree. It had been raining hard, and her father had tried to make coffee in the can over a small fire. Suddenly she remembered the hogan—it had only been partially built back then.

When she tried to recall exactly where it was, her thoughts became fuzzy again. Ella began a soft chant her mother had taught her many years back, a *hozonji,* or a good-luck song. Apprehension and fear seemed to pass through her and fade away. Then, at long last, she remembered.

Ella pressed down on the gas pedal, speeding across the rugged terrain. Time was running out, but now she knew her destination. Before long, she saw the hogan. Wilson and her brother were outside, talking. She was downwind, and they hadn't heard the truck. Realizing how vulnerable they were, Ella stopped the pickup and hopped into the back, scouting the area with binoculars. No one was near, but they couldn't be far behind. Ella jumped back into the truck and sped toward the hogan.

As she raced across an open spot between the piñons, she saw Wilson reach for a rifle. Clifford quickly stayed his hand. She'd counted on them recognizing the truck right away, and now breathed a sigh of relief.

Ella came to a skidding stop near them. "You've got to get away from here. There are others on their way, planning to kill you both."

Clifford gave her a disbelieving look. "Our enemies? In daylight? I think you're mistaken, Little Sister. The ones after me will only attack at night; that's when their powers are strongest."

"No, I'm not wrong. Guns work fine, day or night. But I

don't have time to explain it all now." She saw Wilson turn toward his truck. "No! You can't use that. You'll both have to ride with me. There's a transmitter hidden on your truck someplace."

Wilson's face suddenly turned ashen. "I led others to this hiding place?"

"It wasn't your fault; you had no way of knowing. But we have to leave right now."

Clifford started back toward the hogan. "I need to retrieve a few things."

"There's no time!" Seeing her brother disregard her warning, she jumped out of the truck. "Wilson, keep a lookout. Get down behind the truck with your rifle."

Ella drew her pistol and watched Clifford enter the hogan. A second later a shot rang out behind her. The bullet impacted only inches away, shattering the windshield and ripping away the metal trim on the driver's side.

"Time to leave, Clifford!" she shouted, spinning around and crouching low to use the engine block as cover. Seeing movement in the trees, she fired twice. "Give him some cover fire," Ella yelled to Wilson.

Clifford ran from the hogan, carrying two rifles and several ammunition pouches. Zigzagging as he ran, he was at his sister's side in a few seconds. A burst of gunfire whined overhead. "How did you know?"

"It's my job to find things out, Big Brother," Ella said as she looked Clifford over quickly to assure herself he was unharmed. Then she glanced at his weapons. One was his .30-.30, but the other was a .30-.06 bolt-action, heavier but very accurate in capable hands. Clifford had certainly been ready to defend himself.

A volley of gunfire erupted, and bullets struck the top of the hood, just beside them. Caught in a crossfire, Ella fired rapidly into the trees as she and her brother dove to the ground beside the truck.

"Guard yourselves," Clifford warned, then began chanting.

At the sound of her brother's voice, Ella's skin prickled with alarm. The song seemed to wrap itself around her tightly in a deadly embrace, and she had to fight the panic rising inside her.

"Let's go," Clifford said, grabbing Ella's arms and shoving her toward the pickup door.

The shooting had stopped momentarily, so she took a chance and threw open the door to the truck. Wilson and Clifford were right behind her as she scrambled for the ignition key. Ella pressed hard on the accelerator. The starter whirred, but the truck failed to start.

"Damn! I flooded this old thing!"

"Fear holds them right now, but it won't last long," Clifford warned. "Try again."

True to his words, gunfire erupted a second later. Everyone crouched as she tried to start the engine a second time. Suddenly the motor roared to life. Bullets thudded into the top of the cab, and the rear window smashed into thousands of tiny slivers as the truck shot forward.

"We can't outrun them in this old pickup. They're too close," Wilson yelled as Clifford stuck his Winchester out the side window to return fire. "We have to make a stand here."

"No, we'll be trapped. I have no idea how many there are out there." Ella gunned the accelerator and headed for a narrow path between two clusters of trees.

As the old truck jumped forward, the gunfire intensified. Wilson stuck his rifle out the passenger window, aiming forward.

"They're all around us," Wilson said, firing at a shape moving out from behind a clump of brush.

His shot reverberated sharply in the cab of the pickup, and Ella's ears hurt. "They're trying to block our escape," she yelled. Three gunmen stepped into view in front of the pickup in the canyon ahead. "We'll have to go right through them!"

Ella kept her head low and the truck hurtling forward at breakneck speed. The men blocking their way began firing as if in a shooting gallery. Shots struck all around the cab. Wilson and Clifford, now aiming straight forward, through the gap where the windshield had been, returned fire.

Keeping her head down while keeping the truck on a steady course was hard, but somehow Ella managed it. Some of the men's defensive shots hit their marks—two of their enemies were hurled downward as bullets slammed into them. Wilson and Clifford's marksmanship surprised her. She wasn't sure she could have hit anything at this speed, particularly traveling over bumpy ground. A third man broke for cover as they whizzed past in the bullet-riddled truck.

"We may yet get out of this alive, Sister," Clifford said calmly. "I owe you one."

"I'll do my best to make sure you never forget it," she told him.

Ella didn't look back until they were on the graveled road leading to the main highway. Three vehicles, two pickups and a car, were behind them, racing to catch up.

"We have a problem," Ella warned. "Those trucks are newer than this old thing, and they're not shot full of holes.

We're not getting out of this anytime soon. In fact, we're in as much danger now as before."

"So are they." Clifford began a new song as he reached into a leather pouch.

FIFTEEN

Ella didn't know how he'd done whatever he'd done before, but this time she was prepared. She steeled herself for another assault on her senses, but oddly enough, nothing happened. Clifford was singing, but she could barely hear him. She risked a glance at him as they sped down a long, steep hill toward a sharp curve. Her brother's eyes were closed, and he seemed to be deep in concentration. A bead of perspiration formed on his forehead.

As the pickup rounded the bend, Clifford spoke a single word in Navajo and threw what he'd been holding in his hand out of the back window.

In the rearview mirror, Ella saw a white billowing cloud suddenly appear in the road. She felt an explosion. A heartbeat later, the lead vehicle chasing them skidded into the hillside. The truck crashed onto its side and slid to a halt, blocking the road.

"A few minutes, that's all the time we have," Clifford warned Ella.

Their truck bounced across a cattle guard onto the paved road. "We'll be okay now. I can make good time to the nearest police station," she said, pressing down on the accelerator.

"No!" Clifford yelled indignantly.

"Those guys behind us mean business. After today, I don't think they're about to give up. The police could place you in protective custody," Ella argued.

"What the police will do is stick me in jail. You can't do that to me." He paused, and added, "Or to our family."

"I'll find the answers needed to clear you. Trust me, Clifford, please," she responded, looking at Wilson for support. Today, Wilson had truly faced death alongside her and Clifford. She was almost ashamed that she had doubted his loyalty.

"You don't understand what's really going on," Clifford argued.

"Fine. Explain it to me then."

"I know you made our escape easier," Clifford conceded, his sorrowful voice betraying his weariness.

"Try possible."

"No, easier," he repeated, "and safer, perhaps."

"*I* think what she did showed courage and merits answers," Wilson said.

Clifford looked at his friend speculatively, then back at Ella. "What you did today, Little Sister, showed skills and strengths that are far from ordinary. How do you explain your ability to find us? Luck?"

Ella noted his guarded tone. Something about it disturbed her. "I sorted out the clues I'd gathered, then went on a hunch. It paid off."

"Do you always trust your instincts so little?" Clifford said in a disapproving tone.

Ella could feel Wilson's gaze on her, though she kept her eyes glued on the road. "It's not magic, if that's what you mean. The subconscious often has answers that are difficult to recall. I've learned how to tap into that when I need to."

"Your subconscious," Clifford repeated with a hint of a smile. "That's what it was. You've always had a lucky subconscious."

Ella wasn't sure what was going on in Clifford's head, but she was sure she didn't want to know. He was just trying to distract her with his own brand of magical double-talk. "I can help you, but you're going to have to trust me all the way. We share the danger, so this isn't the time for secrets between us. There's too much at stake."

Wilson looked at Clifford. "Your sister has shown you loyalty. She's jeopardizing the career she loves by protecting you from the police, even though she doesn't agree with what you're doing."

"All right." Clifford glanced at the empty stretch of highway before them. "Where are we going, and how long will it take to get there? What I have to tell you is difficult, and not something I can explain in a few minutes."

"I'm still trying to figure out where you'll be safe. For the moment, I just want to get as far from here as possible, and stay off the more traveled routes. To a cop, this truck would stand out like a sore thumb."

"No one else will give it a glance," Clifford said. "Beat-up trucks are a dime a dozen around here."

"I have an idea," Wilson said. "What about that abandoned gas station just east of where they used to hold the turkey shoots?"

"The cinder-block place where the bootleggers store their shipments of beer?" Clifford asked.

"That's the one. Everyone knows about it, but no one says anything, because the Tache family really needs the money. Since it's such a small-time operation, the cops have always left it alone. That's not likely to change soon."

"I like that. Good idea," Ella agreed. She remembered where it was, too.

"All right," Clifford chimed in.

"Now, the answers you promised," she prodded. "We're at least forty minutes from the station."

Her brother took a slow, deep breath, then let it out again. "I believe that the skinwalkers want the area surrounding the church and the college because of the inherent evil that resides there. They want to tap into its strength and use it for their own ends. That's why they have to stop the church from being constructed—they can't afford to have that ground consecrated. It would weaken the magic there. Even if you don't believe in magic yourself, Sister, you must recognize that others do and are willing to act on such beliefs. Believe me, their motivation is strong."

"So the problem isn't really the college, just the church."

"No, not at all," Clifford answered. "They want that area to remain deserted for their rites. The college will bring in a lot more people and threaten their secrecy. Plus, once it's finished, *hataaliis* will gather from everywhere to perform special ceremonies at the dedication. That might also destroy the power the skinwalkers want to harness and protect."

"If Sings would stop these jerks, couldn't our Singers do the ceremonies now?"

"No. Remember, our rites are very specific. It's a lie to perform a ceremony for a building that isn't there. Any ceremony that is false will not be heard. It could even make things worse."

Wilson glanced at Clifford, then Ella. "In the long run," he said, "there's only one answer. We have to expose the skinwalkers hidden among us, identify every single one of them. If we don't, they'll undermine everything the tribe is trying to accomplish."

"I believe that there are specific locations within that area where the evil is particularly concentrated," Clifford said. "I suspect the skinwalkers have already held ceremonies over these places."

"Where?"

"One is right above the old church." A squad car approached; Ella asked Clifford to duck down. The unit went by without slowing.

"The skinwalkers have miscalculated. They've inadvertently turned you into a double threat, Big Brother," Ella mused, after giving him the okay to sit up again. "As the manhunt for you continues, Blalock and the police keep broadening their search patterns. They could easily stumble onto one of these secret ceremonies."

It took over an hour to get to the gas station—the pickup had begun to overheat and Ella had had to ease up on the gas pedal. She hoped the truck hadn't suffered damage that would wind up stranding them somewhere. She drove around to the rear of the building, where they'd be hidden from the road. Ella surveyed the surrounding area. "I don't like this. It's too open."

"That's what makes it ideal," Wilson said. "No one can sneak up on Old Man Tache here. And the phone line works," he added. "All you have to do is put in a quarter."

"How do you know this?" Ella asked with a tiny smile.

Wilson cleared his throat. "Everyone knows it."

"Try again."

"I've bought a six-pack or two here on a hot summer day," he admitted.

Ella chuckled softly. "Wait here for me."

She went inside the building and checked out the gas station's boarded-up office, then the garage area. Finding it empty, she returned to the truck. "It's clear for now, but if they're using this as a drop-off, there's no telling how long that'll last."

Wilson walked inside with Clifford. "I doubt there'll be another shipment for a month, maybe more. FB-Eyes is making too many waves, and it's got people nervous."

Ella joined them. "How reliable are your sources?" she asked Wilson pointedly.

"We're reasonably safe using this place," Wilson said flatly. "Tache follows the old ways. Of course, if you can think of someplace better . . ."

Ella considered. "No," she answered at last, then looked at Clifford. "But it's your call. You're taking the biggest chance. Until we can discover the identity of at least some of our enemies, you have to remain hidden. While they're looking for you, I'll look for them."

"I'll stay here then. I can even pull my truck inside and keep it out of sight, if I have to. I'd prefer to play it safe and hide it in the desert. Somebody will have to bring it here—it's in an arroyo, about a mile north of the hogan, covered with shrubs. I doubt our attackers found it."

"I'll get it. I have to go back anyway," Wilson said. "My truck's still there, too. The ones who ambushed us won't stick around. It should be safe enough, now, for me to reclaim it."

Ella nodded in agreement. "We'll both go. I want to search your vehicle and find that homing device. But we might have to leave your truck where it is," Ella told Clifford. "The police and Blalock are looking for it."

"They won't recognize it; I painted it green, then weathered it a lot." Clifford shrugged.

"That was smart," Ella conceded.

Wilson nodded in agreement, then glanced at Ella. "I understand homing devices are very small. My truck's pretty big. What if we can't find it?"

"We will, don't worry. I'm very good at searches."

Ella and Wilson drove back in her father's truck, which was operating normally again despite the bullet hole and broken or missing glass.

After delivering Clifford's admirably disguised truck to a new hiding place, and stopping at the gas station to tell him where they'd left it, they drove back to the area where the shooting had begun. They had wanted to put that off until last to ensure that their attackers had time to leave the area completely.

About an hour before sundown they arrived at the spot where Wilson had left his truck, some distance from the hogan. They circled the area first, seeing tracks, but no sign that anyone was still around. Ella checked the boot prints, but none was very revealing.

"Looks like I won't be taking that truck anywhere tonight," Wilson said, gesturing to the flat rear tire.

"Don't you have a spare?"

He gave her a sheepish smile. "You're looking at it. I blew out a tire last week and haven't had a chance to get it repaired." He rubbed the back of his neck with one hand. "My cousin Ed will drive out with a spare. He won't ask any questions."

"Let me look it over while we're here. I still want to find that homing device before the sun sets."

"I'll hold a flashlight for you," Wilson offered. "It's dark underneath the truck."

Ella went over the truck with a practiced eye and touch. Locating explosives and listening devices was all part of her training. A homing device was just another form of transmitter. She checked the bumpers, then the wheel wells. Moving inside, she ran her hands carefully over the upholstery, then searched the steering column and underneath the dashboard. Not finding anything there, she went back to the outside. Ella jumped up onto the bed of the truck, but found nothing unusual. Finally she crawled beneath the truck, looking up into the area where the spare tire was kept. Nothing was visible from below, so she ran her hand along the top of a metal bracket that normally held the tire in place.

"Got it!" She removed a small magnetic device, about the size of a large button, emerged from under the truck, and studied the bug for several moments. "You can easily get these through electronic warehouses, and I know of a guy who got one through a survivalist's catalogue. This is going to be difficult to trace. It was placed after you had the flat, but would have taken only a few seconds to attach. I'm afraid it won't tell us much about its owner."

"It doesn't matter; you couldn't have taken it to the police without leaving yourself open to a lot of questions. For one thing, they're sure to wonder why someone would put this on my vehicle. Since they know I'm Clifford's friend, they're bound to start watching me more closely. They may even think FB-Eyes did it, though if Blalock had bugged my truck he would have used a better bug."

"You're right about all that."

Ella hurled the tiny device as far as she could, sending it

straight into the desert. "Maybe some packrat will pick it up and carry it around, and keep them running in circles."

"We can always hope."

"Come on. I'm beginning to see why Dad loved his old truck. They don't make them this tough anymore."

Silence stretched between them as they headed back to the now-familiar stretch of highway. The sun had finally gone down, and something was telling her that they needed to get out of the area fast. She concentrated on driving, turning on the headlights to see clearly.

"Do you feel it?" Wilson asked in a hushed voice. "The gathering shadows, since sunset . . . Well, they just don't feel right."

Ella heard the mournful wails of coyotes or wolves faintly in the distance and had to suppress a shudder. She suddenly felt as frightened as a lost child.

"It gives me the creeps," she answered with deliberate, concealing evenness. "It won't be much longer before we reach the highway, though."

In the beam of the truck's headlights, they saw a large dog ahead, trying to drag itself out of their path. "That poor thing," she said, "somebody hit it with a car. It's leaving a trail of blood."

"Don't even think of getting out of this truck," Wilson said flatly.

"I wasn't," she assured him. "It's feral, and it might not understand that we're no threat to it."

As they drew near, the injured animal seemed to abruptly recapture its strength. Its limp vanished. It whirled to face them. In the blink of an eye it jumped onto the truck's hood, jaws snapping viciously.

"What the . . . It's a coyote!"

"Don't stop. Drive on!" Wilson yelled.

Before Ella could react, another coyote jumped into the bed of the pickup. Growling, teeth bared, it stuck its head through the gaping hole in the rear window.

Ella drew her pistol and fired, hitting the coyote squarely between the eyes. As the animal staggered and fell back, she turned and fired again at the creature on the hood, striking it. She gunned the accelerator. The wounded coyote, yelped and dropped to one side, rolling off as Ella sped toward the highway.

After they'd traveled several hundred yards, Wilson released his death grip on the dashboard. "Okay, slow down. We can't take that thing in the truck bed back into town with us."

"Why not?" Ella's ears were still ringing. She shook her head, trying to clear the annoying buzz. "That's precisely what I was going to do. Maybe there's an outbreak of rabies or something. That was not normal behavior for a coyote. And don't try to tell me those were skinwalkers; those animals were the real thing."

"How do you know that?" Wilson asked.

"Didn't you get a look at them? They were mangy-looking, half-starved."

"And what did you expect?"

She started to speak, then pressed her lips together and slowed the truck. "We've all heard stories that wolves or coyotes with turned-down tails are really skinwalkers, but these animals looked like the real thing to me. They were crazy, out of control, but nothing marked them as anything other than coyotes."

"You're looking for signs of humanity within the form of the beast, but you won't find it. Those who choose to follow evil eventually lose themselves and become more beast than man."

"I don't accept that," she said, shaking her head. "Every instance of magic like theirs has a logical explanation if you look into it closely enough."

"You've seen a lot of things since coming home that can't be explained with conventional knowledge and logic. You're fighting yourself by trying to make sense out of something that operates under rules you don't understand. There's too much at stake for that kind of confusion."

"And what would you have me do with the animal in the bed of the truck? It's dead. You can see that for yourself. No living creature can survive a hollow-point nine-millimeter slug in its skull at point-blank range."

"We have to burn the body."

"At least let scavengers take it," she argued.

"We have to set fire to it," he repeated adamantly.

"Look, are you sure you want to do this now? I really don't want to hang around out here . . ."

"I'm sure," he said, interrupting her. "Let's get to it. This is an open stretch. We'd see anyone approaching in plenty of time to react."

She didn't share his confidence, and the weight of her pistol was of very little comfort. The last thing she wanted was to face another assault. She only had a few rounds left in her clip.

Ella and Wilson worked quickly to build a fire. Once the flames were going strong, Wilson uttered a prayer for protection and dragged the animal into the fire. Flames licked the carcass; a putrid smell rose into the air. Ella began to cough. "It smells like a sewer!"

"Get downwind, but we have to stay until it's consumed."

"Hey, I went along with you on this, but we have to get out of here. The fire won't spread, and I'm not—"

The air was shattered by an unearthly howl. The creature jumped up amid the flames, its body covered in bright orange tongues.

Ella stared at it for an endless instant. It wasn't possible. The animal should be dead. But as the beast leaped for her throat, she fired again and again.

Her finger kept snapping the trigger long after she'd run out of rounds. The thing collapsed back into the fire.

Beside Ella, Wilson kept his gaze on the creature until the flames turned it into a black, shapeless mass. "It's over."

Suddenly wild howling rang out all around them. The sound rose until it became an earsplitting wail.

Wilson grabbed her arm and half dragged, half raced Ella to the truck. "Drive! And don't stop for anyone!"

SIXTEEN

Ella sat beside Clifford in a small depression behind a clump of sagebrush. It was early evening, the next day, and the ground was cool by the old garage.

"I can't believe you actually went out searching for the skinwalkers' meeting places." Ella shook her head slowly. "You're just opening yourself up to more danger."

"I'm doing it during the day, and staying away from the community and the college construction site," Clifford explained. "I'm being very careful."

Ella closed her eyes and shook her head. "It's still one helluva risk."

"Things aren't going anywhere on the case. You couldn't exactly report the attack on us to the police. And your checks with doctors and hospitals didn't turn up any gunshot victims. We have to take the offensive." Clifford lowered his voice and looked around to make sure no one was anywhere near the abandoned building.

"You should trust me to do that, and stay put."

"I'm trusting you to help Loretta and Mom. I don't expect you to do it all, or to work miracles. You're the only one who expects that." Clifford looked her straight in the eye.

"You may have a point." Ella glanced at her watch. "I'd better be going. I've got to pick up Mom at the chapter house. She's at the fund-raising meeting the progressives called on behalf of the college, to pay for landscaping and outdoor sculptures."

"I'm surprised she went to that. I didn't think she'd want to get actively involved, particularly on the night of the Enemy Dance. I realize that these days the dance is mostly a summer social, but some of us still take it very seriously. It used to be done only when needed, to eliminate contamination from outsiders and their influences. Only we traditionalists realize that the tribe is in dire need of it right now." Clifford turned his head to watch as a car full of Navajo teens drove slowly down the highway. The hollow thump of amplified music reached them despite the distance.

"The meeting will be over before the dance starts. Our mother wouldn't have gone if she thought there was a conflict. The only reason she went was because she was invited by an old friend of father's."

"Is our professor friend going to the ceremonial?" Clifford reached for a can of cola Ella had brought him, along with a few sandwiches.

"I don't know. Even if he is there, I'm going to be too busy to socialize. I need to use this opportunity, while most of the community is present, to find out if anybody is talking about our little shoot-out, or if anyone is missing or injured. Hopefully I'll be able to pick up something."

Clifford shook his head. "Remember, part of the evening is still a religious ceremony. For it to bless the tribe, onlookers have to help the participants by keeping their thoughts on the ritual."

Ella could have argued with Clifford. A meeting like that was the ideal time to observe, especially in light of what had been going on recently. But she knew she wouldn't convince him of the validity of her point of view. She'd just do what she had to.

She stood. "The meeting should be over soon." Smiling at Clifford, and giving him a thumbs-up, Ella walked through the brush to a low spot that was out of sight from the road. Her father's pickup was too shot-up to drive around without raising eyebrows. It was parked in Wilson's garage, out of sight. Ella had told her mother it was being worked on, and had leased a new truck in Farmington.

Less than an hour later, Ella arrived at the chapter house, where the meeting was still going full blast. Ella wasn't surprised to hear loud voices coming from inside the building. According to custom, issues were debated until everyone could vote unanimously. That often took a very long time.

Wilson was standing outside the building. Had he been waiting for her? Ella started to cross the parking lot to meet him. Two pickups, each carrying five or more Navajo teens crowded in the cab and back end, pulled up at the chapter house's entrance. Something about the teenagers' expressions warned her of trouble.

Wilson quickly came to stand beside her. "They don't belong here," he mumbled.

"I figured that," she said, as they jumped out of the trucks and crowded through the door. She raced into the building, Wilson at her side.

"This meeting is over. You won't interfere with our religious ceremonies ever again," one of the boys shouted.

Ella brushed past two youths at the entrance, appraising the situation at a glance. The boys, who ranged in age from sixteen to their early twenties, were circling the seated adults like vultures. Suddenly a tall, muscular-looking Navajo boy lunged at Wilson. Ella tripped the youth; he didn't fall, but turned on her with a roundhouse punch. She grabbed his wrist, sharply twisted the boy's arm behind his back, then kicked him away. In an instant another one was on her, grabbing the back of her hair. Ella leaned into the attack, then stomped down hard on his instep and kicked back, spinning. By then, the room had erupted in a free-for-all.

Out of the corner of her eye, she saw Wilson flatten one of the boys with a punch, turn and pull another away from one of the older men, then pitch the boy through the open door. The practical efficiency of the move, and the strength it had taken, surprised her. She wondered where he'd learned to fight like that.

Diverted, she almost didn't see the folding chair one of the boys hurled at her. She ducked at the last minute and the chair caught another attacker in the back. As the teenager advanced toward her, she kicked out hard, catching his knee full force. The boy yowled in pain, falling to the floor. Before Ella caught her balance, another young man lunged at her, but Rose stepped in and smashed him in the face with her purse. She continued hitting him, hard, and he tried to protect his head with his hands. In a flash, Rose was joined by three other angry women.

Ella moved toward an elderly man in a wheelchair. He too seemed to be holding his own. He'd used his chair to trap one of the young men who'd been knocked down against the wall. Every time the boy moved to get up, the man would ram him with one of the metal footrests.

"Someone call the police," Ella yelled.

Her words were lost in the angry shouts and screams that filled the room. She tried to move toward her mother, but one look at Rose jolted worry right out of her. She and the three other women were ganging up on whichever young troublemaker was closest.

Wilson was blindsided with a solid punch to his jaw. As he staggered back, two more youths were on him. Ella deflected an arm that snaked toward her and kicked one of Wilson's opponents in the crotch from behind. He went up into the air about a foot, then crumpled.

Grabbing a broom someone had left propped against the wall, Ella jammed the handle into the stomach of the last boy on his feet, then brought it crashing down on the back of his neck. As the boy struck the floor, Ella heard sirens above the din in the room.

Wilson scrambled to his feet and, with Ella and several other adults, blocked the door. Those teens still able to move retreated to the opposite side of the room.

A minute later, eight tribal police officers came rushing in, batons ready. The defeated attackers offered only token resistance.

Recognizing Peterson in the group of newcomers, Ella sighed with relief. He would be professional about taking statements, and they wouldn't be detained any longer than necessary. Wilson helped the officers, relinquishing custody of two young boys he'd forced to the floor.

As the troublemakers were led from the room, Peterson came over to Ella. "What the hell happened here tonight? How did all this get started?"

Rose Destea approached before Ella could speak. "I may

be an old lady to them, but I can still take care of myself," she said proudly.

Ella chuckled. "Yeah, I saw you. You sure took care of those punks, Mom."

"All that trouble, and from them!" she muttered angrily.

"Who, Rose?" Peterson asked. "Do you know what this was about?"

"Hotheads, that's all. They thought they could teach those who don't follow the old ways a lesson. All they've done is hurt the cause of those of us who still value the old! People of both views were here tonight."

"You mean these boys were traditionalists?" Ella's eyebrows furrowed skeptically.

"That's what one of them told me," Rose nodded.

"But then why would they do this tonight, when there's an Enemy Dance scheduled? You'd expect them to be there, getting ready," Ella added.

"The only answer I can think of is that they were incited by someone," Rose replied. "Some were saying they were here because this meeting would force many of the Dineh to miss the beginning of the ceremonial. But that's not true."

Peterson said, "I'm afraid it is. There was an error in the flyer that went out advertising the meeting here at the chapter house. It reported that the ceremony wouldn't begin until moonrise. Actually, it was set for nightfall."

"So it would have been impossible for anyone here to get to the ceremonial on time," Ella said softly. "Who wrote the text for the flyer?"

"I haven't been able to find that out yet." Peterson glanced at Rose, the unspoken question in his mind.

"I don't know who's responsible," Rose answered. "It seems like a very stupid thing to do. The people conducting the ceremonial were sure to discover the mix-up."

"That's exactly what happened, and it got some of them very angry," Peterson said.

The young people who'd started the trouble were driven to the station, but those arrested also included some who'd fought off the assault but refused to cooperate with the police. Wilson stood beside Ella as the last squad car drove away. "This is really going to create trouble. Everyone will blame someone else, until they're all at each other's throats again. And it will interfere with the Enemy Way too."

"Nothing can be done about it now. But you can bet that whoever planned this little confrontation knew exactly what they were doing." Ella surveyed the meeting room. People were picking up chairs and trying to straighten things up.

"We have to find out just who that was," Ella said. "I'll ask around. I have a feeling the police didn't get much cooperation from this crowd, not when some of their own were arrested." One group of ladies was still arguing about the police response.

"Wilson, shouldn't you be leaving for the ceremonial now?" she asked, her gaze on her mother, who was trying to calm an old man and his wife.

"Before I go anywhere, I'm going to check my answering machine. Clifford has my home number, and the code you suggested we use in case of an emergency," Wilson said.

She'd been with her brother less than two hours ago, but in view of the circumstances, it couldn't hurt. "Let's do that now. There's a pay phone at the gas station across the street."

They walked outside, dodging the cars of a few curious onlookers who were cruising by because of the recent excitement. Several people stood around the gas pumps, drinking sodas and gossiping excitedly about the near riot.

Wilson dialed, covering one ear with his hand as he struggled to hear above the din of voices nearby. "He's in trouble," he said flatly after a moment. "We've got to leave right now."

Ella didn't bother to ask him to explain. There'd be time for that later. Instead, she ran with him back to the chapter house parking lot. Rose had just come outside, looking for them.

"I have to go," Ella said to her mother.

Rose nodded. Sensing their urgency, she asked no questions. "Give me the keys to that rental pickup. I can see myself home. You two can use Wilson's truck."

Ella handed her mother the keys. "I'll be home as soon as I can."

"Clifford needs you more than I do right now," Rose answered, then walked away.

Ella turned to Wilson. "How does she do that? *I* don't even know what's going on yet. You haven't told me."

"Your mother's side of the family is very gifted; you know that."

"What's happened with Clifford?"

"The message he left was the code for trouble, but not an emergency situation." The code they'd worked out included a number of variations.

"I hate to think of him alone out there."

"You've been more alone than he is, living on your own, off the Rez."

Ella didn't respond. As they approached the gas station, she spotted several children, playing on the concrete pads that supported the pumps. "What on earth are they doing here at this time of night?"

"If they're here, that means an adult brought them." Wilson paused. "I don't see any horses or bicycles. A shipment may be on the way."

"We have to get Clifford away fast." She pulled to a stop behind a thicket of Russian olives. "We'll have to go on foot from here."

Wilson commented, "I never thought they'd take advantage of a ceremonial to bring in beer."

"Less traffic, less interference," Ella reasoned.

"I suppose," Wilson admitted grudgingly.

"I'll get Clifford. You stay here and be ready to drive the truck out of here the moment we get back."

"Right."

Ella circled in a wide arc across the desert toward the back of the gas station. She could see Clifford standing in the shadows near the rear exit. His truck was nowhere to be seen. If there was danger, why had he stayed? Surely avoiding a half dozen kids wouldn't have been that difficult for him. He was the kind of man who could hide in a crowd of three. He'd done it even when they were kids.

Her brother saw her and came toward her, staying low but moving with a fleetness and agility that surprised even her. He made no sound. It was as if he had become one with the land.

"I was hoping one of you would get my message quickly," he said.

"Where's your truck?"

"Across the road, hidden in a canyon. Bouncing around in the desert loosened the fuel line, and before I knew it, all the gasoline had soaked into the ground. By the time I found it, even the sand was dry."

"Let's go." Ella led him to where Wilson waited.

Moments later, as they drove down the highway, a large

van passed them, then turned, heading for the gas station that had served as Clifford's hideout.

"I'm sorry," Wilson said. "This is my fault. I thought you would be safe there."

"I don't blame you, so don't blame yourself," Clifford answered. "At the moment, no place is really safe for me." He hunched down in the seat as headlights approached, but the vehicle turned off the road before they passed it.

"But we do have to find a safe house," Ella said pensively. "You need a home base." She saw Wilson's eyebrows knit together as he considered their options.

Wilson looked at Clifford, then at Ella. "I have another idea, but it could get risky." He checked the rearview mirror for cars.

"Go on," Clifford encouraged.

"The tribal government has several portable buildings that eventually will become part of the new college. They're currently unoccupied."

"Where are they?" Ella asked pointedly.

Wilson exhaled softly. "Not far from the construction site. About two miles from there, actually, inside a fence."

"Perfect," Clifford stated.

"Only if you're trying to make yourself a target," Ella countered. She glared at Wilson. "We already know that's where our opponents have been most active. Leaving Clifford there is a lousy idea! He'll be vulnerable."

"No, not really," Clifford interrupted. "I will be on my guard, and my own powers will support me. But to put it on a level you're more comfortable with, let me make one point. That's the last place they'll look for me. Best of all, it'll give me a perfect chance to study the area and familiarize myself with our enemies."

"Or get killed. This is a rotten plan. Let's think of another location."

"No," Clifford said softly, but with such vehemence both Ella and Wilson turned to look at him. "That place is the ideal hideout. Take me there."

"How will you survive?" she challenged. "You'll be on your own, facing danger, with no backup and no way of contacting us."

Clifford shrugged.

Wilson glanced at the row of cars heading to the ceremonial. "Why don't you two keep my truck for now? Drop me off so I can attend the Enemy Way." He looked searchingly at Ella. "That is, unless you need me."

"Do you want me to pick you up later?" Ella asked.

"Come by, but let's play it by ear. If it doesn't look like the right time, I'll catch a ride from one of my cousins and get my truck at your place later."

"Okay," Ella agreed.

After dropping Wilson at the dance, Ella continued toward the construction site with her brother. Ella stared at the road, her thoughts drifting. "You know, this investigation has thrown me more than the usual number of curveballs. Even when I'm sure of an answer, I find I'm wrong." She shrugged. "Maybe this place Wilson suggested is exactly where you should hide; I don't know anymore."

Clifford looked at his sister speculatively. "Something has happened to you," he observed. "Your confidence has been badly shaken."

"On more levels than you can imagine."

"Tell me."

Ella recounted the incident with the coyotes, and the animal that had leaped from the flames. "I was sure it was dead, but obviously I was wrong. It was an awful sight. But if I can't be sure of something as simple as my aim at that close a range . . ." She lapsed into silence.

Neither spoke for several long moments. Clifford cleared his throat. "Was this near the main irrigation canal where it crosses beneath the highway?"

"Yeah," Ella answered, looking away from the road in surprise. "How did you know that?"

"A man and his son died near there in a hunting accident last year. The father accidentally shot the boy, then killed himself after the boy died."

Ella shuddered violently, and not from the cool evening air streaming through the partially lowered window. "What are you saying?"

"That area is contaminated by the *chindi.* It's a place of power for the skinwalkers. You shouldn't have stopped there for any reason whatsoever." Clifford glanced at Ella. "Wilson was with you. He should have prevented it."

Ella shook her head. "If anyone's at fault, I was. I was driving."

"What you lack is knowledge—not of criminals, but of our people's secrets. That's something only time can give you. Unfortunately, that's one commodity we don't have."

Ella started to argue, to protest again that her aim had been at fault, but uncertainty, mingled with fear, kept her quiet. Wilson had insisted they stop and burn the dead animal immediately, right on the spot Clifford now said he should have known to avoid. Was Wilson simply a good actor, working against them? Had he rigged the fire trick to damage her confidence and effectiveness? She hated these questions that circled her mind like a hawk in search of prey.

For distraction, Ella switched on the Navajo radio station. A news report of the disturbance at the chapter house was being aired.

Clifford's hand balled into a fist. "More trouble."

"They made it sound worse than it was," Ella said quietly.

"You were there?" Clifford asked.

"Wilson and I both were." Ella filled Clifford in. "Mom can sure take care of herself," she added, trying to ease her brother's mind. "She's deadly with that purse of hers. There must be a brick in there."

Clifford never cracked a smile. "Do you see the tactic underlying all this? Those we are up against are well-organized people who intend to foster as much chaos as they can. These modern skinwalkers are deadlier than their ancestors."

"They definitely want power," Ella said flatly, without accepting or challenging her brother's insistence that their enemies were skinwalkers. "But to what ends? We've got to find out what they intend to do with it."

Ella drove off the highway into the desert. After a ten-minute ride, she finally pulled to a stop. "We'll leave the truck here," she said, "and take a roundabout path to the buildings." She glanced around. "Where are you going to hide your truck once it's repaired?"

"Just leave it where it is," Clifford answered. "It will throw anyone who's after me off my trail."

"But what if you get into trouble out here?" Ella insisted. "This isn't like the gas station. There isn't going to be a convenient phone nearby. Consider, also, how hot it will be—those things are metal, and you'll bake every afternoon. That's precisely the time when people are around, so you can't come out in plain sight."

"I'll need shelter only at night," he answered, reminding her of what he saw as the real threat. "During the day, the desert itself will hide me."

"More of your illusions?" she whispered, suddenly uncomfortable.

"Survival. Like a lone soldier."

They made their way slowly and carefully toward the trailers, working hard to avoid leaving any tracks. Far off, Ella spotted a security guard with a flashlight, but he didn't notice them as they crossed the open area that led to the trailers. Clifford seemed to have an innate sense of timing that allowed them to move at precisely the right moments.

Seconds later, they were through the fence. A window had been left open in one trailer, and they easily slipped through.

Clifford looked around. "It will do."

"Now what?" Ella asked in a whisper.

"Join Wilson at the dance, but don't just go as an investigator. Learn how things have been done in the past, and how some traditions always continue. Stop trying to avoid our ways."

"I'm not trying to avoid anything. By your own admission, I'm dealing with the type of threat most of our people would do anything not to confront, and I've been doing that since the day I got here."

Clifford held up a hand. "Stop. Let's not argue now. This isn't the time for it. We need to band together. Remember the story of the Big Yeibitchai."

Ella stared at the tiled floor of the portable classroom. She vaguely remembered something about the Twin Sons of Talking God.

As if guessing her thoughts, Clifford continued, "When the children of Talking God were half-grown, they were stricken with two diseases. One was struck blind, and the other's limbs withered. Being useless to their mother's people, they were driven out to die. But the one struck blind gathered up his crippled brother and placed him on his shoulders. They traveled together that way, until they found the help they needed to be cured."

Clifford looked over at Ella. "Neither of us can stand on our own on this, for very different reasons. We need each other, now more than ever. We both have special talents, which make us different from the rest of our people. We are our own best hope."

Ella sighed. She had to bring up a difficult subject, and this seemed like the best time. "I need to discuss something with you, something that's been bugging me for some time."

Clifford said nothing, just stared at Ella, his gaze sharp. Finally Ella took the plunge.

"Wilson," she blurted out, "I know how long he's been your friend, and mother's, and mine."

"But?" Clifford asked simply.

"I don't know if I—if we should trust him very far. He's always showing up wherever I am or go, and knows everything I'm doing about the investigation. Whenever there's trouble, there he is. I wonder sometimes if he's deliberately playing up the supernatural angle, even arranging 'miracles,' like the coyote thing and the skinwalker with the skull, to scare me away."

Her brother thought for a moment, then spoke. "Wilson could have killed me, or you, several times already if he meant to harm us."

"Maybe we're being manipulated—steered toward some specific goal. He can't use us or influence us if we're dead."

"I trust him as I now trust you. Give him the benefit of

the doubt, out of respect for my judgment." Clifford crossed his arms as if settling the matter.

"I'll go halfway with you. Let's both give Wilson our trust, but not blindly. Stay alert not only to what he says, but what he does and its effects." Ella thought Clifford could accept a reasonable compromise.

Clifford nodded. "I think you've misjudged him, but you have a point. We mustn't allow ourselves to become anyone's pawns." He turned toward the door. "Now go to the dance. Wilson will be expecting you. He can help, despite the questions you've raised."

Ella peered out the window. The security guard was nowhere in sight. Behind her, she heard her brother begin a prayer for protection. Hoping it would be enough, she unlocked the door and slipped out silently.

The terrible sense of aloneness she'd known since childhood crept through her. It seemed destiny had found her at last. Her efforts to escape seemed as futile as those of a bird trapped in a sealed room, beating desperately against a pane of glass, trying to find freedom. She had to accept her brother's extraordinary abilities, however she explained them. She had to rely on her own finely honed skills as a federal agent. Together, she and Clifford would support and help each other, like the children of Talking God, until they found a cure to the terrifying threat they faced.

Dozens of trucks were parked at the ceremonial grounds; that Ella was not driving her own truck would not be noticed. She studied the crowd as she approached. She would have preferred to mingle, but there wasn't much chance of that. She'd tried that at the barbecue and had failed. Her best chance was to stay in the shadows of the cedar fire, listen, and learn.

Wilson, an eligible bachelor, was bound to be in demand. He was in a much better position than Ella was to circulate, unattached. During intervals in the ceremony there would be public dancing, and many of the young women would probably ask him to dance. If he wanted to be released from the duty, he would be forced to pay a forfeit to whoever had selected him. It was all done in fun, much like Sadie Hawkins dances outside the Rez, but it would give him the perfect chance to talk to many people. Ella hoped Clifford was right about Wilson's loyalty.

Ella drew to one side. Her above-average height gave her a clear view of the proceedings. The Queen was carrying the medicine man's rattlestick aloft. The wood pile in the center of the grounds was lit. Decked out in their finest jewelry and colorful, traditional, velveteen blouses and skirts, the Queen and her debutantes sat down, surrounded by their chaperones. The voice of the chorus rose in the air, beginning the dancing song.

Bright tongues of orange flames and bursts of sparks illuminated the area, casting lively shadows that swayed in rhythm to the Foot-Together Dance going on around the fire. As an unmarried man, Wilson would be there somewhere. As a widow, Ella was expected to remain in the general gathering, outside the firelit ring. For the first time since she'd returned to the Rez, she felt like she knew where she belonged.

Ella envied the laughing young women, many of whom were still in their late teens. Those not dressed traditionally wore their most attractive western wear, similar to Ella's outfit: a dark red Western-style shirt, blue jacket and slacks.

Although she looked like many of the people around her, right down to her boots, she couldn't remember ever being so carefree.

She caught sight of Wilson, dancing by the fire. From the line of young women already gathered nearby, she had a feeling she wouldn't see much of him tonight. A spark of envy touched her. It would have been nice to be able to have fun, laugh, and take part.

Herman Cloud left a small group of elderly men and walked toward her. He stood beside her and for several long moments they both made a great show of watching the dances in rapt concentration, as if nothing else mattered to either of them.

"I wouldn't have expected you to be interested in a gathering like this. Have you come looking for a husband?"

Struggling not to choke, Ella kept silent. If she tried to answer him right away, she'd sputter like an engine missing a spark plug.

"Wilson Joe maybe?" Cloud prodded.

Ella shook her head slightly. "No, I just wanted to watch. I've been away for a long time."

"Uh-huh," he mumbled, as if he didn't believe a word she'd said.

Suddenly, over the drums and the chorus, she heard a loud pop. An unnatural silence immediately settled over the gathering. As Ella shifted, reaching beneath her jacket for her weapon, all she could hear was the roar of the fire and the crackling of cedar. That had been a gunshot, and whatever was happening was not part of the ceremony.

Ella worked her way forward, looking over the heads of the people backing away from the fire. Dread filled her as low murmurs began; she heard women crying. As the crowd before her thinned, she saw Randy Tsosie lying on the ground. The *hataalii* was dead. Nothing else could explain the total stillness of a body lying at such an awkward angle. His limbs were bent like a marionette's whose strings had suddenly been cut. A deep crimson stain was spreading over his shirt.

Hundreds of people hurried to their cars. It would be impossible to stop any of them now—she'd be trampled. She caught a glimpse of Wilson standing still as the crowd swirled around him. For a moment their eyes met, then the confused mass of people swept him up and carried him away.

The chill of death hung in the air, and the fire looked dim and anemic to her eyes, somehow void of heat. The site would be abandoned now; no other ceremonies would ever be performed here. She saw a few white visitors working their way forward, but knew the *hataalii* was beyond their help. Two Navajo police officers were also approaching. Ella knew if she stayed, they would notice her and start asking questions. She had nothing to tell them.

She turned and headed for the pickup. When she reached it, Wilson was leaning against the cab.

"How did you get here so fast?" she asked.

"I let the crowd carry me out, then jogged around the fringes to find the truck," he answered somberly. "Did you see what happened?"

"No, I was too far away. When I saw the police move in, I left." She shrugged.

As people continued to race past them to get to their cars, Ella and Wilson sat together inside the truck and waited for traffic to clear. He told her, "I heard a sound like firewood popping loudly. Then the Singer staggered back, clutching his chest, and fell to the ground. His eyes were still open, but he'd stopped breathing. I thought it was a heart attack until I saw the blood staining his shirt. People panicked right after that, and, well, you know the rest."

"We're thirty miles from the construction site. Do you think people are going to link this to the troubles there?"

"It's already started. I heard some claiming that the figure of a coyote appeared in the flames."

"Group hysteria."

"Maybe. But then again, maybe not."

She looked around. What had been a field full of cars now held fewer than ten vehicles and a cloud of dust. Ella muttered a curse, knowing she had to get involved whether she liked it or not. Her training as a law enforcement officer just wouldn't let her walk away. She got out of the truck; Wilson followed her.

"Let's find the police before they find us. Head for the first cop you see, and make sure you don't look hostile. They don't know if the killer is still around and are probably pretty jumpy," Ella advised, turning in a complete circle as she looked for the tan-uniformed officers she'd seen only a few minutes earlier.

Wilson searched too, and in a few minutes, as the dust thinned a bit, they found the officers near the body.

Wilson identified himself and related what he'd seen, then answered questions about the events preceding the shooting. After they gave the officers as many names of potential witnesses as they could remember, Ella took the opportunity to ask them for news of her father's case. Chief Clah wasn't around to stop her, and she was hungry for any new information the department might have uncovered. Unfortunately, they could tell her little other than that they'd been sent everywhere by Blalock, looking for Clifford.

When asked, Ella said she had no idea where Clifford

was. Technically, this was not a lie, since, at that precise moment, she really didn't know. It was, however, enough of a deception to cost her her career.

Hearing that a forensic team had been dispatched, Ella realized Blalock was probably on his way too. Since she and Wilson had given statements, and Blalock knew how to get in touch with them, they were free to leave.

The air was still dusty, and it wasn't until they reached the highway that fresh clean air streamed through the truck's windows. Ella took a deep breath. Wilson wiped the sweat and dust from his eyes with a handkerchief.

The killing at the dance had taken Ella by surprise. What worried her most was how her mother would react to the gossip that would soon get around. First a Navajo Christian minister was killed, now a *hataalii.* Would Clifford get the blame for this too? Undoubtedly there were people who might claim he resented Tsosie, an older and more prominent *hataalii.* As she rocketed down the highway, she wondered how much more her mother would be able to take. Rose was a strong woman, but everyone had limits.

As Ella turned down the dirt track that led to her home, she saw an ominous glowing light just over the rise. Her heart began to hammer against her ribs.

"What the . . ." Wilson spoke for the first time since they'd left the ceremonial grounds.

Ella increased her speed, though the ground was too uneven to be safe. "Hang on. Mom's in trouble!"

Several times she hit deep ruts that sent both of them bouncing against the roof of the car despite their seat belts. Closer, the glow became a stream of orange that rose into the night like a sunlit curtain.

The unmistakable smell of smoke drifted through their open windows. Ella's pulse was racing, her skin clammy. A heartbeat later, she realized her worst childhood nightmare had come to life. The whole right side of the house, where her mother's bedroom lay, was engulfed in bright orange flames.

"No, not Rose too!" Wilson uttered in a horrified whisper, but Ella did not hear.

SEVENTEEN

Terror gripped her. Breaking the paralysis that had claimed her, Ella slammed on the brakes and shot out of the pickup.

"Mom!" She screamed at the top of her lungs, but the fire spoke with a voice of its own. The wood framing the stucco house crackled and snapped, a window shattered, spraying glass out into the yard. "Mom!" Ella raced toward her home. A few feet from the door, Wilson knocked her to the ground. "Let me go!" Ella struggled to kick free of his grip.

Rose came around the side of the house, carrying a large hose, the faithful mutt by her side. "Stop fighting and help me, you two!" she yelled angrily, as if they'd been nothing more than naughty children.

Ella almost cried with relief. "You're all right!"

"Of course I am. Now start up another hose. I've already called the volunteer fire department. They should be here soon."

Wilson yanked Ella to her feet. "I'll get the hose. Give your mother a hand."

Ella helped her mother keep the line unkinked as they sprayed the base of the flames, trying to slow the fire's spread. "What happened?"

"I've been having problems with the generator lately. Maybe it caused a power surge. Maybe there was a short in the wiring." Rose took a breath. "I was in the bedroom when I saw a trail of smoke coming from an outlet and smelled a funny odor. By the time I ran outside and turned off the power, the curtains had caught fire. It spread quickly."

The fire was responding to their efforts to douse it. The thick smoke that billowed from the windows and the roof had turned almost white. "By the time the firemen get here, we'll have this under control," Ella muttered, a nasty suspicion crowding at the edges of her mind.

"I left a message, but it's a long way out here from town."

"Neighbors should have come. The smoke would have been seen for miles."

"Many went to the dance, I suppose," her mother said hesitantly, trying to find some reason for their absence.

Remembering what had happened there, Ella felt a chill travel up her spine. First the *hataalii*'s death, now this. Someone was trying to terrorize the community, and not just to cover the motive for a murder.

As they continued to spray water on the house, the flames were smothered, but still-glowing wood made it clear the fight was not completely over.

Rose didn't take her gaze—or the hose—off the smoking embers. "Something's wrong. What happened at the dance?"

"I'll tell you all about it after we get the fire out," Ella said. "For now, this is more important."

After fifteen minutes, Rose left Ella holding the hose and peered through the open window. "The fire is out," she said, "and the damage isn't as bad as it could have been. We're going to be just fine, once the water is mopped up. Turn off the hose. We'll go inside and look around and you can tell me about the dance."

Wilson, who'd been busy with the second hose, shut off the water and joined them. "Hang on—it still may not be safe in the house, though the fire has been extinguished. Let me get the flashlight from my truck, and I'll check out the structure."

Rose nodded, then turned to look expectantly at her daughter. "Well?"

Ella took a deep breath of cold desert air. It had a smoky tang that reminded her of the bonfire at the dance. She told her mother about Randy Tsosie's murder, then added, "I'm hoping this won't give rise to more talk about us. Clifford is still at large, and I hate to think they'll blame this on him too."

"I suppose that's possible."

Wilson entered the house. Rose moved to follow him in, but Ella stopped her, placing a hand on Rose's arm. "Wait. He'll be out in a minute."

"It's *my* home," Rose insisted.

"You may have to move out while repairs are made. Is there anyplace in particular you'd like to go?"

"Dog and I are staying right here. I'll repair it myself, if no one will help. *Nothing* is going to drive me out of my home." Together, the women moved toward their home.

Wilson met them at the door. "Two rooms have extensive damage and a lot of water in them, but the rest seems okay."

"There," Rose said, looking at her daughter. "We'll live in the undamaged part of the house while we repair the rest. And we can cook with the woodstove until the electricity is working again."

"I'll help you rebuild," Wilson said, staring down the dirt road, an angry expression on his face.

Ella knew he'd noted there was still no sign of a fire truck. "What do you think happened to them?" she asked softly. "I know it's volunteer and all that—"

"You said it yourself. Volunteer. No one wants to come out here," Wilson spat out. "They'll probably say they didn't get the message, or the truck wouldn't start, or some excuse like that."

In the kitchen, Rose retrieved the flashlight she kept hanging from a hook there. "Fear is keeping them away, but they're not to blame. The ones who are guilty are those who are taking our beliefs, twisting them, and using them for their own purposes." With her back ramrod straight, she walked down the hall, the mutt by her side.

Wilson stared pensively at the smoke-damaged walls. "She's right. What really angers me is that what happened here will play right into their hands."

"What are you talking about? This wasn't arson, not according to what my mom said."

Wilson met Ella's gaze. "Don't you get it? If anything had happened to your mother, *you* could have been blamed."

"How could I be blamed for an electrical fire—" Comprehension dawned slowly, filling her with horror. "You mean people would have thought I sacrificed my mother so I could become a skinwalker?"

Rose came out into the living room. "That's how they drove people away from your brother after your father's death and the death of your newborn nephew. It could happen to you too."

Ella glanced at her mother, then at Wilson. "I think we need to have the wiring checked. This may not have been an accident after all."

"There's something you're not taking into account: their powers may be great, but this is *my* home. They cannot enter here, nor touch me. My son and I have both seen to that."

Ella walked along the hall, checking out the damage with Wilson's flashlight. "It does seem like luck is on their side, doesn't it?" But she didn't believe in such coincidences. She stood by the soot-covered door of what had once been her room. Smoke, fire, and water had blackened everything, ruining all her mementos of childhood. The quilted throws, the high school pennants, even her yearbooks were covered in black, oily water, or singed and charred. At least the interior of the closet on the far side of the room had been spared, along with her clothes and extra ammunition.

Rose came and stood beside her. "I'd say we proved that things are finally turning around for us. No one was hurt, the fire was checked in time, and the damage, considering how bad it might have been, is slight. By the time we're through redoing your room, it will fit the person you are now. The master bedroom will also be changed. The fire cleansed us of the past. Now it's time to move forward."

Ella hugged her mother tightly.

Wilson came down the hall holding a brightly lit gas lantern, two mops, and a bucket. "No time like the present to start."

* * *

Mercifully, it didn't rain that night. Wilson had patched the roof, where the shingles were burned away, with boards and plastic, but it wouldn't have held up against a driving summer rain. Ella and her mother slept in the living room, Ella in a sleeping bag that had once belonged to Clifford, Rose on the sofa. Ella was sure she'd never be able to relax enough in the smoky room to get even a wink of sleep, but exhaustion made its own demands. She shut her eyes and knew nothing more until daylight.

The next morning, Wilson and Herman Cloud arrived with supplies and began the job of properly repairing the roof while Ella and Rose worked inside. The women started by removing the fire-damaged curtains, mattresses, and furniture. As each treasured piece of her past was stacked in a pile, Ella felt as if a part of her heart was being discarded.

Ella untacked the Shiprock Chieftains banner and pulled it away from the charred surface of the wall. The felt disintegrated beneath her fingers, dropping to the floor in shreds.

She picked up the water-swollen remains of a high school photo and tossed it into the trash. She'd spent so many years trying to disassociate herself from the past; why was she mourning it now? To her, the future had always been far more exciting and important.

Rose glanced around the room. "It's looking so much better already! I think once the roof is patched and we get the room painted, it'll be almost as good as new. Then we redecorate. Do you know what you want to do with the place?"

"You've always wanted a sewing room, Mom," Ella said. "Maybe we should make my room over that way."

"No, this is your room. That's what it'll always be, until you marry again."

Ella laughed. "Plan on this being my room for a long time, then."

Wilson knocked on the open door and came in. "The tar covered well, and should hold even if it rains this afternoon. We've repaired the windows and fixed the door frames. Although the fire destroyed most of the wiring in your mother's room, the rest wasn't quite so bad. I've shut down the damaged circuits at the fuse box, so you can use the generator again. Herman had to leave, but he said he and his son-in-law could come back tomorrow if you needed him."

Hearing a car approaching, Ella walked to the window. She shook her head in disgust. "*Now* we get an official presence," she muttered. "It's a tribal police unit."

Wilson gave Ella a worried look. "More trouble, you think?"

"Probably more questions about what happened at the dance."

The vehicle stopped out front. Peterson Yazzie climbed out and waited beside the car.

Ella walked to the porch and waved him inside. "What can I do for you?"

Peterson looked around, his eyes wide. "What the heck happened here?"

Ella explained about the fire. "We called the fire department. No one showed up," she said, leaving all emotion out of her words.

Peterson stared at her. "How could that . . ." His voice trailed off. "I'm going to make a few calls on my radio. I'll be back in a minute or two."

He returned to his unit and picked up the mike. Watching, Ella saw flashes of anger cross Peterson's features. At the moment, siding with her was a risky proposition, even for a tribal cop, yet he'd never hesitated. Peterson had turned out to be a staunch and loyal friend, more than she had a right to expect. Then again, maybe sharing a career in law enforcement—in addition to their tribal and family ties—*had* made a bond between them.

He returned several minutes later. "There's no record of your mother's call. In fact, there were *no* calls to the fire station last night."

Rose stood behind Ella. "When I called, I got the answering machine. I didn't worry because I know it also rings at Harvey Ute's home or Charley Kodaseet's."

Peterson shook his head. "I'm sorry. They claim they have no record of the call. The tape is blank."

"That's bullshit, and you know it," Ella snapped. "Someone erased the message."

"Maybe," Peterson answered, "but I can't prove it, and neither can you. Without that, my hands are tied."

She exhaled softly. "Well, everything's under control now."

Peterson glanced at Rose. "If there ever is a next time, or any emergency, ask for me. The dispatcher will pass along the message."

"I'll remember that," Rose answered.

Wilson gave Peterson a long, pensive look. "What brought you out here today?"

"Business," Peterson said brusquely, then glanced at Ella. "Can I see you outside?"

"Sure."

Peterson glanced at Wilson. "I may need to ask you a few questions later too."

Wilson nodded. "I'll be around."

Ella watched the men. There was an animosity between

them that she couldn't quite understand, but it obviously went deep. She would have to ask about it later.

Ella took Peterson into the shade of the tall old elm tree at the front of the house. "What's on your mind?" she asked when they were alone.

"There's lots of gossip going on about the dance last night," he said succinctly, "but not when a cop shows up. People are even more afraid, now that a *hataalii* has been killed."

"I figured as much."

"Anything you saw, or would like to tell me about?"

"Without a look at the medical examiner's report, I don't have an opinion. I only got close enough to see the blood on his chest."

"Did you talk to him, either before the ceremony or during the dance?"

"No. The only person I spoke to was Herman Cloud. I actually only got there a few minutes before the shooting."

Peterson kicked at a pebble by his boot. "In some ways that's even worse."

"Yeah, I know. They'll say our family brings only trouble."

"Word of the fire here will get out too. Things are going to become very difficult for you, particularly since there have been some new developments in the case."

"Like what?" she asked, struggling for a cool, professional detachment to mask her feelings. Finally she was going to get some answers, but from Peterson's expression, she wasn't going to like what she heard. The tension in Peterson's tone of voice made her want to shudder.

"This is difficult," he admitted, "but I thought you should know."

"I'm listening." She wished she could shake him, make

him stop drawing it out. Had something happened to Clifford?

"We found three bodies by the river, south of the old high school. Two were mutilated like your father's had been. The third died of gunshot wounds, a .30-.30 perhaps. Your brother owns a rifle of that caliber, doesn't he?"

Ella remembered the shoot-out near the hogan. There was no doubt in her mind that their enemies had carried their dead to the river and dumped them there—after carving up the bodies. "Yeah, I'm sure my brother has a rifle of that caliber. So do three-fourths of the men on the reservation!"

"Yeah, but only a handful know about mutilation specific to a medicine bundle."

She tried to lead their conversation back to ground more familiar to her. "Have the bodies been identified?"

Peterson nodded. "That's another piece of circumstantial evidence that also points to your brother. One of the men was Gene Sorrelhorse. Remember, I told you about him? He's bad news, a self-styled vigilante."

She nodded. "He was one of the volunteers looking for my brother?"

"Once the news got around that Clifford was involved with witchcraft, Sorrelhorse decided to go after him. He's been asking questions, searching for your brother, and driving around with a rifle. And now he's dead."

"You think they met, and my brother shot him?" She saw Peterson nod. "From the way you described Sorrelhorse, what makes you think it wouldn't have been self-defense?"

"I won't know that, not until we find Clifford and ask him some questions."

"Do *you* believe my brother is guilty of all they accuse him of doing?"

"No," he answered slowly. "I've known your family a long time. But that's not going to help. Blalock plans to get your brother—that's no surprise. Although he alienates everyone he comes in contact with, he also has good police instincts. He had us searching along the river. That's how we found the bodies."

She wanted to tell Peterson to look further north, near the mesas, until he found the hogan. Maybe, if he saw evidence of the assault on Clifford's hiding place, he'd understand why her brother had to remain on the run. Yet she couldn't say anything without revealing her own complicity.

"I'm on your side. Remember that," Peterson said. "But play it straight with me. If you learn where Clifford is, come to me first. I can make sure he's safe, and that his rights aren't trampled over. FB-Eyes is starting to get impatient, and I'm afraid he'll start cutting corners soon."

"How so? Any ideas?"

"No, not really, but I can't see him sitting back, waiting for the case to break."

"No," she admitted grudgingly, "neither can I."

"Just be careful around Wilson Joe. I know you're relying on him quite a bit."

"Not as much as you might think," she answered, deliberately being vague. "I keep hearing about his violent streak, but I haven't seen any evidence of it."

"It's there, believe me. A few years ago, I came across him really beating up some guy in a parking lot."

"I heard. A relative?"

"His cousin." Peterson shook his head. "And at the

chapter house the other day, I understand he threw a boy out a door." He grimaced, then shrugged. "Just watch out for yourself, okay?"

For a moment, Ella was uncertain how to respond, but she quickly recovered. Just yesterday, she'd warned Clifford to be cautious in trusting Wilson. Now Peterson was saying essentially the same thing to her.

"I'll be careful around him. Thanks," she said. "On a different subject—have you received any reports about grave-robbing?"

"Sorry. We've been so busy with Blalock. I'll try to ask around when I get back to the station." Peterson checked his watch. "Tell your friend I may need to talk to him about last night. Right now I have to go to a meeting."

Before she could say good-bye, Peterson turned and left. Ella stood on the porch and watched Peterson walk to his car and drive away. A cloud of dust rose in the air behind him, and lingered there.

Rose came to stand beside her. "What did he have to say?"

"Peterson's keeping me current on the investigation. He's turned out to be a good friend to our family, Mom."

Rose remained silent. "I don't think Wilson would agree."

Ella nodded pensively. "There seems to be some bad blood between them. What do you think's behind it?"

"You." Rose chuckled softly at the surprised look on Ella's face. "Wilson's jealous."

"No, you're misinterpreting it. I'm sure of it." Before she could argue the point further, Wilson came down from the roof and joined them.

"I bought some paint when I was in town. Do you want me to give you a hand inside?"

"You've already done too much," Rose said. "If my son had been here . . ."

"Look at it this way," Wilson answered with a grin. "Back in high school, when I was caught writing on the wall with a marker, I had to repaint practically the whole school in punishment. Clifford helped me. Without him, I would have been at that all year. It's a debt I never had a chance to repay until now."

Rose laughed. "If I recall, my son also had a part in the mischief. Only he ran faster than you did."

"Well, true, but he didn't *have* to come back."

"Oh, yes he did," Rose answered with a tiny smile. "It would have gone against his nature to let you face the music on your own. He could no more have done that than I could forget I'm Navajo." She turned and went back inside. "Come on, I'll fix us all a snack. We've worked hard and deserve a break."

"I'll be right there," Wilson called. "Let me put the tools away." He took down the ladder and hauled it toward the shed.

Rose had left a pile of burnt items on the porch. Looking at the rubble, Ella noticed a short length of electric cable still attached to a plug. A badly melted aluminum wire extended from one of the burned outlets. Ella moved it with her foot. The wire had been cut.

"I had to cut away three of the damaged outlets. You'll be without power on that circuit," Wilson said.

"We're grateful for all you've done, but you shouldn't have cut that box away. It's evidence." Ella tried to show patience in her voice, but she couldn't quite hide her annoyance.

"What's so special about the box? It can't be repaired." Wilson shrugged.

"Look at it carefully. Someone stuck a piece of wire in there. It got hot and wore away the insulation, shorting out the box. I bet that's where the fire started. You should have left it in place for an arson investigation," Ella explained.

"Where's the closest arson squad? Farmington? Albuquerque? Even if the fire was no accident, how would that change things?" Wilson's tone showed that he found Ella's attitude irritating. "This isn't L.A., remember?"

"You're right." Ella relented, wanting to avoid any further argument for now. She still was going to take the outlet to Blalock. If he didn't send it to a lab, she would. "Let's go have a bite to eat. You've been working all day." Ella smiled and motioned toward the house.

Later, when Wilson was leaving, Ella walked outside with him. "You must be dead tired."

"Yeah, but I've still got some papers to grade. Afterward, if you don't mind, I'm going to pay your brother a visit and make sure he's okay."

"Excellent idea. If someone saw you, your presence wouldn't create the same problem mine would."

"Anything you want me to tell him?"

Ella considered, then nodded slowly and recounted what Peterson had told her, omitting the personal observations. "He's in danger from every side now. I don't know how to keep him safe. He has to turn himself in soon."

"Your support, and your faith, are what matter to him the most. And in case you need to hear it, he's worried about you, just as much as you are about him."

"He shouldn't be." Then, remembering the coyotes and the men who had attacked the hogan, and the fire, her expression became somber. "Then again, maybe he should."

"One bit of advice?" Wilson saw her nod and continued. "You're being asked to accept and act according to rules of behavior that conflict with the law enforcement career you worked hard to attain. You can't expect to become comfortable with that overnight. Be patient with yourself. We're all trapped in something we have no control over. Be thankful that at least we're not alone," Wilson said.

Yet Ella was alone. A gulf as wide as the desert separated her from her people. Wilson's life had been punctuated by normality. His father and mother had been educators, like him. Their life had been predictable and comfortable, framed by stability and common ground. Despite the mistakes he'd made today, something told her he wasn't the wolf in sheep's clothing Peterson had described. All the violence she'd seen in him had been purposeful, not self-serving.

"You've never known what it's like to need to define yourself apart from those around you," Ella argued softly.

"Everyone goes through that to one extent or another."

"I'm not talking about a search for individuality. I'm talking about fear and survival," she affirmed.

"In my own way, I've known both." Wilson had a faraway look on his face.

Before she could ask him about that, or for his side of the story Peterson had told her, he walked away without another word. Ella let him go, and waved as he started the pickup.

There was no way Wilson would ever understand her or what it had been like for her to grow up as part of a family that people stood in awe of. All her life, her family, and traditions she couldn't understand, had called to her, even as they pushed her away. The battle was one she'd fought as long as she could remember, and one whose outcome was still undecided.

* * *

Ella and Rose spent the next two days working to restore the house. They brought in an Anglo technician to get the wiring back in operation. Ella hadn't yet told her mother about the possibility that the short circuit had been induced. Maybe she never would. She'd cajoled Blalock into sending the fused outlet to the bureau's crime lab, but it would be weeks before they got a full report.

Hearing the telephone ring, Ella put down her paintbrush. The doorway trim was almost finished, and that would be the last of it. The smell of fresh paint seemed a victory over those who were persecuting her family. Her mother reached the phone first. Holding the receiver, Rose staggered back into the easy chair, her face ashen. "Have you called the police?"

Ella's heart began to race. "What's wrong?" she mouthed.

Rose looked at her daughter. "Thanks for calling," she said, and hung up.

Images of Clifford in trouble raced through Ella's mind, each more frightening than the last. She jammed her hands inside her jeans pockets to keep them from shaking. "Tell me what has happened."

"That was the church's construction foreman. They set up their trailers today, getting the site ready for on-site work. About thirty minutes ago, someone called in a bomb threat. The police advised them to evacuate. The foreman was calling from the construction office back in town."

"This bomb threat sounds like another way to scare people off. I'm going over there to take a look. The bomb squad's been alerted?"

Rose nodded and stood. "I'm going with you."

Ella didn't like the idea of her mother being anywhere near a bomb, but she disliked the idea of leaving her alone at the house even more, especially since it seemed no one would come to help if she called. No one but Wilson, Peterson, and Herman Cloud, she reminded herself. But guarding Rose was *her* job, not theirs.

"This is also my business," Rose continued softly. "It's your father's church. I'll go, either alone or with you. That choice is yours."

Ella sighed. "All right. Let's go, but please, if there's any trouble, promise me you'll stay back and let me handle things."

Rose nodded her acquiescence.

As they drove quickly to the site, Ella's thoughts were centered on Clifford.

"Where is your brother hiding?" Rose asked.

"Near the new church site," she answered, momentarily unnerved by her mother's perceptive question.

Rose closed her eyes and remained very still for several long seconds. Finally she glanced at Ella. "They don't know where he is," Rose said calmly. "They're just hoping to draw him out. You have to warn him."

"I will."

The dry countryside passed by quickly; the telephone poles looked like fenceposts at the speed she was going. Her mother glanced over to the speedometer once, adjusted her seat belt, and didn't look again.

When they passed through Shiprock, Ella whipped through traffic like she was on a Los Angeles freeway. Fortunately, there were no police cars around.

Something odd was lying by the side of the road near the turnoff for the church construction site. The smell reached them about the same time as they realized that it was the bloated corpse of a cow. Very dead, the distorted beast lay on its side, eyes open, staring at nothing.

Minutes later, Ella parked a few hundred yards from the newly set-up construction foreman's trailer and made a visual search. "The police aren't here yet, but it looks like the area's been completely evacuated."

Ella opened her car door, but remained inside. Suddenly the cry of a child pierced the stillness. The sound made her heart lodge in her throat. "Stay here."

"No, don't go. Wait for the police." Rose's expression was one of wariness.

"I have to go. You heard that. There's a little kid in there. I'll watch my step, don't worry."

"It's more than that. Something feels very wrong." Rose looked around the site cautiously.

Ella stayed still, her gaze darting around the area. There was danger close by; her mother was right. A familiar, unmistakable sensation washed over her. It made her skin prickle, like the electricity that charged the air before a lightning strike or a big bust. Something was going to happen, but she wasn't sure what that something would be.

"Stay here," Rose repeated sternly.

"I can't." Ella left the truck, weapon in hand.

As she approached, Ella listened carefully for the child, or for anything that would indicate a trap. She wouldn't linger. She'd check out the place fast, grab the kid, then get the heck out.

Ella crept steadily toward the trailer. The opened door creaked in the breeze. It looked like the crew had left in a hurry. The all-enveloping silence around the place was unnatural and set her nerves on edge.

She stood still for a long moment, considering turning

back, then heard crying. The sobs were soft, somehow muffled.

"Who's there?" The crying stopped abruptly. "Don't be afraid."

She took another step forward—then threw herself to the ground as she heard a sharp crack. The trailer exploded with a vicious, ear-shattering thump, sending a million particles of steel and metal into the air. The blast rocked the earth beneath her, expanding air buffeted her. Bits of searing-hot metal rained down on her. She held her arms over her head and rolled desperately away from what was left of the trailer, trying to protect herself from the merciless steel rain and incendiary heat.

Through the ringing in her ears, Ella thought she heard a child's singsong voice ring out, then mean, childish laughter.

EIGHTEEN

Ella stared at the gutted trailer. What was left of the metal building looked as if it had been ripped apart with a jagged can opener. Black smoke curled from inside, but there were no open flames.

Standing, she brushed off her clothing while checking herself for injuries. She had a few tiny lacerations, nothing more. She'd been lucky. Hearing running footsteps, she turned her head. "Mom, get back. I've still got to go inside; there was a kid playing in there."

"There's no child. Don't you understand? It was only a trick to draw you closer."

"A trick?" Her thoughts cleared. It had all been a ruse. "A tape recording," she muttered to herself.

"We have to talk to the construction foreman and his crew," Rose said adamantly. "This"—she gestured at what was left of the trailer—"is going to scare them all. We have to find a way to reassure them, so that their work will continue. This is what my husband would want."

"That isn't going to be easy," Ella answered.

Hearing sirens wailing in the distance, Ella turned to see flashing lights approaching on the gravel road. Two minutes later, three squad cars came to a screeching stop about twenty yards from them.

Peterson Yazzie was first to emerge from the units. Staring at Ella in surprise, he jogged over to her. "What are you doing here?"

She briefed him quickly, omitting nothing.

"A *child?*" he asked skeptically.

"Or a trick. Your guess."

"What's yours?"

"A trick."

He ran to the other tribal police officers, who were fastening on flak vests. Ella saw the wary look on the men's faces as he spoke to them. Well, at least they'd search carefully for more bombs, just in case any were still hidden or unexploded.

Peterson returned. Ella said, "If you don't need me here, I've got other things to deal with. My mom's worried about how this will affect construction. She wants to talk to the foreman."

"Before you go, I've been meaning to ask you something. Did you ever find any of the threatening notes your father was supposed to have received?"

"They were thrown out. Sorry about that."

Peterson nodded. "That's what I figured." He escorted her to where Rose waited. "What will you tell the construction people?" he asked. "I doubt they'll be real eager to start work tomorrow."

"I'll ask them to hire more security guards," Rose said flatly, "and I'll talk to the church committee. I didn't want to get involved in this, but construction on the church must continue, according to my husband's wishes."

"Be careful, both of you," Peterson said.

Ella nodded, then returned to the pickup with her mother.

They drove home quickly. Rose telephoned the construction company and several members of her husband's church committee. The construction foreman agreed that security guards were needed and said he would make the arrangements. He also told Rose that work on the church would not stop.

Later that afternoon, Wilson arrived with word that Clifford was fine. He and Ella stepped onto the porch. "Your brother hinted that he's getting closer to finding the places the skinwalkers are using for their ceremonies. He refused to say anything specific. He's convinced that the explosion was meant to force him into the open," Wilson confided.

"Mom agrees."

"And you?"

"I think the bomb was meant to serve more than one purpose, and it did." Ella knew that with all the recent deaths, and the fire, tension had to be growing in the community.

Thankfully, the rest of the day was quiet, though Ella felt worried about something she couldn't quite define. The dog stayed within sight of her or Rose, as if he were watching over them.

The following morning, Rose walked back slowly from the mailbox, sharp lines of anger and worry framing her eyes. Wordlessly she handed Ella three letters, envelopes still in her hand.

Ella handled the pages by their edges. Letters cut from newspapers spelled, "YOU WILL FIND ONLY DEATH," "ENE-

MIES OF THE TRIBE," and finally, "DO NOT INTERFERE. DEATH STALKS YOU."

"I have to take these in," Ella said, reaching for the envelopes and noting they were postmarked from inside the reservation. "The bureau has state-of-the-art equipment, and with a bit of luck maybe they'll get prints."

"First, I want to see if the construction crew is working on your father's church," Rose said flatly.

"Mom, they're probably still trying to get the wreckage hauled away and get reorganized."

"We'll go anyway."

Ella took a large manila envelope from her father's desk. After dropping the letters and envelopes inside, she retrieved her truck keys from a hook in the kitchen. "Why does it have to be right now? Couldn't this wait a bit?"

Rose walked with Ella to the pickup. "If we received these notes today, it's possible they got some threats too. I want to make sure they don't lose their courage and cave in to our enemies."

Ella didn't dispute her mother's logic. She'd considered the same possibility. What worried her most was how her mother would take it if the construction company pulled out of the deal.

"I'll stop by on the way to see Blalock, Mother. No sense in making yourself a public target."

"Haven't you realized you can still protect me when we're away from our home?" Rose asked. "Where is your faith in yourself?"

The question surprised her. "Of course I can protect you. I trust my instincts and my training."

"That's not the faith I had in mind," Rose answered. "I'm talking about what is part of you, your birthright—what you insist is only intuition."

"I can use logic to explain the insights you call magic," Ella said. "Clifford accepts your explanation. I admit, he's really talented, a natural magician. I never could figure out most of his tricks. When we were growing up, half of the kids were terrified of him because they really believed he could do, or see, things they could not."

"He never harmed anyone."

"True, but he played with other people's beliefs—too much, in my opinion. He played the role of medicine man to the hilt."

"He eventually learned to put it into perspective, but being a *hataalii* is a major part of his life. Still, there are other things he values just as much, if not more," Rose answered. "His natural abilities, like his charisma and his leadership, are at the center of everything he's become. But he's paid a high price for following that life path. The ordinary goals, the hopes and dreams that most people have, are completely foreign to him."

"Is your love for the career you've chosen so different from his?"

"Of course it is. My career gives me purpose and direction, but it isn't the center of my life."

"What is?"

Ella opened her mouth to speak, but to her own surprise, she had no ready answer. "I guess, my dreams of the future."

"And those are?" Rose was relentless.

Ella shook her head. "Don't you see? Dreams shouldn't be too structured. That closes a person off from the best part of all: the possibilities."

"Sometimes that part is what turns on you and destroys. Look at the skinwalkers. They want power, and they get it, but at the expense of their humanity. You have to look closely at what you want and see it from all sides. To walk in beauty, one must search out balance."

"I do have balance. I rely on logic and common sense to find firm ground. My job has taught me about myself, and about other people. I know the pitfalls we all face better than most. My abilities may not be the kind you admire in Clifford, but I've cultivated them through hard work and training. Whether they stem from police instinct, or are the results of some mythical inheritance, isn't as important as the fact that I use them, that I've taken them as far as they go."

"How do you know, if you constantly refuse to acknowledge their possible origin?" Rose shook her head sadly. "You never wanted to be set apart because of who and what you are, but pretending you're not different doesn't alter the facts. No matter where you go, you'll never be just like everyone else."

Ella said nothing, her thoughts whirling. She wished, more than anything, to avoid the question her mother had raised. It would stay in her mind, preying on her, until she found an answer. There could not be any more running away.

"Well," Ella finally spoke. "Are you ready to go to the construction office?"

"No. You're right, I'll be safer here. Besides, I'd be a fifth wheel at the police station." Rose folded her arms, signifying an end to the conversation.

"You mean after all that . . . ," Ella blurted out, then shrugged in defeat. "Mothers."

* * *

Ella pulled into the parking lot beside the construction company's office in Shiprock. The Anglo-owned company leased the space from the tribe.

When she stepped through the front door, it was obvious that threats had been received here too. Phones rang incessantly at empty desks. Only one harried-looking Navajo secretary remained behind the front counter, trying desperately to answer all incoming calls.

She glanced up when Ella closed the door. "I'd like to see the church's project manager," Ella said.

"Sorry. He's not seeing anyone today. We've received more threats, and everyone is scared."

"There's a signed contract binding this company. I won't leave until I speak to the project manager." Ella spoke in the same tone she used to place a suspect under arrest, then held out her bureau I.D. and gold shield.

The girl blinked, and for the first time seemed to really focus on Ella. Ignoring the still-ringing phones, the receptionist stood and hurried down the hall to an office in the back. She emerged a minute later and said, without crossing the room, "Mr. Washburn will see you now, Agent Clah."

Washburn was a tall, light-skinned Anglo with bright red hair. He stood as Ella came into the room and gestured toward a chair. "I apologize for the chaos, but we're closing this office today."

"I came to find out the status of the church project," Ella said clearly.

"At the moment, work has stopped, and unless I can keep insurance coverage and bonding, I can't continue. When I reported getting threatening letters to the police, my insurance company canceled our coverage. Without insurance, I can't even stay in this building. The owners have asked us to leave as quickly as possible. Their insurance premiums will skyrocket if we don't have our own coverage."

"Surely there's a company somewhere that will underwrite this project," Ella challenged. "You're a businessman. You've run up against obstacles before. The contract you have with the church is still in effect."

"Well, it won't help you to throw your weight around here, FBI agent or not. I am trying to find another company who'll insure this project, but it's going to take some time. That doesn't mean we won't build the church, just that the work will be postponed."

"If you don't resume operations, church officials will take whatever legal means are available. Your company won't do any more business on the reservation." Ella knew that could happen; it had been done before.

"This isn't my doing," Washburn protested. "The tribe has this hassle with your family and the site chosen for the church."

"This is *not* between my family and the tribe. Don't confuse the issue. This is about your company upholding its legal obligations." Ella was surprised to find herself fighting for her father's church. She had stepped off the fence when she entered this office.

"I won't risk the safety of my men. I'd have to add to the security already there, and that's going to add steeply to our costs."

"How soon can you get back to work?" Ella asked pointedly.

"At least two weeks, maybe more. Some of my men have quit, and others, especially the Navajos, won't work on that site anymore." He shrugged. "These are circumstances beyond my control. If you want to do something, arrest the people behind the bombing. Then my job can continue on schedule."

Anger spiraled through Ella, made worse by the fact that the man had a point. "The law enforcement agencies will do their job. Just make sure you do yours." Ella strode out of the room without looking back.

Outside, she stood fuming on the sidewalk for a moment, then walked back to her truck, considering the problem from a more rational point of view. She knew a few independent insurance agents in the area. Maybe she could pull some strings and help get the project under way again.

Ella knew her mother needed this. The church had become a way to keep her husband's memory alive, to focus her anger, and to avoid the pain, at least for a while. Rose wasn't used to being alone, not yet.

Ella stared out at the desert, filled with a subtle blend of greens and grays, sand and rocks. Its rugged sameness seemed comforting in a way she'd never experienced before. It spoke of endurance, and of the strength of spirit that had allowed the Dineh to survive.

Alone. That word suddenly had many meanings to her. As a girl, the feeling she had attempted to describe with that word had really been the desire to find someone who could understand her needs and fears. Denied that, she'd eventually tried to become another person entirely, hoping to ease the chill inside her. But she'd never quite fit in anywhere.

Now, as she gazed at the empty stretches of desert, she knew that she was truly home. Here, others could love her as she was. For the first time, Ella realized that her brother and her mother had each known that solitary walk between the ordinary and the borders of darkness. What bonded them was infinitely stronger than whatever separated them, and that was their greatest strength.

Hours before, after Ella had driven away from her home, a figure in a khaki uniform stood up from behind some concealing brush and walked slowly and silently toward the house. Dog, who'd been lying on the front porch, noticed the movement, and his ears came to attention.

NINETEEN

Wilson sat on the summit of the mesa behind the police station. He felt ridiculous up here, using his hunting binoculars to keep watch on the police. He shouldn't have let Clifford strong-arm him into this. Then again, convincing people was one of the things Clifford did best. One could always count on him to word things in a way that made refusal impossible.

Wilson checked his watch. It was four o'clock in the afternoon, but the temperature today wasn't bad, and there was a breeze. Fall was approaching, and good thing, too, or he would have baked.

He wondered if he should have warned Ella about Clifford's plans. Then again, Clifford hadn't given him much of a chance. He'd called from somewhere near his mother's house and asked Wilson to go to the station and search for any signs of trouble. He'd be vulnerable while at his mother's house, and he wanted no trouble from FB-Eyes.

The news had alarmed Wilson. For Clifford to come out

in broad daylight seemed foolish to the point of stupidity, and he'd said so. But Clifford had been adamant. He needed to talk to the one member of his family who fully understood his strengths and limitations when dealing with their enemies. He also needed knowledge his mother possessed, and a few hours of safety in which to prepare.

Wilson had strongly recommended that Clifford speak to Ella and ask for her help. She'd be better able to protect him since she was familiar with police procedure. If any unusual activity occurred, she would spot it. Clifford had said something very odd. He'd said that Ella wasn't ready, that her own fears might hold her back at a critical time.

Wilson had started to argue that he too was afraid, and that fear hadn't prevented any of them from doing what they had to, but something had stopped him. Then Clifford had apologized for saying too much, and asked him to forget it. As if he could. An ever-curious mind had spurred him on through college and further higher education. Dozens of speculations passed through his mind.

Wilson continued watching the entrance to the police department. Abruptly, several officers rushed to their vehicles, carrying weapons and wearing SWAT gear. Focusing the binoculars, Wilson spotted Peterson Yazzie and Randall Clah. Seconds later, Blalock appeared, wearing a bulletproof vest and carrying a shotgun.

A chill seeped through Wilson. This was what he'd feared. Someone must have spotted Clifford, and now they were gearing up for an arrest. As Wilson watched the squad cars race down the highway, he admitted that there was a slim chance that they were going someplace else entirely. But even the possibility that they were on their way to Rose Destea's home filled him with dread.

He had promised Clifford he'd call and warn him, but at

the speed the squad cars were going, Clifford wouldn't be able to get far. Still, he had to try. Wilson ran to the public phones at the gas station down the road.

Wilson's hands were sweating as he held onto the receiver. One thing was for sure: he was no macho television cop with nerves of steel.

Rose answered the phone and, using their code, Wilson warned her to expect trouble. He heard her sharp intake of breath, but she recovered fast, and her voice became steady. "Thanks for your dinner invitation. I'll ask my daughter."

She was telling him to stay away. Had they needed or wanted his help, she would have countered his invitation with one of her own. He hung up, unable to suppress his growing fear.

Wilson checked his watch. Almost five, but not quite. Ella had gone to see an old friend who was an independent insurance agent on the Rez, hoping to convince him to underwrite a policy for the construction firm. With luck, he'd catch her at John Todacheene's office.

Wilson dialed. She was still there. He filled her in quickly. As he spoke, he could feel her distancing herself from him. By not taking her into his confidence earlier, he'd severed the trust that had begun to grow between them. She'd hold him accountable for whatever happened from this point on, and he had no doubt Ella could make a formidable enemy.

Ella drove across the alkali flats, thankful that she'd rented the most powerful standard pickup the dealer possessed. The truck was leaving a trail of dust that could be seen for miles, but, fortunately, no one was around. The bottom of the truck scraped something hard, but she ignored it, never slowing down. She had to get to her mother's home before Blalock did. At least she was starting from a place much closer to home than the police station.

It would take her a long time to forgive Wilson for not coming to her immediately. At the moment, she was furious with him. His allegiance to Clifford was admirable, but this time it seemed to have come at the expense of his intelligence. She had a right to know Clifford's movements. Wilson Joe should have found a way to let her know. Even as the thought formed, she realized Clifford had manipulated his friend into doing precisely what he'd wanted. Her brother was as much to blame, if not more, than anyone else.

There were other things to worry about now, however—like how Blalock had known her brother's whereabouts. Slowly the answer became clear, and that inescapable truth angered her far more than her brother's ill-fated decision to visit home. Though Blalock had been in the Destea house only a few times, somehow he'd planted a bug.

Ella slammed her hand against the steering wheel. She prided herself on being an excellent investigator, but she'd been outsmarted and betrayed by one of her colleagues.

As she approached her home via a back way, she saw Clifford moving fluidly through the shadows. Although he was scarcely an outline in the bramble of sagebrush and rocks, there was no mistaking her brother. They'd played hide-and-seek too many times as children for her to be fooled by his tricks. He was wearing a tribal police uniform. Great. Add impersonating an officer to the list of charges Blalock already wanted to hang on him.

She swung the vehicle in his direction and pulled up beside him, slamming on the brakes. "Come on. I've got to get you out of here fast!"

Clifford jumped inside the truck. "The others are almost here; I could see them turning off the highway."

"This was the stupidest idea you've ever had! Why didn't you tell me first? I could have brought Mom to see you instead. Hell, anything would have been better than this. And where did you get the uniform?"

"A distracting noise at the Laundromat accomplishes much," he said.

"What on earth did you hope to accomplish?"

"I needed our mother's knowledge and support. And I needed her where she was strongest, at home. I've become an outcast, discredited throughout the Rez. Every crime imaginable has been assigned to me. Even my wife looks at me as if she's not certain of who or what I am."

Ella's heart twisted inside her. Clifford was even more isolated than she was. Even people he loved were beginning to doubt him. No pain could be greater than that betrayal.

"You should have come to me," she said.

"And what could you have told me? You've spent most of your life running from yourself."

"If you think I was ever able, even once, to get away from who or what I am . . ." Her voice trailed off, and she shook her head sadly.

"You've managed to blunt it. You found a way to shield yourself by committing to ideas and ideals, but never to people. I used to think that you would end up cheating yourself of everything that made life worthwhile, but now I'm not so sure," he admitted sadly.

"If I wasn't committed to people, you sheep turd, I wouldn't be here with you now," she snapped. "I'm jeopardizing the career I spent years nurturing, not to mention my life."

"You're doing what you feel is the right thing. It's a principle you're giving your allegiance to, not me."

"At one time that would have probably been true, but that's not the case anymore," she answered honestly.

"Turn and head toward the church site," Clifford said as they reached the highway.

"Why do you want to go there?"

"I'm going to do a Sing. I have to finish it before sundown."

"Wait a second. Did you tell Mom you were going there?" He nodded. "Then you can't go. It's out of the question."

"I'll be all right. Mother would guard that secret with her life."

"Yeah, but I think Blalock has planted a listening device in the house. You can't carry out any plan you told mother about because he knows all about it already. You'd be walking into a trap."

"Then where are you taking me?"

"There's only one place I know of where you'll be safe." She gestured at a mesa in the distance. The letter C, for the Shiprock High School Chieftains, had been spray-painted in white on the side. "The shrine, remember?"

Clifford looked at her in surprise.

"I hadn't thought about it in years, but it came to mind just now." Ella recalled the circle of pollen-covered stones, and her own disdain at having been brought there. Her mother had claimed the ancestral shrine was a place for their clan to renew their strength and gather power. At the time, however, all she'd seen were rocks. She'd envisioned their cold hardness encircling her like armor, shielding her heart. She'd argued that she wasn't like Clifford, or their family. She'd vowed to follow her own path.

She remembered the smile on Rose's face as she'd said, "Your path will lead you back here, to us, to yourself."

She'd left in a fit, abandoning her brother and mother to whatever ceremony they'd performed, swearing that she would never return to that empty, desolate place. Now she had to. "I know you'll be safe there."

"Why do you say that?" Clifford goaded. "It's on high ground, but no higher than any of the other mesas around here." He paused. "It's near Wilson's home, though. Is that what you meant?" His voice was soft, though his gaze was eagle sharp as he studied her face, watching for an answer that would transcend her words.

"Wilson is your friend, but your safety doesn't rest on him. There are certain things we all have to face alone."

Clifford nodded slowly. "You know, I wish that when you ran you could have escaped these choices you're being forced to make. If you had succeeded, then I would have seen it as a possibility for me too. But there's no getting away from this. All we'd ever find is illusion, a mirage that promises escape but leads us right back to the danger."

"I've faced armed men. The day of the tragedy here I had my own brush with death in L.A. I had to kill a poor man who was so full of hatred he was scarcely human anymore. But I've never felt fear like this before. I know I'm changing inside; I'm discovering things about myself I've never wanted to face. I envy your ability to influence others, and I'm certainly tempted to use my own intuitions about things and people to achieve the same results."

"Then your time of danger has come, and it has nothing to do with those we fight."

"I may also find that the temptation is moot, because I'll never have your charisma."

"If that's what you discover, will you be glad or disappointed?"

"I don't know," she said slowly. But something whispered the true answer deep inside her. The realization frightened her, and she mourned for the part of her she'd lost.

TWENTY

When Ella got back to the house, it was surrounded by half a dozen cars and twenty armed men. Blalock was shouting orders through a bull-horn. Leaving the pickup, she approached, keeping in plain view of the officers. A few heads turned briefly, and Blalock grinned with smug satisfaction.

"Your brother's inside, or hiding somewhere nearby. We're going after him."

"Why the hell are you blaring orders to my brother through that noisemaker? If he was there he would have come out by now. All you're doing is upsetting my mother."

Rose came out of her home to stand on the front porch, followed by the mutt, who growled low, once, then sat beside her, teeth still bared. Rose transfixed the officers, many of whom she'd known since their childhood, with a cold glare. "If you would like to come in and search, do so, but stop that shouting this instant! I'm no criminal, and I refuse to be treated this way. Besides, you're annoying my dog."

Ella blinked, then smiled. That had held just the right touch of righteous indignation. Her mother had a lot of nerve. "What are you waiting for, FB-Eyes?" Ella challenged Blalock. "Even if my brother was hiding inside, he'd be no match for twenty armed men."

"Mrs. Destea, please step away from your house," Blalock ordered through the bullhorn.

Ella went through the line of cars and escorted her mom and the wary mutt back behind the blockade. "It's just a power play, Mom, it'll be over in a few minutes," she assured her, loud enough for others to hear.

Making sure the exits were covered, Blalock led a team of four SWAT officers inside the house. After ten minutes, he emerged, anger and frustration etched clearly on his face.

He strode over to Ella and Rose. "Clifford Destea was inside your home. Where did he go?"

Rose Destea remained silent. Dog growled, and Blalock stepped back a foot.

"You're obstructing justice," Blalock warned, his voice hard.

"One second," Ella countered. "What makes you think my brother was here?"

"I have my sources."

"I don't believe my brother was here. Did one of these officers see him? Which one? Let's ask him again."

"Stay out of my way, Agent Clah. I'm warning you," he snapped.

"Maybe you're psychic, Blalock. Did a little voice tell

you to come looking for him today?" Ella added, letting him know she was on to his bug.

Blalock's eyes narrowed. "What do you mean, a little voice?"

"You tell me," Ella replied pleasantly.

"Your brother was here. My information is correct. Clifford Destea will be in custody by tonight. Count on it." He moved away and spoke to two of the others in a low voice.

From his gestures, Ella knew FB-Eyes was giving directions for an all-out search of the area. No doubt the church construction site would also be covered. She smiled. This round was theirs, but their luck couldn't hold forever.

Ella took her mother back to the house, accompanied by the still-protective mutt. Once they were inside, Ella placed a finger to her lips, gesturing for her mother to remain quiet. Ella walked around looking for the bug, chattering on about her meeting with the insurance agent and her plans to redecorate her room. If Blalock was listening, she intended to bore him into a coma.

Searching the house, Ella went through a long discourse on the merits of eggshell versus cream-colored walls. She then proceeded to discuss, at length, the advantages of building a greenhouse where they could grow vegetables year-round.

After twenty minutes, she still hadn't found the bug. Anger knotted her insides. She'd gone through every room Blalock had ever been in.

Finally she walked to her father's study and sat down on the couch. Rose watched worriedly, but kept silent as Ella leaned back, closed her eyes, and tried to clear her mind. It was here. It had to be. Where hadn't she searched?

When she opened her eyes, her gaze settled on the commendation binder Blalock had given her. She stared hard at the binder, then grabbed it and rapidly leafed through it twice. Nothing.

Holding the binder open, facedown, Ella peered between the hardboard cover and the metal bar containing the ring mechanism. Near the middle was a small, gray, button-sized device. How could she have been so trusting and so stupid? He'd made her a traitor to her own family. Rage shook her. Taking a letter opener from a shelf, she pried loose the device. Clutching the bug, she strode out of the house. The police had left.

Ella jumped into her pickup and drove to the highway. Her first urge had been to find Blalock and shove his sneaky gift down his throat. But now, another idea appealed to her more. He'd undoubtedly left a receiver at police headquarters.

Ella drove to Blalock's motel in Shiprock. Jean Neskahi, her cousin, ran the desk during the day. It didn't take long to get a spare key to Blalock's room. Placing the bug in his bed, Ella carefully replaced everything the way it had been, down to the toothpick he'd stuck in the door jamb. She smiled. Tomorrow morning, when he got into the office, FB-Eyes would have lots of hours of snoring, bathroom noises, and possibly a private phone call or a visitor or two to explain.

As Ella drove home, her temper began to cool. Turning the tables on Blalock had made her feel infinitely better. At the house, her mother was sitting on the porch, enjoying the cool evening breeze while the mutt lay stretched out on a step, asleep belly up.

Rose glanced up from the blouse she was mending as Ella sat in an empty chair. "What's on your mind? We can speak freely now, I take it."

Ella nodded. "You told me, over a decade ago, that

someday I'd need to learn about things I'd shown no interest in."

"That time is certainly here," Rose acknowledged with a sigh. "Where would you have me start?"

"Tell me about this family 'legacy' of ours. How did it all begin?"

"That's a subject no one has ever discussed openly with anyone who hasn't received one of the gifts."

"I need to know, Mom."

Rose nodded wearily. "Your father never thought much about my abilities. I think he thought of it as legend, not something true. Of course, when we first married, my gifts were minor, just intuitions about things that usually were proven out. Then, after I got pregnant, those feelings became certainties. Sometimes I just *knew* what was going to happen to someone. That terrified your father. He turned to the white man's religion for security and spiritual comfort. As it often does, his faith grew in proportion to his fear. He wanted to protect all of us, particularly Clifford and you, from our own destiny. He thought the white people's god would destroy the 'demons' within us."

"Tell me how the legacy began. Who was the first to discover they were different?"

Rose leaned back and stared at some indeterminate spot in the tall tree by the gate. "It was generations ago, before the Dineh had a reservation, before our war with the white man. Mist Eagle, a woman of our clan, fell in love with Fire Hawk, a warrior who was also of our clan. Obeying the taboo, they went their own ways. Fire Hawk married another. But as the years passed, Mist Eagle's love for him continued. One night she waited until Fire Hawk's wife left for one of our ceremonies, then went into the hogan and seduced Fire Hawk. She became pregnant."

"Did Fire Hawk leave his wife?"

"No. Knowing the shame he'd brought on his family, Fire Hawk took his own life. Mist Eagle eventually gave birth to a girl child, but both she and the child were shunned. Sorrow was Mist Eagle's constant companion. Alone, Mist Eagle learned about herbs, and about healing. Skinwalkers sought her out—her crime, incest, was one they encouraged and frequently practiced. Mist Eagle was taught by them, and her powers grew, but she never truly became one of them. Then one day, she helped an old man who had gone to the desert to die. He was not a skinwalker. Word spread. Slowly, people began to seek her out in secret. It was said that she could kill her enemies as easily as she could heal, and those who came took considerable risks in doing so. Mist Eagle taught her daughter all she knew, and finally died during a cold winter. Her daughter tried to use her knowledge and power only for good, but the darkness that shadowed her from the day of her birth eventually consumed her."

"If this legacy was passed on, Mist Eagle's daughter must have had a child of her own."

Rose nodded. "A girl, by her father's brother. In each generation, the abilities each child received changed, becoming as individual as the people who bore them. Only one thing remained constant: the darkness and fear that came with the power. No matter how much good was accomplished, its evil roots were always there."

"Have some in our family used these abilities for harm?" Ella's mind was already gauging the possibility that the attacks against her family and their goals were rooted in revenge.

"Not many, but enough so that members of our clan decided generations ago to always have two children; no more, no less. It was hoped that if the darkness seduced one, the other would fight to restore the balance. And that's the way it's been, as far back as anyone remembers. The last time the darkness showed itself was with my great-grandfather. According to my mother, he killed his sister with an ax and then hung himself." Rose paused, then continued. "I believe the evil we've controlled since then has finally risen to challenge us."

That much made sense, particularly, Ella mused, if that evil was in the form of a man or a woman bent on revenge for some real or imagined crime. She still didn't believe the family "legacy" was real, but motivations rooted in religious beliefs could be deadly.

"But, you know, even those of our clan who were corrupted by the abilities they'd inherited, weren't truly evil," Rose added. "They simply failed to bring temptation under control, and allowed it to ruin their lives and those of the ones around them."

"And the children of those who failed? Did they also fail?"

"Some did; others didn't. Each person makes their own choices," Rose explained. "There's something else you should know. The power, even within the same generation, is not given in equal measures. The women have always had greater power than the men."

"Until now," Ella protested. "Clifford can sway people with a few words. I've never been able to match him in anything."

Rose's eyes found her daughter's and held them. "I believe that your powers will someday exceed Clifford's, though they will take a different direction."

"Different how?"

"I can't be more specific than that. You see, how much

you accept, how much you choose to develop, isn't foreordained. It's up to you."

Ella didn't argue; she agreed, at least in part. Any talent or gift needed to be developed. That's what she'd done with her police instincts and training. Her effectiveness was a result of a concerted effort to use all the knowledge and intuition she possessed.

"Someone's coming," Rose said. At that instant, the dog rolled over and sniffed the air, ears erect and gaze focused.

Ella strained to see through the darkness. Finally a vague outline appeared among the gray nighttime shadows. She automatically felt for her gun, then forced herself to relax. The man was on foot, coming from a direction that would have been impassable by truck or car. Only a member of Clifford's family was likely to approach from the north. She glanced down and saw that Dog's tail was up. No growl had escaped his throat.

"It's Paul," Rose said. "I recognize the way he walks. He always looks like he's lost something on the ground."

Ella began to laugh. Her mother had just reminded her of the one thing she thought she'd never forget. Observation and patience were an investigator's best allies. Many other things could help, but, without those, progress was often impossible.

Paul approached as Rose waved at him, inviting him up to the porch. Paul's downcast expression represented utter defeat, and Ella held her breath, fearing bad news.

"May I come inside?" he asked.

Ella noted the jagged cut that crisscrossed his arm. Blood had caked over it, but it still looked raw and painful. "What happened to you?" she asked quickly as they stepped toward the door.

"I've let my family down."

Rose gave Ella a look of alarm, but her voice was gentle and soothing. "Come inside. Let me take care of that cut."

Paul shuffled across the living room. The wound wasn't deep, but he looked like a man who was dead inside.

Ella felt the icy grip of fear spreading through her, and her throat went dry. Paul sat at the kitchen table, staring at Rose as she cleaned the wound on his arm. His silence seemed to stretch endlessly.

Finally he reached into his pocket and pulled out a piece of paper that had been meticulously folded. Paul handed the note to Ella while Rose, at the sink, prepared one of her herb poultices.

Ella opened the note and studied the odd writing while holding the pages only by the edges. Each letter looked like a child's scrawl formed with a turkey quill. Yet the runny, red liquid was no ordinary ink. The message, she suspected, was written in blood.

As she began to comprehend the note's contents, Ella turned so her mother couldn't see the words.

"Wait." Rose placed a hand on Ella's shoulder and drew her back around. Rose read the note at a glance, then took a stumbling step backward, falling hard into the chair. "No," she whispered.

Ella took her hand and gave it a reassuring squeeze. "I'll handle this. It'll be all right."

"But . . . they have Loretta."

Ella glanced at the note again. The message was succinct. It read, "If Clifford does the Sing, his wife dies." She met Paul's gaze. "Who delivered this and when?" she asked in a crisp, confident style. She had to break through the barrier created by shock and restore hope.

"I don't know who, but it happened about an hour ago."

"Tell me everything," Ella said, sitting across the table from him.

"I heard Clifford—I was sure it was him, calling from the bushes behind the house. I thought he was afraid to come into the open, or that he didn't want Loretta to see him and get upset. I went outside to meet him, but the voice seemed to be coming from farther away than I originally thought. I walked toward the sound, toward a stand of junipers, and caught a glimpse of the one calling me. He was taller than Clifford, and heavier-set. I realized that it was a trick, so I ran back to the house as fast as I could. I'd only been away for a minute, but Loretta was gone. She'd been reading, and her book and glasses were on the floor. They also took my rifle."

"What did you do then?"

"I ran outside; I was going to go after them. A dark pickup rushed past, and someone threw a huge rock right at me. It almost hit my head, except I dodged at the last second. That's when I cut my arm, on a broken-off tree branch. The note was attached to the rock."

"After you read it, you came straight here?"

"Yeah, as fast as I could. I didn't want to go to FB-Eyes. I don't trust him."

"We'll have to go to him now. We have to get Loretta back. To do that, we're going to have to find out where she is, and that'll take manpower."

"Skinwalkers have my sister, and you want to go to an Anglo? He doesn't know enough about us, or what we're fighting."

"That's true, but we don't have a choice. Whatever the motive, this is still a kidnapping, and that's something the bureau trains its agents to handle," Ella answered. "We have to find Loretta quickly. The danger to her increases with every minute that passes."

Paul nodded. "All right. What should I do?"

"Help me load something into my truck, then stay here while I talk to Blalock and try to get an operation going. In the meantime, I want you to visualize the man you saw. Did you recognize him? Try to remember his voice, or anything else that might help you identify him or the others. Then try to think of where they might have taken Loretta."

"I have no way of knowing all that! I barely saw the man who tricked me! You're asking me to do the impossible!"

"*Think.* You said he was heavier than Clifford. How much heavier? Is there anyone you can think of who's about the same size?"

"Samuel Pete, but it wasn't him. I'm certain of it."

"Why?"

"He moved like a younger man."

"See that? You do remember some things. Keep working on it."

Ella quickly checked the contents of her equipment trunk. Everything seemed to be in order. Together she and Paul carried the trunk to the pickup.

Seeing the look on her mother's face, Ella's throat tightened. "I'll be back soon. In the meantime, call Herman Cloud, or his son-in-law. Better yet, go see them."

"No. Paul and I will watch out for ourselves. And if we need help fast, I have the police dispatcher's number."

Recalling Peterson's instructions to her mother, Ella nodded.

"We will be all right," Rose answered. "You be careful."

"I'll be back as soon as possible."

Ella's heart pounded as she drove way. She had to find her brother's wife. First he'd lost his son, then his father.

Now this. They wanted to bring him to his knees and then destroy him. She wouldn't allow that to happen.

One fact was very clear. The skinwalkers could only have found out about her brother's plans to do a Sing if they'd had access to the listening device Blalock had planted. She'd have found a second bug. Blalock owed her big now, and she would get his cooperation if she had to wring it out of him.

Ella made the forty-minute drive to the station in less than thirty. As she pulled into the police station's parking lot, she saw Blalock unlocking his car door. She screeched to a stop and saw him instinctively reach for his weapon.

"Don't bother pulling your gun, just get in. You're coming with me."

"You have a death wish or something? I might have shot you!" he bellowed angrily.

"There's no time for this. Get in."

"What the hell's the matter with you?" he argued, getting inside the truck and slamming the door.

"You and I have to talk, so shut up and listen."

She filled him in as she headed quickly down the highway. Spotting a dirt road ahead, she turned on to it and parked. Ella shifted in her seat to look at Blalock. "Who else knew about that listening device?"

"Only a handful of people—the receiver was inside my temporary office at the police station."

"Who?"

"The police chief, Yazzie, and the desk sergeant who mans the telephones."

"That's it?"

"I didn't want the news to get out, and let's face it, every clan has a bazillion cousins, nieces, and nephews. There are at least five other Clahs in the department."

"Then someone monitored that conversation at the same time you did. That's the only explanation. Who heard that conversation, and, more important, who had the chance to leak the information to someone else?"

"A tip could have been passed at any time. Someone let your brother know we were coming."

"No, there wasn't enough time. The kidnappers went on the offensive just about the time you raided my mother's place. They launched their attack while you were busy with us."

Blalock's face grew hard and angry. "Then there's a traitor at the tribal police department."

"Which officers were in on the operation, and did anyone leave the room right after you decided to make the raid?" she asked insistently.

"The police chief was the only one who left. He'd brought us some of the assault gear." Blalock paused. "Is it possible that someone else planted a bug in your house?"

She gave him an incredulous look. "Get serious. I've searched, and besides, it's far more likely they used yours."

"Then the only suspect I can think of is your father-in-law."

The information weighed heavily on her. Randall wasn't very likable, but she would never have thought of him as an enemy. She shook her head in disbelief. There had to be another answer, an explanation Randall could give. But for now, this was the only lead she had to pursue.

"What do you want me to do?" Blalock asked.

"I need your help, and you need mine. You don't want news of this mess getting back to the bureau, and I want my sister-in-law back safely. If the police department can't be trusted, then we have to rely on each other."

"I have no idea where to begin searching. Unless you

do, there's nothing we can do except go back to the station and round up as many men as we can, hoping the good ones will outweigh the bad. We can have a crime-scene unit go over to your brother's house and see what they can find."

"That will take too long. While we investigate, the kidnappers could easily kill Loretta." She shook her head. "I have a better idea. If my father-in-law is involved, I have a few suggestions about where we can start looking." The thought made her sick inside.

"I'm listening."

"He used to have a hogan near Wilson Joe's place. I can't remember exactly where; it was a long time ago. The family abandoned it after a relative died there one summer."

"Let's check it out."

"First, let's find out exactly where it is." She drove to the public phone outside the gas station. She dialed Wilson's home number, and breathed a sigh of relief when she heard him answer. "I need directions," Ella said briskly, "but I don't have time to explain why."

To his credit, Wilson gave her the directions without any hesitation. "I'll meet you there."

"No. Blalock is with me. I'll talk to you later."

Heading east, Ella drove through a grove of trees and across a narrow wooden bridge. Below, the irrigation canal was half full of muddy water. Heading toward the river, they passed several corn- and alfalfa fields and a small wood-frame house. Two children played beside an old car up on cinder blocks. A single, bright light, high on a pole, illuminated the yard.

As they drove past, one of the kids, a long-haired girl in a T-shirt and jeans, made a face at Blalock. He laughed, then sobered when Ella looked at him in surprise. He checked his pistol, placing his extra clips in his jacket pocket for easy access.

About a mile from the hogan, Ella headed into a shallow arroyo and parked. "We'll have to go in on foot from here. I don't want to tip off a sentry, if there is one."

"It's already too dark for us to spot any guards if they're in the shadows. Then again, the darkness can work in our favor."

Abruptly, Ella held up a hand, signaling Blalock to remain still. A soft, muffled sound was coming toward them.

Ella tensed and drew her pistol. Blalock, weapon already in hand, cocked his head to one side, indicating that he'd go around and try to take the person by surprise.

Ella crouched down and waited. Blalock wasn't about to take anyone by surprise, regardless of what he thought. He was making enough noise to wake the dead. What he would do was flush the person toward her, and that suited her just fine. She scarcely breathed as she listened for the muted steps that Blalock's passage almost obscured.

Then she heard a soft rustle in the outcropping of tumbleweeds a few yards to her right. Someone was there. She aimed her weapon and kept it steady as the man appeared. The barrel of her pistol was trained on his chest, and when he saw it, he stopped abruptly, his eyes widening.

Recognizing Wilson, Ella broke her stance, quickly pointing the barrel up. "What the hell are you doing here?" she said in a harsh whisper.

"I came to help," Wilson answered. "My pickup is just ahead, around the bend."

Blalock emerged from the bushes amidst a symphony of snaps and crackling twigs. His gun was aimed at Wilson's head. "Don't move, pal. Don't even breathe."

"It's okay," Ella whispered quickly. "Put your weapon down."

"He appears out of nowhere and you're ready to trust him? Not with my neck, you don't," Blalock challenged, a hint of anger in his voice.

"Chill," she snapped. "He's the one I called to get the location of this place."

Wilson's face was a carefully crafted picture of serenity. "If I'd wanted to harm you, I wouldn't have approached you so openly."

"What openly? You scarcely made a sound. Good thing our hearing's sharp."

"There might be others around," Wilson replied softly. "We must keep quiet. What's going on, anyway?"

"Loretta's been kidnapped, and Police Chief Clah could be responsible," Ella said quickly, and explained about the bug.

"Are you sure about this? He's your father-in-law." Wilson was as surprised as she had been.

"The more I think about it, the more I know I'm right," Ella muttered sadly.

"Then Randall is one of them," Wilson said.

Ella knew he meant a skinwalker, and her stomach sank even further in revulsion.

"His hogan has a death hole punched in the side, but that wouldn't stop them," Wilson continued, disgust apparent in his tone and attitude.

"We've got to know exactly how many people we're dealing with, and where they're positioned. Loretta is probably being held inside the hogan. We have to come up with a strategy to get in there and free Loretta," Ella whispered.

"If guards are posted outside, we could take them out

and raid the hogan," Blalock said. "Let me take a look. I'll come up with a plan that'll work."

"You can't go," she said flatly. "You make too much noise. Wait here for me." She slipped through the gathering shadows and disappeared.

TWENTY-ONE

Wilson watched Ella go, then stood silently, looking all around him. FB-Eyes did the same. Wilson had never hunted a man before, but he knew the agent had. Would FB-Eyes be better than his opposition today? Wilson hoped so, for the sake of Loretta, Ella, and himself.

Blalock stared at Wilson, then mouthed, "How much time do you estimate she'd need to get there and back?"

"Five minutes. Unless she's discovered." Wilson rubbed his bottom lip with his index finger in a calculating gesture. "But she won't be."

"Oh, excuse me. You have a crystal ball?" Blalock spat out. "What's your part in this, anyway?"

"I'm on her side," Wilson answered calmly, knowing it was probably not enough for FB-Eyes.

"And what's she after? It used to be her father's murderer, but it's more than that now."

Wilson remained silent.

Time seemed to drag as the men waited impatiently for Ella to return. When she finally appeared, deadly intent and determination were etched clearly on her features. Wilson didn't need more than one glance to know they were about to take action.

"I counted four armed men. One stays by the hogan; the other three are patrolling. They're nervous and at each other's throats. One almost shot another by mistake just a minute ago. The hole in the side of the hogan has been patched. The entrance is no longer covered with a blanket. There's a solid wooden door that's padlocked from the outside."

"Big deal. We'll force the padlock with a lug wrench," Blalock said.

"Fine, but you'll have to get past the armed men first," Wilson replied quietly.

"Get to the point, Clah. Is your sister-in-law being held there?"

"Yes."

"You saw her?"

"No, but they've got someone inside. They took food in, and from one of the disgusting remarks I overheard, I know it's a woman. I don't need the I.Q. of Einstein to figure out the rest."

"Let me call the bureau and get a SWAT team in from Farmington."

"Are you crazy? The minute they come onto the reservation, word will get out, and Loretta will be dead."

"If there's four of them and only two of us, then she's liable to end up dead anyway."

"Three," Wilson corrected.

"Yeah, right. Just what we need. Civilian cannon fodder." Blalock shook his head. "All you'll do is add to the casualty list."

"Wilson Joe may be a civilian, but out here, people learn to shoot and hunt early in life. It's part of our way," Ella said.

"Yeah, but the game we're after shoots back," Blalock replied acidly.

"More incentive for me to be accurate," Wilson countered. "Tell me, FB-Eyes, what the hell are you complaining about? I'm offering to help you, and it sure looks like you're going to need a hand."

"Three against four does improve the odds," Ella agreed.

"Let me round up a few of my cousins," Wilson offered. "It won't take long, and then we'll outnumber them easily."

"No," Ella replied flatly.

"The ones I'll pick will never betray us, no matter what happens," Wilson insisted.

"Just get Paul. He's at my mother's house," Ella said. "Then it'll be four against four." She considered sending Wilson for Clifford, but she couldn't trust Blalock not to arrest her brother and she didn't have time to argue with him about that. "We'll sit tight, then move in at dawn. If we're lucky, they'll be half asleep."

As Wilson left, Ella turned to Blalock. "You still with us on this?"

"Do I have a choice?"

"Not really. You started this with your damn fool illegal bug. I think it's only right you see it through."

Blalock glared, then nodded reluctantly.

"I have some equipment—I shipped it in. It should give us an edge."

Blalock smiled slowly. "I should have known you'd have something up your sleeve."

"Let's just say I came prepared."

"With what?"

"Flash-bangs and enough tear gas to choke an army."

"This is starting to look more like a workable plan." He smiled again, but there was no joy in it.

Ella led Blalock over to her pickup and unlocked the trunk.

It was nearly dawn by the time they were all ready, at the ridge east of the hogan. Ella gave Blalock four flash-bang grenades.

"What are those?" Paul asked, worried about his sister's safety.

"They're like enormous firecrackers. They're called flash-bangs because there's a flash, and a bang, and that's about it. But they do incapacitate, and that'll give us time to move in."

She picked up the tear gas canisters. "I'll use these. My goal is not to exchange gunfire anywhere near the hogan. I don't want a stray round to hit Loretta, and we have no way to warn her."

Wilson had been keeping watch; now he joined the others. "We have to move now. There's a pickup heading this way. It should be here in about ten minutes."

"Let's get to it," Ella said.

They split up, moving toward the hogan from four different directions. If the assault was simultaneous, the element of surprise, and their enemies' confusion, would all work to increase their chances of success.

Ella watched the hogan, then glanced at her wristwatch.

Another minute passed. Right on time, the loud flash-bangs landed to the left of the hogan door, where two of the men were talking. The concussion wave rushed past Ella like a wall of air, and she flinched.

Ella hurried forward, shotgun ready. The two men were lying facedown, stunned, and would remain that way for a while, but there were two others, undoubtedly behind cover somewhere. She crept silently through the brush, stalking the missing pair.

She advanced cautiously, searching for signs of the two guards. It was as if the earth itself had swallowed them. She kept her senses sharp and her weapon ready.

Finally she heard a barely perceptible shuffling noise, about fifteen yards to her left. Ella froze, listening until she heard it again. Pinpointing the sound, she saw a rifle barrel poking through some scrub bush, aimed at the hogan.

She moved closer. With the rifleman in her sights, Ella opened her mouth to order him to surrender, when a shot cracked through the air. On instinct, she dove to the ground, rolling and firing a round at the gunman in front of her. She didn't hit him, and he was gone before she reached solid cover.

The shot had come from the direction of the hogan. Ella crawled forward. Abruptly she saw Clifford staggering away from the door of the hogan, clutching his chest. Blood poured through his fingertips.

For a moment, Ella couldn't breathe. When had her brother come here, and how? The world seemed to spin out of focus. With effort, Ella shook herself free of the anguish that knifed through her as Clifford fell to the ground.

Blalock advanced toward her brother, pistol in hand, ready to shoot again. Ella fired into the air, shouting, "Don't!" The thought that Blalock had been their enemy all along turned her blood to ice. She brought her pistol to bear, intending to shoot Blalock, then noticed the horrified look on Blalock's face as he stared at the body on the ground.

Blalock stepped back, shock etched plainly on his face. Ella realized he hadn't known who he was shooting at. Her brother had created a disguise, making use of shadows and an ordinary wig. As usual, Ella had recognized him anyway—but Blalock hadn't.

Hearing a car engine start up, Ella spun around. The two gunmen had reached a Jeep at the bottom of the rise. As they sped away, she felt relieved—she wouldn't have to contend with them now. She started running toward her brother, but before she'd taken more than a few steps, she suddenly heard the metallic rasp of a shotgun shell being fed into its chamber.

"Stop." The whisper-soft voice had come from directly behind her. "He's a dead man, Daughter-in-Law. It's over for you and for your family. We tricked you. My men will double back and take out the rest of your companions. You've lost."

Ella slowly turned around to face Randall Clah. "Why are you doing this?" She didn't want to believe he was involved, but the truth was there in the twilight before her. His eyes gleamed unnaturally, illuminated by the approaching dawn.

"For power. More power than you have ever dreamed of. It's right there, just waiting for us to take. People like you hold us back. You're afraid. You don't even try to use the advantages that real magic can give you."

"You've lacked for nothing all through your life, Randall, and your family lives very comfortably. What more do you want?"

"All the abilities you and your family have. For generations, your ancestors have been able to command respect and fear. Then you and your brother came along. You both waste your powers by not using them to get what you want. Your loss is our opportunity."

Ella knew now why he had never liked her, and had opposed her marriage to his son. "My brother is a Singer. How can you say he's thrown anything away? He's using everything he knows, all that he is, for the benefit of the tribe."

"Neither of you has developed your abilities fully. You both saddle yourselves with useless rules. That's why we're stronger, and why we will win. After your clan has ended, the People will come to us. We'll be in control, giving or withholding our help as we see fit, and destroying those who get in our way."

"Jealousy and envy are poor excuses for what you've done. You'll still lose. We have many relatives. What makes you think this legacy, handed down through generations, will die with Clifford and me?"

"You two are the only ones with any real power. First we destroyed your brother's reputation. Now we've taken his life. That order will be reversed in your case, but the outcome will be the same. In the end, we'll be the ones people respect. The Dineh will consider us heroes for getting rid of your family and their hold over us."

He raised his shotgun. A single rifle shot rang out. For an instant she wasn't sure what had happened. The pain she expected did not come. She glanced down at herself, noting in muted shock she wasn't injured. Looking up, she saw incredible surprise in her father-in-law's eyes. Without a sound, he fell to his knees, then crumpled to the ground, lifeless.

Wilson stepped out of a thicket of junipers, rifle still smoking. His eyes were narrowed, and he stared at the corpse before him transfixed. "I couldn't let him kill you," he finally managed.

Stunned, Ella walked over to Randall Clah's body and took the shotgun. Outrage, and a sense of being cheated, spiraled through her, choking the air in her lungs. It shouldn't have ended like this. Justice hadn't been served. The law enforcement system he had betrayed should have had the final word, not a carefully aimed bullet.

Her father-in-law had understood nothing about her family. Her family had never coveted power. Randall Clah was a prime example of why they'd done their best to avoid it. And as far as her own so-called powers, they were those of any seasoned law enforcement officer. Randall had given his life for nothing at all.

Bitterness filled her, but she forced it aside as her instincts came back in a rush. Ella glanced around warily. "The other two are doubling back," she said quietly.

Blalock rushed toward them and spoke reassuringly. "No, they're long gone, along with the two we stunned with the flash-bangs. The guys in the pickup saw the chief fall, then hauled their buddies into the truck and took off like a lightning bolt. I was too far away to try for a shot. I would have gone after them, but . . ." He glanced back at the hogan. "Paul's gone for help. We need a medical team." He cleared his throat. "I bandaged him and stayed with him while Paul freed Loretta, but I think it's already too late."

"My brother is dead?" Ella's voice came out a broken whisper, and suddenly she was empty inside.

Blalock hesitated, his face lined with strain. "I hit him square in the side. How was I supposed to know he'd be there? I knew it wasn't one of us, and hell, it didn't look like him!"

"I know what happened. Don't blame yourself."

From the look on his face, Blalock had expected recrimination or rage from her, and her calm answer had stunned him. "How did he know we were going to be here? Was he behind his own wife's kidnapping?"

Ella suppressed a desire to shake Blalock. "You're putting it together all wrong. As usual." Now her tone was razor sharp, and he flinched.

Ella joined Loretta, who was kneeling beside Clifford and holding his hand. Although her brother's eyes were closed, and his chest scarcely moved, Ella knew he would be all right. She sighed audibly in relief. The wound was serious, but her conviction was nothing short of certainty. It might have been wishful thinking, or a conclusion drawn from instinct, based on experience. Still, she knew her brother would live.

Loretta glanced at Ella, tears in her eyes. "He came for me. I knew he would."

Ella placed a hand on Loretta's shoulder. The naked sorrow on her face made her ache with compassion. "He will be all right," she assured her sister-in-law. "I've never been more certain of anything in my life."

"He has to be," Loretta answered, lifting Clifford's hand and brushing it with a kiss. "He just has to."

As fear for her brother faded, confidence filled Ella. She pulled Blalock aside, anger and determination blending to a lethal combination in her mind. "If the chief was involved, others high up in the department may be part of this as well. We have to keep everything under wraps for now."

"We need reinforcements."

"We bring in outsiders, and the perpetrators will go to ground. We'll never find them. We can't let that happen." She considered it carefully. "On paper, Clifford was the man you were after, right?"

"The initial evidence all pointed to him. You've got to admit—"

Ella held up a hand, interrupting him. "Report the shooting. Tell them you're unable to get answers from Clifford, and you've placed his wife in protective custody since she's a witness. They'll come after her, count on it." She'd started to say more when they heard the wail of the emergency vehicle.

Wilson stayed with Ella while Blalock went to guide them in. "Clifford was at your mother's when I went for Paul," Wilson confessed. "He knew something was wrong, and your mother confirmed it. I had to tell him what we were planning. It was his right to know."

Familiar doubts crowded in her mind, but she tried to dismiss them. It was hard to keep anything from Clifford. Once he decided to wring information from a person, he always succeeded. He'd done it to her often enough when they were growing up.

"What I don't understand," Ella said slowly, "and find hard to forgive, is that you didn't tell me he would be here. How could you have withheld something as vital as that?"

"I intended to tell you, but I wanted to do it privately. I was afraid Blalock would try to arrest him and blow everything."

Ella stared off into the distance, trying to get her temper under control. She didn't need anger to confuse her thinking. She needed cold rationality. "We'll discuss this later," she said coldly.

Ella saw Chester Bowman emerge from the rescue squad vehicle and breathed a sigh of relief. The Bowmans had been friends of her family for generations. She would be able to get a special favor from him.

Ella went to Loretta and whispered a few quick words in her ear. Loretta nodded, then got up and took Blalock aside. Ella crouched beside Chester, who was just opening the medical kit. His partner was retrieving other supplies from the squad vehicle.

"He'll make it," Chester assured her.

"Not if his enemies find him again. That's why I need you to do something," she said.

Chester regarded her with interest, but said nothing. The lines around his eyes sharpened.

"I need you to pronounce him dead in front of FB-Eyes," Ella said. Blalock wouldn't go along with her if he thought Clifford was still alive.

Chester nodded slowly. "I'll do it. Your brother healed my mother and my little brother. I'm glad for the chance to help him. My partner will go along with it too. I'll tell him in our language, so FB-Eyes won't understand."

He tended the wound as best he could, then spoke hurriedly to his assistant in Navajo. The men appeared to work urgently for several minutes. Finally Chester stood with a somber air and sent his assistant to retrieve a sheet from the ambulance. "We have to take him to the morgue. He's dead."

Blalock's face went as white as chalk. He stared at the body as the EMTs covered it with the sheet. Ella could feel his tension. This could mean the end of his career with the bureau.

"We'll get through this, Blalock. It wasn't your fault. But you've got to keep Loretta in protective custody. That's the only chance you'll have to explain what happened here. Take Paul with you too, to help. I doubt he'd leave her with anyone else right now anyway."

Blalock nodded robotlike, as if he was glad to follow someone else's lead. "There'll be a review board about this shooting. I have to find answers for them."

Ella could taste the bitter sorrow of a man who saw a lifetime of effort eradicated by one single moment. As far as Blalock was concerned, Ella was the best person to explain Clifford's abilities with disguises, back up Blalock's story, and justify the shooting.

Ella led the way to her truck, pulled out some gear, then handed Blalock the keys. "Pick up Paul, then take Loretta to my mother's home. She'll help you. Drive my sister-in-law off the reservation, up to Durango. Stay at the ski lodge. And try to get my mother to go with you. Tell her about my father-in-law's involvement if you have to. Tell her not even the police can be trusted. I can't guard her now. If all else fails, get Paul and Loretta to help kidnap her."

"How long do you want us to stay undercover?"

He hadn't questioned her orders, just the particulars. Now she'd be able to count on him. Fear was a great motivator. "A few days, no more. I'll get word to you as soon as possible. If you have to stay somewhere else, leave a message telling me where I can reach you."

As Blalock left with Loretta, Ella returned to the emergency vehicle. Clifford needed medical attention, but she wasn't sure how to get it for him under the circumstances. "How's he doing?"

Chester pulled the sheet away from Clifford's face. "He doesn't need my help," Chester said, his voice filled with awe. "His body is healing itself."

"What do you mean?"

Chester lifted one end of the bandage taped loosely over the wound. Although her brother had taken a nine-millimeter round through his side, the bleeding had already stopped. Chester opened his palm and showed her the bullet. "His body, or the movement of carrying him, pushed the bullet right out. When my partner and I placed him in the ambulance, I checked the wound again and found this on the surface."

Ella stared down at her brother. He was unconscious, but his breathing was even. "He needs careful nursing, and time to heal. Like this, he's easy prey. I'm not sure where to hide him so he'll be safe."

"Will you trust him to me?" Chester asked. "I can take him to my mother's. She'll know what to do."

Angela Bowman had taught Rose Destea all she knew about herbs. She was traditionalist, and fiercely loyal to what Clifford had been trying to do. "That's an excellent idea," she agreed. "But how will you explain this emergency call to your superiors?"

"False alarm," he answered with a shrug. "We'll bring back doughnuts and everyone will be satisfied."

Ella gave him a grateful smile. "I won't forget this."

Ella watched the emergency vehicle until it disappeared from sight. "It's just you and me now," she said to Wilson.

"I know."

"Do you regret your involvement with my family?" she asked, holding his gaze.

"No, not at all. Your family may be the target now, but the threat is to all of us," Wilson answered. "To be honest, I'm not a fighter by nature. I'm glad I'm an academician. In my world, intellect rules; the environment is more civilized, gentler. Had this issue not endangered the very people whose children I hope to teach, I would have done my best to avoid the entire thing. But there are some things worth fighting for."

"Yes, you certainly can be quite a fighter at times," she said warily.

He gave her a puzzled look. "What's that supposed to mean?"

"Well, I saw how you handled yourself at the chapter house, and I've heard of another instance too."

"Like when?" he asked, puzzled.

"Peterson mentioned he had to pull you off someone once," she said, keeping her voice casual.

"Oh, that!" Wilson answered. "He still holds a grudge because I wouldn't tell him what was going on, and my cousin wouldn't either."

"Your cousin?"

"Yeah, Aunt Emma's kid. He'd been breaking into cars and I caught him. We'd tried everything else to get him to stop. Had the police caught him, they'd have sent him to jail as a repeat offender, so I decided I'd do what his own father would have done, had he been alive. I tossed the kid around, tried to scare the living daylights out of him. Then Peterson showed up. Neither of us was going to tell him what was going on." Wilson paused. "I'm not surprised he remembered, but why tell you?"

She shrugged, weighing what he'd told her. It made sense. "Right now we've got more immediate problems." She shook her head slowly. "My father-in-law's involvement has really thrown me!"

"He was a very persuasive man, a natural leader. If he chose that path, you can be sure he talked plenty of others into following him. Do you have a plan?"

"For starters, we need everyone to believe that Clifford is dead. I'm hoping that'll make the skinwalkers less guarded. They won't be as well organized, having lost their leader, and I want to take advantage of it. With luck, they'll start to make mistakes when I push them a little." She ran a hand through her hair.

"Everyone in the department, guilty or innocent, will be looking for the chief. How do you plan to get around that?"

"I'll have Blalock call the department and say that he and the police chief are checking some out-of-town leads. Those who aren't involved in what happened here will believe him. The others, who know the real story from the two who escaped, will start getting nervous.

"I'm betting that they'll think that the chief is still alive, being held under guard in a medical facility. Before taking the offensive though, they'll search for ways to strengthen themselves ceremonially, like using Clifford's body to make a medicine bundle. My guess is that they'll go straight to my family's traditional burial ground."

"But there's no body . . ." His eyes grew wide, guessing her plans. "Your mother will never consent."

"I'm not going to tell her. In fact, I haven't told anyone this part of my plan, except you."

"When do you want to do this?" Wilson asked.

"You and I will take my father-in-law's body. After I telephone Blalock at my mother's, we'll head for the bluffs. If we go the long way, the trip will take half a day, if not more. That'll give Randall's men enough time to get the news and head out there. With luck, they'll see us burying the body, believe it's Clifford, and that their plans are working."

Ella walked to the chief's body. She had no desire to touch the corpse. Whether she believed in magic or not, the thought of encountering the *chindi* of someone this twisted gave her the creeps. "We don't have a choice," she whispered, mostly for her own benefit.

"No, we don't." Wilson glanced down at the man he'd killed, then turned away with a grimace. "I'll go get something to wrap the body in."

Ella stood alone and looked down at the remains of Randall Clah as the first rays of dawn spilled over the Chuska mountains. "In your own way, you underrated the powers of evil. It destroyed you long before you were dead."

TWENTY-TWO

It was shortly after two P.M. when Ella pulled her father-in-law's body closer to the large hole they'd dug. It repulsed her to wrap in a blanket that had belonged to her brother the body of the man who'd betrayed them. The ceremonial blanket, in natural colors of walnut, tobacco, and tan, had taken Clifford six months to weave. Ella was sure that anyone watching would recognize the distinctive diamonds within diamonds pattern, bordered in bold stripes, as her brother's handiwork.

Wilson and Ella worked slowly, deliberately inviting the scrutiny of anyone who might be watching. Once the task was finished and the body interred, they walked to Wilson's pickup and placed their digging tools inside.

"If your brother knew what you'd done with his blanket, I believe he'd strangle you with his bare hands," Wilson said softly.

Ella smiled. "Yes, I think you're right. That's why I was considering having you tell him."

"Me? No way. In fact, I want to be in Arizona when he finds out."

"Not a bad idea. We'll both go, then call him on the phone."

"What now? Where do you want to set up surveillance?" Wilson asked, putting the pickup in gear.

"In that canyon to your left."

"There's not much ground cover there."

"I know, but the boulders are enough to hide us. I would have preferred higher ground, but we might run into our enemies inadvertently and be forced into a premature confrontation."

"Okay, I'll leave the truck in that stand of salt cedar." He pointed to the gray-green cluster. "We'll have to hike about a quarter of a mile back to the canyon, but that's the only cover big enough to hide this vehicle."

They were in place twenty minutes later. Ella lay on the sand, using Wilson's hunting binoculars, her gaze fixed on the area around the grave. "We won't be able to see them until they're almost there."

"We'll have some advance warning. From my position, I can see a stretch of open desert surrounding the grave." Wilson paused and looked across at Ella. "Do you think anyone will take the bait and show up tonight?"

"Yeah, I do. I'm sure they'll want to gather a medicine bundle. Clifford was their most powerful enemy."

"No, not their most powerful one," a low voice said from behind them.

Ella rolled onto her back, drawing her pistol. She was already starting to squeeze the trigger when she recognized Clifford, squatting behind a bush, rifle in hand. She stared at him, aghast. "How—"

Wilson fell back to the ground, his breath coming in rapid gasps. "Damn, healer, you're supposed to fix heart attacks, not give them."

"I didn't mean to startle you," Clifford said, inching forward, between them, and peering ahead. "I thought you would have heard me coming."

"You made no sound," Ella protested.

"Ah, then I'm still in practice," he said with a nod.

"Why are you here instead of in bed?" Ella demanded. "What's the matter with you? Your body isn't ready for something like this."

He shifted and winced. "Oh, I still hurt. Quite a bit. But someone had to keep watch over you two." He smiled thinly. "Besides, you aren't the only ones who want to know who the other skinwalkers are."

"How did you find out we'd be here?" Ella demanded.

"Blalock called the tribal police from our house before he left with Paul and Loretta. Mother put together the rest, and filled me in when she got to the Bowmans'."

"And she approved of this?" Ella demanded in a harsh whisper.

"Actually, no. But she saw the need, so she and Angela Bowman gave me some herbal drinks, and my body did the rest."

"You don't exactly look full of energy, my brother, so if anything does happen, stay here and cover us, okay? The last thing we need is for you to fall into our enemies' hands." She knew Clifford had almost superhuman willpower, but she'd never expected him to be able to do this. Perhaps the herbs had blunted his pain, and he was operating mostly on sheer stubbornness.

"I won't take foolish risks." He glanced around. "We

should spread out more. I'll take a different observation point. Below the summit of that hill, there's a spot clustered with boulders. I'll hide there."

"No, you stay here," Wilson said. "We'll go."

"You don't have to be concerned about me," Clifford argued. Ella saw her brother's jaw set.

Wilson was right, but Clifford hated admitting weakness. Hoping to outthink him, she said, "You saw us burying my ex-father-in-law, right?"

Clifford scowled, caught off guard by the abrupt change of topic. "Yes, I did," he replied harshly, "in my beautiful ceremonial blanket."

"Okay, we both owe you one. So we'll move—it's the least we can do." Not giving him a chance to reply, she led Wilson away.

"Good strategy," Wilson whispered after they were in position once more. They were now slightly above the grave, but a little farther away than before.

"I had to think fast. This could be a long stakeout, and I wanted to make sure he had a vantage point that would provide him with substantial shade no matter what the position of the sun."

"Do you think they'll go after what they need for the medicine bundle while it's still daylight?"

"My guess is no, but then again, they've had the guts to attack in daylight before. There's no second-guessing them, and that makes them doubly dangerous."

Time passed slowly. Twice, Wilson checked on Clifford, bringing him water.

At around four that afternoon, thick clouds gathered, giving them some respite from the heat. Strong gusts blew swirling masses of sand and dust all around them. Lightning forked across the sky. Each thunderous blast sent its reverberations clear through her.

"Nothing goes easily for us, does it?" Ella murmured, not really expecting a response.

Rain poured down in torrential sheets that obscured everything beyond a hundred yards. Ella huddled behind the largest boulder.

"At least it isn't freezing," Wilson observed, rain dripping down his forehead.

Ella turned up the collar of her denim jacket, trying to keep the rain from slipping inside. Sandy mud splattered her clothing, only to be washed away by the steady downpour. The lightning flashes intensified, becoming a spectacular display, slicing horizontal jagged lines across the dark skies in great forks she'd never seen anywhere other than the desert. Or maybe she'd never bothered to look for such simple beauty anywhere else. It was a different world in the city; diversions and other concerns filled each waking hour.

Ella tried to keep a lookout on the grave site, but the rain was coming down in such thick sheets that her visibility was severely limited. The binoculars, though waterproof, were useless. She could hear torrents of water flowing through the arroyo behind them. She hoped the pickup was on solid ground and would not be carried away or trapped in the mud.

The rain continued, at varying levels of intensity, for several hours. The warmth had long since leeched out of her; once the sun vanished below the horizon, she grew even colder. An uneasy twilight descended on the valley. The lavender hues that blanketed the ground were as striking as they were unusual.

"They're coming," Ella whispered to Wilson, then wondered how she'd known. Still, there was no doubt in her mind that she was right.

The soft, whistlelike call of a mourning dove floated through the air. She recognized the sound as her brother's signal. "He's seen them," she said to Wilson.

Wilson tensed. She could see the muscles of his back and shoulders become more pronounced beneath his rain-soaked clothes. "Your pistol, is it dry enough?" he whispered, checking his rifle.

"It'll work," she assured him.

She heard a coyote wail. A heartbeat later, another answer, then still another. Ella felt her skin prickle, but she shook off the dread she knew came from superstition. Concentrating on the job at hand, she reached into her backpack and pulled out an infrared scope. Scanning the area, she said, "Coyotes are drawing near, but I don't see anyone close to the grave site." She handed Wilson the scope. "I wish I had two more of these."

"Your brother won't need it. His night vision is incredible. I've gone camping with him lots of times." Wilson looked through the scope, then handed it back to Ella. "This is very strange. I can hear the coyotes, but I can't see them anymore."

"Something's happening. Do you feel it?" she asked softly.

"Not even the insects are making noise," he whispered. "I don't like this at all."

Ella spotted a lone figure cautiously approaching the family grave site, but couldn't make out his face. "Here." She handed Wilson the nightscope. "The walk looks familiar. See if you can figure out who that is."

After watching for several long moments, Wilson said,

"I have no idea. Why don't we just go down there and take him?"

"No, I want this guy for more than grave-robbing. Let's hang back. Hopefully he'll lead us to the others."

"If we lose him, we could wind up with nothing at all."

"While he's busy digging up the body, I'm going to move in and get an I.D. Then we'll tail him."

Ella bided her time until she was certain her prey's energies were focused on the job he was doing. Finally satisfied, she moved closer.

"Try to approach from the opposite side, but remember, he's not alone," Wilson whispered.

Ella had just slipped behind the thick cover of a cluster of sagebrush when the skinwalker reached down and struggled to pull up the corpse. He tugged the body away from the grave, then unwrapped the blanket. As the body rolled free, he jumped to his feet. In that split second, he turned toward Ella and she finally saw his face.

Sergeant Peterson Yazzie, her cousin, stood staring at the corpse. She felt sick to her stomach. He was her friend. At least it had appeared that way. Now she knew that his kindness, and the consideration he'd shown her, had been nothing more than a skinwalker trick, meant to get her to lower her guard. He'd lied to her, and he'd stalled her, again and again.

Before Ella could fully come to terms with his betrayal, she saw Peterson throw his head back, mouth open in a silent cry. Grief? Was he still capable of that, or was it a curse of rage?

Peterson glanced in her direction, then slowly turned in a circle, studying the ground. She held her breath, wondering if she'd given herself away. A breath later, he shifted his attention and scattered pollen over the blanket. His action made no sense to Ella. Pollen was a blessing, the opposite intention of a skinwalker who sought to harm. Then he pulled a handkerchief from his pocket, used a small lighter to set it aflame, and tossed it onto the blanket. To allow pollen to be burned by fire was to destroy hope. In his rage, he would commit an ultimate act of desecration and burn blanket and pollen together.

She resisted the urge to stop him, knowing it would ruin their plan. Suddenly Clifford raced past her, running toward Peterson, rifle in hand. The fierce determination on his face frightened her.

Alerted by the sound of Clifford's footsteps, Peterson spun around. He stared in terror at Clifford, and Ella realized Peterson believed he'd come face to face with a vengeful *chindi.* Peterson took a step back, dropped the smoldering blanket, and ran away across the mesa, disappearing into the darkness. The long, mournful wailing of coyotes rose all around them, but none appeared.

Ella jumped out of hiding, gun in hand. Her brother, in his anger, was making himself a perfect target! "Get down!" Ella shouted.

Clifford dropped to the ground only moments before shots rang out. Ella fired at the flashes, trying to cover her brother.

She glanced behind, wondering where Wilson was, why he wasn't firing. A breath later, she heard the sound of a truck engine, strained to the limit. Wilson's truck appeared, the vehicle virtually leaping out of the low spot, tires spewing mud as it fishtailed to a stop next to Clifford. Ella was at Clifford's side a second later, helping him into the pickup.

"I'm okay," Clifford said, clutching his side. "I just wasn't up to a chase."

Ella took a deep, relieved breath. "Then why did you interfere? He might have led us to the others!"

"No. You were so intent on trapping him that you missed the signs. He knew you were there, Little Sister. You were casting a shadow. That's why he kept sneaking looks in your direction. He probably would have pretended to leave after setting fire to my blanket and the pollen. Then, when you went to put out the fire, he would have shot you."

Ella felt ashamed. She'd seen Peterson look in her direction and had wondered if she'd been seen, but allowed his actions to divert her.

"We can't let Peterson get away," Clifford said. "He'll warn the others and they'll all go into hiding. Then the danger will increase even more."

"We can still catch him. He's heading north, not for the highway," Wilson answered.

"He might be leading us into a trap," Ella warned.

"I'll hang back a bit, to give us time to avoid an ambush," Wilson answered.

They followed Peterson's mazelike route for nearly an hour, going back and forth down farm roads in a crisscross, zigzag pattern that defied prediction. Slowly, however, one trend began to emerge. "He's heading someplace specific." Wilson's grip tightened on the wheel. "We're working our way west. Help me keep an eye out."

They turned off a dirt road and continued cross-country. The recent rain had created large quicksandlike areas. Twice they got bogged down and the tires spun wildly, almost trapping them in the ooze.

The moon finally broke free of the clouds; the silvery glow made their passage easier. "Why the hell doesn't he slow down? This terrain is tearing my truck apart," Wilson muttered through clenched teeth.

"Peterson's been this way before," Clifford answered. "Look at him go."

Peterson was heading directly for a grove of trees and brush. Fear spiraled through Ella. It was a trap, but she wasn't sure what kind.

Wilson slowed down instinctively. "That's a great place for an ambush."

"Go around the way he did," she snapped, watching Peterson's truck swing out to the right around a tree, then cut back to the left so they could see him.

"No. We can gain some ground on him by going straight through," Wilson argued.

The second Wilson cut to the left, Ella felt a chill that pierced her to the core, as if death itself had touched her. She glanced at her brother, and saw the lines that framed his eyes.

"Stop!" Ella and Clifford ordered in chorus. Wilson slammed on the brakes, and the truck slid to a halt beside a tree. Ella heard a deep rumble overhead. "Get out!" she yelled.

Clifford dove out the passenger's side. Wilson threw open his door and jumped out, pulling Ella with him. After they'd rolled clear of the vehicle, Ella saw a thin wire stretched taut across the windshield, shimmering in the moonlight. As she studied it, trying to figure out where it led, it suddenly snapped with a twang.

Before she could take a breath, something dislodged from the cottonwoods overhead. A split second later, a massive tree trunk, its end sharpened to a point, crashed onto the cab of the truck. They heard the sickening crunch and squeal of metal as it transfixed the pickup. The ground trembled.

For a moment they were frozen in place, then Ella ran uphill through the trees. Peterson's truck was moving eastward at a moderate pace.

Clifford came to join her. "This trap has probably never failed before. He thinks one or more of us are dead."

"No, I don't think so," she responded. "I think he figures we're trapped here, and he's going for reinforcements. He'll be back with everyone he can round up. We've got to get out of here."

Wilson walked slowly uphill. "Well, my truck isn't going anywhere for a very long time." He exhaled softly. "How am I going to explain this to the insurance company?"

Clifford grinned. "Logging accident?" They both laughed.

Ella shook her head. Men! They had bursts of humor at the oddest times. "Okay, guys, we've got to get moving. We're at least three hours' walk from the main road, but if we keep a steady pace, we'll be fine," she said, casting a worried glance at Clifford.

"No. That's not where we should be headed," Clifford stated. "I know where Peterson's going," he continued, still staring at the retreating pickup, which had almost disappeared from view. "Remember when I told you about areas where the evil seems stronger?"

Ella had been studying her brother. "Even if you know Peterson's destination, you're in no shape for a long hike, and probably a fight."

"She's right," Wilson agreed. "Let's head for the road. Maybe we can flag someone down."

"Hiking all the way to the road will sap my energy. Then I won't be able to see this through—and you *will* need my help." Clifford pulled his knife from its sheath, then went back toward Wilson's truck. "You'll both just have to trust me."

"We do trust you," Wilson said, following him. Wilson reached into the truck and retrieved his rifle and a box of ammunition. Fortunately they had been behind the seat and were undamaged. "It's your judgment we don't necessarily agree with."

"Well put," Ella said as she joined the men, unable to suppress a smile.

Clifford pressed the blade of his knife against the palm of his hand. Blood oozed from the gash.

"Are you crazy?" Ella demanded furiously. "You're weak enough."

"I would have asked you to volunteer, but I know you've always had a problem handling pain."

"I avoid it whenever possible—so what? That just means I've got sense!" she challenged, outraged.

Clifford held his hand over the passenger seat, allowing his blood to stain it, then wiped the steering wheel with his bloody palm. "We have to use all the tricks we can think of to even the odds."

Suddenly she realized what he was doing, but Wilson was a step ahead of her. Taking Clifford's knife, he sliced a thin line down his arm. "Let them think we've been injured. It'll make them underestimate us." He smeared his blood around the truck.

"You're both crazy."

Wilson grinned at her. "You have a better idea?"

She shook her head in disbelief and frustration. "I won't slice my hand. I may need it to shoot."

Clifford's cut clotted quickly, but the wound on Wilson's arm continued to bleed even as Wilson wrapped a handkerchief around it. "It's not deep," he said in response to Ella's worried look. "It'll slow down soon."

"Why don't you hold your arm up for a bit? That should help."

Clifford reached into his medicine pouch and pulled out some bits of dried leaf. "Put this on the wound. It'll help." Wilson nodded and did as Clifford had said.

For the first time, Ella found herself envying her brother's knowledge of healing. "Let me tear off one sleeve of my shirt. You could use the extra bandaging."

With a grin, Clifford said, "Have you noticed how soft-hearted my sister is? She tries to hide it, but the truth always comes out."

Wilson unwrapped the handkerchief, then looked at his arm. "Keep your sleeve. The bleeding's stopped."

Ella nodded. She felt relieved. "Good. Let's get going. Once the shooting starts, you'll be glad I've got two good hands." As they walked into the darkness, Ella realized she hadn't said *if*.

TWENTY-THREE

The long hike across the desert valley was made tolerable by the evening air and the fact that their wet clothes had dried. Still, Ella was worried about Clifford. He hadn't said a word in over forty minutes. "Let's stop and rest for five minutes."

Clifford shook his head. "We're in danger, exposed out here. We can't even afford to slow down."

"We'll be in greater danger if you fall flat on your face and we have to carry you," Ella countered.

"She's right," Wilson agreed. "Even in the dark, you don't look so good."

"Glad to hear you think so. I'd hate to discover you found me attractive."

"I think you both lost too much blood back there. It's affecting your thinking," Ella mumbled, annoyed at their banter.

"Little Sister, don't you ever lighten up?"

"Not when I know I could be jumped at any moment."

Clifford smiled. "Nah, I don't think Wilson would get out of hand with me around."

Wilson laughed softly, seeing the startled look on Ella's face. "Would you have us march into a fight in total silence, thinking about it every step of the way?" he asked her quietly.

She forced a smile. "Sorry. Never did have a lot of patience with the male-bonding thing."

"Jealousy, that's all," Clifford teased, then grimaced.

"Are you okay?" Ella asked quickly.

"I'll make it," Clifford said, taking a slow, deep breath.

"How close are we?" she asked.

"Another fifteen minutes, but we'll have to take a very tough route to avoid being seen." He gestured toward the rugged cliff they were approaching. "Straight up."

"You're not serious. No way you'll make that," Wilson said.

"It's our only chance. They won't be looking up there for anyone. It's too difficult an approach, and very noisy if you take even one misstep."

Ella heard low voices up ahead somewhere. "I think we may have underestimated their number," she said quietly.

"It sounds like there are too many people for us to risk a confrontation," Wilson said, moving to steady Clifford, who was weaving slightly.

"Time for a change of plan. We'll take a quick look around," Ella said, "try to identify as many people as we can, then steal a car and leave."

"No," Clifford whispered. "There's no time to waste. A few nights ago, I found one of their gatherings. It was small, but the power they're able to call up is great—it drew me to the site. That night, I heard one of the men mention this place. This is the center of their power."

"How many people did you see that night?" Wilson asked.

"Only six, but their numbers are not important. There are only a few whose power we need to fear."

"Their leaders?" Ella asked.

"Yes, but it's their abilities we have to guard against, not their standing," Clifford answered.

"Because their powers are a match for yours?" Wilson asked.

"Perhaps superior," Clifford admitted. "But we're strong as long as we fight as one." At Wilson's nod, he added, "I mean all three of us. We each have something unique to contribute."

"Ella has her training; you, your abilities as a *hataalii*. What do I add?" Wilson asked.

"Your knowledge of the past and of our people. Most of all, your loyalty and courage. Those are not to be discounted."

Clifford was nearly exhausted by the time they reached the summit of the mesa. About twenty yards away, a wooden building stood almost hidden in a cluster of piñons. "Six cars," Clifford whispered. "They came up from the south end of the mesa."

"So your count was about right," Wilson said, matching the softness of his tone.

"I'm going on alone," Ella murmured. "Stay here and cover me while I take a look around. Maybe I can identify some of the cars—and I'll try to steal whichever vehicle looks easiest."

"No, I'll go," Wilson offered. "I'm the one who's most expendable."

"None of us is expendable," she said harshly. "Besides, do you know how to hot-wire a car?"

Wilson smirked. "No, I took drafting and P.E. that semester."

"Then I'm the logical choice," Ella answered with a tiny grin. "My education has been more varied."

"Your greatest strength still lies in the things you've never had to be taught," Clifford said softly.

She didn't want to think about what he meant, focusing instead on what she had to do. Ella crept forward, feeling as clumsy as a newborn colt. Every sound she made, crossing the rocky mesa, seemed magnified. Her heart hammered against her ribs. She'd tried not to show any fear in front of Wilson and her brother, yet the terror pounding through her made Ella sick to her stomach. What she intellectually derided as superstition still had the power to touch her deepest emotions. She was coming face to face with her darkest nightmares.

Ella inched slowly toward the building. Perspiration covered her body though the temperature was in the low sixties. Keeping carefully behind cover, Ella waited, watching and listening. Nothing moved, yet she was reluctant to cross the flat empty stretch between her and the building. It was unnaturally quiet. She shuddered.

After several minutes, when nothing had changed, she made up her mind to jog over, make her way to a side window, and peer inside. On the way, she'd check the vehicles for ignition keys. That might save valuable time later.

If she didn't see any keys, she'd disable the vehicles by using her pocketknife to cut the valve stems on two tires.

Ella took a deep breath, pulled out her pocketknife, and opened the largest blade. Then, drawing her weapon, she ran a zigzag course to the building. As she dodged around the parked vehicles, she saw a Bronco with the keys still in it. That would be their ticket out. She left its tires alone.

Reaching the building, she pressed herself against the wall. She could hear a slight hiss from the cars as their tires flattened, but that was all. She still couldn't hear any voices. Something was wrong. She should have been able to detect at least some sounds by now.

Bracing for trouble, she slowly peered over the window ledge. The small, one-room building was empty. A bolt of fear slammed through her. Maybe the enemy had heard or sensed her approach and circled around after her brother and Wilson. They'd be no match against so many.

She ran back to the Bronco, started it, and sped down the road the skinwalkers had used. Ella glanced back, wondering how soon they'd come after her, but no one appeared. She drove around to the north side of the mesa, half expecting to be ambushed at any time. As she pulled to a stop, Wilson and Clifford ran down toward the vehicle.

"What happened? We saw you shoot out of there like a rocket," Clifford said. "How come they didn't chase you?"

"There's no one there. The building's empty."

"Where did they go?" Wilson asked.

"I don't know."

"We had a clear view from the top of this mesa. No one came out," Clifford assured her. "They must have been in there. Somehow you missed them."

"I didn't. I'm telling you no one was inside," Ella maintained.

"They were hiding," he insisted.

"It's possible, but why? They didn't know I was there."

"I don't have any answers," Clifford replied. "Not yet."

Ella raced toward the highway. "We can't go back there alone. We're badly outnumbered. It would be suicidal."

"Not if we prepare ourselves adequately. Trust me; I know what to do. Drive to the sacred mountain, to the cave our mother showed us when we were kids." Clifford leaned back into the seat, weariness etched on his face. As if to himself, he said, "Each mountain is a being that thinks and breathes. The water that channels through them gives them life. It's there we'll gather the strength we need, and appeal to First Man and First Woman to protect us."

"The gods that have control over witchcraft," Ella said, remembering the stories.

"Properly appealed to, they can be persuaded to help us. I've kept prayer sticks at the cave, and ancient weapons have been hidden there for decades. Those will help us now."

Ella kept her doubts to herself. Weapons sounded good, but not ancient ones. In lieu of manpower, they needed firepower. Still, she was confident that when the time came, she'd be able to appeal to Clifford's practical side.

It took ninety minutes to get there, but the ride helped Clifford recapture his energy.

Ella parked halfway up the mountain, aware she couldn't drive any farther without risking the vehicle. "We'll have to hike from here."

"Now I know where you're going," Wilson admitted. "I came here once, a very long time ago, with my father. He showed your mother the cave."

"I didn't know that," Ella said, surprised. She couldn't remember her mother ever mentioning Wilson's parents.

"My father was in love with your mother once, although that was a long, long time ago."

"I certainly didn't know that!" Ella looked at Clifford, but he didn't seem surprised by the revelation.

"What happened between them, do you know?" Ella asked, unable to suppress her curiosity.

"When my father was dying, he told me all about it. I

think he wanted to relieve himself of all the guilt he'd felt for years." He cleared his throat. "Dad had wanted to marry your mother, but she never trusted him. You see, he wanted to father children who'd have the power given to those of your family. Your mother knew that and realized his reasons for wanting her were selfish. She chose your father instead."

Ella sat there in stunned silence.

"For years, our families were in competition. My father wanted me to prove that I was better at virtually everything Clifford ever tried. He even had me study with a *hataalii* and learn everything I could about our ways. I did it to please him, but I always knew that my life's walk would take me in a different direction. He died while I was still in high school. Suddenly I was free—and eager to discover my own strengths and weaknesses. As I found myself, Clifford and I became friends."

Clifford led the way through the narrow opening to the cave, lighting the path with a flashlight they'd found in the Bronco. "All our lives are at stake now. We'll need to use every shred of knowledge we have to stay alive."

"I'm still not sure who actually killed Dad," Ella admitted slowly. "And that's the man I really want."

"Only someone he trusted could have made him stop on the highway that night," Clifford said.

"Maybe it was my father-in-law," she observed. "No, that makes no sense. As police chief, he didn't have to use lethal force to make sure my father didn't interfere with the skinwalkers. He had too many legal options open to him." She paused abruptly as the full brunt of the betrayal her family had faced dawned over her. "Peterson Yazzie!"

Clifford nodded. "He's the logical choice. He was our father's favorite nephew. Peterson loved him."

"How can you say that? He killed him."

"Peterson had to kill someone he loved, someone dear to him, for the skinwalker magic to work. He had no brothers or sisters, and his parents passed on years ago. Our father was the person closest to him."

Ella tasted bile at the back of her throat. "He's mine," she whispered. "Leave him to me."

Clifford gave her a long look, then nodded. "All right."

"Don't talk to him when you meet; don't let him distract you," Wilson added. "When you face him, remember that it's a battle to the death. He won't surrender to you, no matter what he says."

"I'll take him down, trust me, but not by sacrificing my honor. He'll either surrender or die."

Clifford moved a large tumbleweed away from an opening in the wall of the cave, revealing two metal footlockers. Wilson and Ella helped Clifford pull them into the center of the cave. Clifford opened the first one, and the preparations began.

While Clifford prepared an herb mixture, Wilson sprinkled cornmeal as an offering to First Man and First Woman.

"This offering serves a dual purpose," he explained. "Their help is never assured, understand. But if we appeal to them, then we can at least count on them not to interfere with whatever good may come our way tonight."

Clifford started assembling a medicine bundle for each of them to carry. "Flint to repel the *chindi*, and to confuse our enemies. Do you remember the story?" he asked Ella, showing her the stones.

"Flint originated when the supernaturals who preyed on the land were destroyed. It has power because of its hardness, and the flashes of light from its facets represent lightning and the time before dawn."

Clifford nodded in approval. "We'll carry flint-tipped arrowpoints, and other flint-tipped weapons, plus a small piece of turquoise to give us power and strength. Remember that when Sun placed the Turquoise Man inside his child, he promised it would make him invincible to any evil he encountered."

He added rock crystals to the contents of the leather medicine pouches beside the turquoise. "At creation a crystal was placed on the tongue of each person, so that everything he said would come true." Clifford sprinkled pollen into each bag. "The pollen is for well-being; the crystal for prayer."

"So the medicine bundle becomes like a holster, meant to hold our weapons."

"Only this is to attract good, not just repel evil."

Wilson started a small fire as Clifford crouched next to a pile of herbs that had been stored in the footlocker.

"We need to burn these five chant herbs," Clifford explained, spreading out a small rug taken from the footlocker. "Then we'll dip the flint in the ashes and use the rest for Blackening." Blackening, the rite traditionally used to frighten evil away, might work against skinwalkers whose beliefs were steeped in tradition. And if nothing else, it would be good camouflage.

She watched the two men prepare the mixture. Clifford placed the flint in the chant dish, then poured water from a sealed jar in five directions. At length, the dish was set on the blanket with the other bundle items. After her brother completed the chant, they each reached for the ashes, applying them to their faces. Ella was surprised at how natural she felt during the ritual. She would have expected to feel silly doing any such thing.

"Now we're ready for the rest." Clifford brought out the traditional weapons from the second footlocker and sang over them. He kept the flint ax and handed Ella a large flint knife. Last of all, he handed Wilson a short-handled stone spear.

Ella noted the more conventional weapons stored inside the second footlocker with a relieved sigh. "Don't forget these." She handed Clifford a carbine and a box of cartridges. His own rifle had been smashed by the pointed log when it struck the truck. She kept the shotgun, a nice Winchester pump model with an eight-round capacity.

"No chance of that," Wilson answered, opening the breach and checking his own rifle, which hadn't left his sight since they'd abandoned the truck.

Fifteen minutes later, they were headed back down the mountain in their stolen vehicle, Ella at the wheel. "Let's hope they're still there."

"They will be," Clifford assured her.

"Let's get something clear," Ella warned. "We'll use only as much force as necessary to subdue them. I'm primarily interested in Peterson Yazzie. If the others make no move against us, we hold our fire."

"We can't," Clifford said quietly.

Ella took her foot off the gas, ready to stop. "This isn't a vigilante raid. We'll identify and capture those we can, then turn everything over to the tribal council. Let them decide what they want to do about it."

"The evil ones will resist," Clifford stated calmly. "Navajo witches cannot permit themselves to be taken alive. The minute their activities are exposed, their lives will be ruined. They have to fight."

"If they don't attack us, we won't use force. Is that clear?" Ella snapped.

Wilson and Clifford exchanged glances, but it was Wilson who finally spoke. "Do you honestly believe the skinwalkers will give up and go quietly into captivity? They're all accomplices to murder, and a host of other crimes. They've given up everything to protect one of their own."

Ella exhaled softly. "We'll do whatever has to be done, but not in a way that makes us no better than they are. Are we all agreed on this?" She waited until Clifford and Wilson nodded, then pressed the accelerator and continued on their way.

When they reached the top of the mesa, the cars were all still there, each with two flat tires. No alarm appeared to have been raised. At Ella's insistence, they split up and approached the building from three sides. They crept up slowly, each watching for signs of danger.

The continued silence was as unnerving as it was puzzling. Ella could sense her brother's position and, looking through the darkness, caught a glimmer of a shadow she knew was Wilson. At the moment, she was closest to a window. She would have to look inside.

She rose slowly and peered in. The building was as empty as before. Hearing a soft footstep behind her, she spun around, shotgun ready.

"Whoa!" Clifford whispered.

"No one's in there."

"Close your eyes for a moment. Feel. They're there."

Ella shut her eyes. Her other senses seemed to become more finely tuned. The air around them seemed to vibrate, or hum. It made her skin crawl and set her nerves on edge.

"We have to go inside," Clifford said.

"They're close by, yet not," she said and shook her head. "I'm not making sense."

Wilson approached. "The back door's not locked. Let's go get some answers."

TWENTY-FOUR

Ella led the way; Wilson brought up the rear. Clifford, the most vulnerable, would be safest between them. They slipped into the building noiselessly and looked around, but no one was there.

Ella stopped beside some cardboard boxes, her back pressed against the wall. Her gaze stayed sharp, and her body was tensed in anticipation. An odd humming noise, hard to pinpoint, came from everywhere and nowhere. She glanced at the others and knew they heard it too.

Clifford gestured to a wooden pallet in the center of the room. "There," he mouthed.

Ella approached carefully. The humming grew more intense as she drew closer. The sound seemed to pierce her, winding around her, icy cold. Her scalp prickled.

Fear descended over her in waves that made it difficult to keep her thoughts focused. The sound heightened every terror she'd held in check.

Taking a deep breath, Ella forced the fears away. "We have to move this," she whispered.

Clifford took one side and Wilson the other, lifting the wooden barrier noiselessly, revealing a large, dark opening, like a sightless eye. A ladder had been propped against one earthen wall of the vertical shaft. Ella peered down, trying to gauge the depth of the cavernous drop-off, but it was impossible. She suppressed a shudder, thinking it would be like climbing into your own grave.

Ella handed her shotgun to Wilson and thumbed off the safety on her pistol. Then, with one last glance at the others, she descended. The loud monotone chant rising from below repelled her, making Ella long to turn back. With effort, she kept going. At the bottom of the ladder, she saw that the tunnel led into three passageways that seemed to swallow the light.

The chant was more distinct. She listened for a moment, then shook off the spell cast by the rhythmic, repetitive notes. They seemed to weave themselves into a fog around her mind.

Clifford and Wilson joined her a moment later. "Fight it," Clifford whispered.

A pinpoint of light suddenly pierced the gloom, and she saw that Wilson held a penlight in his hand.

"It's not much," he whispered, "but it shouldn't give us away."

"We'll follow the sound," Ella said softly.

They made their way slowly down the hand-carved tunnels, but twice they ended up in blind alleys or passageways that looped back to the beginning. Ella shook her head. "I can't make heads or tails out of this place."

"Take your best guess," Wilson suggested.

"No," Clifford whispered. "Use your intuition. It'll lead us down the right path."

Walls of solid earth engulfed them on all sides, and for a panic-filled instant, Ella could scarcely breathe. There was a strange smell in the air. The place seemed to be pressing in on them, challenging her courage to the limit.

She forced herself to take another slow, deep breath. The walls were stationary. It was just her imagination, and that damnable chant. For a moment she had the sensation that they were being lured in, that the skinwalkers would be waiting to spring a trap on them.

"We're okay," she said softly, trying to bolster her own courage. They walked for what seemed like miles, Wilson's faint light their only ally. Each time they came to a junction, Ella did not hesitate before deciding. She didn't know if it was her instincts, or decisions based upon subtle clues she was aware of subconsciously, but they encountered no more dead ends.

She could sense Clifford and Wilson's apprehension. None of them knew what to expect at the end of the tunnel. What if the ceremony ended while they were still searching, and their enemies started returning? Could they remember which of the tunnels to take to avoid the skinwalkers?

Instinctively Ella touched the medicine bundle looped to her belt. The panic passed.

With every stretch of tunnel they traveled, the sounds of chanting became stronger. Her outward senses finally agreed with her instincts; they were heading in the proper direction. The walls changed from earth to stone. Ella had to work hard to stop the trembling that shook her body. She'd always hated caves. Clutching her pistol firmly, she pressed onward.

Finally a flickering light appeared ahead, and the tunnel

seemed to widen. Ella pressed her back against the wall, allowing Clifford and Wilson to look ahead.

The chanting rose to an unbearable crescendo, each note reverberating in the confines of the tunnel. Clifford's grip on his flint ax tightened. His face was mapped by the eerie firelight ahead. "Go," he murmured. "Embrace your fear until it becomes an ally."

Ella's body was covered in perspiration. The way she figured it, her pistol would probably rust in her hand, despite its Parkerized finish, if this didn't come to an end soon. And here was Clifford spouting something about *embracing* her fear? Hell, it had invaded every cell in her body. She couldn't have avoided it if she'd tried.

"If they have skinwalker powder, don't let them touch you with it," Clifford whispered, barely audible. "It's red."

At the mouth of the chamber, Ella flattened herself against the limestone wall of what was apparently a natural cave, dissolved from the earth by time and water. The stone felt cool against her sweat-soaked back. She took another deep breath to calm her ragged nerves. The chanting had become strangely mesmeric, growing strong then faint in an even cadence.

Six men and two women sat in a circle inside the limestone cavern, around a strange stone altar. The altar was stained with a reddish-brown substance Ella suspected was dried blood.

Skinwalkers didn't erect altars, nor practice blood sacrifices—so far as she knew. As she studied the cavern's interior, she realized several human skulls littered its floor. Without a doubt, it was an ancient ceremonial place, but not one that had belonged to their tribe.

"Toltec," Wilson whispered.

"Appropriate. The Toltec practiced human sacrifice.

This is a place of the *chindi*. The evil is here," Clifford added as the chant grew loud again.

Ella slipped into the chamber, staying in the shadows, and took her first clear look. The skinwalkers had painted their shoulders red and white, and drawn yellow spiders on their arms. At the far side of the circle was a small basket filled with a reddish substance.

Ella struggled to see the face of the man who was leading the ritual, but it was concealed in shadows. He dipped one hand into the basket and sprinkled some of the powder onto something on the ground before him. She edged in closer, keeping a low profile, and saw it was a human leg. The skin seemed to be festering and rotting. She swallowed quickly, afraid she was about to vomit.

The leader began to chant again, all the while sprinkling more powder on the leg. The skin seemed to shrivel right before her eyes. The woman beside him took some of the dust and placed it inside a pouch.

Ella angled for a better vantage point, but before she was completely in place, she heard her brother's voice rise in a chant that countered the cadence of the skinwalkers' rite. The clash of sounds echoed frighteningly in the confines of the chamber.

The leader jumped to his feet, and she recognized Peterson Yazzie. "Don't move. You're under arrest," she snapped, bringing up her pistol. She felt foolish—the words seemed so out of place here. Should she read him his rights next?

Two of the men threw some powder in the air and flooded the cavern with a bloodcurdling cry. Ella coughed as the reddish cloud filled her lungs.

Suddenly a large bear appeared where no animal had

been, forcing Wilson back into the tunnel. Four wolves with turned-down tails appeared from the further recesses of the cave and ran directly toward her and Clifford. Their teeth flashed in the dim firelight. Their eyes glowed. Clifford raised his ax and lightning seemed to fly from its razor-sharp blade, incinerating the animals before they could complete their leap.

A woman skinwalker came toward Ella, chanting and unafraid. Ella felt herself sinking into murky blackness. She struggled to make her hand work, but her fingers seemed frozen around the pistol.

Then something flew past her, and an instant later the woman fell to the ground, transfixed by Wilson's stone spear. Ella turned around and saw him trying to untangle her shotgun from the rifle sling. She had no time to grab it. Catching a glimpse of movement, she pivoted and spotted Peterson running down one of the side tunnels. She snapped off a pistol shot, but it ricocheted and he was gone.

Three men and one woman remained standing, held at bay by Clifford and his flint ax, which he was swinging back and forth menacingly. Wilson struggled to get into a position to use his rifle without hitting Clifford.

Clifford shouted, "Go after him! We can handle things here."

Ella needed no further encouragement. She shot into the darkened tunnel, determined to catch Yazzie before he escaped the cavern. She wasn't sure where she was going, but she could hear the hollow sound of running footsteps ahead. She increased her speed, her thoughts clearing and her instincts awakening. Then she ran around a natural bend of the passageway and into an ambush. The woman's eyes glowed fanatically in the harsh light of the lantern she carried. Before Ella could bring her pistol to bear, the woman threw a handful of white powder directly into her face.

Ella choked and gasped for air. She staggered. The woman's image shimmered and grew. Ella blinked furiously, unable to focus clearly.

The woman seemed to slowly split in two. Ella stared intently, trying to figure out which was the real image and which was the illusion. Both images came closer, and Ella fired once at each as she staggered back, slamming against the tunnel wall. Her heart was hammering too fast for her to draw in a breath. She sank slowly to the ground, her knees weak.

One thought pounded through her hallucinogen-clouded brain. Peterson was going to get away unless she got moving again. Ella felt a rumble, then the cavern walls shook. Or was that an illusion?

Using all her willpower, Ella slowly rose to her feet. At first her steps were halting, and once she fell, hard, on her knees. The effort to remain upright seemed to take all her energy. Surely Peterson and the woman had reached the exit by now, but she had to maintain pursuit.

The cave rocked beneath her again, but this time she managed to stay on her feet. No, she would not give up. Peterson would not elude her.

A new surge of energy shot through her limbs, and she felt steady once again. Now if she could only figure out which way to go. She closed her eyes and took a deep breath. Instinct was the only ally she had in this all-encompassing darkness. Still, she'd relied on it often as a federal cop, and had always come through alive.

The cave continued to shake as she moved on, and several times she felt the vibrations of a tunnel collapsing somewhere behind her.

Finally she saw a faint glow of moonlight ahead. She hurried on, knowing she didn't have far to go. As she stepped outside, through a narrow crack in the rocks, the ground shook again. She drew in a breath of fresh air, and her mind seemed to clear.

Before she could even glance around, the tunnel behind her collapsed. Dust flew out, then slowly settled. In anguish she stared at the rubble where the cave opening had been. Her brother . . . Wilson. Had they made it out? Ella glanced around, hoping they would somehow appear in the dark, unharmed. She shut her eyes for a second, reaching out mentally. Surely she would feel it, somehow, if anything had happened to them.

Ella didn't want to be the only one left to continue the battle. But now it was up to her. She wouldn't give up. She gathered her courage and walked away from the blocked entrance, trying to figure out exactly where she was.

She stood amid the low walls of the old church ruins, the wooden foundation forms of the new church just yards away. The skinwalkers' chamber had been directly beneath the old ruins. The ill-fated church, with its blood-soaked catacombs below, had been the perfect place to foster fear and welcome the *chindi*.

The wail of a coyote rose slowly from the top of the mesa. Its ululating cry sounded almost like human laughter. Ella broke into a run, heading toward the residential community just a mile or so away. She'd borrow or steal a truck there and continue the pursuit.

* * *

Ella was out of breath when she reached the construction site for the new college. A vehicle was speeding up the road toward her—probably someone investigating what he or she had perceived to be an earthquake.

As the pickup drew near, she recognized Samuel Pete behind the wheel. She wasn't sure whom she could trust, but she'd take her chances with him.

Ella stepped into the center of the dirt road and flagged him down.

"I need your truck. I have to get someplace fast!" She yelled, wondering what he was thinking. At the moment, she had to resemble a crazy woman, what with her dirty, haggard appearance, her flint knife, and the pistol still in her hands.

"Get in, I'll take you. Does this have to do with the earthquake?"

"That was no earthquake. Tunnels and caverns beneath the church site were collapsed, probably with explosives. Let me take your truck. You can wait here. It'll be extremely dangerous for anyone to be with me right now."

"Then it's begun," he said, and again waved for her to get in. "Your brother warned us that a confrontation was coming, and that no one would be able to stay on the sidelines." He gestured to the rifle rack behind the seat of the cab. "I've got a Winchester with me, and I can use it. My eyesight's as sharp as it ever was."

"I could use the help, but you'll be risking your life," Ella said bluntly.

"I've been your family's friend for a long time. If you need my help, you've got it."

Ella gave him directions to where she'd first entered the tunnels. "Go as fast as you can."

Samuel nodded. "I understand you're afraid to trust

anyone, but I have a right to know what I'm facing if I'm to fight it alongside you."

Ella considered his words. They'd all trusted Peterson Yazzie, and he'd been working against them from the beginning. On the other hand, she didn't really have anything to lose by telling the old man what had happened. She filled him in, concluding, "It's possible Clifford and Wilson were able to backtrack and get out the way we came in."

"If there was a way out, your brother and his friend would have found it. They could be on Yazzie's trail right now."

Ten minutes later, they could see the disabled vehicles, still parked outside the building. Ella looked around, searching in the glare of Samuel's headlights for her brother and Wilson.

"Drive closer, but stop before we reach the cars. Then I can use the truck for cover while I look around."

As Samuel parked, Ella spotted two figures hurrying toward them. She had her pistol out in a heartbeat. "Stop! FBI!" she called out.

Then she recognized Wilson, who was supporting Clifford's weight and hauling him along. Her brother's arm was looped around Wilson's shoulder. Ella lowered her pistol and rushed to help. "I've never been so glad to see anyone in my life. I was so worried about you both."

"Two skinwalkers escaped," Clifford said, forcing himself to stand unaided, "but they're somewhere nearby. We made sure they couldn't reach their vehicles. Somebody made it to the Bronco, though. I heard it leave."

Samuel Pete, hurried toward them, Winchester in hand. "We can't stay, Nephew," he said, using the term out of custom, not kinship. "You're in no shape to fight now."

"Neither are they," Clifford answered with a tiny smile. "We'll stay."

His bravery tugged at Ella's heart. He was exhausted, and injured, yet he'd never lost the courage to fight. "It must be Peterson who got to the Bronco, but I think I know where he went," Ella said with certainty.

Clifford had his rifle in a sling over his shoulder, and a bloody-looking stone ax in his hand. Wilson carried a rifle and a big flint spear. Samuel Pete held out his keys to Ella. "Here. Take my truck. If your brother wants to remain here, I'll stay and help. Both of these warriors look like they still have some fight in them."

"We'll be okay," Clifford told Ella reassuringly. "Do you still want to run Peterson down and arrest him?"

"You couldn't keep me from it. He's gone bad as both a cop and a Navajo. He's betrayed everything I value."

"Then go," Clifford said.

Samuel Pete took an ammunition box from a shelf behind the driver's seat, then stepped back. "She's all yours. Good luck."

Ella headed straight for the highway. Time was short. She couldn't allow Peterson to leave the Rez. As a cop, he'd know only too well how to hide deep within the Anglo world, covering his trail.

As she raced down the highway, the indigo skies started turning to purples and deep blues. Traces of light fringed a few thin clouds on the horizon. Dawn. She felt relief washing over her. She preferred the daylight, where any fight would be stripped of the overtones traditional beliefs might give it.

Ella pressed down on the accelerator, watching the needle climb to ninety. The truck was out of tune and lurched frequently in complaint, but she refused to let up on the gas.

As she prepared mentally to face her enemy, Ella knew she'd be shouldering the full weight of expectations—expectations others had of her and ones she had of herself. In her worst childhood nightmares, she'd been utterly alone, fighting an evil monster she couldn't defeat. Now she wondered if those nightmares hadn't somehow foreshadowed what would come.

Nothing mattered more than the capture of Peterson Yazzie. Her father's murderer would face justice, and she would bring him down, or die trying.

Ella slowed down, took the truck out of gear, shut off the engine, and coasted to a stop in front of the police station, in hopes of achieving the element of surprise. There was only one vehicle in the parking lot—the Bronco, as she had anticipated. The office staff wouldn't be in for at least two hours, and the field units were out on patrol. Ella glanced at the horizon, already lit up in magenta and orange, and smiled grimly. The sun would be up very soon.

Walking silently toward the entrance, she heard an animal growling nearby. Immediately her heart started pumping overtime. She drew her weapon and glanced about. The stone knife was in her belt. She hadn't forgotten the coyote she'd shot at close range, but hadn't killed.

The growling stopped.

Ella hurried toward the door, checking both sides of the station's long, covered porch. If her hunch was right, Peterson would be acquiring weapons. As she approached the entrance, an old woman wrapped in a gray blanket stepped onto the porch.

Something compelled Ella to stay behind a big round porch support. Despite the blanket that kept the woman's face in shadow, there was no doubt in Ella's mind that this was a trick. As the old woman moved closer, she realized what had alerted her—the woman moved like a man. Ella kept her pistol in hand, but didn't bring it to bear. She kept her distance and waited, studying the situation.

The first rays of dawn came over the horizon, striking the rooftop of the two vehicles in the parking lot. The golden beams filled the air with the promise of warmth, and a curious calm fell over everything.

The figure stepped toward the wall, seeking darkness. "I don't fool you, and you're not fooling me," Yazzie said loudly. "Don't try to keep me from leaving. I don't want to kill you."

The barrel of a riot gun had risen from below the blanket and was pointed in her direction. "My powers fade at daybreak, but the buckshot is real. It'll do the job as well on you as it did on the dispatcher inside. Move aside."

Ella had raised her pistol as Yazzie had moved, and now had it aimed at his chest; both hands gripped the nine-millimeter in a combat stance. The stone knife—magic or not—was no match for his shotgun. "You're not going anywhere, not unless you have a death wish."

"Don't be a fool. There are other places on the reservation like the one that's been destroyed. The evil that you're trying to fight is as old as the desert itself. We didn't create it, we just used it. Even if you kill me now, there are others to contend with, perhaps even some you think close to you. It wouldn't be over. So what purpose would it serve?"

"I'd capture the man who murdered my father."

"I wasn't alone. Others stood with me while I stole the strength from the preacher. What about them?"

"I'll see that each of you face's justice, one at a time if necessary." The horrific image evoked by his admission filled her with rage. Ella held her gun steady, refusing to let it waver for even a second. "You're not going anywhere.

Put down the shotgun. That's your only chance. I won't warn you again."

"I've always loved you, Ella," he said, then squeezed the trigger.

The porch support splintered into kindling and buckled. Ella dove to one side, off the porch. She was trying to roll behind the Bronco when she felt buckshot from his second blast sear the side of her leg with fire.

Blood flowed quickly, soaking her pants leg. She crawled to the opposite end of the vehicle, staring at Peterson.

He fired again, crouched behind an overturned bench. "You're wounded and outgunned, and in no position to fight. I'll give you one chance. Stay behind cover if you like, but throw your pistol out onto the ground where I can see it."

"Why are you being so generous?" She clutched her gun firmly and ignored the damp warmth creeping down her leg. If she was going to die, she'd take him with her.

"There are secrets in your past about which you know nothing. The evil will call to you too, and soon."

"Yeah, right. Well, I've fought you to a standstill and I'm still here. Most of your buddies aren't."

"You're kidding yourself. You've accomplished nothing, unless you count killing your father-in-law a victory. But even that is not over. The chief's *chindi* now occupies another living body. He'll take your life unless you join us."

"Right. And the tooth fairy is your sister."

For his answer, a blast of buckshot peppered the ground beside Ella, stinging her face with sand. "Enough. Either throw your weapon over here or die alone. You're too stupid to realize what you're dealing with. You'll be forgotten before the next sunrise."

Bessie Tso came out from behind the corner of the building. "No, she won't be forgotten," she said, her voice clear. "I was offering my prayers to the dawn when I heard gunshots. I came to see if I could be of help, and it seems I'm just in time. You're not alone in your fight anymore, L.A. Woman."

"So I kill two bitches instead of one. This whole area will be the playground of skinwalkers. There's nothing you can do to prevent it," Peterson said and swung around, firing at Bessie and missing her by inches.

The middle-aged woman moved with surprising speed, and the buckshot only tore a chunk from the corner of the building. Ella squeezed off a shot of her own, forcing Peterson to the ground. He grunted as it struck.

Suddenly at least a dozen more adults came toward the police station, advancing warily, but approaching nonetheless. The sounds of violence had apparently alerted other early risers in the neighborhood. Ella heard Herman Cloud's voice. "What's going on?"

As Bessie filled him in, Ella shifted her vantage point to the other end of the Bronco, searching for the opportunity to gain the upper hand. "Give it up Peterson, it's over."

Ella's heart stuck in her throat as she saw Herman step out into full view, six others beside him. "You can shoot one, maybe two of us, but you won't escape the rest. Or our justice." His voice was harsh and convincing.

Ella knew they would tear Peterson apart with their bare hands if he fired again. She waited, scarcely breathing.

Peterson stood up, leaving his weapon on the ground. Blood ran from a bullet wound below his collarbone. "I'll take my chances in the courts," Peterson said, raising his arms as much as his injury would allow.

Ella saw the murderous intent on the faces of the people

moving forward. Part of her would have liked to hand Peterson over to the angry civilians, then just turn her back and walk away. "If one of you will open the door for me, I'll take him inside to a cell."

Bessie came up to her. "You shouldn't move. You're still bleeding."

"Not badly. First we'll take care of Peterson, then I have to get help for Wilson Joe, my brother, and Samuel Pete."

Herman smiled. "No need. The old man called me on the CB ten minutes ago, from one of the pickups out by the warehouse. Everything is over up there. In fact, it was that call that brought the rest of us here. We don't live as close as the professor, or we would have been here sooner." Herman nodded to three men, who grabbed Peterson's arms.

Ella holstered her pistol and pulled out the flint knife. "Hold this at his throat while I search him for weapons or keys." She gave the blade to Herman, who looked at it for a second before swinging it to within a quarter inch of Peterson's throat.

Yazzie froze, then began whimpering softly in obvious terror. Ella searched him thoroughly, dropping everything in his pockets on the ground, including his wallet, keys and a large lock-back pocketknife. Removing his belt, she stepped back and nodded to the men, who hauled him into the station none too gently.

Ella limped toward the building, with Bessie supporting her. Hearing a vehicle speeding up the road, Ella stumbled around to face it, gun out again. A familiar voice shouted, and she saw Wilson at the wheel.

The truck came to a sliding stop in the gravel, and Clifford jumped out. He studied her wounds. Then, taking her arm, he helped her move toward the building. "You did well, Little Sister."

"Just barely."

"You accomplished what you set out to do," he said.

"We're not finished yet," she answered hesitantly. She was about to tell him what Peterson had said when Herman Cloud came toward them.

"We need one of you to accompany us. We've put him in a cell and locked the door, but none of us can make sure we do everything necessary to keep him there." He handed Ella a ring containing a single large double-cut key.

"Legally, he's not about to get off, so I guess they want the services of a *hataalii,*" Ella said, glancing at Clifford.

Clifford helped her through the door and down the corridor to the holding area. "We each have jobs to do. You completed yours. Now it's my turn."

From her vantage point in the hall, she saw her brother sprinkling sacred pollen on the bars that held Peterson prisoner. He was standing against the back wall of the enclosure, deliberately looking away from Clifford's activities. For one brief instant, Peterson's eyes met and held hers.

"We're not finished with you," he uttered.

A shudder rippled through her, and she looked away, toward Clifford.

TWENTY-FIVE

Two weeks later, Ella sat outside on her mother's porch, listening to Blalock's account of the legal proceedings against Peterson. The agent was in much better spirits now that he knew Clifford had not been seriously wounded and no charges would be brought against him.

"We worked on Yazzie for eight hours. He just sat there and smiled. Then the temporary police chief—the guy appointed by the tribal council—came in and told Yazzie that he'd personally post bail for him. All the time he talked, he kept thumbing the blade of a nasty-looking stone knife. Then he reminded Yazzie that he would notify the community of the time of release, for their own protection, of course.

"Yazzie turned whiter than me, then damn near choked. He started foaming at the mouth, claiming that little voices told him to kill your father. He's obviously decided to start working on an insanity plea. He said the voices told him it was either your father's life, or his own."

Ella shrugged. "There might be a tiny element of truth to that. But an insanity plea, that's weak, even for him. He participated willingly in the murder, and had a definite motive, no matter how warped that motive may seem to the courts."

Silence stretched between them. Blalock looked away. In the distance they could hear the rhythmic beat of ceremonial drums. Blalock's expression grew taut. "Doesn't that annoy you after a while? It's really getting to me. It's been going on for nine days now. I don't know how I'm going to stand this godforsaken country another two years."

"Full credit for the collar went to you. I thought you said they'd be letting you transfer out."

"Hell, that's what I thought too. But I was told that my success with this case shows I understand the Indian mind. The bureau decided I could serve best by staying here." He shrugged. "Who knew?"

The sounds of the drums intensified. Blalock pursed his lips. "How much longer is that going to go on?"

"Tonight's the last night. It's a Night Way chant."

"Everyone's down there—must be thousands of people."

"Troubled times make people come together."

"But now that it's over—"

Ella shook her head. "That's the problem. Some people don't believe it's over."

"Do you?"

She took a deep breath and then let it out slowly. "Our way teaches that whatever happened once may happen again."

Rose came outside. "It'll be time to go soon," she told

her daughter. She glanced at Blalock with an "Are you still here" look that was hard to miss.

"I'll be ready."

Blalock waited until Rose went back inside the house. "How long before you return to duty? Your leg is healed up pretty good. I hear the L.A. office is eager to get you back. Somehow you came out of all this smelling like a . . . gardenia?"

"I sent in my resignation yesterday."

Blalock just stared for a moment. "You did *what?* I don't believe you! You're tossing away your career just like that?" He snapped his fingers. "What for? What could you have been offered that's better than what you already have?"

"Not a thing. At the moment, I'm unemployed. Believe me, it wasn't an easy decision to make."

"So what are you going to do for a living? Law enforcement is in your blood."

"I filled out an application for the tribal police. There are a few positions open right now," she answered with a wry smile, "and I'm qualified. I've got a whole binder full of commendations."

Blalock guffawed. "You're trying for the police chief's job?"

"Why not? I have excellent training and experience."

"Do you think you'll get it?"

"I don't know, but I'm sure they'll find room for me somewhere."

Wilson joined them on the porch. "Ella's needed here, and the People know it. She won't have a hard time finding a place for herself in our police department."

Blalock shook his head. "Well, I wish you the best of luck," he said finally, shaking his head. "I'll be seeing you again, one way or the other."

"Thanks." Ella watched him go, knowing that a chapter of her life was coming to an end.

"Do you regret resigning?" Wilson asked softly as Ella's mother emerged from the house.

"No. I belong here. I've never been as certain of anything before in my life."

Moments later, the three of them set off for the new churchsite in Wilson's new truck. "Today," Rose said in a heavy tone, "I fulfill my last obligation to your father."

"It's time to let go, and look to the future," Ella said softly.

"For all of us," Rose answered.

The silence that settled around them was a comfortable one that no one seemed eager to break. Finally they approached the dirt road leading to the new church. "It's still too close, just a mile from the previous site," Wilson muttered. "This place will always make me uneasy."

"That's why we're all here early. The first church service won't be for several hours, and Clifford needs to do a *Hoh-chon'-jih Hatal* to clear the area of *chindi*. Then he'll do a blessing on the land that will keep the skinwalkers away from here for good."

As they reached the church—still only a foundation and concrete pad—they saw Loretta and Clifford, waiting hand in hand. "She looks happy at last. I'm glad," Ella said softly.

"A young woman is too alone without a husband," Rose answered dryly.

Ella tried not to look at Wilson, but she knew he was smiling. "Real subtle, Mom," she whispered sternly, shaking her head.

As they left the vehicle, Clifford greeted them. "Everything's ready. Now that you're all here, I can begin." He moved away from the others and invoked the four Lightnings.

Clifford stood back for a long moment and gathered power into himself. At last he led them toward a sand painting prepared on buckskin that had been placed on the ground. The Sun was depicted in blue and the Moon in white. Black and Yellow Wind completed opposite corners of the picture. As he sang over the painting, incense burning in a small pottery bowl sent a wholesome scent into the air.

Ella concentrated on her brother's song, accepting the duty of supporting his prayers to aid the ritual. Fear no longer held her back. She was stronger than she'd ever been.

After the Sing, Clifford destroyed the painting with his hands, in the order it had been constructed. Completing the ritual, he swept up the sand and carried it north, where he released it.

"It is finished in beauty," he said at last.

Clifford's face looked worn and Ella knew he was still very tired. As Rose and Loretta walked back toward the church foundation, Clifford, Ella, and Wilson stood looking at the nearby mesa.

"It'll start again," Ella said. "We all know that. And next time, they'll be wiser and tougher."

"How much time do we have?" Wilson asked.

Ella shrugged and looked at her brother.

"I'm not sure either," Clifford answered quietly, his eyes on the horizon.

Ella glanced up at the thick dark clouds gathering. "It'll rain again soon," she said. A strong gust of wind whipped against them, and for a moment she thought she heard a strange wailing sound. She glanced at the others.

"A coyote, at this time of day?" Wilson asked in a hush.

"Not likely," she protested. "It's just the wind."

"Wind carries only the truth," Clifford mused softly.

Thunder rumbled in the distance. Ella, her brother, and Wilson Joe turned to face it.